TEMPTING

CRYSTAL KASWELL

Copyright

This is a work of fiction. Similarities to real people, places, or events are entirely coincidental.

Also by Crystal Kaswell

Sinful Serenade

Sing Your Heart Out - Miles

Strum Your Heart Out - Drew

Rock Your Heart Out - Tom

Play Your Heart Out - Pete

Sinful Ever After – series sequel

Dangerous Noise

Dangerous Kiss - Ethan

Dangerous Crush – Kit

Dangerous Rock – Joel

Dangerous Fling – Mal

Dangerous Encore - series sequel

Inked Hearts

Tempting - Brendon

Hooking Up - Walker

Pretend You're Mine - Ryan

Hating You, Loving You - Dean

Breaking the Rules - Hunter

Losing It - Wes - coming 2019

more coming in 2019

Standalones

Broken - Trent & Delilah

Dirty Rich

Dirty Deal - Blake

Dirty Boss - Nick

Sign up for the Crystal Kaswell mailing list

About This Book

**He's my best friend's older brother, off limits and
incredibly tempting.**

I shouldn't peek into Brendon's sketchbook, even if the
tattoo artist is as brooding and stoic as the day is long. I
can't help myself. I peel it open, run my fingers along the
paper, soak up every ounce of him.

His drawings are as beautiful and bold as his dark eyes
and his cocky smile. Only, there, on the third page--that's
no tattoo mockup. That's me.

Naked.

Ready.

Waiting in his bed.

There's no denying it--those are my blue glasses, my
green eyes, my flushed cheeks.

Brendon wants me.

The smoking hot, ten thousand miles out of my league
bad boy wants me-- a good girl virgin with thick glasses
and no game.

It's perfect.

Only it's not.

He's my best friend's older brother. He's off limits.

But damn is he tempting.

A standalone romance with a best friend's brother theme

for everyone who needs a little extra help finding normal

Chapter One

BRENDON

Kaylee plants her palms on the table. Her cheeks spread to her ears. They're pink. Then red. She's laughing so hard her tits are shaking.

Damn, that tight blue dress, the same blue as her glasses.

She looks amazing, like the sweet, innocent angel she is and like the sex goddess I'm desperate to unleash.

But I still hate that scrap of fabric with every fiber of my being.

I hate every ounce of air between us.

Every flint of wood in this table.

Every guy here looking at her the way I am.

Fuck, if I don't get ahold of myself, I'm going to break a few arms. And maybe my hand. And I can't exactly finish Alex's back piece at nine a.m. tomorrow with broken fingers.

Em wraps her arms around Kaylee.

Kaylee laughs, pushing her long blond hair behind her ears and gathering it at one shoulder.

Her eyes flit around the room.

They catch mine.

They scream *I'm about to wish for you to take me to your room.*

Or maybe that's in my head.

Today is the day.

She's no longer a temptation that can get me locked up. Just a temptation that can rip away everything that matters to me.

Em leans in to whisper in her ear. I know my sister. I know exactly what she's saying. *Wish for someone to fuck tonight.*

Not happening.

Not as long as I'm here.

I hate to be a cunt-blocker, really, I do, but there's no way Kaylee is taking home anyone on my watch.

I have no idea how she's managed to stay single this long.

She's beautiful. Smart. Funny. Kind. And innocent... fuck, the way her cheeks are blushing.

The way she's leaning over the table, letting her eyelids fall together, parting her lips...

I could teach her so many things.

I could teach her everything.

But I can't.

She's my sister's best friend.

And as much as Em is a brat, she's all the family I've got.

These two are the most important people in my life.

My cock is going to have to cool it.

It's not getting anywhere near Kaylee.

———

I SIT ON THE KELLY GREEN DECK CHAIR, THE ONE UNDER the old lamp with the too yellow bulb.

Even though we're in one of the most crowded cities in Southern California, the beach is empty. Still. All the voices and laughter are coming from the house. The roar of the ocean isn't enough to muffle the party.

I should head inside and kick out Emma's friends. Insist on driving Kaylee back to her place. Lecture both of them about drinking too much.

But I'm not in the mood to play Dad today. I'm tired of playing Dad, period. Emma and I never got along, not exactly, but we used to have a rapport. We were a team. A *you're annoying, but not quite as annoying as Mom or Dad* team, but we were still a fucking team.

Now, the majority of my relationship is lecturing her and yelling some equivalent of *go to your room*.

And her yelling back *you're not my dad*.

I force myself to look out at the ocean.

It's beautiful. Dark water. Soft sand. Stars bright enough to shine against the black sky but dulled by light pollution all the same.

None of it distracts me.

None of the eight million things going on in my life distract me.

I need a way to get Kaylee out of my head. I've tried everything—work, play, other women, fucking myself, not fucking myself.

Nothing helps.

I pull out my sketchbook and flick my pen a few times. A few more. My warm up sketch is a messy abstract shape. It means something, I'm sure, but I don't have a clue what that is.

I turn the page. Outline the octopus going on Will's bicep tomorrow afternoon. Attempt to fill in the shading.

The details don't come. The only image in my mind is Kaylee. The brightness in her green eyes, the smile spreading over her pink lips, that coy hip tilt. Like she knows how badly I want my hands on those hips.

Like she's going to roll that dress up her thighs, place her palms on the table, and shoot me a *please, fuck me now* look.

I don't need a tattoo mockup.

I need her naked in my bed.

"Hey." The side door slides open and Kaylee steps outside. Her steps aren't soft the way they normally are.

They're messy. Quick.

Her eyes are brighter than normal.

Bolder.

She sits on the lounge chair, next to me. Her thigh presses against mine. Her fingers skim the edges of my sketchbook.

She leans over my shoulder, pressing her chest against my arm, looking up at me with those doe eyes. "Can I see?"

Not the sketchbook. The shit I have in here, of her, will terrify her. Kaylee is sweet. Innocent. I haven't asked, but I'd bet—I have bet Dean—she's a virgin.

My cock rouses at the thought of being the first inside her. Fuck, my lips, my tongue, my fingers—every part of me wants to be her first.

Not happening.

"You looking for a nautical tattoo?" I shoot back.

Her smile spreads over her cheeks. "Maybe. What do you suggest?"

I drag my fingertips over her shoulder, drawing the shape that best suits her. It's a bad idea, touching her like this. It's doing shit to me.

And from the way her eyelids are pressing together and

her lips are parting with a sigh, I'm pretty sure it's doing shit to her.

Fuck, I need a thousand cold showers.

Even if Kaylee wasn't Em's best friend, she's a sweet girl. Someone who deserves a nice guy. A guy who can give her a normal life. Not an asshole who destroys everything he touches.

Even so, I trace the outline of a would-be tattoo up to the tip of her shoulder. "A mermaid."

"I like it."

"I know. You've seen *The Little Mermaid* a thousand times."

"At least two thousand." She looks up at me. "What do you say? Right now? I'm finally old enough to sign the form."

"Okay." I take her hand and pull her to her feet. "Let's walk to the shop. One topless mermaid."

Her eyes go wide. She stammers, presses her toes together. The plastic of her heels clicks. Her teeth sink into her lip. "I, uh..."

"Hate having your bluff called?"

"No, I just... I need to think about it a little more."

"Bullshit." I can't help but smile. She's adorable flustered.

"No, just regular... uh... that isn't why I came out here."

I arch a brow.

She scoots toward me. It's a tiny movement. Soft. More like the Kaylee I know. The sober one.

"Well, it's my birthday." Her fingers curl around my wrist. "And I want a birthday kiss."

How about a birthday fuck? How about a birthday coming on my face until my lips are numb?

"I only give birthday spankings." My voice is steady even though my heart is pounding against my chest.

Fuck, the thought of bending Kaylee over that table and—

"Okay." She presses her lips together. "Let's go. Right here, right now."

"You can handle eighteen?"

She nods.

She can't, but it's tempting anyway...

"Let's go, Brendon." She takes my hand and places it on her hip. Her eyes meet mine. They bore into mine. They demand every thought in my head. Or at least all the ones about stripping her naked. "Or did I call your bluff?"

"Bend over and set your hands on the glass if you want to find out." She *is* calling my bluff. And now I'm calling hers.

Only this is one time—

My sister saves me from my filthy thoughts. She bounces out the door, throws her arms around Kaylee, and pulls her from her seat. "Stop hiding from all the guys at the party."

"Your brother is a guy."

Emma scoffs. Her nose scrunches. It lights up her dark eyes—the same deep brown as mine. She runs her fingers through her violet hair and just barely restrains herself from rolling her eyes.

Kaylee's fingers brush the back of my hand as she turns toward Emma. "Sorry, Em, but it's undeniable. Just look at him."

Emma sticks out her tongue and mouths *gross*. "Mr. Look What a Brooding Bad Boy I Am will be here tomorrow." She grabs Kaylee's hand and pulls her toward the door. "These other guys won't." Emma looks to me. "You don't have to stay and supervise."

"Nice try," I say.

Emma laughs. She blows me a kiss then turns back to her best friend. "Don't wait up."

Kaylee's eyes meet mine. "Did you mean it?"

One part of me did. The rest of me knows better. I play coy. Shrug.

"I'll collect eventually."

"Birthdays only."

"Even so."

I watch her round hips sway as she walks away.

Fuck, that dress...

Fuck me.

How the hell am I going to get this girl out of my head?

Chapter Two

KAYLEE

I'm never drinking again.

Ever.

The pounding headache, cotton mouth, and torn up stomach are reason enough.

But the loss of inhibitions?

No. Thank. You.

I push myself out of Emma's bed—she's still in her shiny silver cocktail dress and most of her makeup—and slink to the bathroom across the hall.

There's noise downstairs. The drip of a coffee maker. The scratch of a spatula. The steady footsteps of a man I can never look in the eyes again.

Not after last night.

I want a birthday kiss.

Ugh.

Inhibitions are underrated. Criminally underrated. They keep you from making a fool of yourself.

They keep you from stepping out of line.

They keep you safe, period.

If it weren't for my inhibitions, everyone would know. And no one would look at me the way they do now—like it's possible I'm on my way to becoming a strong, independent woman.

I pee. Shower. Brush my teeth. Grab my pastel pink makeup bag—the one I adorned in song lyrics—and pick out exactly what I need.

Emma is the one who got me into makeup, but we wear it so differently. For her, it's fun. A way to express herself. To experiment.

For me, it's another necessary component of my shield. No one asks if you're okay if you look polished and awake. Nobody dives past the surface. Which means nobody gets closer than they should.

After I clean every spilled drop of powder foundation from the counter and towel-dry my hair, I head back to Emma's room.

She's out like a light. Her shoes, bag, and jewelry are strewn around the room. I take a moment to put everything away—hers and mine.

I practically live here. Which is why the room is as clean as it is.

I love Emma. She's my best friend, the only person I trust. Well, besides Grandma.

I say this with love.

She's a slob. A proud slob. One who insists she prefers her room messy. Supposedly, it inspires her creativity.

I don't care.

I can't stand it.

We fight about my clean-up efforts all the time. Usually, I get Brendon on my side. Usually, he delivers one of those *I don't care if you're technically an adult, my house, my rules* dad lines of his.

But right now...

I'm not sure how I'm going to face him after last night.

I check my phone. No texts from my parents, not since the *see you after work tomorrow, sweetie* ones I got last night. My Facebook is still flush with Happy Birthday notifications from people I haven't talked to since middle school.

It's kind of nice to feel popular. Even if it's obviously fake. Don't get me wrong. I'm friendly with lots of people. Most of the people I know, save all the reporters on the school paper who complained about my high standards, think I'm sweet, nice, easy going. And they're right. Sort of.

But they're not my friends.

They don't know me. They only know the pretty, polished Kaylee who gets straight As and smiles a perfect customer service smile no matter how ridiculous the complaint.

My stomach growls as the smell of bacon wafts into the room. Then it screams *food, no thank you*.

Bacon isn't happening.

But I should eat something.

I should get this torture over with.

Brendon is my best friend's older brother. I can't avoid him forever.

I pack my bag, change into my work clothes, and slink downstairs.

The white light of morning falls over the wide-open room. It casts Brendon in an angelic glow—so not him, but so right all the same.

God, those dark eyes, that black hair, the strong features—

I want to drink in every inch of him.

And I'm not even gawking at his chiseled torso or his ink yet.

He moves from his spot in the kitchen, behind the oven, and turns toward me. "Hey."

"Hey." I keep my voice even. Casual. Like I didn't ask him to kiss me. Like he didn't offer to spank me. Like I get that he was teasing, that it didn't mean anything, and not like I spent the entire night imagining him pulling me onto his lap.

"You look fucking awful, Kay."

"Hey." I brush my hair onto my right shoulder. "It's not my fault Emma threw away her blow dryer so she wouldn't fry her hair further."

His lips spread into a smile that lights up his dark eyes.

My knees knock together.

That's all it takes for me to crumble—his smile.

But, God, it's a gorgeous smile.

Has it always been this hard to breathe around Brendon? I'm not ashamed to say I've had a crush on him since the first day I saw him on that couch all tall, handsome, and brooding.

But it's been the better part of a decade.

There have been other guys. Dates. Boyfriends. Sloppy make out sessions at parties.

And that big chunk of time last year where I didn't want anyone or anything.

"You always look good." He motions to the table *sit*. "It's your expression."

"Yeah?" I don't want to take orders from him—well, not while we're both dressed—but with the hangover and the lust mixing together sitting is all I can manage.

I take a seat, cross my legs, smooth my button up shirt. The restaurant switched to black shirts six months ago. They hide stains better, but they also suck up all the energy in the room.

"You want tea?" he asks.

"I can make it."

"I know."

"I want to make it."

He shoots me that same stern look. "Which one?"

I press my lips together. I keep a dozen boxes of different teas here. "Iron Goddess of Mercy."

He chuckles. "Suits you."

"You've used that one before."

"It still suits you."

My laugh breaks up the tension in my chest. I'm nowhere near close to badass enough for a label like that, but there are ways that it fits.

Brendon turns on the kettle. Grabs a mug and a tin of tea from the top cabinet.

I try not to obsess over the way his t-shirt hugs his broad shoulders. "You're up early."

"You too."

"I couldn't sleep."

"Hmm."

"What's hmm?"

"It's hmm."

"It's something."

The kettle steams. He pours water into the mug with those strong, steady hands of his. It's not just that I think about what his hands would feel like on my body.

I do.

But I also watch him work.

It's a thing of beauty, watching Brendon draw on paper or on someone's skin. Okay, everything he does is a thing of beauty. But when he's working on a tattoo, he gets this look in his eyes.

Like there's nothing else in the world.

Like he's exactly where he belongs.

I want that. To know what I'm supposed to do, where I'm supposed to be.

There are only two times I feel at home: when I'm reading and when I'm writing.

But neither of those are a career.

I can't write *Hunger Games* fan fiction full time.

I'm too embarrassed to show anyone but Grandma said fan fiction.

"I'm not gonna lecture you about drinking too much." He crosses the room, sets my cup on the table in front of me. His eyes lock with mine. "I'm just glad you feel like shit."

"You're cruel."

"You're just figuring that out?"

My smile spreads over my lips as I shake my head. "Why are you up this early?"

"I'll give you one guess."

"A tattoo."

He nods.

"Doesn't the shop open at ten?"

"Yeah. This guy is an old friend."

"You mean an interesting tattoo."

He smirks as he scoops eggs onto plates. Two plates. "You know me too well."

"Can I see?" I love seeing his work, but he's secretive about his faded black sketchbook. When he isn't reading or watching TV, he's drawing tattoos in that book.

"If you eat."

My shoulders tense.

Who the hell does he think he is telling me when I should eat?

I'm the only person who says what I do with my body.

But I should eat.

And I need to see that sketchbook.

If Brendon wants to believe I'm taking his bribe, that's fine by me.

I nod an *okay*.

Brendon brings our plates to the table. He sits across from me and fixes his coffee with a splash of milk and a hint of sugar.

He brings his mug to his lips and takes a long sip.

I do the same with my tea. Mmm, sweet, sweet caffeine. Nutty, rich, warm oolong.

"So," I say. "Where's the tattoo mockup?"

He grabs his worn black sketchbook from the chair next to his and starts flipping through the pages.

This is a normal morning.

Like nothing happened last night.

Like we're still friends. Just friends.

And as much as I hate that we're just friends, it's better than pretty much every other reasonable possibility.

———

MY OPENING SHIFT DRAGS ON FOREVER. IT'S A SLOW Friday morning, but my manager Jake talks me into staying late to cover for someone who called in sick.

Em chides me about being a pushover, but it's not like that. It's about taking responsibility. If I don't do it, no one will.

Besides, I need the tip money.

I get home a hundred dollars richer—and that's not counting the California state minimum wage that comes with my paycheck.

I live with my parents, in an apartment in Santa Monica. It's a nice place a dozen blocks from the beach.

It's small, but it's ours.

And it's calm. Quiet. Especially on Friday afternoons.

Only it's not.

My parents aren't at work.

They're sitting at the kitchen table, looking at me with regret in their eyes.

Mom motions to the seat across from hers. "Kaylee, sweetie. Will you sit down? We need to talk."

Chapter Three

KAYLEE

My stomach twists. It's not the hangover. That's down to a dull ache.

It's all the dread in Mom's green eyes.

The frown on Dad's face.

He's in his suit. He just came from work. And Mom is in her usual trendy outfit—she does hair at a nice place by the beach. And she usually works on Fridays. She usually works Wednesday through Saturday.

Neither one of them should be home.

Even though my feet are throbbing, I don't move. "I'd rather stand."

"Please, honey." Mom motions to the dining chair. "How about I put on some tea?"

She's nervous. Scared. Which means it's bad.

I don't want to make it harder for her.

But my feet refuse to move toward the table.

I'm not ready for a blow. Any kind of blow. Things are finally good. College starts in a few weeks. I've got my school schedule and my work schedule ironed out. I've got a nice chunk of change in my savings account.

And I'm healthy enough I'm not thinking about how I'm healthy every three minutes.

Mom moves into the kitchen and turns on the electric kettle. She's the person who got me into tea. We still spend afternoons lingering in tea shops together, talking about books and movies and clothes and boys.

Or we did. Until last year.

My parents don't know much, really. Only that I wanted to see a shrink. But that's enough they treat me differently. Like I need to be handled carefully.

Like right now.

Mom fills the tea maker with four scoops of vanilla black. My favorite. Brendon never let me forget my favorite is vanilla.

Dad looks up at me with a sad smile. His hazel eyes are as streaked with regret as Mom's are.

This is something awful.

I tap my toes together. Then my heels. My non-skid shoes are special order Converse knock-offs. They're actually approaching fashionable.

They're a lot more comforting than the looks on my parents' faces.

I continue staring at my scuffed black shoes.

Mom strains the tea into two cups and brings both to the table. She lets out a heavy sigh as she takes her seat.

Again, she motions to the chair opposite hers.

This time, I sit.

I press my knees together.

My toes. My inner feet. My heels.

My shoes are still worn in all the same places.

"Kaylee, Grandma, she isn't doing well. Mike, I mean your dad, had an opportunity to take a promotion that will put us back in New Jersey." Mom's voice is steady, like she's talking about the taste of the tea and not our lives uproot-ing. "He's taking it."

I continue staring at my shoes.

"We talked to the Kanes."

Does she really see Brendon as another parent enough to call him by his last name? When we first moved here, and Emma and I became instant friends, she used to complain about him being a bad influence. That was before the accident. Before he became Emma's dad as much as her brother.

Still, he's only twenty-six.

That's young.

At least that's what I tell myself. That an eight-year age difference means nothing. That there's a chance he sees me as something other than a naïve kid.

"We agreed. It's best if you stay here." Mom folds her arms in her lap and straightens her back. Her posture is stiff. It's *this is our decision and you don't get a say*.

"What if I want to be with Nana?" There's no if. Of course I want to be with Grandma. She lived with us until we moved here. She was my first friend, my closest friend. She still is. We still talk about *Days of Our Lives* and *Harry Potter*. She still tells me every piece of my fan fiction is amazing. "What if I want to watch soaps with her all afternoon and listen to her complain about whatever terrible reality show she's watching all night?"

"I know it's hard, honey. It kills me thinking about my mom all alone, especially when she's ill. But you know this is what she'd want. She wants you in school. She's so proud of you." Mom's smile is earnest. Sweet.

She's right. Grandma has always talked about the importance of school. She's always the first one cheering when I bring home straight As—and I always bring home straight As.

"Brendon made a generous offer," Dad jumps in. "He said you can stay with him and Emma."

What? My lips press together. When the fuck did he do that? He acted normal this morning. And last night...

"He's not my first choice, honey, but this is for the best. Especially with everything that happened last year. Grandma's care is going to be expensive. We're going to have to sublet the apartment. We can try and stretch things so you can stay here. But we'd have to rent out a room. And we figured you'd rather live with your friend than with a stranger." Mom's throat quivers. It's her tell.

They can't stretch things.

They can't afford to help me financially.

And I can't afford to cover half the rent here. Not if I want enough time to ace my classes.

This is an obvious solution.

A smart solution.

But fuck them for not involving me in this decision.

For forcing me to choose school over Grandma.

For treating me like a child.

I push myself to my feet. "When are you leaving?"

"We're flying out Sunday," Dad says. "We need to clear out by the end of the month."

"That's a week and a half away." That's bullshit.

This is all bullshit.

Still, I nod an *I understand*.

I take calm steps to my room.

Press the door into the frame.

Plop on my bed.

Then I hide under my headphones, blast my best angsty playlist, pull the covers over my head and try and fail to feel okay.

When I'm tired of wiping tears off my cheeks, I grab

my Kindle and try to lose myself in all the shit going wrong in Katniss Everdeen's life.

This series is usually instant comfort—I've read it at least two dozen times now—but it's not sticking today.

Nothing is.

Chapter Four

BRENDON

"**Y**ou fucking asshole!" A pillow smacks into my bedroom door.

It's not a brick.

Or a knife. Or Emma's fist.

That's something.

I hit pause on my music. Emma's ragged breath replaces the rhythmic hum of The Clash.

It's funny. My sister is as punk rock as it gets. She doesn't give a fuck what anyone thinks of her. She stands up for her friends no matter the circumstances. She dyes her own hair and sews half her clothes.

She's everything I wanted to be at sixteen.

Whereas—

I'm not exactly a square. I'm not sure you can be a square tattoo artist. But I'm a mortgage paying, Kelly Blue Book checking, Starbucks drinking upstanding member of society.

More or less.

If Mom could see me now...

She'd still think I'm a waste of space.

But she'd have to admit I have my shit together.

"Why the fuck am I hearing this from Mrs. Hart and not from you?" There's the fist against my door. "Brendon. Don't be a coward. Look me in the face when you admit you're conspiring to ruin my best friend's life."

My stomach drops.

Em is pissed.

She's right to be pissed.

And the only thing I can do is insist I'm the adult here.

That's being a parent. I knew what I was signing up for when I lobbied to be her legal guardian.

But that doesn't mean I like it.

Kaylee living here is what makes sense. She's a bright girl with a great future ahead of her. She should be in school. Even if it kills her not being with her family.

"Brendon!" Emma bangs on the door. "I'll give you twenty seconds to explain before I... I don't know. Do something to hurt you back."

"The door is open."

"I know. But—"

We have a strict *ask permission before you enter* policy. It saves both of us from a lot of awkwardness.

I close my sketchbook. "Come in."

She does. She's fuming. Her face is red. Her eyes are blotchy. Her hands are fists. "Well?"

"Her parents are moving back to Jersey."

Emma raises a brow. *And?*

"They think she should stay here. Start school right away."

"And you agree with them?"

"Think about it, Em." It's not like I want Kaylee here. I don't trust myself enough to have her in the next room.

It used to be Kaylee was just Emma's friend. She was a girl who was always good for a late-night conversation about books and movies.

But one day, something snapped. She wasn't Emma's friend. She wasn't a girl at all.

She was a woman.

She was still adorable.

But in a fucking intoxicating way.

I've been thinking about her for months.

It's torture every time she spends the night. Every time I see her on the couch in those tiny shorts she sleeps in, hugging her knees to her chest as she loses herself in a book.

It's torture not touching her.

And it's only going to get harder.

I'm a sick fuck, lusting after the girl I'm supposed to protect.

The girl younger than my kid sister.

But that knowledge hasn't done shit to slow my heart rate when Kay's around.

"Okay. Maybe Kay is better off starting UCLA rather than moving back to New Jersey right away. But you conspired with her parents." Emma folds her arms. "Did you even ask her what she thought?"

I know what Kaylee thinks. If I close my eyes, I can see her miserable and lonely, hiding behind her Kindle the way she always does, pretending like nothing could ever upset her the way she always does.

"I'm your legal guardian." Even if that doesn't matter now that Emma is eighteen. "This is a parent decision."

Emma scowls. "That's a no."

"It's the best option, Em."

"Maybe. But you should have asked her. And me."

"You don't want her here?"

"That's not the point." She turns and spins on her heel. "You should have asked me. Period." She stops at the doorframe. "When is this happening?"

"As soon as possible. Her parents are moving out end of the month."

"You should turn this back into a spare room." Emma nods to my office. "Right away."

"I will."

"And get her an actual copy of the key." Emma's voice softens. "And everything she needs. If you're going to ruin her life, you could at least make her comfortable."

"You think I was gonna leave her on the floor?"

"I didn't think you'd conspire with her parents. How should I know what you'd do?"

"Come by the shop tomorrow. I'll have her key."

"I'll tell her."

"I will."

Emma scoffs. "She's not gonna want to talk to you."

"We'll see."

"Yeah. We will." She slams the door on her way out.

———

THE OFFICE IS A SPARSE ROOM—A DESK, A BOOKSHELF, A few framed prints on the wall. Kay can make use of most of this. But the decor isn't right. It's bold, angry, loud.

She's soft. Quiet. Subtle.

She needs Monet not Lichtenstein.

I did pay attention during one class. The one class I wasn't supposed to take.

Successful guys don't know shit about art.

And certainly not about tattoos.

I move everything but the desk into my room.

There. The black workstation is too dark for Kaylee, but there's no way it's staying black for long. Within a week it will be covered in some mix of lyrics scribbled in silver Sharpie, magazine tear outs, and band stickers.

We argue all the time about the merits of pop-rock and pop-punk vs. punk. Sometimes, I admit I actually enjoy Blink 182. Other times, I tease her about her habit of falling for the broken bad boy. Then I turn over the words in my head, obsessing over the way her green eyes light up every time she sees me without a shirt.

Which is a lot more often than it should be.

Fuck, I'm already thinking about Kay. About the way she takes slow, careful steps when she's modeling a new outfit for Em. About the way she sings along with Emma's favorite Disney movies—with every ounce of emotion in the world. About the way those blue glasses frame her eyes.

I sit on the sprawling four poster bed in my room. I've given this thing a workout over the years. But not lately. Lately, every time a woman so much as touches my arm, I feel sick.

Like I'm betraying Kay.

But I'm not.

We can't be anything.

Ever.

I'm a million years older than her.

I'm her guardian.

Her caretaker.

And, fuck, as much as I'd like to say Mom was wrong, she wasn't. I'm not the kind of guy who brings home the sweet, smart girl. Not unless she's trying to piss off Daddy.

There's no way I'm avoiding Kaylee now.

Which means I need to figure something else out. Some way to resist her that doesn't involve locking myself in my room when she's around.

I stare out the window, watching the waves crash into the sand. Same dark sky. Same silver moon. It's comforting, but it doesn't offer any clarity.

I want Kaylee.

I can't have her.

Sheer willpower is still my only technique for resisting her.

Part of me hopes she hates me for this move thing.

It will be easier to stay away if she isn't looking up at me with those sweet green eyes.

Giggling as she rests her head on my shoulder. *How can you like action movies when you hate "sell out music"? Is anything more by the numbers than yet another Die Hard sequel?*

Better to get this over with.

I pull out my cell and I text Kaylee.

Brendon: You okay?

Kaylee: About what you'd expect.

Brendon: I'm getting a key made for you. I'll leave it at the front desk. You can pick it up whenever.

Kaylee: Thanks. I'll stop by before work.

Brendon: You want to talk about it?

Kaylee: What's there to say? My parents are moving across the country and they aren't asking my opinion about it. I hated it when I was ten, and I hate it now. At least then they invited me to join.

Brendon: Would you move with them if they'd asked?

Kaylee: I don't see how it matters.

Brendon: Your grandma okay?

Kaylee: No. But I'm not in the loop with the details. I have no idea if she has a few weeks left or a few years.

Brendon: I'm sorry she's sick.

Kaylee: Thanks. This isn't on you. You made a generous offer. I do get that. And I appreciate it. Really, Brendon. I do.

Brendon: It's nothing.

Kaylee: It's a lot. I just...

Brendon: Wanted to be consulted?

Kaylee: Want things to be different. But that too. I'm tired. I'm going to go to bed. I'll see you tomorrow.

Brendon: Sweet dreams, Kay.

Kaylee: You too.

Chapter Five

BRENDON

The bell rings as Kaylee steps inside the shop.

She's in her work outfit—dark jeans, a black button up shirt, black non-skid shoes.

She hugs her pink purse to her shoulder as her eyes flit around the room.

Ryan nods hello. Runs a hand through his shaggy brown hair.

She nods back. Smiles a polite *I'm trying to act like everything is great* smile.

The client sitting in his chair isn't at all shy about giving Kaylee a long once over. His eyes are practically bugging out of his head.

My hand curls into a fist. It's a reflex.

Nobody like him is getting anywhere near her.

"Hey Kaylee," Ryan calls. "How are you?"

"Good. Thanks." She presses her lips together. "I'll just be a minute."

He nods.

She crosses the room to my spot at the front desk.

Leighton is running late. My next appointment is in

thirty minutes. So I'm working on a mock up here instead of in my chair.

The light is better here.

But there's not enough privacy.

I need the space to think.

To let images flit through my mind and fit together.

Kaylee's steps are soft but steady. "Hey. This... I know you're only trying to help."

I nod as I pull her spare key from my pocket and hand it over. I wouldn't assign myself such charitable motivations, but I'm not going to argue with her. "You have a moving date in mind?"

"I'm off Monday."

"I'll meet you at your place at nine."

"I'll be okay on my own."

"I know."

"I don't need your help."

"Take it anyway."

She tilts her head to one side. "Fine, but only because I'm running late and I'm not in the mood to argue." She taps her fingers against the counter. "I... I guess I'll see you... everywhere. Since I'm your new roommate."

"It will be a good thing."

She nods. "Eventually."

I want to wrap my arms around her and refuse to let go.

That can't happen.

Neither can a handshake or some equally painful brush off.

Kay and I hug. Period. I need to find a way to be okay with that.

I step out from behind the counter.

She leans in to the gesture.

It's quick but tight.

And, fuck, I feel her everywhere.

I have to force myself to pull back. *She's a kid. You're supposed to protect her.* "You sleeping over tonight?"

"Maybe. Em's trying to convince me to go out. But I think I'd rather crash at home." Her eyes go to the clock. "Shit. I gotta go. I'll see you soon."

I nod goodbye.

Watch her ass sway as she walks away.

This time next week, Kaylee is going to live in the room down the hall.

I'm going to have to resist her twenty-four seven.

Will power isn't gonna cut it.

I need something a hell of a lot stronger.

———

MY TWELVE O'CLOCK IS SITTING IN THE TEAL CHAIR, HER face pressed against the wall, her tongue between her teeth.

She squints.

Bites her tongue.

Squeezes her thigh with her free hand.

Her gaze goes to the mirror. She watches me work.

At first, it bothered me. But I'm used to it now.

Clients love watching ink mark their skin.

I can't blame them.

I love it too.

And this girl—she's barely older than Kaylee—is a trooper. It's nearly two now, and she hasn't asked for a single break.

I check in. "You okay?"

She murmurs something. When I arch a brow, she nods.

"This is the last line."

"Thank fuck," she whispers.

My lips curl into a smile. This is her first piece of ink, and it's a big fucking tattoo—a teddy bear with its arms hanging off, stuffing spilling from its guts, its eye missing, its nose askew.

I don't ask what it means. I never do. Tattoos are personal. People talk when they want someone to listen.

Mostly.

Some people don't say shit, even when they're desperate for someone to listen.

Besides, there might not be a backstory. It might be as simple as a love of teddy bears.

It's better to skip assumptions.

I place the needle over her skin, work the angle until it's just right. My eyes meet hers through the mirror. "You ready?"

She grits her teeth as she nods.

I turn the gun on and draw the last line down her shoulder, all the way to the middle of her upper arm.

She's done.

I pull the gun away, set it down. "That's it."

Her shoulders slip from her ears as she sighs. She shifts her torso so she can see the reflection.

Her eyes are saucers.

Her smile is spread over her cheeks.

"Oh my God! It's perfect." She jumps out of the chair and throws her arms around me.

I'm not used to *this*. I should be. Getting ink releases all sorts of endorphins. Adrenaline. Dopamine. *I'm a badass, I can't believe I did that* vibes. It's easy for people to mistake the rush of a tattoo for the rush of lust.

Or she thinks I'm hot.

I'm well aware of my effect on women.

It hasn't done me any good in a while. Not since I gave

up on finding someone who would push Kaylee out of my head.

Shit. There goes my clear mind. When I'm in the chair, my hands on my tattoo gun, I slip into this trance. There's nothing in my head but the work. Not my doubts, not my desires, not my parents' voices. Hell, I'm not even thinking about the client. Or about our owner.

It's all about the ink itself.

It's nirvana.

I'm leaving a mark on someone's skin. Something that will last forever.

It's the best job in the world.

Worth almost any amount of bullshit.

"Sit back down. I need to clean you up." My voice drops to that demanding tone. The one I use when women are naked. Or about to get naked.

Not the kind of shit I do at work.

She doesn't mind the Dom voice. She settles into her seat, staring at the reflection of her tattoo with a goofy smile on her face.

Her enthusiasm is infectious.

And she's cute. Light hair. Bright eyes. Ample tits. The kind of girl I used to take home every other night.

I slip back into my trance as routine takes over. Wash. Pat dry. Photo. Plastic covering.

I go through my usual aftercare speech, take her to the counter to pay, grab some A+D ointment for her, accept another hug, take a few more pictures, listen to her gush to Leighton.

Fuck, it feels good, seeing someone that happy over their new ink.

Nothing else fills me with that kind of pride.

It doesn't even faze me when she slips me a business card and smiles. "I'd love to get a drink sometime. The bar down the street is great. Or we could go to my place. You haven't had a dirty martini until you've had one of mine."

Anna. She's an assistant at some place with a corporate name.

She wants to fuck me. She's nearly screaming it.

But I'm still tempted to toss her card.

She sways her hips as she walks out the door. It's a showy gesture. A *look at my ass*.

Dean waits until the door swings shut to move into the lobby. He shoulder taps me. "You got her number. Nice."

I shoot him an incredulous look.

"Did you not see those tits? She was fine."

"And?"

His smile spreads over his cheeks. His blue eyes light up. "And she wants to tear off those black skinny jeans of yours. What the fuck are you trying to prove with that outfit anyway? You look like an emo musician."

I struggle not to roll my eyes. This is a tattoo shop, not a runway. And he only pulls out that emo label to annoy me. Because he knows Emma's room is decorated with posters of eyeliner wearing musicians. And that nothing annoys me more than her blasting that shit.

"It wouldn't hurt, honing that damaged musician look," Walker calls out from his suite. He stands up, shakes his head, shaking his long, wavy hair in every direction. His dark eyes get bright. "I doubt Kaylee would mind."

Fuck, I know it's a Saturday afternoon in the middle of summer, but I can't deal with all four of us here. Dean and Walker together isn't so bad. The two of them give me a lot of shit, but it's good natured.

Ryan's fine on his own. He's curt but it comes with a quiet professionalism.

The three of them together—

It's too many opinions.

They're like children throwing a tantrum.

Reacting only encourages them.

"Yeah, I know, you know, Ryan knows, everybody here knows. Everybody but Brendon," Dean says.

Ryan rolls his eyes. "You here to work or to gossip?"

"Gossip." Dean smiles at his brother. Runs his hand through his hair exactly the same way Ryan does. "Especially about fucking cute blondes rocking the librarian look. You have anything to say about that?"

"I have shit to say about work." Ryan folds his arms.

Walker chuckles. "You really think Kaylee would give you the time of day?"

Dean shrugs. "I'm speaking metaphorically. We can all appreciate a woman with a nice ass and fantastic tits. Especially when she wears tiny sun dresses and sweet cardigans."

"And she has hypothetical green eyes and blue glasses? And a heart that beats only for Brendon?" Walker asks.

"I'm not talking about her heart," Dean says. "I'm talking about her body."

Walker laughs. He shoots me that *you gonna take this* look?

"How do you think she'd sound screaming my name? More high pitched?" Dean imitates a woman's moan. "Oooh, Dean," he squeals. "Fuck me, Dean. Harder. Harder." He drops the put-on voice. "Or more low and breathy?" He groans. "Oh. Dean. Yes. Right. There."

Dean has no intention of fucking Kaylee.

And Walker is right. She'd never give him the time of day.

Dean wants me to snap and tell him to go fuck himself. It's not happening. The shit that goes through my head is a lot worse than this.

He presses on anyway. "The girl looks at you like you

set her panties on fire. You could snap your fingers and have her on her knees."

"You want to hear this shit or not?" Ryan's voice hits that *I mean business* tone.

Dean nods. "I have a lot more shit to give Brendon, but fine."

"Manning is selling the shop," Ryan says.

Fuck.

Every bit of joy falls from Dean's expression.

Even Walker looks surprised.

"He's giving us the option to buy him out. Any of us. Or all four of us. It's not cheap, but it's doable." Ryan stares back at his brother. "You listening now?"

Dean nods.

Ryan takes a minute to go into the numbers. I'm the only person with enough to buy out the place. But that would mean adding more time to the mortgage.

There's no way I'm doing that.

But there's no way I'm letting this shop slip through my fingers either. This place is the best thing in my life.

"We have two weeks," Ryan says. "Think about it. Check your shit. We'll talk."

He nods goodbye to his brother.

Ryan shakes his head as he watches Dean and Walker return to their suites. He runs a hand through his shaggy hair. Shakes his head. "They're such kids."

"They are kids," I say.

His expression gets sincere. Caring. It's a rarity for him. He's been sulking over his broken heart, avoiding anything that even resembles earnest emotion, for ages now. "They're fucking immature, but they're right."

"I ask for your opinion?"

"I ask you to invite your crush to hang out here so you can stare at her ass?"

"She was here for two minutes."

"Yeah, she never hangs out here."

"She helps out for free."

"That's why she's here, love of our bottom line?"

"You have a point?"

"My idiotic brother is right. She's not gonna wait around for you forever. And you shouldn't either." He motions to the business card in my hand. "She was cute."

"Not interested."

"You don't need to marry her. Just go out. Have fun. Realize there are more fish in the sea."

"Really?"

"Fuck off. I can be a hypocrite if I want." He is. He's been scorched Earth about romance since his ex left. There are no other fish in the sea. Not for Ryan.

"She's almost as young as Kaylee."

"She invited you to a bar." Ryan shrugs. "Your life. Do what you want." He motions to Anna's number. "You keep saying you don't want to be with Kay. If you mean it, then prove it. At least to yourself."

Chapter Six

KAYLEE

There are a dozen boxes in the living room. The space is empty. Sparse. Soulless.

Mom is sitting on the couch, one hand in her lap, the other playing with the silver palm-tree tag attached to her plain black suitcase. She might as well scream *we're leaving California, we're leaving you, we're leaving our lives entirely*.

She stands.

Her gestures are small. Quiet.

Her steps are nearly silent.

She picks her purse off the kitchen table and slides it onto her shoulder with tender care. Like it's some piece of fine China and not something we bought at TJ Maxx for forty dollars.

The table—the one that gives me bruises every time I bump into it in the dark—is one of the only things of ours left.

Okay, that's not fair. Most of the furniture is here. We're subletting the place furnished. For college kids, the ones that go to Santa Monica College on their parent's dime, the ones who can afford to have fun.

I shake my head. I'm not going to get jealous. Emma is one of those people. She can't help that she and Brendon inherited a fortune. She can't help that she isn't wound tighter than a ball of twine.

I have time, money, and space for fun.

The only thing stopping me is me.

"I wish we had more time." Mom's voice is as sad as her smile. She unwraps her arms, opening herself and inviting me in.

I don't want her invitation.

I want to tell her to go fuck herself. She can't un-invite me from my life then offer comfort. That's bullshit.

Them being vague about the details of Grandma's condition—that's bullshit.

It's not like Grandma is some relative we never see. She's practically my best friend. She taught me how to curl my hair, how to make an almond butter and jelly sandwich (cooking is one thing I still can't master), how to tell which games at the boardwalk were rigged (most of them).

We used to play with dolls and Legos and even Dad's *Star War*'s figurines.

Now, it's more talk about boys and hair and school, but we're just as close. She calls every week. At least.

I want to yell and scream.

But I won't. I never do.

Someone has to be the one in control. The one who keeps it together.

Someone has to be the one everyone can count on.

I accept my mom's hug. I sink into it. I try to find comfort in the embrace, but it feels like betrayal.

They should have asked me.

This is my life too.

I don't want things to change. I don't want them to leave. I don't want Grandma to die.

But I can't stop any of it.

I'm not in control here.

Not even a little.

I release my mom's embrace and take a step backward.

Dad is waiting at the kitchen table, his hands in his pockets, his eyes on the floor.

He looks up at me. His hazel eyes fill with pride. "Kay, I'm going to miss you so much. We'll call every day. And visit as soon as we can." He smiles. "Or we can fly you out to visit with Grandma. How would that be?"

I want to tell him to throw away his shitty consolation prize, but I don't. The thought of visiting Grandma is too inviting. The affection in his voice is too earnest. "Okay."

He steps forward and pulls me into a hug. "I'm so proud of you. We all are. You're going to ace your classes."

My mouth gets sticky. Everyone is sure I'm going to excel. Everyone expects me to get everything right, all the time. It's a lot of pressure. Even if most of it comes from myself. "Thanks, Dad."

"You're such a bright young woman. I'm not sure what we did to get so lucky. I love you so much, baby girl."

"I love you too."

He steps backward. Reaches for his suitcase, the black one with the plain red tag.

He looks to Mom. "I guess we better go. Security at LAX is always a nightmare."

Mom nods. "Are you going to be okay alone, Kay? We can drop you off at the Kanes' house."

I shake my head. I need to say goodbye to everything.

And I need to figure out how I'm going to survive constant proximity to Brendon. He's off limits.

I know that.

I just don't know how to convince my body or my heart to get on board with the get over Brendon plan.

My eyes go to the clock on the wall, the plain black one we got at Target last year. It's the only thing in here I picked out.

Their flight takes off in an hour and a half. They've been waiting for me to get home. To say goodbye.

Warmth crawls into my chest. It threatens to break up the stone growing around my heart.

But that's not happening.

If they want forgiveness, they should apologize.

"I'll be okay. Let me know when you get in." I hug Mom and Dad one last time. Go through one last round of goodbyes.

Then I watch them walk out the door.

And I settle into the couch.

And I soak in all the feelings whirring around my chest.

I'm alone.

I have Brendon and Emma, but as long as I keep everything to myself, I'm alone.

————

I HATE EVERYTHING ABOUT THIS.

I could talk to Emma, but she's angry on my behalf. She starts ranting about how awful my parents are, about what a traitor Brendon is for siding with them, about how everything in the world is unjust.

She's right.

But I don't want her being pissed for me.

I'm plenty pissed myself. It's just... I can never quite find the words to express it. Not verbally. Not to anyone else.

The only place where I can really get my feelings out is my journal.

I've always loved pouring my feelings onto the pages.

Though love isn't the right word. It's more of a frantic need. If I skip a few days, my thoughts turn into a jumbled mess. I get fuzzy. Overwhelmed.

My head goes to dark places.

Last year, my head started going to dark places all the time. It was before Grandma got sick. It wasn't for any reason, really.

It was like falling asleep. It happened slowly, then all at once. Food stopped tasting good. Everything I read—even *The Hunger Games*—failed to grab my attention. Class was boring. Parties, hangouts, and study sessions stopped appealing.

I didn't hang out with anyone but Emma.

And I didn't even want to see Emma. It was some combination of her insistence and inertia that got me watching Disney movies at her place every afternoon.

Otherwise, I didn't do anything but go to school and work. But even that felt so hard. Like there was always a ten-pound weight on my chest.

I couldn't sleep. I couldn't think. I didn't even want Brendon.

I was empty.

I started seeing a therapist. According to her, I have high functioning depression. Instead of falling apart and doing nothing, I channel my self-loathing into achieving.

Apparently, it's my broken brain. Instead of telling me I'm not good enough, it latches onto grades. They aren't good enough. But then they never are. Even when they're straight As.

It took a while to find an anti-depressant that took the edge off without dulling me completely. The first one made me tired. The second kept me from coming. The third gave me nightmares. This one is tolerable. It pushes all those thoughts about hurting myself to the back of my head.

If I keep up my routine—healthy diet, not too much sugar, just enough caffeine, cardio every day, journaling every night—those ugly thoughts stay at bay.

But they never go away.

And they never will.

I'm broken.

I'll always be broken.

I've accepted it, mostly.

But no one else has. No one else knows.

If they find out, they'll leave.

So, I keep it to myself. I keep all my writing—the poems, the stories, the journal entries—to myself.

Fan fiction is fine, but anything personal—that's mine.

I write things from my heart all the time. Words get caught in my throat and I spill my guts on the page. It's like that expression. How do you write? It's easy. You just cut yourself and bleed on the page.

Only there's nothing in the expression about guarding your scars with your life.

Writing in my journal makes me feel at peace.

Writing, period, makes me feel at peace.

It's my favorite thing in the world.

But I'm not brave or foolish enough to share it with anyone.

That means it's staying a hobby.

That means it's staying mine.

I fall back on my bed. It's still covered in my *Little Mermaid* bedspread. I've had it since I was a kid. Emma's addiction to Disney movies is contagious. I love all the Disney princesses too. Every one of them.

But there's something special about Ariel. She knows exactly what she wants. She's fascinated by the human world. Even though it's strange and foreign, she wants to be a part of it. And she's willing to do whatever it takes to make that happen. Even give up her family. Her home. Her voice.

I want to be that bold.

That sure of myself.

But here—my journal—is the only place I can really hear my voice.

I bring my pen to the page and I let all the ugly thoughts in my head flow through my pen.

I want to show this to someone.

No, not to someone.

To him.

But there's too much risk. He might run in the other direction.

One day, I'll be brave enough to open my heart.

I close my journal and trace the Latin saying scribbled over the back.

Serva Me, Servabo Te.

Save me and I'll save you.

I want that. One day.

But it's as much of a fairy tale as *The Little Mermaid*.

Chapter Seven

KAYLEE

I'm still in my pajamas, fixing coffee and tea, when Brendon knocks on the door.

"Hey." His steady voice flows through the wood.

"Give me a minute." I've worn this exact outfit at his place a hundred times. But right now it feels too revealing, too personal.

I move to my room, grab the outfit I laid out last night. High-waisted shorts and a v-neck t-shirt. Cute. Flattering. Practical.

I change as quickly as I can, dart back to the door, pull it open. "Hey."

Light surrounds him like a halo. It casts highlights over his dark hair and his strong shoulders.

God, his shoulders are bare.

He's wearing a muscle tank and shorts. It would look douchey on anyone else. On Brendon, it screams *trace all the lines of the ink running down my shoulders. Don't you want these arms around you? Don't you want every bit of everything I have to give?*

I can't have that.

I can't have a single bit of it.

It would kill Emma.

Even if it wouldn't, Brendon doesn't want someone broken. He ends all his "relationships" when things get complicated.

He nods to the boxes sitting in the living room. "I'll start loading."

I motion to the carafe on the counter. "Coffee first?"

"Coffee after."

"As long as I can have tea first."

"I'd never deprive you."

He's talking about tea, but my body doesn't catch the nuance.

My skin tingles. My stomach flutters. Heat spreads down my torso, collecting at the apex of my thighs.

I allow myself a moment to gawk as he picks up the first box and carries it to his car. Okay, then the second.

He shoots me an *are you going to watch or help* look.

I make my way to my bedroom and finish my last bits of packing. It's just clothes now. I have a lot of them. Nothing compared to Emma, but when my entire bed is covered with a quarter of my wardrobe...

Maybe I have a problem.

I pack my last set of dresses. Then all the toiletries I left out for this morning. I do one last wipe down of the bathroom, so everything is pretty and pristine.

Now, it's just my...

Oh God.

Brendon is in my doorframe, his eyes on my bed. Not just on the *Little Mermaid* comforter, but on the collection of underwear on top of it.

It wouldn't be so bad if I owned anything remotely sexy. But that's all cotton and comfort bras.

Not what I want him imagining when he...

No.

It doesn't matter.

Brendon doesn't look at me that way.

I think.

He's not saying anything.

I'm not saying anything.

We're just standing in this room with my underwear on display, saying nothing.

His gaze moves to the walls. "I'm sorry I missed seeing it in its glory."

"Huh?"

He nods to the bare walls.

"Oh." He's never been in my room. With the way my heart is pounding and my body is buzzing, it makes perfect sense. He's here. My bed is there. It would be so easy to combine those two things. "I'm going to attempt to recreate the majesty at your place."

"Our place."

"Our place." It feels funny on my tongue, but I will get used to it. The house in Venice Beach isn't Brendon and Emma's place. It's our place. My place.

I live with Brendon.

I live with the guy who refuses to leave my head.

I can handle that. Totally.

He nods to the bedside drawer. "I can make myself scarce if you need to pack anything personal."

"Why would I..." Oh. My blush spreads to my chest. I stammer. "No. I don't. I don't have one of those."

He arches a brow. Teasing. Maybe.

"No. But. Um." I'm going to die of embarrassment. "I don't use those."

"You're missing out."

"What?" I manage to look at him for an entire second. Two even. His expression is light, but there's curiosity in his eyes. He really wants to know. "Why do you care?"

He shrugs. "You should get one."

"Oh." This is... My head is spinning.

I can't place his tone.

Is it *you should get one so I can use it on you?*

Or is it *masturbation is healthy and awesome, you should get a vibrator* awkward but necessary mentor/Dad/older brother talk?

I...

Uh...

My body goes straight to the former.

I can't think.

The only thing in my head is the glorious mental image of him peeling off my panties and pressing a vibe to my clit.

Fuck.

We're going to live together. We're going to be roommates. Or even... it's more like he's my legal guardian.

He doesn't see me that way.

We're friends.

We're only ever going to be friends.

I need to act like this is normal. Like we're two adults talking about sex toys like adults do. "I thought guys were bothered by—" I can say the word. "Vibrators."

"In your vast experience?"

"Yeah." Okay, so I've never exactly had a guy over here. I've never had a guy's hands below my waist. Or mine below his. But I listen in class, at work, at the shop. I've heard guys talk about sex toys like they were only for desperate women.

"It's a tool. That's it."

"And that doesn't threaten you?"

"No."

"You're that... confident?"

He gives me a long once over. His eyes settle on mine. "We're not having his conversation."

"You brought it up."

"Even so."

There's something in his eyes.

An awkwardness I don't recognize.

Because he sees me as a sister?

Or because he's desperate to use a vibrator on me?

———

IT TAKES THE ENTIRE MORNING TO UNPACK MY STUFF. The room—my room—has a desk but it's lacking most of the other furniture I need.

We get lunch at the taco place down the street, make plans to get furniture tomorrow, argue about who is going to stay in the master bedroom until we get my bed. I insist he stays in his room. He insists the couch.

Eventually, I break and agree. And it has nothing to do with how much I want to be in his bed, wrapped up in sheets that smell of him.

It's not like that's the only reason why I relent.

Not at all.

———

GOD, THIS REALLY IS AMAZING.

I fall back onto Brendon's four poster bed.

I sink into the smooth sheets.

They smell like him. Like his earthy soap and like something distinctly Brendon.

God, they smell good.

I let my eyelids flutter closed and let my head fill with dirty thoughts.

Him next to me.

Pulling my t-shirt over my head.

Unhooking my bra.

Sliding it off my shoulders.

Dragging his fingertips up my torso, between my breasts, around my nipples.

Pressing his lips to mine.

He thinks I'm sweet. Innocent.

Everyone does.

And I am.

I'm a virgin, sure. But I'm not naïve.

I know what I want.

It's him.

A knock on the door pulls me back to the moment.

"I'm heading to work. You gonna be okay alone?" Brendon asks from the hallway.

He explained it at lunch—he and Emma have a strict knock, enter only if invited policy.

"Yeah. I have to get started on my summer reading."

"Call me if you need anything."

"I'll be fine."

"Promise."

"Brendon—"

"If you'll be fine, it will be an easy promise to keep."

It's a compelling argument. Even if I have no intentions of calling him. No matter what I need. "Okay. I promise."

"See you tonight."

"You too."

His footsteps move down the hallway. Then the stairs.

I can just barely hear the front door shut.

Emma is at work—she works at a department store at the promenade.

I'm alone here.

I've never been alone here before.

It's the perfect chance to work out some of this tension.

But not yet.

It sounds stupid, but I can't touch myself in the middle of the afternoon. That's so... intentional.

I only ever masturbate before bed. So it's for insomnia relief as much as anything else.

Still, I should take advantage of being alone in Brendon's room somehow.

Reading isn't quite as exciting or naughty as masturbating to thoughts of my new roommate slash guardian, but hey—

I have dirty books on here.

I'm capable of fun. Of sexy. Of bad.

Just, I'm going to do it by myself in my pajamas.

I toss my sleep shorts on the bed.

Set my Kindle on the dresser.

Right next to the faded black sketchbook.

Wait.

That's Brendon's sketchbook.

It's right there.

I've never seen it by itself.

In his hands? Yeah.

On his lap? Absolutely.

Nestled under his arm? Of course.

It never leaves his sight.

And he snaps it fast whenever I get close.

This is it.

All the secrets to what's in that beautiful head of his.

His secrets.

None of my business.

I pick it up. Run my fingers over the worn leather cover. Undo the snap holding the pages together.

This is his.

It's private.

Yes, I want to know why his smiles are so rare.

I want to know what it is he's thinking about when he's sitting on the deck alone.

When he's alone, period.

God, I want in his head so badly I'm shaking.

This is wrong. What if it was your journal?

I force myself to set the book down.

To sit on the bed.

To cross my legs. Fold my hands. Keep my gaze on the floor.

I shouldn't look.

But this is the only chance I'm going to get.

If I don't look, I'll never get inside his head.

I'll never know what he's thinking.

I'll never know if he's thinking about me.

I place the book in my lap and pry it open. The first few pages are familiar tattoo mockups—Brendon always shows off his finished work. Or maybe I check the shop's Facebook religiously. Either way.

Then there are figure drawings. More tattoo mockups. A fierce dragon defending a castle. A giant octopus destroying a sea monster. A topless mermaid sunning on a rock.

A librarian pin up.

Only...

No.

She looks like me. Same champagne blond hair. Same green eyes. Same pretty pink cardigan. Same thick blue glasses. These aren't exactly standard frames.

And she's wearing a Mockingjay pin.

Exactly like the one attached to my backpack.

That's nothing. Lots of people like *The Hunger Games*. Even Brendon.

There's no way he's looking at me like this.

My heartbeat picks up.

My breath flees my body at an alarming rate.

I shouldn't turn the page, but I can't stop myself.

It's that same pin up, only her cardigan is unbuttoned. Her breasts are exposed.

In the next picture, she's lying on her back, her arms over her head, her cardigan binding her wrists.

The next.

That's me. Splayed out over this bed. Naked. Bound to the railing.

I turn the page.

Fuck.

I suck a deep breath between my teeth.

I press my thighs together.

I'm on my knees, resting on my heels, looking up.

Naked.

Waiting.

Hungry.

He wants me.

Brendon wants me.

Chapter Eight

BRENDON

Kaylee pushes her glasses up her nose. "I think I have everything."

It's Tuesday morning. Our furniture date. More than twelve hours since this place officially became Kay's.

A night on the couch didn't do shit to help with my head space.

I'm exhausted. It lowers my inhibitions. Gets me saying all the shit I want to say to her.

Looking at her the way I want to.

"You have everything?" she asks.

I nod and try to keep my eyes off her tits.

Fuck, the way her sun dress is falling down her chest—

I know she doesn't wear this shit to torture me. I know Emma curated half of Kaylee's wardrobe.

But I don't see my sister's handiwork when I look at her. I don't see the kid I'm supposed to protect.

I see long legs, lush tits, soft lips, sweet green eyes—

I want to rip off her cotton panties.

I want to pin her to the table and lick her until she's groaning my name.

She's not going to stay a virgin forever.

Someone is going to be her first.

It should be someone she trusts.

Someone who will make sure she comes.

Someone who will teach her every fucking thing she needs to know.

"You... you ready, Brendon?" She looks up at me with those soft green eyes.

What the hell is wrong with me?

This isn't about my cock.

Or my hands or lips or my tongue.

Kaylee is here because her parents bailed on her. Because her grandma is sick. Because she needs someone to protect her.

That's what I signed up for.

There's no way I'm taking advantage of that trust.

Yeah, this isn't how I imagined my life when I was her age. That guy would kill somebody if he knew he was going to grow up to get his furniture at Ikea.

And, fuck, if he had any idea how much pop-rock he'd listen to on the way—

I'm not proud of what a judgmental shit I used to be. But I did stand for something. Well, against something. Against all the bullshit my parents jammed down my throat.

Now that I am a parent—legally, at least—I get it.

It's hard taking care of someone. Wanting what's best for them. Trying to figure out where to draw the line.

That doesn't excuse my mom's constant reminders that I'd never be good enough.

But it does explain them.

I promised myself Emma would never go through any of the shit I did. That she'd never hear that who she was or what she wanted was wrong. But fuck, it's hard. She tests my resolve all the time.

Even Kaylee pushes my resolve.

"Brendon? You okay?" Her voice is soft. Caring.

"Yeah." I push myself to my feet.

She stares at my empty coffee mug. "You're going to leave that there?"

I nod.

"I'm fine with that." She slides her purse onto her shoulder. The grey one with the gorilla key chain. "Really, I am."

"Of course."

She tries and fails to pry her eyes away. "Really?"

I chuckle. "Not that it bothers you."

"You're doing it on purpose."

"Why would I do that?"

"Cruelty." She grabs the mug, brings it to the sink, shoots me a *you win* look. "Why else?"

She's adorable flustered.

Too adorable.

It's sending my thoughts straight to my bedroom. To her splayed out on my black sheets, wearing nothing but those glasses and that tiny turquoise cardigan.

"Brendon?" Her fingers curl around my forearm. Her index finger slips. Traces the lines of my sleeve tattoo. "We can leave later if you have something to do."

Yeah, I do, but it's going to take all fucking day.

Go to my room, take off your dress, sit on the bed and wait for me.

"And delay our three-dollar meatballs?" I force my voice to something light. "I don't think so."

She follows me to the car. Her cheeks flush as she folds her arms over her chest. She tugs at her purse, pulling it closer. "Three dollar meatballs?"

"Ikea."

"Ikea?" Kaylee arches a brow. "Really?"

I nod.

She pushes her blue glasses up her nose. "Why?"

"Three-dollar meatballs are enough of a reason."

"Ew."

"They're good. Try them." I let the back of my hand brush against her arm as I lead her to the car.

She moves around the back and reaches for the passenger-side door. "I'll consider it."

I unlock the car and pull the door open. "You trust me?"

She shoots me a *really* look as she slides inside. "It has nothing to do with trust."

"Nothing?"

"Yeah, nothing." She clicks her seatbelt. Sets her purse in her lap. Plays with its strap. "No offense, Brendon, but don't you have more money than that?"

I can't help but chuckle. "I'm a humble craftsman."

"With a million-dollar house on the beach. Or, um, I guess I've never asked about your finances."

"Don't. I've got it under control."

Her lip corners turn down. "I... Did my parents offer to help you out?"

"Yeah."

"And?"

"I turned them down."

"And you can afford that?"

"Yeah."

She stares at me, those green eyes wide. "If you don't convince me with some numbers, I'm going to start buying groceries. And trying to cook dinner. And no one wants that."

My chest warms. Kaylee's a terrible cook. It's the only thing she isn't good at. I nod. "That's horrifying."

"Yeah, even worse than what those assassins did to John Wick's dog."

Fuck, it's like she's trying to drive me out of my mind.

Kay always joins me when I watch action movies on the couch. She spends the entire time hiding behind her hands or complaining about how everyone is quick to violence, or about how the plot is incomprehensible, but she keeps watching them.

She doesn't like the movies.

She watches them to hang out with me.

Fuck, I'm not stupid.

I know she doesn't like me as a brother or a parent or a friend.

"My parents bought this place before I was born. Mortgage is almost paid off. And it's cheap. Based on the value from nearly thirty years ago." And they had good life insurance. My dad was careful before he was anything else.

"How cheap?"

"I can cover it in a week of work, easy."

"Oh. Good." She presses her lips together. "You probably know already."

I shake my head. The Harts didn't explain much. They didn't have to. I get it.

"They want to stay in Jersey. Permanently."

That's a knife in my chest. I can't imagine how she feels.

I turn the car on and pull onto the street. "I'm sorry, Kay."

"Thanks. I... I don't know. I guess, if they gave me the choice, I probably would have stayed here. But I hate feeling like I'm not in control of my life. And I miss

Grandma. She was my best friend when I was a kid. Still is."

"You can stay as long as you want."

"Yeah?" Her fingers skim my wrist. "That won't get in the way of your... relationships?"

"My what?" I arch a brow.

"You used to *date* a lot. Not as much lately."

Not for the last few months, give or take. Not since she found her way into my brain.

"I wouldn't want you to feel... deprived."

"Deprived?"

"You know what I mean." There's this tone to her voice. One I can't place. "You're a young guy. Prime of your life. I'm sure you want to be having fun."

"You saying Ikea isn't fun?"

"I don't know. We aren't there yet." She leans back in her seat. "Do you still date?"

"Why?"

"Don't friends talk about this kind of thing?"

Yeah, technically. Dean and Walker brag about their conquests. Ryan... well, everyone knows where Ryan stands. "Do you date?"

"Sometimes. You know Em and her double dates. You?"

I can't tell her it's been awhile. That will encourage her. But I've got to say something. "There's a lot going on right now."

"Like?"

"This."

"This just happened."

"Manning is selling the shop."

"Oh." She runs her fingertips up my arm. "Brendon, I'm sorry. Will you have to go somewhere else?"

"Maybe. He's offering it to us first. Any of us."

"Hmm."

"Hmm?"

"You only have a few years left on the mortgage. What's a few more to be the proud owner of Inked Hearts?"

"It's Emma's house too."

"You know she'd say yes."

She would. She's always wanted to run her own business. This would be perfect training wheels.

Which is why she can't know.

I protect Emma from this kinda thing.

I'm not sacrificing her stability.

There's got to be another way.

"I'll think about it," I say.

"Lies, lies, lies." Kaylee laughs. "You've already decided."

She knows me too well.

"Someone at the shop will tell Emma. You really want her finding out from Dean?"

She has a point. But I will find a way to do this without sacrificing Emma's future. Period.

"How much cash do you have on hand?"

"Why? You pitching a business."

She folds her arms. "Could you buy a quarter of the company?"

I nod.

"You could buy it together."

I've thought about it. A lot, actually. I could stretch to cover half the company. But if anything happened, shit would be hard.

A quarter is safer.

Half of me is over the moon at the idea of owning Inked Hearts with the three guys who are essentially family.

The other half is screaming *hell no, I don't want to be legally tied to those annoying assholes.*

Either way, I don't want her worrying. "I've got it under control."

"You always do."

Huh.

There's something in her voice.

Like she knows about my penchant for handcuffs and riding crops.

Dean has a big mouth.

She might know.

It's not like I hide my tastes.

But there's something in Kaylee's eyes.

Something more than *Dean told me this rumor.*

I shake it off.

It doesn't matter.

This trip is staying clean. Period. "How is your grandma?"

"I'm not sure, really. My parents aren't giving me all the details. She seems okay. She texted me yesterday asking when I was going to write her another... never mind."

"Another what?"

She shakes her head. "Nothing."

"Something."

"No... Nothing."

"Tell me."

"It's embarrassing." She leans in to turn the stereo on. It's on the alternative station and it's playing some pop-rock song. "Oh, I love this one." She settles into her seat. Her eyes go to me. "Let me guess. Too polished for you?"

"It's a crime, enjoying punk music?"

"It's a little 1980s."

"Arrest me."

Her laugh dissolves the tension in the car. "Sure. But,

really, Brendon, you seem more like the type to cuff someone."

Fuck.

She knows something.

But my brain is skipping right over that.

It's skipping right to handcuffs slapped over Kaylee's wrists.

This car is way too small for how badly I want to bind her to my bed.

New topic.

"What is it that's embarrassing?" I ask.

"How much you secretly love pop music."

"In your dreams."

She smiles. "Sounds like a waste of a dream." There's a gleam in her eyes.

I know women.

And I know Kay.

She's flirting.

What the hell?

I take a deep breath. Turn to the road. Attempt to get my thoughts in order.

Nothing has changed.

I'm the guy who's supposed to protect Kay.

Even from herself.

That means we need a new subject.

"Is this that band Emma is in love with?" I ask.

"The *one* band?"

"One of the bands."

"Yeah. But it's more the lead singer and that sexy, breathy voice of his." Kaylee motions to the radio. "He sounds like he's in the middle of... you know."

"I know?"

"Sex."

He does. Which means it is the band. And even though

the singer does sound like he's in the middle of a fuck, this is a much safer topic than handcuffs. "You know two of the guys get their work done at Inked Hearts."

"They do not."

I nod then attempt to turn my attention back to the road as I take the 10 to the 405. It's a straight shot for another fifteen miles. Luckily, we're late enough into morning to skip traffic. Mostly.

Kaylee turns toward me, her smile brightening her light eyes. "Brendon Kane, I can't believe it."

"Yeah?"

"You're a name dropper."

"Didn't say a name."

"Brendon Kane, the celebrity name dropper. Who else do you work with, oh great tattoo artist?"

"A lot of musicians."

"Yeah?" Her voice perks. She clears her throat, trying to play down her interest. Kaylee and Emma were obsessed with a few bands for a while. And I mean know the guys' birthdays, tattoos, and favorite foods obsessed.

Only all those bands sound the same to me.

"Not that you care," I tease back.

"Yeah. Of course not." She smooths her dress. "Who was it?" When I don't respond, she motions to the stereo.

"Artist client confidentiality."

"Tease."

Fuck yeah. "And that's a bad thing?"

That gets her chest flushing red. She still manages to hold my gaze. "Don't make me beg."

So much for a safe topic. There's no way I can handle her begging. Not right now.

I turn back to the road. "What's his name?" I don't forget my regular clients' names, but I don't recall their professions either. Rock star, secretary, bartender, CEO—

it's all the same to me. Skin is skin. Ink is ink. "Joel Young. He's a regular."

Her eyes go wide, but she nods like this is no big deal.

"And Ethan Strong. And his girlfriend."

"A couple's tattoo?" She lets out a long sigh. "That's sweet."

No, but it is sweet. "I could introduce you next time he comes in."

"No way," she squeals. It's a rarity for her.

Fuck, the things that excitement in her eyes does to me...

I'm not going to survive the drive at this rate.

"I'm sure he'd offer tickets," I say.

Her eyes go wide. "Really?"

"Backstage passes even."

"No fucking way." Her voice rises to a squeal. She claps her hands together. "You wouldn't tease me?"

Fuck yes. Lose the panties if you want to see how badly. "Not about this."

"Em would kill me if I went without her."

"So go with her."

"But..." Kaylee turns to me. Her green eyes fix on mine. They fill with earnest affection. "You'd have to come. Or it would be too much fun. Really, Brendon. Who would complain the music is too generic?"

"Anyone with taste."

"Anyone who's a judgmental jerk?"

"And your comments on *Die Hard*?"

"I like *Die Hard*. It's that third one where it gets iffy."

"Not that you get judgmental."

She laughs. "Never." Kaylee leans down to place her purse on the floor. There's no frustration in her eyes. She's just happy. "What was the couple's tattoo?"

"It wasn't. It was something for her. An in memoriam for her brother."

She makes that *aww* sound. "That's sweet."

"It was."

"You do a lot of couple's tattoos?"

"A handful. Would you get one?"

"I don't know. That's a lot of commitment. One person, on your skin, forever. Would you?"

"If it was someone I couldn't get out of my head. Someone I needed under my skin." Someone like Kay. "Yeah. I don't see how I could avoid it."

Chapter Nine

BRENDON

K aylee steps off the escalator and surveys the expansive room. "This is huge."

Her smile spreads a little wider. She turns back to the warehouse packed with fake rooms and apartments and takes another step down the glossy white-grey path.

Usually, I find this place depressing. Manufactured. Fake.

But the way Kay is trotting to the faux studio apartment on our left, running her fingers over the light wood bookshelf, crouching down to pick up the thick dictionaries on the bottom shelf...

Fuck, her joy does something to me.

Something I'm not used to.

She puts the dictionary away, pushes herself to her feet, and moves into the room.

The faux apartment suits her.

There's a tiny silver and white kitchen against the "wall." A white cloth futon next to the bookshelf. A TV nestled into a tiny stand—one adorned with vases flush with silk flowers.

Kaylee plops onto the couch. Smooths her floral print dress. Takes my hand and looks up at me with those doe eyes.

It's like she's screaming *please*.

Fuck, the thoughts going through my head...

We're not here as foreplay.

We're not here so I can order her to strip for my viewing pleasure.

We're here because everything in her life is changing.

I'm here to be her friend.

Not to think about her hands on my zipper and her lips around my cock.

I need to get a hold of myself.

Her fingers skim my outer thigh. "The embarrassing thing... I'll tell you if you agree to help me with it."

She's sitting there waiting. Exactly where I want her.

I channel every other thought I can. Baseball. Dodgers blue. Dad whining about trades and salary caps. Explaining that if I want to waste my time playing video games, I should play one that actually teaches me something. Like his baseball management simulator.

My cock cools it.

I manage to sit next to Kaylee. "I'm not agreeing until I have more information."

Her chest spills over her dress as she leans closer. The top of her bra peeks out from the neckline. It's beige. Nearly the color of her skin.

I force myself to stare into her eyes. "That's your invitation to offer more."

"Would you rather own the shop outright or share it with Dean, Walker, and Ryan?"

"Don't worry about it, Kay."

"I'm not worried."

I've been thinking about that too. I'm a control freak.

There's no denying that. But there's another part of me. One that wants teammates. That wants to let people in.

That wants someone to lean on.

"You need help with something. It's not my finances," I say.

She shakes her head. "I have this idea. We could take thirty minutes, try to find the best collection of stuff to decorate Inked Hearts properly."

"And your room?"

"That after."

"You gonna tell me?"

"If you agree to help."

I shake my head.

"Then let's go." She pushes herself to her feet. Offers her hand to shake. "Thirty minutes. We'll meet downstairs. See who gets the best stuff."

Fuck, the brightness in her eyes.

There's no way I can deny that.

This is a good idea.

Something fun.

To fill both our heads.

I nod. "You're on."

We shake. Set our timers. Go for it.

I give her a head start.

All right, I watch the way her dress falls over her ass as she walks away.

Same difference.

———

THIRTY MINUTES LATER, I'M DOWNSTAIRS WITH A CART full of cheap decorations. White Christmas lights. Simple black frames. Rectangular black pillows. Planters full of cacti.

Eighteen-year-old Brendon would fucking kill me.

I'm yuppie scum.

And there's Kaylee with a full cart. Pink string lights. Heart pillows. Same planters full of cacti. One of those mass-produced paintings of the ocean.

She holds it up. "I just wanted to see your face."

"And?"

"Perfection." She sets it aside. "The corporations have us, huh?"

"Pretty sure I'm doomed."

"If you buy stuff at Ikea to decorate your small business, is that corporate or not?"

"Don't look at me. I didn't go to college."

"Me either. Not yet."

I never thought about those kinds of technicalities. I was an angry kid without responsibilities. One who'd never ever wanted for anything. Who'd never worried about anything.

Easy to decry three-dollar meatballs and cheap decorations when you have the time and money to make your own dinner, sew together your own jeans.

You get older. Start making compromises. Realize some of your ideals were naïve.

But owning my own business—even one adorned in Ikea decorations—that warms me like nothing else does.

She smiles. "You're going to do it."

"I was always going to do it."

"No... you weren't. I know you. I know every single one of your facial expressions."

"I have expressions?"

"Barely. But you do."

"You have a room to furnish."

"You saying you can't handle it?"

"You baiting me?"

She shakes her head.

But she is.

She has no idea how much she's baiting me.

———

WE PICK OUT A BED, A BOOKSHELF, A CHAIR, A HANDFUL of decorations. It's not a lot. Just enough for the room to scream *Kaylee*. Just enough for the room to feel like home.

Her eyes go to the sign next to the elevator. The ones that label the cafe on the third floor. "I guess I can give the three-dollar meatballs a chance."

"Generous."

"I think so too."

The elevator dings as its doors slide open. I motion *after you*.

She steps inside and presses her back against the metal wall.

I pull out my phone. Check my texts from Ryan. Manning has been an absent owner for years. Ryan and I more or less manage the place.

We try to check with each other about any changes— schedules, pricing, difficult clients, even what brand of coffee we keep on hand—but it's a formality.

Neither of us listens.

Brendon: I want to do it. Me and you. Or the four of us.

Ryan: You know I'm off relationships.

Brendon: And I?

Ryan: Only have eyes for Kaylee. You sure about this?

Brendon: Yeah.

Ryan: You call Anna?

Brendon: You call anyone?

Ryan: Fair enough. I'll let Dean and Walker know. Can you meet with a lawyer Friday?

Brendon: I'm booked all day. But I'll make it work.

"Ryan?" Kaylee asks.

"Yeah." I slip my phone into my pocket. Try to wipe my smile off my face.

She notices. Bites her lip. "You told him."

I nod.

"It's really happening?"

"There's a lot of legal shit first, but—"

She throws her arms around me and buries her head in my chest. "Congrats."

"Thanks." I press my palm between her shoulder blades, over her cardigan.

It's not like with other women.

I feel Kaylee in my bones.

She doesn't hide her sigh when she pulls back.

There's something up with her. Something she isn't saying.

Her eyes find mine. "How is he?"

"Same as always."

"Pining and moody?"

I chuckle. "Don't let him hear you say that."

"He knows."

He does. Again, I motion *after you.*

Kaylee nods a thank you and steps into the lobby. The cafe is around the corner. It's set up cafeteria style, with food in fridges, steam trays, baskets of fruit everywhere.

She grabs a teal tray and places it on the metal railing in front of a sneeze guard. Her gaze flits to the picture menu board. "Veggie meatballs too. This is gourmet."

I grab a tray and place it next to hers. My body begs me to move closer. To wrap my arms around her. To throw her on that table, roll her skirt up her thighs, and rub her over those cotton panties.

I'm imagining her panties.

76

That blue pair with *Paradise* written on the crotch in black.

Fuck, has there ever been an article of clothing that accurate?

I force myself to stay in place. So there's room between us.

She orders the veggie meatballs.

I get the regular meatballs. And two fountain drinks. Kay fills them. I pay.

We find a table by the window.

Yeah, it looks out on a parking lot then on the 405, but it's still a nice view. The sky is a beautiful blue. And the light from the sun is casting highlights and shadows all over the room.

Kaylee slides into the seat across from mine and hands over my iced tea. She wraps her lips around her straw and takes a long sip. "Not bad."

I motion to our plates. "All for under ten dollars."

"And..."

"Food tastes better when it's cheap."

"I get half off everything at The Pizza Kitchen. I never want to eat cheap restaurant food again." She picks up her fork, stabs a veggie meatball, holds it up and examines it. "No offense."

"If you don't like it, I'll make you something when we get home."

Her lips purse. "Or I could have an almond butter and jelly sandwich." She offers me her fork. "You want one?"

"Sure." I let my fingers brush hers as I take her fork, bring it to my lips, suck the snack off the metal silverware.

It's better than what I'd expect for three dollars, but it's not exactly fine dining.

I hand back the fork. "Not bad."

She stabs a veggie ball and stares at it like it might just

kill her. "Okay. I'll give it a shot." She bites half of it, chews, swallows. "Not horrible." She stabs a piece of broccoli—her plate comes with steamed vegetables—and holds it up. "No one could mess this up, right?"

"I have faith in you."

She flips me off. Chews. Swallows.

"If you're not going to tell me, I'm going to guess."

"Huh?"

"The thing that embarrasses you."

"Oh. Well, if you agree to help..."

I nod. "Shoot."

"Fan fiction. I write fan fiction sometimes."

"Yeah?"

"Don't laugh."

I want to, but not for the reasons she thinks. Not because it's lame. Because it's so fucking Kay. "How could I possibly help?"

"Well, there's this theme I want to include in my next story. And I'm pretty sure you're the person to ask."

"Only thing I know shit about is tattooing."

She shakes her head. "No. Dean... He mentioned something." Her eyes bore into mine. "That you like to tie women up."

Fuck. Blood flees my brain at an alarming rate. It's replaced by the image of Kaylee tied to my bed, squirming under me, begging me to let her come. "Sometimes. It's not an obsession." I like having a woman on the edge. Having her desperate for me. Tying her up is the easiest way to do that. But I'm into all sorts of shit.

"Oh. Well. I, um, I thought I'd ask. If there's anything you think I should know. Or resources."

No. No fucking way. I'm not explaining bondage to Kaylee. But I don't want Dean explaining it either. "I'll send you a few links."

"Sure." She forces her lips into a smile. It's not what she wants.

She wants me explaining it.

I want to do a lot more than explain it.

"Do you... do you do that a lot?" she asks.

"Sometimes." It's been awhile. Longer than it's been since I've fucked. Playing hasn't felt right. Rough hasn't felt right. Ever since my parents died, nothing has felt quite right.

It's like Mom is in my head now.

Shaking her head *of course you're into this shit, you degenerate*.

Doesn't exactly help the mood.

But the thought of bending Kaylee over my knee—

Of her wrists tied to my bed—

Her thighs against my cheeks—

"You can tell me more, Brendon. I'm not an innocent flower. I read all sorts of books. I can handle an explanation."

Maybe she can.

But I can't. "There're a few good books. I'll make a list."

She nods, but there's something about it.

Like she knows exactly what I'm thinking.

Like she knows how badly I want to make her mine.

Chapter Ten

BRENDON

Fuck, it's hot in here. The air conditioning never quite balances out. Downstairs is freezing. Upstairs is a sauna.

I wipe my brow with my t-shirt.

Kay is behind me. I'm not sure how I know, but I do.

She's staring.

Of course she's staring.

I'm practically putting myself on display.

I need to be more careful. But that's a lost cause. This is my house. I strip. I shower. I walk around in a towel.

Making a point of being fully dressed at all times—that will make things weird.

"It's hot, huh?" she asks.

"Yeah." I let my t-shirt fall over my torso. Turn back to face her.

Her cheeks are flushed. It's hot yeah, but that's not it.

She has that look. That *mmm, I want more* look. I know it well. Fuck, when I bring a woman home, that look is my goal. I like having someone begging, panting, screaming for more.

"You look hot." She presses her lips together. "I mean, flushed. Like it's hot."

I nod.

"How about I run to that coffee shop down the street. Cold brew for you, iced tea for me."

"Thanks." I need the space. And the chance to put something in my head besides *damn, Kay is so considerate. She'd make the perfect girlfriend.*

She will.

For someone.

One day.

I reach for my wallet to pull out a twenty, but she shakes her head.

"No way. You bought me a room full of furniture. This is on me." She takes a step backward. "Besides, you need to start saving if you want to own a quarter of Inked Hearts."

"Not that you're smug about it."

"No. Never." She smiles. Waves. Spins on her heels and moves down the stairs.

My eyes refuse to get in line. They trace her path out the door. They fix on the way her hips sway as she walks.

I pull my t-shirt off. Toss it aside.

It's not enough.

I'm still burning.

My thoughts are still fixed on that flush in her cheeks. On the way she looks at me. Like she wants me. And like I'm someone worth wanting as more than an easy fuck.

Nobody looks at me like that.

Like I'm worth something.

I move into my bedroom. Bright light flows into the room. It falls over the perfectly made bed and bounces off the shiny hardwood.

And off that mirror across from the bed.

The one I use to watch.

Does she realize that?

There's no way she thinks it's for checking out my outfit. The only time I wear something that isn't jeans and a t-shirt is... never. Em and Kay's graduation.

That meeting with our lawyer Friday. The one where we make this shit happen.

My head fills with other images. Kaylee and me at some fancy dinner. Her in that blue dress. Me in a suit. Staring into her eyes as I take her hand.

Fuck.

This isn't working.

I move into the bathroom, run the water until it's freezing, splash it over my cheeks.

It's not enough.

I pull my cell from my pocket. Go straight to the last voicemail Mrs. Hart left. I need the reminder that I'm supposed to protect her. That she trusts me. That her entire family trusts me.

"Hey Brendon. How are you? I hope work is going well. Mike is happy to be back in New Jersey. His old team is still here, and they're much easier to work with than the team at the Santa Monica office. And being near my mother—it's been wonderful."

She lets out a heavy sigh.

"You're doing so much for us. I want to repay you, but here I am asking for more. Kaylee hasn't been picking up my calls. I know she's angry with us for leaving her out of the decision. And I understand. We knew she wouldn't be happy about this or about us deciding to stay here. But we couldn't give her the choice."

She pauses.

"We wanted to protect her from that. She'd never choose herself over Grandma. And if she did, can you imagine the guilt she'd have over putting her future first?

Sorry, I'm rambling again. I'd like anything you have. A text even. My mother is doing better. She hasn't needed as much help. But she would love to hear from Kaylee. We're going to fly Kaylee out in a few weeks, but we don't want to interfere with school. If you have any suggestions for a weekend, we'd appreciate it."

The message beeps.

My head gets it—I'm supposed to take care of Kay, not picture her naked in my bed.

But my body—my body is whining for more of her in that sweet sundress.

Maybe Ryan was right.

These blue balls aren't helping any.

This isn't what I want to do.

But it's a lot better than crossing the line.

Chapter Eleven

KAYLEE

D amn, I'm tired. My back is tight. My arms are aching. My legs are trembling.

I collapse on the bed—my bed. It's a simple white frame, a cheap but comfy mattress, white sheets.

I stretch out like a snow angel. Try to breathe deep, something to soothe my sore muscles. It doesn't help.

Am I this out of shape?

Or is Brendon that fit?

We've been working to unpack and put together furniture all afternoon. And it was mostly him. And now he's heading to the gym to lift more heavy things.

How the hell does he have any energy left?

Maybe it's me. That's another side effect. Fatigue.

Only it's also a side effect of my medication.

Do other teenagers feel this heavy all the time?

Are they always wondering if what they're feeling is them or their medications?

Normal is a lost cause. Usually, that doesn't bother me. After all, Emma isn't anywhere near normal. Brendon isn't either. Grandma is a weirdo. My parents, they aren't quite on Grandma's level, but they have their moments.

I just... I want to fit in somewhere. Me. All of me and not just the parts I show everyone.

I want someone to love me, all of me.

Or at least see all of me.

I do a good job keeping up appearances, convincing everyone I have my act together, that everything is okay.

And, mostly, everything is okay. I'm not having an episode. I'm not struggling to drag myself out of bed. I'm not thinking about hurting myself.

I am not happy, not exactly, but I'm okay.

I roll onto my back and stare up at the ceiling. It's still dotted with plastic stars. They're Brendon's. This used to be his room.

They suit him. Specks of brightness that only come out in the dark. That only reveal themselves to people who are patient enough to wait until the lights are off.

I let myself drift into a half sleep and wake to Emma walking through the open door.

She sits on the bed next to me and tugs at the sheets. "I hope you're not naked under there."

"Would you actually care?"

Emma laughs the way she always does, with her entire body. "No. Of course not. I don't want you embarrassed all night. Not with the plans I have for us."

I groan. "Everything hurts."

"Everything? Even your pinkie?"

I nod.

"How about your ass?"

"What?"

She lies on her side, next to me. "Don't worry. I'm planning an epic housewarming party for you. But not tonight."

My exhale is heavier than I mean it to be.

Which only makes Em laugh. "It's at the shop. We'll have snacks. Well, in the lobby. Ryan and Brendon were very clear about their no food near the chairs policy."

"You talked to Ryan to make this happen?"

"That's how much I love you." She props herself up on one elbow. "I didn't invite anyone else, but I can. If you want."

No. I don't want. "That's plenty of party." It's small enough, and filled with enough people I like, that I might enjoy it without three shots.

Emma's expression gets sincere. "You can tell me if you hate the idea."

"No. It's sweet. I'm just—"

"Don't worry. Tonight's plans only require your ass." She doesn't give me a chance to agree. She pushes off the bed and offers her hands.

I take them and let her pull me to my feet. "I didn't know you liked me that way."

"In your dreams." She takes a step backward. "Disney marathon."

My ears perk. My eyes too. I nod, yes.

Emma laughs. "See. I know how to make you happy."

"You do."

"We just need pancakes—"

"Chocolate chip?" I ask.

She nods. "And tea. I'll make them. So long as you measure the chocolate chips."

"You're too good to me."

"I know."

———

THE TV SCREEN FLICKERS, CASTING LIGHT OVER ME AND

Emma. Hercules is kicking ass and taking names. Same as always.

Is there a Disney movie I don't know like the back of my hand?

I might have a problem. Though, it's not really *my* problem. It's *our* problem.

Right now, I don't care.

My stomach is full of pancakes. My brain is buzzing from the mix of sugar and tea. Everything is good.

I want more.

Even if it's a bad idea.

I push off the couch and turn to Emma. "You want more coffee?"

She raises a brow. "You planning on starting a novel tonight?"

I laugh, but I don't quite sell it. One day... Maybe... in a million years.

"You know I can go all night, babe." She winks at me. "I'll take some chocolate."

"Your wish is my command."

"Different movie."

"You want to watch it next?"

"Is Brendon moody and annoying?"

"Well... Not to me. Not usually."

Emma rolls her eyes. "I don't know what you see in him."

"He's your brother." When that fails to get a reaction, I press on. "He let me move here. He bought me a room full of furniture."

"I thought we agreed to stop talking about that."

We did. I couldn't take anymore of Emma getting mad on my behalf. "He's hot, Em. Even you can see that."

"I guess it runs in the family."

I laugh. "Humble as always."

I move into the kitchen before she can press the subject further. There's way, way too much I see in Brendon.

His eyes.

His smile—the rare times I get it.

That protective stare.

Those strong shoulders.

The tattoo spreading over his chest.

The other going down his arm.

That look he gives me when I'm sitting on the couch, when he asks if I'm reading something *good*.

Just... everything.

I let my head fill with thoughts of Brendon as I make another cup of vanilla black and grab chocolate. Enough chocolate for my thoughts to turn to the bliss of the cocoa bean instead of the bliss of Brendon.

God, I have it bad.

There's no getting over him. Not with those drawings of his in my mind. Not with the way his eyes lit up when I mentioned dirty demands.

He wants me too.

How will I ever think about another guy?

I move back to the couch, hand over Emma's chocolate, settle in.

We get lost in the flow of the movie-talk about nothing combination. It's familiar. Comforting.

It feels like this is a normal lazy summer day. One where I'm sleeping over because I want to, not because my parents bailed on me. One where I look at Brendan as Emma's hot older brother, a guy so far out of my league we're playing different games. One where Grandma is okay.

Everything else feels far away. It's just me and my best friend in our own world. I'm not alone. I'm not medicated.

I'm not aware Brendon's sketchbook is full of dirty drawings of me.

I'm just home. Safe. Happy.

"Hey." Brendon's voice flows into my ears. He moves into the hallway. Then down the stairs.

He's wet. Fresh from the shower. Wrapped only in a towel.

I... he... Fuck.

There's water dripping off his dark hair. Down his chest piece—the shaded black and grey roses. It drips down his side, across The Ramones lyrics, all the way to the Latin quote jutting out from his towel. *Sic Transit Gloria*.

Glory fades.

What does it mean to him?

What would it feel like to trace every link of ink?

To have that warm, wet body pressed against mine?

On top of mine?

I'm pretty sure my jaw is on the floor.

My cheeks are burning. I must be every shade of red.

Emma grabs a pillow and tosses it at her brother. He moves into the main room just in time to dodge it.

She folds her arms over her chest. "You're not wearing clothes because...?"

"There's this thing called a shower. You use it when you want to get clean."

"And what do you know about being clean?" She taps her fingers against her bicep. "You think the girls you throw away stay quiet about your preferences?"

Brendon raises a brow.

Emma looks to me and rolls her eyes. *Isn't he annoying?* "What are you trying to prove? We know you're sculpted out of marble. Who goes to the gym twice a day?"

"People who are sculpted out of marble." Brendan moves into the kitchen. "Smells like pancakes."

"You want some?" Emma asks.

"No," he says. "I have dinner plans."

"Oh." I press my palms into my thighs. "You and Ryan meeting to talk about the buyout?"

"Huh?" Emma looks to me. *What are you talking about?*

Brendon shakes his head. "No. I have a date."

Chapter Twelve

KAYLEE

B rendon has a date.

He's seeing another human being.

Romantically.

I'm going to throw up.

Emma presses her hands together. "You could make us more pancakes before you go."

"I'm running late," he says.

"Who are you dating?" Emma's voice is casual. Like this isn't the worst news in forever.

Okay, that's not even close to true. Everything with Grandma is worse. But Brendon on a date...

Touching some girl.

Kissing her.

Binding her to her bed.

I... I'm going to throw up.

"We're not dating." His voice is curt. Obvious. *We're meeting for dinner and a fuck.*

I try to settle back into the routine of watching and laughing and teasing, my body refuses to relax.

Nothing helps.

Not even my dirty thoughts.

They all go wrong. He's touching me, stripping me out of my clothes, dragging his lips over my neck.

Then she's there.

Some girl with big tits and pretty lips and a tight dress that screams *please take this off*.

He'll fuck some girl he barely knows.

But he won't even talk about sex with me.

It's bullshit.

Total bullshit.

He moves into the kitchen. Comes out with an apple between his hands.

Takes a bite.

He shoots Emma a stern look. "No guys or drinks while I'm gone."

She rolls her eyes.

He shakes his head *you're a brat*, but there's concern in his eyes. "Kay. Promise. No drinks or guys."

"I'm not Emma's keeper," I say. I don't add *fuck you for this date bullshit. Fuck you for acting like it isn't a knife in my chest. And for doing it in a towel, just to add insult to injury.*

But he doesn't know I know.

He doesn't know I'm crazy about him.

He...

He must have some idea. There's a connection between us. He gets me in a way no one else does.

And he's different with me. He smiles. Laughs.

I watch him walk away. Watch his back tense and relax. Watch that towel slip lower and lower on his hips.

My body screams *all of him now, please*.

My heart is more reluctant.

He's going on dates.

I... I can't deal with this. Even if it's inevitable.

"Excuse me." I tug at my dress. "Pajamas."

Emma nods. "He's weird, huh?"

"Yeah. Annoying."

"Finally, you see it my way."

I do. I see exactly why Emma has a problem with her brother.

He demands his way.

But offers nothing.

I just barely restrain myself from stomping up the stairs.

Okay, that's bullshit. My steps are as light as they usually are. I'm still the good girl. The one who keeps things together. Who doesn't cause a scene.

The hall is dark.

There's light coming from Brendon's room.

And his door is open a sliver.

And there he is, in front of his bed.

Turned toward the wall.

Naked.

It's only his back.

His ass.

His legs.

Fuck.

I've never seen a guy naked before. Not in person. Not one I wanted to see naked.

But Brendon...

Heat pools between my legs. I want him. Every inch of him. Every way I can have him.

I want the sight, the sound, the taste, the smell, the feel of him.

I want him owning every one of my senses.

I...

He pulls on a pair of boxers.

Steps into his jeans.

Turns.

I jump out of the way just in time. I think. I hope.

God, I hope he didn't see me gawking.

He can't.

That's so...

I dart into my bedroom. Fumble out of my dress and into my pajamas.

A tank top. Panties. Sleep shorts.

That's it.

I'm barely wearing anything.

And he's there, barely wearing anything, thinking about me naked.

About to go on a fucking date.

I move back into the hallway. Nearly run downstairs.

A few moments later, Brendon walks through the main room. He grabs his keys from the table and slides them into the front pocket of his skinny jeans.

"Text me when you go to bed." He looks to Emma. "Or if you need anything."

She nods. "I won't wait up."

"You too, Kay. Text me if you need anything." He holds my gaze. *Promise?*

I'm pretty sure I can't request him naked in my bed. So I force my lips into a smile. "I'll be fine."

He takes that as a yes, turns, walks out the door.

On the way to his date.

With some girl.

Some girl who isn't me.

Chapter Thirteen

BRENDON

This place is all squares—the stools, the tables, the couches, the patrons.

Candles flicker. The soft yellow lamp in the corner offers just enough illumination to make out the menu.

This place isn't my scene. It's hers. Upscale. Pretty. Filled with people in suits. The kind of people who gush over sauvignon blanc.

I don't get it. Wine tastes the same to me.

We're ten minutes into conversation, but I'm not absorbing any of it.

I'm thinking about that look on Kay's face. Like I stabbed her in the gut.

Anna's laugh grabs my attention.

She turns to show off the ink on her back. "It still looks good."

"It does."

"That's a compliment."

"Mine too. You designed the tattoo."

She tilts her head to one side. "I'm not sure I buy you

as humble." Her smile lights up her blue eyes. They're hard to see from under her silver makeup.

And her lips are red. Bright red. *Think about where these lips could be* red.

But I'm not thinking about ordering her onto her knees.

I'm thinking about how Em wears her lips that color.

I try to ignore that Emma has a sex life. She's an adult. She can do what she wants. I'm not going to tell her that sex is wrong or dirty. Not like I can talk.

But I still prefer to not connect the dots.

I try to shake it off. "No?"

"No." She leans into the table enough for her breasts to press together.

She has nice tits. They'd feel good in my hand. Or around my cock.

"You seem like the type to brag."

"About?"

Her laugh is bold. Knowing. "I guess you don't have to. Not when you have a reputation."

I try to imagine Anna in my bed. Pressing her against the wall. Rolling that dress to her waist and tearing off her bra.

The image flickers in my head. For a second.

Then it's Kaylee against the wall.

My hand up her skirt.

Those doe eyes of hers looking up at me with every ounce of trust in the world.

This isn't how tonight is supposed to go.

I'm supposed to smile at Anna. Return her flirty glance. Go back to her place—I only bring women home when Emma isn't around—and get her begging for release.

But none of that appeals.

I force myself to look back in her eyes. Force my voice to that *I know you want to fuck me* tone. "Do I?"

She laughs. "Now, I'm pretty sure you're playing coy to mess with me." She wraps her fingers around the stem of her wine glass. Takes her last sip. "I got here early. Right after work."

I nod.

She motions to the bar. "Let me back up." She pushes her empty glass away. "How about a drink?"

"You're buying?"

She laughs. "Well, I did invite you out."

"Doesn't matter."

"You're old fashioned, really?"

In some ways, yeah. I nod.

"The old-fashioned tattoo artist. Hmm... I guess I can see it. Just don't tell me you have a problem with feminism. I can overlook a lot of deal breakers with someone so... well, you know you're handsome."

I nod. "Why would I have a problem with feminism?"

She shrugs. "A lot of guys I... date. They're threatened by women with power. Or a woman who knows what she wants. Or wants to pay."

"I always pay for a first date."

"And the second date?"

They're rarer. Third dates too. Fourth dates—it's been a long, long while since I've had a relationship that lasted longer than three dates. "You negotiating?"

She laughs. "I guess so."

There. The waitress is walking by.

I hail her. Motion to Anna.

She orders another glass of white wine, some specific label, and a brussel sprout salad.

I order Jameson and sliders. Good whiskey, but not *look at how much money I have* showy.

Anna leans a little closer. "I think you might have me if you tell me you're a feminist."

"I have you already."

Her voice lifts. "You sure about that?"

"Yeah."

"Not so humble, I guess."

No. Not so humble.

I lean forward. Stare into Anna's blue eyes. Try to find something to latch onto—something I want.

She's hot. Smart. Funny.

But all I can think about is Kaylee.

Those big, green eyes.

All the hurt in them.

Because of me.

Necessary hurt, yeah. She needs to know I'm not available.

I need to know it.

I need to convince my body and my heart that there's no way I'll ever have Kaylee in my bed.

But, fuck, the thought of stripping her out of that sweet sundress, dragging those cotton panties to her ankles, and diving between her legs—

"So." She stares back at me. "Are you a feminist?"

"Who wouldn't be?"

"You'd be surprised."

Not really. I'm well aware of how shitty people can be. "I was punk rock when I was a teenager."

"Yeah? Red hair?"

"Once." I run my hand through my dark hair. "My girl-friend did it for me." It was more of a fling, but close enough. "My hair practically melted. Had to get one of those half-shaved haircuts."

"I can't imagine that."

I tug at my t-shirt. "Imagine this with an anarchy symbol."

She laughs. "And now?"

"I've lost an appreciation for chaos."

"And your hair?"

"I no longer strive to piss off my parents."

She laughs. "Good. The dark hair suits you."

"Yeah?"

"Yeah. You've got the whole tall, dark, and handsome thing down pat."

The waitress drops off our drinks. "Your food will be out shortly."

"Thanks." I take a long sip. It's too fast. A waste of good whiskey. But I need something quieting that voice that keeps reminding me that Anna isn't Kaylee. That no one else in the universe is Kaylee.

It's a quick fuck.

I'm going to make her come.

It shouldn't matter that she isn't Kaylee.

It's not like I've ever required an intense connection with a woman. Sure, it's a perk. Especially if we're moving past vanilla.

If I want to tie someone up, I need them to trust me. And I need to trust them to be honest about their limits.

But that comes easier than you'd think.

I take another sip. A slower one. It's good. Rich with that hint of toffee.

Anna brings her wine to her lips. Leaves a red stain on the glass.

That lipstick could be staining my cock.

But picturing those red lips straining around me—

It isn't doing anything to get my blood flowing south.

"So..." She traces the outline of her wine glass. Shoots

me that *aren't you going to bring up your reputation* look. "Are you still punk rock?"

"I still listen to The Clash, but the rest of it—"

She nods. "Life forces you to be a square." She taps the table with her French-manicured nails. "I never was punk rock, but I was pretty sure I wouldn't grow up to be this."

"A woman with a badass teddy bear tattoo who invites guys out to bars for one-night stands?"

She laughs. "An executive assistant. But that too." She takes a long sip of her glass. "It's funny. This would have been a nightmare job to be at fifteen. But I love it."

"I know what you mean."

"And the other part... I think my past self would be proud."

"Yeah?"

"But you give yourself too much credit. I haven't decided if I'm sleeping with you or not."

That's bullshit. It's in her eyes. She's picturing me naked. She's even licking her lips.

It's not my personality or my conversational skills.

At the moment, I'm a terrible date.

But I can't muster up the enthusiasm to do better.

I finish the last drop of my whiskey.

I try to find something to latch onto.

She runs her fingers over the neckline of her tight, black dress. It hugs her tits in a way that should beg for my hands.

Only it doesn't.

I shoot her a sly smile. "You sure about that?"

Her laugh is flirty but nervous.

Her eyes spark.

She's reacting to me.

She wants me.

That used to be enough.

Pretty and willing used to be enough.

I've always been eager to get out of my head.

But now...

Her fingers wrap around my wrist. She's reaching out. Touching me. Making sure I know she wants me.

This is the part where I touch her back.

Where I smile and whisper something about what we'll do at her place.

But, fuck, her hand feels so wrong on my arm.

There's no way it will feel good around my cock.

There's no way I'm inviting myself back to her place.

Chapter Fourteen

KAYLEE

Eleven.

How is it already eleven?

The numbers are there. A bold white against my cell background—the picture of the beach I took with Emma last month. The waves are crashing into the sand. The sky is bright and beautiful. And everything is simple.

Because Brendon isn't on a date.

A date that's going past eleven.

I don't know anything about her. I don't know her name or what she does or if she's pretty.

No, I'm sure she's pretty.

He used to *date* a lot. He didn't have a type, not as far as I could tell. Tall, short, curvy, thin, red hair, blond, brunette, tomboyish, girly, punk rock, corporate, white, Hispanic, black, Asian—there was only one thing all those women had in common.

They were all beautiful.

I've been through this a million times.

It never hurt this badly.

But that was when I was sure he saw me as a kid.

I don't know when things changed. But they have.

It was tolerable knowing Brendon was sleeping around when I was sure I'd never have him.

Now that I know he wants me too—

This is supposed to be what distracts me from everything with Grandma.

But it's even worse.

At least, with Grandma there's hope that it's not really that bad. That my parents are over-reacting.

I turn the page on my e-book even though I haven't absorbed a single word. This is the book Brendon recommended.

It should be fascinating.

It should be filling my head with thoughts of him tying me to his four-poster bed.

But it's not.

Every single word is a knife in my chest. Every single one is making me think of her. Whoever she is. This girl smiling at Brendon, looking at him with those *I want you on top of me* eyes.

I hate her.

I hate everything.

I pull out my cell phone and try to find a distraction.

Another message from Mom. My voicemail inbox is littered with my parents, and Grandma, reaching out. I pick up sometimes. But their check ins always come with excuses about why they're trying to run my life for me.

And I don't want to hear it.

I don't want to hear that tone.

The one that reminds me that Grandma is sick. I still don't know how sick she is, how little time we have, what exactly it is, but I know it's bad.

Even Grandma gets that tone.

It's not like her. Nothing scares her. When I was little,

Mom would threaten to hire a babysitter if Grandma kept teaching me dirty words. And that was only the tip of the iceberg. Mom didn't like the ridiculous stories we made for my dolls. Or Grandma curling my hair. Or letting me use her lipstick.

Mom wanted to protect me from growing up too fast.

But Grandma never backed down. She insisted that this was what I needed. Even when Mom really did hire a babysitter—the world's most boring babysitter, who made me watch wholesome kids shows and refused to let me make my own almond butter and jelly sandwiches.

Grandma held her ground until Mom caved.

I play her voicemail. Soak up every bit of strain and worry in Grandma's voice as she insists I need to call my mom, give her a proper update.

I will.

Soon.

Tomorrow even.

Grandma gives the best advice. She'll know what to do about this. She'll know the exact steps I need to take to get from lovesick puppy to over him. She always knows.

Only soon...

No. I'm not thinking that. Not yet. I don't even know if it's true. She might have years left. A decade even.

I place my phone on the couch face down and sink into the leather.

That same page is there in my Kindle. I have no idea what it says. I don't want to. I don't want anything.

Eleven ten.

It's been nearly three hours.

Is that enough time to go back to her place?

My head fills with awful images. They're at the bar in some cozy booth. He's spreading her legs and sliding his hand between them.

They're outside, in some dark, dirty alley. He has her pressed against the wall. Her back is arched. Her skirt is at her waist. He's sliding his jeans to his knees and growling something in her ear.

They're in the backseat of his car. She's under him. There's no space. His legs are hitting the seat. Her head is pressed up against the door. But neither of them care. That's how good it is. How much they want each other.

I force my eyes to my Kindle. The words refuse to enter my brain. It's mush. Meaningless. Nothing.

Eleven fifteen.

I'm nearly due for my medication.

For bed.

I need my routine. It's what keeps me together. That's why I work the same days every week. Eat the same thing every morning. Take the same post-lunch walks. Read for an hour before bed every day.

I take a deep breath and exhale slowly. Too much is going through my head. All the things I want that I can never, ever have. Grandma being well. My parents respecting my decisions. Brendon.

A normal, healthy relationship with a normal, healthy guy. Hell, even a friendship where I don't have to hide all the ugly things in my head.

I could tell Emma. She'd understand. Maybe. Or she might run away. Or she might crumble from the burden of my problems. The ones I'm responsible for carrying. Alone.

There's something outside. Footsteps. Louder than the normal traffic—there are always people moving around in their neighborhood, even in the middle of the night.

Keys jangle in the lock.

The handle turns.

The door pulls open.

And there's Brendon, surrounded by the black of night and the shiny silver moonlight.

It bounces off his hair, his eyes, that sliver of bare skin below his chin—his neck, collarbones, chest. He's dressed the same as always. Grey jeans. Dark t-shirt. Black sneakers.

And his clothes are just as neat as before. Nothing is wrinkled or stained or inside out.

I hug my knees to my chest. Stare at my Kindle like I've been reading it all night. And not like I've spent the last few hours obsessing over his date.

He tosses his keys on the table and kicks the door shut.

"You're still up?" His eyes stay on the ground.

That isn't like him. But why?

"Looks like it." My voice is more curt than I mean it to be. But who the hell does he think he is, going on dates while he's drawing dirty pictures of me?

He doesn't know that I know. He doesn't know that this is a knife in my chest. But, still, it hurts.

He moves into the kitchen. Grabs something from the top shelf. "You eat dinner?"

"The pancakes with Emma. Remember?"

"Yeah." The freezer door opens. Ice clinks in a glass. "You want something to drink?"

"Are you offering whatever you're having?"

He pauses. He's blocked by the kitchen wall. I can't see his face. But I can picture it, that way his eyes get sharper when he's thinking.

"You like whiskey all of a sudden?" His voice is even. Like this whole date thing means nothing.

"Sure." I need to loosen the knot in my gut. This is the wrong way to go about it. Alcohol is a depressant. It's for special occasions only. "You never let me drink."

"I don't?"

"Yeah. Only on my birthday."

"A drink doesn't have to mean booze."

"I'll have whatever you're having."

"Hmm."

I set my Kindle next to my phone. I smooth my sleep shorts. Adjust my tank top. This is a flattering outfit, as far as pajamas go. Plenty of cleavage. Lots of leg.

I have a nice figure. I got it from Mom. Between all the exercise I force myself to do and biking to and from work and school, I stay in pretty good shape. Not Brendon good. But good.

He moves into the dining room—well, this is all one big room, but he's in the dining area—and sets two glasses on the table.

He takes a seat and motions to the other glass.

"What was her name?" I push off the couch and move toward him. Slowly. Casually. Like wondering about this isn't tearing me apart.

"Why?"

"Making conversation." I pick up my drink and take a sip. My lips curl into a half smile. "This is apple juice."

"Is it?"

"Tease."

He shrugs.

"Did you like her?"

"She was nice."

"You're just like Em."

He arches a brow as he brings his drink to his lips. He tries to hold a poker face, but he doesn't quite manage it. His eyelids press together. A soft groan falls off his lips.

The man loves his whiskey.

But that's not where my head is going.

"Whenever she says a guy is nice, that's it. She's never seeing him again," I say.

"I liked her."

"But you didn't..." I clear my throat. But that doesn't get a reaction. "You're home early. Considering."

"Only takes half an hour to fuck someone properly."

"Oh." I stare back into his eyes. There's something missing. A satisfaction. He didn't sleep with her. I think.

"You should go to bed. It's late."

"I work later than this all the time."

"Still. School starts soon. You need to get into a routine." He takes another sip then sets his glass down on the table. "Your parents left another message. They want to hear from you."

"I know." I sip my apple juice. It's better than whiskey, but this much sugar this late is a bad idea. "I'm still pissed at them."

"You consider telling them that?"

Sort of. Telling people how I feel isn't my strong suit. "Did you sleep with her."

"That's not your—"

"I thought we agreed friends talk about sex."

His eyes trace my body. It's quick. Almost imperceptible. "What have you been doing all night?"

"Reading."

He nods *sounds like you*.

"That book you mentioned."

"And it's helping with your research?" He draws out the last word, like we both know this isn't for research.

"Yeah. But it's not enough. Reading about the theoretical is one thing, but I want to know what it's really like. How it feels. So I can capture it properly."

"What exactly are you writing?"

"It's um..." I'm not writing anything. That's all bullshit. I go through my favorite character pairings, trying to find one that makes sense. There's no way Peeta is tying up

Katniss. Or Katniss and Finnick. Or Finnick and Annie. Nobody in *The Hunger Games* is getting tied up. But Draco and Harry—I could see that. "It's a *Harry Potter* fan fiction."

He arches a brow. "Harry doesn't have it in him."

"Yeah. He's not. Draco is."

Brendon chuckles. He's disarmed. He's not thinking about how I'm pushing him to illustrate his sexual preferences. He's endeared by me writing dirty male/male fan fiction. "I didn't realize—"

"I wrote about guys going at it?"

He nods.

"It's a favorite pairing. They have a certain chemistry."

"Yeah." He laughs.

"Yeah. And I... I don't really understand the psychology of it. Not from reading. It's not enough." I swallow hard. I can't believe these words are falling off my lips. Him going on that date is making me reckless. "You... you have experience with that."

"You want me to show you what it's like to be ordered around?"

"Not, you know... not sex. But maybe you could walk me through it."

He shoots me a *really* look.

"Or I could ask Dean."

There. His jaw cricks. He's armed again. But he's armed with exactly the right tool. He hates the idea of Dean ordering me around. Of Dean touching me.

"If you're not interested. Or busy. I'm sure Dean would help."

"You have a boss at work. It's the same thing."

I shake my head. "But that's not sexual."

"It doesn't have to be." He stares back at me. "Put your glass on the table."

I stare back. "Huh?"

"You want to see what it's like, listen and do exactly what I say."

I nod.

His voice drops to a tone I've never heard before. One that demands all my attention. "Put your glass on the table."

I do.

"Push it aside."

I do.

"Now sit on the table." He pats the spot at the edge of the table. It's as far away from him as it could be. "And wait for my next command."

My lips press together. This is weird. But I like everything about it.

I move to the table. Take a seat. Press my legs together.

His eyes bore into mine. He waits. And waits. And waits.

My skin starts buzzing. I'm not sure why, but there's something thrilling about waiting for him.

When he speaks, his voice is firm, but not demanding. "You get the idea?"

"I'm starting to."

"What else are you curious about?"

"Everything."

His pupils dilate. Something sparks in his expression. This desire deep inside him. It's only there for a second, then he's back to a poker face.

"Keep reading. You'll get it." He picks up his glass and takes the last sip. "You thinking about doing this with someone, Kay?"

"Sort of."

"Make sure it's someone you can trust." He moves into the kitchen and leaves his empty glass in the sink. "You can get pretty deep into it. None of it's wrong, but some of it's dangerous." His brow furrows. It's like he's fighting himself. "If you're not sure about anything, ask me. I'm not an expert. But I'll figure shit out for you."

I nod. "I trust them."

He stares back at me, staring at my expression. It's like he's trying to figure out who I'm talking about.

It's like he knows it's him.

Chapter Fifteen

BRENDON

My Friday morning leg routine fails to bring clarity. I'm still easy to bait. I'm still giving in to all my thoughts of Kay. To her bullshit about asking Dean to order her around.

Fuck, it's like she can see into my head.

How the hell does she know exactly how I want her?

It wakes up every single muscle in my body. It's a hell of a lot more effective than squats or deadlifts. Nothing gets my blood pumping like she does.

I finish my last set and wipe off the squat rack. This is a nice place. The kind of place my mom would have gone. If it had been here when she was.

She spent half her time staying beautiful or keeping the house beautiful. It worked. Everyone mentioned her looks. Jo, the beautiful, perfect homemaker. She had the same dark hair as me and Em. The same dark eyes.

The same good looks, I guess. Dad was tall, but he wasn't typically handsome.

She always talked about the importance of fitness. Always tried to get me to sign up for some sport. Soccer.

Little League. Jr. Lifeguards. Surf Camp. Summer league swim team. Then the high school one. I did it freshman year. Right before I hit that *team sports are bullshit; all organizations are bullshit* phase.

That was the moment she gave up on me—the day I quit swim team. I still remember all the disappointment in her eyes. The way her knife slapped across the cutting board as she diced chicken. She'd never say she was pissed off. She'd just look at me like I was a failure and recite something about my future.

Would she be proud of my fixation of getting bigger and stronger?

Maybe.

It's hard to imagine Mom proud. Even if it's easy to imagine her on the stationary bike in some two-hundred-dollar outfit.

I toss my towel in the hamper on the way out the door. Yeah, it's that kind of gym. It costs a fortune. But it's the only thing that clears my head, besides work and sex.

Besides premium coffee beans and good whiskey, it's my only indulgence.

It's bright outside. Traffic is already clogging the roads. Damn, it's early for both. And I'm without my sunglasses.

I shield my eyes as I jog home. It's only half a mile. But tons of the drivers I pass shoot me a *what's his problem* look. This is Los Angeles. We all drive twenty minutes to spend an hour on the treadmill.

My head clears as my feet pound the pavement. Today is the day. We're meeting our lawyer to talk about buying the shop. To get everything sorted out.

That's what I'm focusing on.

Not Kay.

Not those tiny shorts or that tight tank top or the way

her eyes went wide when I ordered her to leave her glass on the table.

She wants to be under my command.

And, somehow, she knows I want that too.

How the fuck does she know that?

I stop at a red light. Bend over to stretch my hamstrings. I'm not going there. I'm not thinking about her sitting on my bed, naked, desperate, waiting for my command.

The light turns green. I take off. Run as fast as I fucking can. Until all my thoughts are dedicated to dodging pedestrians and turning cars.

By the time I get home, I'm back to clarity. And I'm sticking with that.

Emma is at the kitchen table with a bowl of cereal and an oversized mug of coffee.

I nod hello as I toss my keys on the table. Move into the kitchen. Fuck, that coffee smells good. Nutty. Rich. Strong.

I force myself to grab a glass and fill it with water.

"Why did I spend half of yesterday interrogating Kaylee about you having the opportunity to buy Inked Hearts?" Emma's voice is as curious as it's accusatory. It's mild, for her.

I down half my water in three gulps. "Ryan must have mentioned it."

Emma folds her arms. "I called Dean."

My shoulders tense. I don't like Emma talking to Dean. He's my friend, yeah, but he's a pig. He wouldn't think anything of fucking her and throwing her away.

"He explained." She takes a long sip of her coffee. "The four of you are going to buy it together."

"Yeah." I finish the water and fill it again. The last thing I need today is a headache.

Emma's dark eyes get intense. She has something up her sleeve. "Why didn't you tell me?"

"I don't want you to worry."

"Is that how it's going to be—you keep me out of all your decisions because you don't want me to worry?"

Pretty much, yeah. "This is *my* decision."

"No. I did some digging. With Kaylee's help. You don't have enough cash on hand to buy a quarter of the business. Not with the numbers Dean quoted."

"None of the guys do. We're getting a loan."

"With a shitty interest rate. If you refinance the mortgage—it would only add a few years to it."

"Kay put you up to this?"

"No." She taps the table with her purple nails—they match the violet tint to her hair. "But why did you tell her and not me? You trust her more?"

"I'm not sacrificing your future, Em."

"I thought we were a team. That it was 'our future.' It's our house, isn't it?"

"Yeah." Both our names are on the deed. Our parents left it to us.

"Refinance the loan. Get the cash that way. It's what I want."

"That's what you want, me buying Inked Hearts?"

"I think about things besides myself."

"I'm not—"

"Yeah, you are. You're annoying, Brendon, but I do love you. You're my only brother." She pushes herself to her feet. "If we're a team, I want to be part of your decisions. Like Kay staying here. Or you becoming a small business owner. I want that. You know how I dream about owning my own boutique."

She does. She'd be great at it. But not until she finishes school. "You need to focus on college."

She rolls her eyes. "You didn't go to college and you're doing fine."

"Even so."

"I thought about it. You don't have to refinance. Not if I loan you the money."

We inherited equal parts of Mom and Dad's life insurance. Most of mine went to keeping shit together the first few years, while I was still training. But I made sure she never had to touch hers. "No way, Em."

"I won't ask for interest. I just... I want to be able to see the whole process. To see the day-to-day."

"I've offered a million times." Ryan and I basically run the shop now.

"And I'm finally saying yes. You don't need that much. I'll still have plenty for college. Even if I do my last two years at some expensive private school." Her expression is fierce.

This is what she wants.

My sister, the future small business owner.

Usually her stubbornness is a thorn in my side. Right now, it's filling me with pride. What the hell did I do to get Emma to grow into such a confident young woman?

That's one thing I can do right.

Taking care of Em, looking out for her—that fills me with a pride that nothing else can match. Not even finishing a perfect tattoo.

"You want to be a part of this?" I ask.

She nods. "Of course."

"Come to our meeting today. It's at two."

"I don't get off work until two. But okay. I'll figure it out." She smiles. "Thanks, Brendon. You... You aren't always the worst."

"High praise."

She nods. "I know." She pulls me into a quick hug. "I

have to go. But, um, make sure Kay is all right. She's been quiet the last few days."

"Yeah. I will."

"You have any idea what's going on with her?"

No, but I want to. "A lot's changing in her life. And then there's school."

"Yeah, I guess you're right. You're free tonight, right?"

"Yeah. Why?"

"Her party. Well, Ryan and I agreed to combine it. We'll tell her we're celebrating you guys buying the shop. But it's for her too. To say welcome to the family."

"That's sweet."

"I told you. I think about more than myself."

"You're a good friend."

"Thanks, Captain Obvious." She moves to the couch to slide into her black wedges. "You think this is nice enough for the lawyer?"

Her black dress is way too tight and low cut for an office. It's perfect for her job shilling lingerie, but it's not formal. "Wear a blazer."

"Could you get it from my closet? Bring it?"

"Yeah. Sure."

She grabs her purse from the table and waves goodbye. "I love you."

After Mom and Dad, we always close with an I love you. Even if we want to kill each other. "I love you too."

She runs out the door.

I'm focusing on this sale. On the shop. And even on how I'll really fuck things up with my sister—my only family, the most important person in my life—if I give into all the thoughts running through my head.

———

THE MEETING IS QUICK. SEAMLESS.

We've all got our finances figured out.

We're going to make everything official next week.

And Emma is sitting there with a serious, studious look on her face. It's a side of her I never see. It makes me so fucking proud.

I'm over the fucking moon.

Until we're walking back to the parking lot.

And Dean is nudging me and leaning in to whisper. "What do you think Kay's going to wear tonight?"

I say nothing.

"What do you think she'll say if I offer to take her to the back room? You think she'll be into it."

"Go fuck yourself."

"Nah. I'd rather save myself for her."

I know he's saying it to fuck with me.

I know Dean has no intentions of touching Kay.

But, fuck, I still want to punch the smugness from his smile.

Chapter Sixteen

KAYLEE

"**K**ay-bear, you're going to have to be more specific if you want my help." Grandma's voice is irritated. It's the fourth time she's pressed for details, and the fourth time I've denied them.

Not that she can talk. She's being just as secretive about how she's doing. She's still towing the party line. *I need more help, but, really, I'll be fine. Focus on school. Don't worry about me.*

"It's not like I'm gonna know the guy," she says. "Aren't you too old to keep your crushes a secret?"

"Are you ever too old for that?"

"Hmm. I guess not. I've taught you too well." Her voice lifts. Back to hearty. Vivacious even.

But that only makes me think about the possibility she isn't full of life. "Are you really okay?"

"I'm not the one with boy problems."

"Okay, answer this. Are you doing better or worse than just after your heart attack?"

"Better."

My shoulders relax. Then tense. She almost died. It's a low bar.

"You'll tell me if you're there again?" I can't say the words. "If it gets that bad."

"Yes, Kay-bear, of course. Now tell me about the guy. You're making me feel old."

"He wants me. I know he does. But he keeps pretending otherwise."

"How do you know?"

"I just do."

"But do you know? Or do you want it to be true? You wouldn't be the first woman to convince herself of a man's interest."

"No." I turn my phone to speaker so I can check my outfit. "I'm putting you on speaker, Grandma."

"You know I prefer Gigi."

"You know I'm never going to call you Gigi."

I set my cell on my desk. This is outfit four. A plaid skirt and a white blouse. It screams schoolgirl. It screams I'm practically jail bait. It's hot. But it's not what I want.

"I know," I say. "I... I have evidence."

"Yeah? What? He accidentally post it on Facebook or something?"

"Something like that."

"Hmm..."

"What?" I undo the buttons of my blouse and slide it back onto its hanger. "Trust me, Grandma. I know. I have evidence."

"I could help more if you'd tell me the evidence."

And I could help more if she'd tell me the truth about her condition. But I'm not bringing that up. I don't want to fight. "I have it on good authority that he wants me. At least physically."

"Well, of course, Kay. You're a knock out. Every guy you're friends with on Facebook must want you after those pictures Emma posted."

"Grandma—"

"Hey, you got those boobs from your mom and she got them from me. Let me brag. Don't post bikini pics if you don't want attention."

"I didn't. Em did."

"She's a heartbreaker too. So tall and such long legs."

"Yeah. She is." I laugh. Heartbreaker is putting it lightly. "Guys go crazy for her, but she never gets attached."

"Kay-bear, if you want a guy's attention, it's easy. Show off your boobs. It will work. I promise."

I push my skirt off my hips. "But I need more than him wanting me. I need him to admit it."

"Boobs and booze. That's it."

"That's all it takes? Really?"

"Hey, you're the one asking a divorcée for guy advice."

My smile spreads over my cheeks. Grandma has the best sense of humor. She makes the cloudiest day feel bright. Not that there are many cloudy days here. "You promise you're okay?"

"Okay is relative, but I'm not dying anytime soon."

Soon is relative too. But I don't say that. I'd rather believe her. "I have to get ready. There's a party tonight. Emma's brother, you know—"

"Of course I know him. He's fine."

"Him and his friends are buying the tattoo shop."

"Ah."

"What?"

"The timing is interesting."

"Timing of what?"

"You needing guy advice. This guy gonna be at the party?"

I can admit that. "Yeah. But—"

"He have a name?"

"Bye, Grandma. I'll call you soon."

"A push up bra never hurts."

"I love you."

"I love you too."

I end the call.

Maybe she's right.

Maybe showing off my boobs is enough.

It can't hurt.

There. My cream dress, the one Emma made for me, it's perfect.

I slide it on and check my reflection. It hugs my curves. It scoops low enough to show off my chest. It only barely covers my ass.

It's perfect.

I'm not sure exactly what I'm trying to do.

But I'm sure I'm going to drive him out of his head.

I'm going to make it hard for him to pull that *I don't want to talk about this, we're friends, we're nothing* bullshit.

———

I TAKE A SHAKY STEP INTO INKED HEARTS.

The lights are dim.

The walls are adorned with purple, teal, and hot pink tinsel.

There's even a *Welcome Kaylee* banner hanging from the wall. It's in Emma's messy scrawl with a drawing—a tattoo mockup—in each of the four corners.

One from each of the guys. I recognize their styles.

It's...

I blink back a tear.

Emma bounces out from behind the desk. "Surprise. Sort of." She throws her arms around me. "I really am glad you're here."

"Me too." I hug her back. Emma is the best. This would be impossible without her.

"Didn't you throw her a party last week?" Dean moves out from his suite.

"It was her birthday." Emma steps aside. "This is different. And it's for you too. It's so cool that you're buying the shop." She turns to me. "You should have seen that meeting. Dean actually wore slacks."

"Really?" That's hard to believe.

"Don't worry. I don't mind you picturing me without my jeans." He winks. "All these parties too much fun for you, yet?"

"No. It's sweet." It really is.

He moves in to hug me hello. It's sincere—a rarity for him. I really do feel like he's glad I'm here.

I pull back with a smile. "Why are you complaining about the chance to get drunk and make a fool of yourself?"

He laughs. "That's why I like you. Sharp tongue."

My gaze flits around the room. There's Ryan and Walker lining up bottles on the front counter. But where's Brendon?

"I'm not complaining." He releases me and turns to Em. "I'm making sure I get an invite."

"You're a little old..." She smiles, reveling in her teasing.

He mimes being stabbed in the gut. When that gets her laughing, he takes it further. Pretends to double over. Falls to his knees. Mumbles his last words as he falls backward and lands on the floor, splayed out.

Emma nudges him with the toe of her shiny silver stilettos. "Dead. Let's check his pockets."

"Pervert," he mumbles.

"Not the word I'd use." Ryan steps forward. He nods to

me in that *I don't think there's any reason why we need to show compassion toward each other* Ryan kind of way. "You're always welcome here, Kaylee."

"Thanks." I study his expression. Should we hug? Shake hands? Uh... I step forward. Move my hands out from my sides.

Ryan pulls me into a hug. It's quick. Messy. Awkward. He steps back, wipes his brow, sighs. *Let's never do that again.*

Dean jumps to his feet. He actually jumps from his position flat on his back. That's circus acrobat stuff.

He looks to Walker. "You joining this party too?"

Walker shrugs, effortlessly cool. He's the type who takes everything in stride. Nothing bothers him. Or so he claims.

He's a lot like Brendon, really. He's tall and broad with dark hair and dark eyes. He has that same tendency to keep everything to himself. But, with Walker, his typical state is fun, party boy. With Brendon it's serious, quiet artist.

They're the same, but they're opposites too.

He takes his turn hugging me then motions to the booze set up behind us. "What are you drinking?"

Uh... making a fool of myself at my party was bad enough. I'm not doing it in front of everyone.

But I'm not going to be the weird girl who doesn't drink either.

"Jack and diet," I say.

"A girl after my own heart." Walker winks. He brings me to the counter/bar, pours a generous cocktail for me and a straight whiskey for himself. "You're starting school soon, yeah?"

"Two weeks."

He looks to the party—Dean, Emma, and Ryan are in some triangle of teasing. Ryan is actually laughing. Weird.

"Where's Brendon?" I take a sip of my drink. Not bad.

Like a richer version of soda. One that destroys my inhibitions. Gets me saying all the things I need to keep secret.

"Something about *mind your own business*." Walker laughs. "I think he's making something for you."

"Yeah?" My voice jumps two octaves.

"The glimpse I caught looked fucking amazing."

"You're not gonna give me a hint?"

He shakes his head. "More fun this way."

"Cruel."

"Maybe."

"How was the meeting? Was he excited."

"Yeah. Well, for Brendon. You know him. Deadpan."

"And you?"

"Hey, I'm charming. He's—"

"He's charming."

"Well, yeah." He looks me in the eyes. "You tend to find people charming when you're into them."

"What?"

"Everybody knows."

"Who's everybody?"

He motions to the room.

"Not Em."

"Maybe." He places his hands on the counter behind us. "But everybody else."

"It's just... I, um..." God, it's hard to talk. Or think. "Don't say anything."

He brings his fingers to his mouth and pulls an invisible zipper. *My lips are sealed*.

I bury my nose in my drink. The booze only makes my cheeks warmer. It only makes my throat drier.

Everyone knows?

As in everyone talks about it.

As in—

"Hey." Brendon's steady voice flows into my ears. He

sits next to me, on the other side. His eyes go to Walker. "You mind?"

The tattoo artists share a look. It says a lot and it's all about me.

Still, Walker takes his leave.

Brendon moves closer. The back of his hand brushes mine. His thigh presses against mine.

He leans in to whisper. "I have something for you."

"What's that?"

"Close your eyes." His breath warms my neck. It sends shivers down my spine. It sends heat to my core.

"Okay." I do.

His fingers skim my shoulder. Then it's a cotton swab. Rubbing alcohol on my skin.

He pats it dry.

Presses something against it.

Wets it.

Oh...

I turn toward him.

He grabs my other shoulder. Stops me. "I didn't say you could open your eyes." His voice is low, demanding. That same tone he used the other night. "One more minute."

My tongues slides over my lips. My knees knock together. My breath hitches.

Slowly, he peels off the paper sticking to my skin. Then it's cool air on my shoulder. And his fingers curling around my wrist. Peeling my hands from my eyes.

He takes my other hand, leads me to his chair, and turns me toward the mirror. "What do you think?"

It's the topless mermaid he promised for my birthday. She's sitting on a rock, her long blond hair covering her chest, her green eyes on the book in her hands.

It's perfect.

"I love it." I can't help myself. I throw my arms around him and squeeze tightly. "Would you do it right now, if I asked?"

"You've been drinking."

"But tomorrow?"

"In a week, maybe. You're not impulsive."

"What if I asked Dean to do it?"

"No."

"No?"

His voice gets stern. "No, Kay. There's no way Dean is touching you." Regret streaks his eyes. Like he wishes he hadn't said that.

It could be normal *I'm responsible for your well-being, I'm taking care of you* protectiveness.

But it's not.

I know it.

He knows it.

But does he know I know?

I stare into his dark eyes, but that doesn't offer any illumination.

"Hey! No private conversations." Dean moves toward us. "We've got plans. Important ones."

Brendon shoots him a *really* look.

Dean shoots back a sly smile. "We're gonna play Never Have I Ever."

"You're going to be drunk in five minutes flat." That's Leighton, the girl who works at the counter. I guess I didn't hear her come in.

Even Ryan laughs. "I'm not carting your plastered ass home."

"You overestimate me. It's all rumors." Dean moves toward the lobby—to the benches for customers. "Everybody get a drink. Then we'll see who wins."

"Don't you win by losing?" Leighton asks. She runs a

hand through her short, pastel pink hair. "And isn't this game for kids?" She looks to me and Emma. "No offense."

"I think it's more for high school kids," I say.

"But it's fun." Emma looks to Dean. "Just bring cups and whiskey."

"Demanding," he teases back.

"You're not used to taking orders yet?" Walker plops on the bench on the right. "Brendon and Ryan are always bossing you around."

"You too." Dean flips him off.

Walker shakes his head. "I don't live to irritate them."

"You don't?" Ryan takes a seat on the other bench, as far away from Walker as possible. "That's news."

The guys flip each other off.

Slowly, everyone fills in the bench seats.

Grabs a drink.

The guys, save Ryan, are all on the other bench.

I'm sandwiched between Emma and Leighton.

I'm staring at Brendon, trying to figure out what the intensity in his eyes means.

I don't know.

I smooth my dress. Tap my toes together. Gather my hair on my right shoulder.

This is a game you win by losing.

Which means I don't have a chance.

I haven't done *anything*. Not unless you count getting straight As and writing dirty fan fiction.

I...

I'm going to lose.

And everyone is going to know.

Everyone is going to know I'm the sweet girl who doesn't get the guy.

Chapter Seventeen

KAYLEE

Ryan holds up his drink. "Never have I ever fucked a client."

Dean shakes his head. "Lies and slander." He takes a swig.

Leighton taps her drink. "Define client."

Brendon laughs. "That's a yes."

My eyes fix on him. His drink is resting on his thigh. It's nowhere near his lips.

He's never fucked a client.

All he does is work and go to the gym. That means it's been awhile. It must.

That's something.

Maybe this game isn't totally horrible.

Maybe it's somehow useful.

"I could fire you for that," Ryan says.

"You can't fire me. I'm about to be a co-owner." Dean's voice is bouncy. Joyful. He's reveling in rubbing that in. "Besides it wasn't a client here." He stands up to take his turn and offers Ryan that same sly smirk. "Never have I ever gotten a hard-on while doing a tattoo."

Ryan mutters under his breath. He takes a swig, wipes his mouth with the back of his hand.

Brendon and Walker stare at him, surprise in their eyes.

"You gonna explain?" Brendon asks.

Ryan sets his drink on his thigh. "No."

They stare at him.

He stares back.

I tap my heel against the floor. Look to Em with a shrug. She shrugs back.

This... this isn't too bad. It's fun when it's other people getting thrown under the bus.

Ryan folds his arms with a frown.

Dean laughs and blows him a kiss. He nudges Brendon. "Your go."

Brendon shoots Dean a *you're annoying* look. "Never have I ever embarrassed my brother in front of all his friends."

"Bullshit. You don't have a brother." Dean looks to Emma. "And I've seen him embarrass you."

Emma nods. "He's the worst."

"Nah, that's me." Dean holds up his drink. "Fair is fair. You've embarrassed your sibling, so—" Dean takes a long sip.

Brendon nods *fair is fair* and drinks.

Everyone but me drinks.

Ah, for once it's a good thing being an only child.

Walker takes his turn. It's something about tattooing. Leighton's too.

Then it's me. I rack my brain for something that won't out me as a naïve virgin. "Never have I ever fooled around at work."

There are half a dozen fucks at once.

Everyone but Emma drinks.

Ryan shoots Leighton an incredulous look. "Who?"

"Nice girls don't kiss and tell." Her plum lips press into a smile.

"And that's relevant, how?" Dean teases.

They flip each other off.

Emma holds up her drink. "Never have I ever gone to the gym twice in a day."

Brendon takes a drink.

Ryan chuckles.

One of the other guys groans.

Someone complains. "Boring."

Emma shrugs. "I got what I wanted. It's to you, Ryan."

Ryan's expression sticks on Dean. It's like he's a sniper and he's lining up the perfect forehead shot. "Never have I ever lied to a woman about being in love with her."

Dean holds his ground. "You looking at me?"

"Yeah." Ryan stares back at his brother. "You're looking awfully sober."

"I don't have to lie about that shit. I've got a unique charm," Dean says.

Leighton laughs. "Okay."

Walker joins her.

Dean looks to Emma and me. "Back me up, ladies. You'd do me, right?"

Emma laughs. "I like quiet guys."

He mimes being stabbed in the gut.

"And you, Kay?" Dean's gaze flits to Brendon. He's reveling in this too.

I press my lips together. According to Walker, everyone knows. Which means Dean knows too.

This is an opportunity.

I smile back at Dean. "You have a certain charisma."

Dean's smile gets even smugger. "Told you."

Ryan shakes his head. "It's pity. That's it. She feels sorry for you."

"Yeah? Want to hit the clubs and see who's got more charisma?" Dean's voice is a challenge. A playful challenge, but still.

"No." Ryan just stops himself from rolling his eyes. "I have shit to do."

I rest my cup on my thigh and focus all my energy on the amber liquid. This is supposed to be a fun game. The point is getting your friends drunk. That's it.

I hang back for a few more rounds, laughing as the guys take shots at each other. *Never have I ever used "That's nice ink" as a pick-up line.*

Never have I ever dyed my hair.

Never have I ever worn eyeliner.

Then Dean is standing.

Well, trying to stand. He's well past tipsy.

He surveys the room with the same sniper-like precision as Ryan.

He looks to Brendon. Then to me.

"This may be a suicide mission, but I don't care." He holds up his glass. "Never have I ever had sex."

My fingers slip.

Plastic bounces off the hardwood.

Then my drink is spilling on the floor.

And my blush is spreading all the way to my chest.

Everyone is looking at me.

And they know. I can see it in their faces. They know I'm a virgin.

They know I'm head over heels for Brendon.

They know it's never going to happen.

"I... Um... I'll get a towel," I say.

"I've got it." Ryan shoots his brother a death glare.

"What?" Dean tosses his empty cup to the floor. He

pulls his wallet from his jeans, pulls a hundred-dollar bill from it, and slaps it into Brendon's hands. "That's yours."

Brendon stares daggers, but he takes the money.

He bet Dean I was a virgin.

"Fuck you." Brendon pushes himself to his feet.

"It was your idea to bet," Dean says.

"Only 'cause you wouldn't shut the fuck up." Brendon's voice is angry.

It's never angry.

Leighton clears her throat. "It's no big deal, Kaylee. You're better off waiting. I didn't have good sex until I was twenty-one. High school guys can't fuck for shit."

Dean turns to me. "Being a slut is overrated."

"Can I get that in writing?" Walker asks.

"Yeah. I'd like to check the court record on that." Ryan tosses a towel on the spill.

"Not everybody is as soulless and empty as I am," Dean says.

Em looks to me. She mouths *are you okay?*

No. Yes. Maybe.

What the fuck is Brendon doing betting his friends I'm a virgin?

"I think it's great you're waiting for someone special, Kaylee." Dean slurs his words. "But if you're not." He motions to the private suite in the back. The one reserved for especially intimate tattoos. "I'm more than happy to pop that cherry for you. I'll show you the night of your life."

"Right." I plaster on a smile. I know Dean is joking. I can tell he's trying to get a rise out of Brendon.

But it's not funny.

It's not funny that everyone is laughing about the inexperienced girl with a crush on the guy way out of her league.

I push myself to my feet. "Excuse me. I'm going to get some air." I reach for the door.

Walker laughs. "Dean, you're that repulsive."

The door swings shut.

A tear rolls down my cheek. Then another.

I move around the corner. Find a spot against the wall —one where no one can see me—and I slink to my knees.

Tears stain my skin.

This is all fucked.

I can't even enjoy a party.

I can't enjoy anything.

I'm a broken freak. I'll always be a broken freak.

Why would Brendon want me anyway? He has his pick of any nice, normal girl. Plenty who are prettier, smarter, funnier, bolder than I am.

I suck a breath through my teeth and let out a slow exhale. It does nothing to ease the tension in my shoulders. Or back. These heels are awful. How does Emma wear these things all the time?

The bell rings as the shop door opens.

Steady footsteps move toward me.

Then it's Brendon's voice flowing into my ears. "Dean's an asshole."

I press my fingers into my thighs. "It takes two people to bet."

Brendon stops next to me and drops to one knee. "I'm sorry, Kay."

I keep my eyes on my legs. "Why?"

"Huh?"

"Why are you sorry?"

"I shouldn't let him talk about you like that."

"Why?"

"It doesn't matter if you're a virgin," he says.

"But why don't you want Dean talking about me like that?"

He sits next to me. His fingertips trail over the backs of my hands. "You're barely eighteen."

"So?"

He draws a star on the back of my hand. "Look at me, Kay."

I shake my head.

He peels my hands off my knees. Takes one between his thumb and his palm and runs his thumb over my fingers.

I force myself to look him in the eyes. "If you're going to tell me I'm a sweet girl, you can leave now."

"It's not an insult."

"It feels like it. Like I'm a puppy."

"You're not. Puppies are energetic."

I can't help but laugh. And flip him off.

"You're more like a cat. Independent. Smart. Patient."

"Moody and difficult?"

"No." He moves closer. "It doesn't matter if you're a virgin. No one cares."

"I care."

"I don't believe you."

"Fuck you."

"It wouldn't be hard for you to find a guy to fuck."

"How do you know?" My temper flares. He's such a fucking know it all. "Maybe I haven't slept with anyone because no one wants me."

"Bullshit. Every guy in that room would kill for a chance with you."

"Kill who?"

"Me. That's the only way it would happen." His eyes bore into mine. "You're fucking irresistible, Kaylee."

"But you..." *You're resisting me just fine even with all the illicit things you want to do to me.*

I've seen your journal.

I know how you think of me.

I...

I stare back at him. "Do you mean you..." My voice is soft. Barely a whisper. "Do you want me?"

He rests his palm against my check. Wipes a stray tear with his thumb. "It doesn't matter. I'm your guardian. That's it."

"What if you weren't?"

"I am."

"But what if that didn't matter? What if we were just two people who wanted each other? If I had my own place and my own life?" I lean into his touch. "Would you want me then?"

Chapter Eighteen

BRENDON

There's vulnerability in Kaylee's green eyes.

No matter what I say, my answer is going to break her.

I don't want you.

I want you, but we can't be together.

She presses her fingertips into her knees. Her eyes stay fixed on mine.

They demand an answer.

God, I wish I could tell her what she wants to hear.

I wish we lived in some alternate universe where this could happen.

"Brendon." Her voice is shaky. "I'm not leaving until you answer."

"You're my best friend, Kay."

She stares back at me as if to say *and?*

"If a million things were different, yeah. But they're not. Why focus on what ifs?"

"But you... you want to be with me." She sits up straighter. "You want to fuck me."

"If you were some girl I knew, one who wanted me, then yeah, I'd fuck you."

"But you... do you want it now?"

Fuck yeah.

Let's go home now.

Straight to my room.

I'll strip you out of that dress.

Pin you to my bed.

Teach you every fucking thing you need to know.

Her voice gets firm. Confident. "You must have bet Dean for a reason. Because you like the idea of me as a virgin."

"No. It didn't mean anything."

That's bullshit.

I fucking love that Kaylee is a virgin. I love the idea of being the first person inside her. Of my name being the first on her lips. Of my hand being the first on her ass.

It's not because I'm hot for virgins.

It's because it's Kay. Because she's an angel. Because she's sweet. Because I want to watch her bloom in every fucking way she can.

"It doesn't matter, Kay. We can't." I take her hand and pull her to her feet. "Get the thought out of your head."

"What if it won't go?"

"It will. It just takes time." I take a step backward. I can't lie to her. Not when she's looking at me with those gorgeous green eyes. "Forget about me. Find another guy. One you actually want to be with."

"But I..." Her eyes turn down. She wraps her arms around her chest. "I need to get my purse."

"I will. Stay here."

She nods.

I move back into the shop.

Everyone—save Ryan and Dean—is sitting on the

benches. Staring at me like I'm holding a hundred-thou-sand-dollar vase.

Emma glares at me. "Is she okay?"

"Yeah," I say.

"Why would you bet Dean about that?" Emma grabs Kaylee's pink purse as she pushes herself to her feet.

"We get bored. Look for stuff to do." More bullshit.

Walker shoots me an incredulous look.

I shoot him a *shut the fuck up*.

Leighton shakes her head *I don't think so*, but Emma doesn't notice.

My sister moves toward the door. "I'll take her home." She grabs the door. "I'm tired anyway."

I nod. "You okay walking?"

"It's only five blocks." Emma steps outside without glancing in my direction. Pure cold shoulder.

Walker shakes his head. "You're lucky Ryan didn't hear that." He looks to Leighton for support.

She wraps a pink strand around her finger. It matches the cherry blossom tattoo on her forearm.

"You have something to add?" I ask.

She brings her hand to her other arm. "Kaylee deserves better."

"I'm aware of that."

"But the heart wants what it wants. And she's clearly in love with you." Leighton pushes herself to her feet. "If you care about her—and we all know you do—then grab onto her or let her go."

"I do—"

"No. I see the way you look at her. The way you flirt with her. You keep tossing her *I want you* breadcrumbs. You're keeping her in waiting." She reaches for the door. "She deserves better than *that*."

At home, Kaylee is on the couch in a tiny tank top and smaller shorts, her arms wrapped around her knees, her hands on her Kindle.

She looks up at me as the door swings shut. Her eyes fill with frustration. Then regret.

"Hey." I toss my keys on the table. Leave my shoes by the door. Like tonight never happened. "Emma go to bed?"

"Yeah." Her voice is shaky. She looks back to her Kindle. Taps her fingers against its edge. "So, we're... we're gonna act like everything is normal?"

Not exactly, but close.

Leighton is right.

I need to let Kaylee go.

To be her friend, and nothing more.

"That's for the best," I say.

"Yeah."

"Oh." Her voice is hollow. "So, we're..."

"We're friends."

I wish there were some way to make this easier for her.

To wipe every thought of me from her head.

But if I can't stop thinking about her, I don't see how I can convince her to stop thinking about me.

"Yeah. Of course." There's no fight in her voice. Because she's tired of fighting or because she understands this is how it has to be?

It doesn't matter. She'll get used to it.

We *are* friends. The sooner we act like things are normal, the better.

I take a seat on the other side of the couch. "I'm gonna watch something."

She sets her Kindle down. Sits so her back is against

the back cushion of the couch, her legs hanging over the edge. "Something dumb with explosions?" There's humor in her voice. It's not all the way to Kaylee teasing me, but it's getting there.

"Not that you'd ever judge?" I tease back. Almost. I'm only at eighty percent.

She forces a smile. "I'd never." Her eyes catch mine as she turns toward me. "What do you like about that stuff anyway?"

"What do you like about *The Hunger Games*?"

Her eyes light up. All of a sudden, the tension between us melts. I don't know she's a virgin. She doesn't know I want her. It's just Kaylee and Brendon on the couch debating movies again.

"What don't I like about *The Hunger Games*? First of all, there's Katniss. She smart, strong, brave. But she's not trying to start a revolution. She's not even trying to resist. She's just trying to survive."

I know exactly how to press this. "Yeah, but she's a Mary Sue."

Kaylee jumps off the couch. "Excuse me? Katniss is all flaws. Mary Sue is a bullshit sex term anyway. You never hear anyone complain about guys being good at everything. You never hear people saying *Harry Potter is such a Gary Stu*. If you actually read the book, you'd know that her moodiness and her struggle to connect with other people is a big hindrance."

Warmth fills my chest. I fucking love seeing her like this.

And it feels normal.

"That guy she's into. He's boring." Truth be told, I enjoy *The Hunger Games* quite a bit. Even the love triangle. But it's too much fun seeing Kay's eyes light up.

"Oh, big surprise. Another guy complaining about Peeta. Where is it guys got the idea brooding and angry is better than supportive and funny?"

I raise a brow. "You could let a guy dream."

She laughs so hard her tits shake. "Is that why you're on Team Gale?"

"Brooding and handsome has to count for something."

He cheeks flush. "Yeah. But a sense of humor is important too. And being able take care of someone. Do you really think you would be able to take care of Katniss?"

"I'm not sure anyone could take care of Katniss."

Kaylee's lips press together. Her voice gets soft. Uncertain. "Yeah. I guess... I guess she's kinda broken at the end. But I like to believe she's okay. That time and love are enough."

"Me too."

She turns toward me. There's something in her eyes, but I don't know what it is. "Why do you love action movies?"

"I can't go after that. Your answer is poetic. Mine is boring."

"Then make it poetic."

"I'm not the writer. If you want something pretty, well, check out your temporary tattoo in the mirror."

She shakes her head. "I want your boring answer."

"The boldness of them grabs my attention."

"Hmm."

"Don't *hmm* me."

"You do it all the time."

"Still."

She laughs. "You're a hypocrite. But I guess I'll forgive you." She sinks into the leather. Her voice gets earnest. "I do forgive you."

"Thanks." My shoulders relax. Then my back. My jaw. A wave of easiness floats through my body. I need her forgiveness. I need her friendship. Hell, I need a lot more than that, but it's all I'm gonna get.

Her voice perks. Back to teasing. "You're going to make it up to me."

"Am I?" *Loose the shorts and the panties and spread your legs. I want to look at that soft pink cunt before you come on my face.*

"You're going let me pick which dumb action movie we watch. Actually, it won't be dumb."

"*The Hunger Games* doesn't count as an action movie."

"Yes, it does. It has fight scenes. It has people killing each other. It even has explosions."

"Okay. But I get to pick the next one."

"I bet the plot will be incomprehensible."

I can help but chuckle. "Maybe."

She leans back against the couch. Crosses her legs. "You're too smart to enjoy that."

I turn toward her. Soak in the way her lips are turning upward, the brightness in her eyes, the softness in her shoulders. "Says who?"

"Me. Obviously." Her eyes spark.

It lights me up inside. "It's not the same for you. You're a writer. You see the strings."

Kaylee shakes her head. Her cheeks flush. "I'm not a writer. I write things sometimes. It's different."

"You write things. Doesn't that make you a writer?"

"No."

"No? I tattoo people. That makes me a tattoo artist."

"Well, what if you'd only done it once? Or only some-times? If it was a hobby?"

"I'd still be a tattoo artist."

"It's different."

"How?"

"It just is."

"I hate to break it to you, but you're a writer. You're always scribbling in your notebook."

The last word makes her tense. Her shoulders go back to her ears. Her teeth sink into her lip.

She shakes it off. "It's just a hobby."

"It could be more."

"No... I don't think so."

"Why not?"

She looks me in the eyes. Her voice gets strong. Confident. "Because it's my life and I can do what I want."

I can't argue with that. But it's not the reason. "I have a proposition for you."

She perks. "I'm listening."

"I'll watch all four movies with you."

Kaylee claps her hands together. Joy spills over her expression. Her eyes get bright. Her lip corners turn upward. Her brow relaxes. "Okay. Right now? All night?"

"Right now. All night. Can you really stay awake?"

"For Katniss? Of course."

"I bet you can't."

Her eyes narrow. Yeah, bets are a bit of a sore subject. But I don't see another way to make this happen.

"Okay." She taps her fingers against her thigh. "I bet I'll stay awake. What are the terms?"

"You're registering for classes this weekend?"

"Yeah. And?"

"If you fall asleep, you have to register for a creative writing class."

"I don't know..."

"If you're sure, what's it hurt to bet?"

She presses her lips to one side. "If I win, I get to pick your next tattoo. And you get no veto power."

148

"Harsh."

"Well, if you're sure, what's it hurt to bet?" She smiles as she throws my words back at me.

"True." I am sure. And I actually trust her not to fuck me over. Even though I deserve it. "You're on."

Chapter Nineteen

KAYLEE

There are arms around me.

Strong arms.

Lines of ink wrap around soft skin.

Brendon's sleeve.

His footsteps are steady as he moves down the hallway.

He kicks open my door.

The room is dark except for those glow-in-the-dark stars. It's perfect. Romantic. Sweet.

I'm in his arms under the stars.

He lowers me onto the bed.

His fingers skim my temples as he slides my glasses off my face. He folds them carefully. Like they're precious jewels.

My eyelids flutter together. Then apart.

He's looking down at me with those dark eyes.

He's going to leave.

He can't.

I reach up for him. Curl my fingers around his wrist. "I guess I lost."

He nods. "You even remember which movie we were on?"

No. I can see Finnick with his trident. Shit, we were in the middle of *Catching Fire*. That leaves two and a half movies to go.

"It's too bad," I whisper. "I had the perfect tattoo picked out." I tug at his t-shirt, pulling him closer.

My hand finds his chest. My finger traces the line.

"Right here. A Latin expression. But I won't say which one."

He smiles, charmed. But it fades. Back to stern caretaker. I think. I can only see so well without my glasses.

"You should brush your teeth," he whispers.

And take my medication.

But I can't leave.

Not with him this close.

It's all I'm going to get.

The way he's looking at me—he's dead set on this just friends thing.

I stare back into his eyes. "Make me."

He shakes his head as he pulls back. "Sweet dreams, Kay."

But not as sweet as him staying.

———

THE NEXT FEW DAYS, I AVOID BRENDON. I EAT IN MY room. Watch TV while he's at work. Insist Emma and I watch movies in her room.

Sunday is the longest day ever. Even though there's a rush at work, my shift stretches on forever. I don't get cut until ten. Don't get home, in my room, until ten thirty.

Only an hour to go.

And I'm not ready.

Shit. Where the hell is my laptop?

It's not on my desk. Or in my closet. Or anywhere under the bed.

There are footsteps in the hall. Then a knock on my door.

"You looking for this?" Brendon's voice flows into my room.

"My laptop?"

"Yeah. Can I come in?"

"Sure." We're doing normal. We're friends. And friends can hang out in each other's rooms.

It's not like I'm thinking about him on my bed.

Naked.

It's not like I'm obsessed with his dirty drawings.

And the smell of his shampoo.

And all the lines of ink that wrap around his arm.

My heartbeat picks up as he opens the door and steps inside.

He looks the same as always. Tall. Broad. Stoic.

He's wearing black jeans and a black t-shirt. It hugs his shoulders. It offers a peek of the roses tattooed to his chest.

I can't decide what saying I want on his chest.

Live so you can live.

Remember your mortality.

Seize the night.

Nothing comes from nothing.

Save me and I'll save you.

That's a hopeless fantasy. No one is saving me. You can't fix the ways I'm broken.

But he...

He could love me anyway.

It's possible. In theory.

He moves forward. Sets my laptop on my desk. "Forty-five minutes to go."

"Yeah. I should prepare."

"You need to prepare?"

"Sort of." Technically, no. But I want to be ready.

"Did you eat dinner?"

I stare back into his dark eyes. "I'm too nervous to eat."

"You need to eat something."

"It's my body. Not yours."

"We'll do this downstairs." He scoops my laptop back into his arms and takes a step backward. "I'll heat up dinner."

"Brendon. I don't have time—"

"You have forty-five minutes. Go shower. Change into something comfortable. I'll have your food ready."

I glare at him.

He glares back.

"You really are bossy and annoying."

"You just figure that out?"

"I'm usually the one on your side when Emma complains about you."

"That's because you're not around me twenty-four seven. Give it a few more weeks. You'll get sick of me."

Fat chance. Being around him all the time only makes me want him more.

He's so close, but he's so far away too.

I hate him for bossing me around. So what if his intentions are good? Nobody tells me when to shower or eat. Especially not someone who's withholding the kinds of demands I want. "I'm only going along with this because you're holding my laptop hostage."

"Tell me something I don't know." He takes another step backward, into the hallway.

I follow. Watch him move downstairs and set up the dining table.

There's my laptop, closed, untouched.

This is the perfect chance to invade my privacy.

But he's keeping his eyes to himself.

I push the thought aside as I move into the bathroom. We need normal. And me telling him I've seen his sketch-book—not normal.

It's an excuse, sure, but it's true.

———

THERE'S A PLATE NEXT TO MY COMPUTER. AN ALMOND butter and jelly sandwich cut into tiny squares.

The perfect snack.

At least he's being...

Ugh, I hate him more for being sweet.

His eyes go to the timer on his cell. "Fifteen minutes."

Fifteen minutes until I set my fate for the semester.

That's nothing.

I take a seat. Try to avoid the lure of the delicious sandwich.

The bread is toasted. Warm.

Strawberry jelly is spilling from its sides.

And almond butter too.

Maybe just one square...

I pop it in my mouth, chew, swallow. It's perfect warm, sweet, gooey comfort food.

But that half-smirk on his face—

No, I love that too.

He's so beautiful.

I could get lost in his eyes. Dark. Like a strong cup of coffee.

Shit. I'm staring.

I force my attention to my laptop. School website. Login. There. I'm ready to register. And I can even handle it.

"Ten minutes." His voice is soft. Sweet. The Brendon only I know. "You nervous?"

I nod.

"You never seem nervous."

"Never?"

"You're the most put together person I know."

"No. I just seem that way." I bite my lip. That's already too much. If he knew the truth, that I'm held together by pretending and antidepressants, that I'm destined to think about all sorts of ugly ways to hurt myself...

"You never talk about it."

"What about you?" I turn toward him. Stare into those dark eyes. "You never talk about anything that bothers you."

"True." There's no admission in his voice. Only an awareness of the facts. He stares back at me. "You're thinking something."

"Nothing important." I stare at the computer screen so I won't have to take his gaze. It's too much. It's picking me apart.

"You love writing."

"Is that a question?"

"But you don't want to take a creative writing class."

"Accurate."

"Why?"

Because my subconscious takes over when I'm writing. I can't stop myself from spilling all my ugly secrets on the page.

If I share that with people, they'll see the seams.

They'll tug at the stitches.

And then all of me will spill out.

My guts will be on the floor.

And everyone will run away.

Nobody knows I have depression. That I'm on drugs. That my thoughts go to dark places when things get bad.

Nobody knows I'm broken.

And I want to keep it that way.

"Kay." Brendon runs his fingertips over my forearm. "You okay?"

"Just thinking."

"You ever share your writing with people?"

"Grandma reads my fan fiction. She's encouraging."

"Show me something."

My cheeks flame. The thought of Brendon reading one of my bad poems... It's horrifying. "Show me something in your sketchbook. Something that isn't a tattoo mockup."

His jaw cricks. His eyes fill with surprise. "I'll jump if you do."

"Maybe later. There's not much time left." And I'm not a good actor. I can't pretend that I haven't seen every inch of that sketchbook.

He nods. "Five minutes."

"Five minutes." I refresh the school's website for good measure. It's the same. The same *Registration Not Available* is there in all red.

"What else are you taking?"

"Huh?"

"Besides creative writing."

"Oh. Advanced American literature. Chemistry. Latin four."

"Latin four?"

"Yeah." I chew on my fingernail. "It was supposed to be my elective. But now I have creative writing too."

He chuckles.

"What?" I move on to the nail of my middle finger. Hit refresh. *Registration not available.*

"That's perfect for you."

"Thanks. I think." Ring finger nail, here I come.

His hand curls around my wrist. "Kay."

"Yeah?" I turn toward him. Get stuck staring into his eyes. God, those eyes are beautiful.

"You're gonna be okay."

In theory.

He moves closer. "You're the smartest, strongest person I know."

The compliment warms my cheeks and chest.

Even if it's not true. I'm not strong. Certainly not as strong as Emma.

But I'm not going to argue. I'm not willing to offer the details to explain it.

He opens his mouth to say something but the timer's beep cuts him off.

Refresh.

Registration Available.

Yes.

I add each class to my schedule. Latin Mondays and Wednesdays at ten. American Literature after lunch. Chemistry and Creative writing Tuesday and Thursday. Recitation Monday and Tuesday afternoons.

There.

It's done.

Brendon smiles as he offers me his hand.

I take it.

Squeeze tightly.

Move the cursor over submit.

Click.

Congratulations.

It's done.

And I'm officially a college student.
I jump to my feet.
Brendon gets to his.
Wraps his arms around me.
It doesn't feel like a platonic hug.
But it feels too good for me to complain.

Chapter Twenty

KAYLEE

It's well past midnight when I finally float down from my high. I'm not sure exactly why I'm buzzing. If it's mostly because of his arms around me or if it's mostly nerves about school.

But I don't really care.

I need both.

So, when Brendon offers to take me shopping for school supplies, I jump. Insist we do it on a day I know Emma works.

It's not like I'm desperate to get him alone.

Not at all.

———

I GRAB BRENDON'S WRIST AS WE STEP INTO MACY'S.

We turn to the right, past the shiny shoes. Through the wall of perfume—I have to turn to my side, to face him, to avoid scents in my nose and eyes.

Past the makeup counters stocked with forty-dollar

foundation and twenty-dollar lipstick. The kind of stuff Emma brags about buying with her employee discount.

Right to the handbags.

Huh?

"You have a Louis Vuitton obsession I should know about?" I tease.

"Who?" He raises a brow.

I point to the designer bags to our left. They're iconic. Brown with a tan logo.

Brendon steps forward. Checks the price tag. "Fuck. Really? For that?"

Several hundred dollars for a scrap of leather is obscene. But, hey, what do I know what it's like to have money? "You never spend on something you don't need?"

"Need is relative."

"Capitalism is for scum?"

He chuckles. "There's a line somewhere, yeah." He sets the bag down. "Would you buy one of those bags?"

"No. They're ugly."

"And I'm harsh?"

I laugh. "The color scheme doesn't do it for me."

"What about this?" He points to a similar bag in bright pink. Moves close enough to check the price tag. "Is this walking advertisement worth two weeks of waiting tables?"

"Not to me."

"But to someone?"

"It's a status symbol."

He raises a brow. "And that's a good thing?"

"I don't know. I'm never going to have status."

"I'm calling it now. When you write the next *Hunger Games*, you're going to spend your advance on hideous overpriced bags." His voice floats to that teasing tone. His dark eyes light up.

"I am not," I tease back. "But so what if I did? What's wrong with wanting people to see you as well off?"

He shakes his head. "That's what my mom was like. She needed a new car. A remodeled kitchen. The latest fashions. Even her nail polish was trendy."

"I remember." Sort of. "Is that really all she was?"

"No." His voice gets soft. "But that was too much of it. She wanted that for all of us. For me and Em too."

"Yeah?" I press my lips together. Brendon never talks about his late parents. Ever. And his expression—there's a softness to it. That's rare. I want every drop of it.

"Yeah. She wanted me to be this guy who wore Dockers and drove a BMW to high school."

"And you wanted to tattoo punk lyrics on your skin?"

"Basically." He takes a step forward. "I was never gonna be the kind of guy she wanted me to be."

"But you... you are a great guy. You know that, right?"

He says nothing. Turns back to me and looks me in the eyes. "Let's say I give you a grand to buy whatever you want."

"You will not."

"It's a hypothetical."

"I prefer actual cash."

"Don't we all." He chuckles. "Say I give you a grand. Say you have to spend it here. What will you buy?"

"One very expensive designer purse."

"Bullshit."

"Em would buy one."

"Em is Em."

"Still... I don't think it's wrong. Your mom was into a certain image, yeah. But you are too. It's just different." I drag my fingertips over his sleeve tattoo, tracing the lines from his wrist up to his bicep. "How much did this cost?"

His tongue slides over his lips. His eyelids flutter together. He's soaking up my touch.

But only for a second.

Then he's looking at me like he can control every one of his senses. "More than that purse."

"How much more?"

"More than you make in a month."

"A summer month?"

"Yeah."

Damn. I'm not exactly rolling in it, but I work a lot in the summer. And summers are busy. Tips are good.

"Don't give me that look."

"What look?" I stare into his deep eyes, trying to find... something. I'm not sure.

"I'm not like my parents." Hurt flares in his expression.

"I know. Just... we all care about how we appear to others. I know I do. I want people to think I'm strong and smart."

"You are."

I bite my lip. I'm not arguing this point, no matter how much I disagree.

He takes my hand. Leads me toward the colorful bags and backpacks to our left. The ones next to the giant silver gorilla. Kipling. My favorite. Half my bags are this brand.

Has he been paying that much attention?

His gaze goes to the backpacks on the wall. He picks up a teal one and turns back to me. "It matches your eyes."

It kinda does. "It's cute."

"Not cute enough for you." He sets it back down. Picks up a pink one next to it.

It's a beautiful shade of pink—halfway between pastel and Barbie bright.

He moves back to me.

His fingertips skim my bare skin as he peels my purse

off my shoulder then slides the backpack over my arms, one at a time.

They brush my neck as he pushes my hair to one side.

I feel his touch everywhere.

I can't do friends.

Not even a little.

Not with the way my body is buzzing.

I want his body.

And his heart.

I want him to know me.

I want to crumble in his arms and let down every one of my defenses. To admit how terrified I am. About school and Grandma and my parents. And everything.

"How's that?" His breath warms my ear.

My knees knock together.

My sex cries out for attention.

My heart too.

Please, someone, somewhere. Please let me have him. I'm losing everything else. I just want this one little thing.

I force myself to turn toward the mirror. The backpack is cute and comfortable. But— "Pink? Really?"

"Pink is perfect for you."

"It's impractical."

"Then explain this." He holds up my dainty pink purse.

"Purses are supposed to be cute. Backpacks are utility."

"What about that bright blue Jansport with lyrics all over it?"

"You used to complain that I put too much pop music on it."

His eyes light up as he smiles. "If you'd just put something by The Dead Kennedys."

"How about The Smiths?"

"I'm not wearing eyeliner no matter how many times you ask."

I laugh and blush at the same time. Mmmm. Brendon in eyeliner. What a beautiful mental image. "How about Garbage or Hole? Something angry with instruments I can hear?"

He gives me a slow once over. "Why do you scribble lyrics on everything?"

I look up into his eyes. "Why do you have ink everywhere?"

"I asked first."

"I guess, I want to make it mine."

"But it's someone else's words."

"But when I put them together, they feel like mine. Besides, did you ever hear of someone getting lyrics they wrote as a tattoo?"

"Yeah."

"Really?"

"I did them once."

"Name. Dropper."

He shrugs, playing coy. "A huge pop star known for how much she hates her exes."

"Bullshit." It really is. "Why do you have so many tattoos?"

"Same reason."

"You want to mark your body?"

He nods. "Honestly?"

"Yeah." I press my lips together. He's going to tell me something he doesn't tell anyone. I need that. Every drop of it.

"At first, I wanted to piss off my mom. To prove to her, and myself I guess, that I'd never be a khaki wearing, golf playing yuppie."

"Did it work?"

"Yeah. She wrote me off right away."

"I'm sorry."

"Don't be. It was for the best. It hurt less when they..." His voice trails off. Like he doesn't believe it.

It must hurt. Even if things were tense. Just thinking about Grandma—it makes my entire body heavy. Which is why I'm currently rocking a nice state of denial. As long as I don't know the details, I can pretend things will be okay.

"It's more than that." I trace the lines on the back of his hand. His wrist. His forearm.

He nods. "It's a rush."

"And?"

"I like feeling in control."

Heat floods my cheeks. My chest. My sex. "Like you do during sex."

His expression gets intense as his eyes bore into mine. "Kay—"

"You don't talk about this with Dean?"

"You and I aren't friends like me and Dean."

"Well, yeah, I'm not an asshole. If you're embarrassed or something—"

He raises a brow *try harder next time*. He motions to the backpack, swiftly jumping over the subject. "It is perfect for you."

"Because it's feminine?"

He nods. "And innocent."

"Yeah?" We are friends and friends *can* talk about sex. "Like an untouched flower?"

"Didn't realize you were into that."

I nod as I slide the backpack off. Examine its pockets. "You know me. Boy crazy."

"You've dated."

This really is a nice backpack. Laptop pouch. Plenty of space for books. "Mostly double dates with Emma."

"You want to go on those?" There's an edge to his

voice. But is it because he's looking out for me or because he's jealous?

"Sometimes." I try to focus on the pouches on the table. They're perfect for makeup. School supplies. Tampons.

He stares back at me. "You ever like any of these guys you date?"

"Sometimes."

He steps forward, planting his foot in front of me. "You kiss them?"

"Sometimes."

"More?"

His posture is strong, powerful, from his all black converse to the tip of his dark hair.

How am I supposed to answer when he's looking at me like that—like he's in control of the entire universe?

I pick up a fuchsia pencil case and undo its zipper. "You want to know this because?"

"Making conversation." His voice wavers.

It's more than that.

I want to know how much more. To know how far along he is on the *I'll never think about you again/we're totally just friends* journey.

I move away from the bags—this is enough—and start wandering through the first floor.

He follows. "Do you?"

I stop at the jewelry counter and pretend to examine a set of silver earrings. My eyes flit between him and the glass display case. Is he jealous? I'm not sure. "I have."

His jaw cricks. His hands curl into half-fists then unfurl.

He is jealous.

The thought fills me with feminine power.

"You let guys feel you up?" Envy drips into his voice.

I stare into his eyes. "Sometimes."

He stares back. "You let them touch your cunt?"

"What?" My cheeks flush. The salesgirl is only a dozen feet away. She's talking to another customer. Did she hear? Did both of them?

"You let guys stroke you to orgasm?"

"That isn't the word you used."

He wraps his hand around my wrist and leads me to the escalator. "It made you flinch."

"No."

"Yeah."

"No." I make eye contact through the mirrored wall. We look like opposites the way we always do—dark and masculine versus light and girly. But we look good together. "It didn't faze me at all."

He raises a brow. Breaks our mirror eye contact to turn to me. "Really?"

"Really." In theory.

Brendon leans in to whisper. He combs my hair back, behind my ear. "Then say it."

I move onto the next step. Then onto the second-floor tile. There's nothing but clothes here.

I turn and step onto the next up escalator.

Brendon follows. It's just us, on the way to the third floor.

"I, uh... do you always use that word?" I ask.

"Yeah."

"It's so vulgar."

"There's a power in vulgar. You're a writer. I'm sure I don't have to explain it to you."

"Right." It is a powerful word. I can't deny that. "It doesn't bother me."

"Bullshit."

"It doesn't."

He lets out a low chuckle. "Then say it."

"I can."

"Go ahead."

I step onto the third floor. Look around. No one nearby.

Okay. I can do this.

I can totally do this.

I take a deep breath, exhale slowly, ready the word on my tongue. "Cu..." My cheeks flush. "Cunt."

"Like it means something to you."

I stare at the white tile floor. The fluorescent lights are casting a yellow gaze. "Cunt."

Brendon laughs. "You can admit it bothers you."

"It doesn't."

"Then look me in the eyes when you say it."

I stare back into Brendon's dark eyes. I have to prove this. That I'm not this pathetic good girl who can't even say a dirty word. "Cu..." God, I'm going to die of embarrassment. But I hold strong. I push past my blush. "Cunt."

A salesguy is moving in our direction. I turn to the left. To the home goods. So no one will hear us.

Or see me blushing like a tomato.

He takes the backpack from me. Replaces it with my purse. His fingertips skim my neck. My collarbone.

It's like he's reminding me I'm his.

But I'm not.

He's made that abundantly clear.

"Have you?" he asks.

"What?"

He shakes his head *no*. "Have you ever let a guy between your legs?" That same jealousy seeps into his voice.

"Did you bet Dean about that too?"

"No."

"Will you tell him?"

170

"No. I shouldn't have told him shit."

Maybe. But I want him bragging to his friends about us. About being with me. I want him so infatuated with me, with my body, with fucking me, that he can't keep his mouth shut.

"Are you going to tell him about this conversation?"

"No." He chuckles. "I don't need anyone knowing I'm corrupting you."

I move forward. To the expensive notebooks. They're muted. Masculine. Dark. I pick up a black one. It's leather-bound with a magnetic snap. "You are?"

"I just got you to say cunt in a shopping mall."

My laugh is more nervous than anything. "I liked it."

"Even worse."

"No, like you said." I force myself to turn back to him. To look him in the eyes. I can't stand Brendon thinking he isn't good for me. Even if this whole hot and cold act of his is driving me bonkers. "It's a powerful word. A tool."

"You're only interested as a writer?"

I nod.

"And I only watch porn as an artist."

Fuck, why does he make it so hard to hold his gaze? My cheeks are burning. I stammer something. "Well... yeah... you need to study the human figure."

"And that's why you read dirty books, to study the prose?"

"Yeah. I don't need them for fantasies. My imagination is plenty active. You... I guess you haven't read any of my fan fiction."

"I'm still waiting on that story about Draco tying up Harry."

"Have you even read *Harry Potter*?"

"I know the gist."

"I haven't... I have to do more research still." I run my fingers over the edges of the notebook.

He brushes a stray hair from my eyes then takes the notebook in my hands. Runs his fingers over the cover. "This is exactly what you need."

"So I can fill it with *cunt?*" I manage to say the word without blushing.

He chuckles. "So you can fill it with whatever grabs onto you and refuses to let go." He flips the snap, bends the spine, drags his fingers over the paper. "This is a serious notebook. For a serious writer."

"But I'm not—"

"You could be."

"Why does it matter so much to you?"

"Because you matter that much to me."

Chapter Twenty-One

BRENDON

Days pass in a blur. Kaylee in workout clothes in the morning. Emma at the breakfast table, groaning about an early shift. A back piece—a tiger hiding in the bushes. Two best friends getting matching ink. A guy who says nothing, simply hands me an abstract design, and tips an extra hundred dollars in cash.

Dean reminding Ryan they're about to be on equal footing.

Ryan growling and rolling his eyes.

The quiet in the house.

My sister attempting her summer reading.

Kaylee's laugh from Emma's room.

A night out with Ryan. A quiet grunt-hey-raise our beers-nod-drink kind of night.

Another long day at work. Dad duties at dinner with Emma. With Kaylee right there, those big green eyes all contemplative and innocent.

Another night out with Dean and Walker at a too loud dance club. They take turns picking out one-night stands. And teasing me about holding out for "sweet virgin pussy."

Sunday night, I get home late. Strip out of my sweaty clothes. Scrub clean in the shower.

I step into my bedroom wrapped in a towel. Something catches my eye. A light in the hallway.

It's a flicker. Then it's gone again.

I move toward the hall. Watch Emma's doorframe. Nothing for a while. Then the light flickers over it.

It's coming from Kaylee's room.

I should ignore it.

Continue avoiding her.

Do whatever it takes to keep my fly zipped.

I don't.

I pull on boxers and jeans. Move into the hallway with soft steps.

She stirs. Her footsteps move toward the door.

"Hey," she whispers through the door. "You okay?"

No. I'm not going to be okay until she's out of my head. Until my fucking head goes back to normal—so it's filled with details of action movies, and punk songs, and tattoo mockups, and one-night stands, and every awful thing my parents ever said to me.

Until that space is mine and not hers.

"Brendon?"

"I got something for you. Give me a minute." Fuck, there's something wrong with me. Too much. I know better than to invite myself into her room in the middle of the night.

This is not how you resist temptation.

Kaylee looking up at me with those doe eyes, her hands on my skin, her body curled into mine—I can barely resist that when we're vertical.

If we're horizontal?

Fuck this. I shake my head. Skip right over thoughts of baseball and action movies, straight to shop finances.

We're signing the papers tomorrow. Making it official.

But there's more to take care of. We need to hire an extra hand. Or two. And Ryan is refusing to even consider it.

The man hates change.

I grab Kaylee's gift and pull on a t-shirt. Force my thoughts to the shop. To salaries and profits and per hour rates. To schedules and how much more we could make if we plugged a few gaps.

Fuck, I should have paid more attention in high school. Taken some business classes at SMC. Something. I was too busy proving I didn't give a fuck about anything to care about the things that mattered.

I move into the hallway.

Kaylee's door is open.

And she's there, sitting up on her bed, in a thin cream tank top and deep blue boxer shorts with white bicycles on them.

I press the door shut behind me.

I let my eyes roam her body. Her strap is falling off her shoulder. Her top is clinging to her tits. Her nipples are hard.

She presses her knees together. Places her palms on her soft thighs. Her nails—painted Bruins blue—dig into her skin.

She looks up at me. "I haven't seen much of you."

"We're busy with contracts. And clients. We need to hire help."

She nods. "What kind of help do you need?"

"Another artist."

"Not my expertise."

"If Leighton decides to apprentice, we'll need someone to take her job."

"You want me working the front desk?"

"Why not? You're there all the time now." Not lately. She's avoiding me as much as I'm avoiding her.

"Because—" She draws a circle around herself with her hand. Turns to show off her bare shoulders, one at a time. "I'm unadorned."

"Guys would fall over themselves trying to convince you to ink up. They'd get their work done at the shop so they could flirt with you." Which is a good reason to discourage her. I want to deck Dean whenever he flirts with Kaylee and I know he's only doing it to fuck with me. If it were some other guy, one who wouldn't think twice about treating her like a cum-dumpster? Fuck, I'd break my hand within a month.

"What if I said yes?"

"As long as I do the work."

"Yeah?" She scoots back on her bed and lowers herself onto her back. "You trust yourself?"

Trust myself with my hands on her skin? Fuck no. But — "More than I trust anyone else."

She turns toward me and props up on one elbow. "Maybe I can help convince Ryan. If there are numbers supporting it. Math isn't my best subject—"

"You got an A minus in Calculus."

"See. Not my best."

I arch a brow.

She laughs. "That was my worst grade."

"Of course it was."

"Hey, I didn't tell you to spend your high school career hanging out with druggies and burn outs."

"You sure? I thought that was you."

This laugh is bigger. It gets her light hair falling in her face. Her strap sliding off her shoulder. "Are you gonna stay awhile?"

"Yeah."

"Good." She grabs her glasses from the bedside table and slides them on.

I take a seat on the bed next to her. "I have something for you. Close your eyes."

"Okay." Her lids flutter together. She turns toward me. Every part of her body is expectant. Her back is arched. Her lips are pursed. Her thighs are pressed together.

She wants me to kiss her.

Touch her.

Fuck her.

I want that too.

Fuck, how I want that...

Snap out of it.

I shake my head as I place the notebook in Kaylee's hands. "You can open your eyes."

She does. Her gaze goes right to the leather-bound journal in her hands. "Brendon. This was too expensive."

"My money."

"But, you—isn't this everything you hate? Some mass-produced notebook that costs way too much."

"I'm not that guy anymore." I'm not sure who I am now. Not beyond work and family. Usually, that's enough. But the way Kaylee looks at me—it begs me to fill in all the gaps.

I want to be the kind of guy who deserves her.

"It's so pretty." She traces a heart on the cover. "I'm not sure I can actually write in it." She places the journal on her bedside table and turns toward me. "Thank you."

"Of course."

She scoots forward. Wraps her arms around me. Buries her head in my chest. "Really, Brendon. Thank you."

Fuck, she smells good. Her touch is soft. Sweet. Like she believes I deserve her. "I brought you something else."

"Where?"

"Here." I pull the folded paper from my back pocket. "Our deal."

"Oh." Her cheeks flush as she unfolds the paper. She takes it in slowly.

It's an old piece. A self-portrait. It was right after the accident. When I carried around the weight of it on my shoulders twenty-four seven.

It's a lighter burden now, but it's still there.

My parents died thinking I was worthless.

My last words to them were about how awful they were.

"When did you do this?" She runs her fingers over the faded paper.

"Forever ago."

She nods as she looks up at me. "It's beautiful. But sad."

I'm not sure what to say. I don't share *my* work with people. Tattoos are someone else's blood and guts. I can show the entire world that.

"There's a lot of hurt there," she whispers. "Do you still feel like that?"

"Less, but yeah."

"I'm sorry. It must have been hard, everything with your parents. And taking care of Em."

"Taking care of Em was the only thing that kept me going."

She turns over so she's on her side. "You're sweet."

I shake my head.

She nods. "You hide it well, but you are."

Her words twist something in my gut. She sees too much of me. More than I can handle. "You can't talk your way out of this."

"This?"

I nod to her purple notebook, the one sitting on

178

her desk.

"Oh." Her cheeks flush. "Right now?"

"Right now." I let my fingertips brush her hip. Her side. "Why are you up so late?"

"School starts tomorrow." She pushes herself to her feet. Grabs the journal. Hugs it to her chest. "I can't sleep."

"Change is always scary."

She nods. "You seem to roll with it."

"What ever changes in my life?"

"Emma's hair color."

I can't help but chuckle.

She climbs back into bed. Brushes her fingers against my upper arm. Then she's tracing the lines of the tattoo going down to my elbow. "This. It's new."

"Depends on your definition of new."

"You're like Em with her hair. You look different every time I see you."

"Every time?"

"Every few weeks."

"I have to slow down." I stare back into her gorgeous green eyes. "I'm running out of skin."

She drags her fingers over my forearm, presses her palm against all the bare skin. "You have plenty." She drags her fingers over my stomach. Plays with the hem of my t-shirt. "And here."

"And there." I soak in her touch as her fingers skim my bare skin.

"You've always wanted to do tattoos. As long as I've known you."

"Yeah."

"What is it about them you love?"

"Everything."

"But specifically." She traces the ink over my hip all the

way to the waistband of my jeans. "You... you practically left your family over them."

Yeah, I did. I was a little shit, but then it was the only way. I was never going to be good enough for my parents. "It feels right."

"That's it?"

"What else is there?" I watch her trace the outlines of my skin. Watch her eyes travel over my body. Watch her lips purse with a sigh.

She wants me.

I want her.

We're both in a fucking bed.

I should pull back. I should at least get vertical.

But I don't.

"When I'm working on someone's ink, I'm a part of something. I'm leaving a mark in the world. On their skin. That's forever. I get to help people channel all that shit in their guts onto their skin. There are a million reasons why people get ink. To look cool. To celebrate. To mourn. Being a part of that... it's fucking amazing."

She nods. "I wish I had that kind of passion."

"You do, Kay. The way you get when you're writing—" I nod to her purple notebook. "It's still your turn."

She lets out a soft groan. "Do I have to?"

"No. You could disappoint me."

"That's such a dad thing to say."

How about I bend you over my knee and spank you? Would that be daddy enough for you? "I'm not going to push you."

She nods as she climbs up the bed and presses her back against her pillow.

She pries open the notebook. Flips through the pages. Her eyes get dreamy. Like she's lost in her own world.

She turns the page. "Okay. This one. It's short."

"Perfect for my attention span," I offer.

Her laugh is nervous. "Maybe." Her eyes bore into mine. "Promise you won't make fun of it."

I nod.

She looks to the paper. Takes a deep breath. Exhales slowly. "Another stitch.

Another time.

Another love that isn't mine.

And all the shiny people say

It's okay

You'll find another way.

But I always poke the bruise.

Spill a lie. Spin a ruse.

I could draw four aces, but, still, I'd lose."

She presses her lips together, staring at me, waiting for my response.

Something in me stirs. Something in my bones.

Fuck, I have no idea what it means.

I want to peel her open and pry her apart.

Where does she hide this ache in her heart?

How the fuck do I get my hands on it?

Her cheeks flush as she slaps her notebook together. "You hated it."

"No. It was beautiful." Not that I'd know.

"Really?" He cheeks flush. She's embarrassed. Or scared. Or both.

"Yeah."

"Thank you." Her hand falls over my arm.

She nestles into my body, resting her forehead against my chin.

I soak in every inch of her.

Her warmth against my skin. Her breath against my neck. The smell of her shampoo—lavender and honey. Calm and sweet. Exactly like Kay.

"You okay?" I drag my fingertips over her lower back.

There's no way I can sell that this is a friendly gesture. Not to her, not to myself, not to anyone else.

But I don't care.

"Yeah. Just overwhelmed. With school tomorrow. And, well... something else. But I... I don't like to talk about it." She leans closer. "I've never told anyone, not anyone who counts."

"You can tell me anything." Fuck, I want to break that lock around her heart. I want to drink her in. I want to be her salve. The stars in her sky.

"I know. But this... it would change the way you look at me."

"Impossible."

"No. It would. I... I couldn't take losing this, Brendon. You're the only person besides Em I trust. And you're more... well, you're easier to talk to. You're just..." She looks up at me. Her eyes fill with affection. Her fingers skim my stomach. The edge of my jeans.

Fuck, I want that hand around me.

I want those lips on mine.

I want to bury myself in her.

To fuck her like I've never fucked before.

I takes everything I have to pull back.

Desire is coursing through my veins. My heart is pounding. My cock is screaming for attention.

I slide off the bed. "You trust me?"

"Why?"

"You want to feel better about school?"

She nods.

"You trust me, yes or no?"

She stares back into my eyes. "Yes."

"Then get dressed."

Chapter Twenty-Two

BRENDON

T wenty minutes later, I'm parking my sedan on a Brentwood street and Kaylee is clutching at my forearm.

She forces her words out. "Are we really doing this?"

I nod as I pull the door open. "Call it a trial run."

She steps onto the street. Nods to the *No Parking 10 PM to 6 AM sign* posted in front of my car. "You're going to get a ticket."

"At three a.m.?"

"Yeah." She digs her cell—the one with the *Hunger Games* phone case—from her purse and stares at the screen. "It's really three a.m."

I nod.

"Why did you get home so late?"

"Walker and Dean."

"They take that long to find women to bring home?"

"Yeah." Or they were dragging it out for my benefit. Their benefit really. They both enjoy mocking my *pining over the one woman I can't have* state.

"Hmmm." She hugs her purse to her shoulder as she steps forward. "You sure about the car?"

"My car."

"Damn. Such an outlaw. What will you risk next?"

I flip her off.

She smiles as she returns the gesture.

I take her hand. Lead her across the small, neighborhood street. All the way to the main drag.

No lights or cross walks in any direction.

No cars either.

I turn to Kaylee. "You ready?"

She nods. Squeezes my hand and takes the first step into the street.

We run across the major road. Through the tuft of Eucalyptus trees on the other side. Over the wet green lawn.

Kaylee clutches her stomach as she doubles over with laughter. "You run fast."

"It's called exercise."

"I exercise. Just not running. Running is the devil."

"No wonder I like it so much."

She laughs. "That was bad. But funny too. I must be tired." She pushes herself up. Wipes her wet hands on her jeans.

I take them. Wipe them on my t-shirt.

Her palm lingers against my chest. She drags it over my torso as she pulls it back to her side.

Her eyes meet mine.

Her lips part.

I can see the words on the tip of her tongue.

And I'm not praying for her to hold them back.

I'm desperate for every fucking syllable.

Tell me you want me, angel.

Tell me you want me to fuck you so hard you get grass stains on your skin.

Tell me you want me to throw you on that bench, rip off your jeans, and lick you until you're screaming.

Her eyes go to the building to our left. One of the science buildings. "It's different than before."

"Yeah?"

"Yeah." She leads me across the campus. "It feels real. Like this is really happening tomorrow."

We move onto the sidewalk. Past the science building. "It is." Toward the foreign languages building. "I remember the first time I walked into a shop looking for a job."

"It wasn't Inked Hearts?"

"No. I met Ryan at this dive in Downtown LA. He knew Manning. Invited me to Inked Hearts. He invited Dean and Dean invited Walker."

"What was that place like?"

"It was cleaner than it looked. Very *go the fuck away*. Band stickers on the walls. A burly guy at the register. A bunch of elitists who scowled at tattoos that weren't traditional enough."

"And you liked that?"

"The bands, yeah. It was a lot of punk. Metal. Hardcore shit. Nobody who listened to KIIS FM would dare enter that place."

"Perfect for you."

Yeah, it was. It still is. I can't say I'm into the elitist bull-shit anymore.

But the whole *I'm pissed and I don't want your opinion*?

I get that.

"You've been seventeen," I say.

"Only three weeks ago even." She bites her lip. "There was a long time that I didn't see you."

"Mom didn't want me around Em. Not once I started apprenticing."

"Oh. I never realized. I thought you were just—"

"An obnoxious teenager who didn't want to be around my family?"

"I guess. I'm not sure. I was young. And I... I mostly thought you were hot."

"And old?"

"Yeah. But the same age as *Harry Potter*."

I chuckle. "I think he's older."

"Probably. But shorter. And—"

"Submissive, apparently?"

"Yeah." Her cheeks flush.

I shouldn't have said that. It's too late. The part of me that knows better is tired.

"How exactly did it happen?"

"I moved out the day I turned eighteen. Moved into a shitty place in Downtown LA. Had too many roommates. But I still came by to hang out with Em. Picked her up from school. Took her out on the weekends. Not like Mom was gonna take her to do the shit she actually wanted to do."

Kay nods.

"It was fall. I'd just gotten my sleeve. I was gonna take Emma hiking up in the Malibu hills. She used to enjoy that kinda thing. If you can remember."

"Sort of. She doesn't ever get dirty now. Unless it's the beach."

I nod. Emma is different than she was before the accident, but I'm not sure how much is her growing up and how much the ache of losing Mom and Dad.

"Mom saw me coming into the house. Asked about the tat in that *why would you do that* voice. I told her Ryan had done most of it. She'd met him once or twice."

"And she hated him?"

"She never said as much, but yeah. She grabbed Emma and made up some excuse about how they had somewhere to be. Then she found me and told me she didn't want me around her daughter. Not if I was going throw my life away."

"Oh, Brendon. I'm sorry."

"Don't be. It was—"

"That's your mom. It must have hurt."

Like a knife in my chest. But that was how it had to be. "Not everyone deserves to be in your life."

"Still. I know how much you love Em. How much you... well, you really are a family man."

"You could say that."

"It must have killed you, that rejection."

Maybe. I've always been angry. I think about it and I see red. I see injustice. I see bullshit. Sadness doesn't seep in.

"Your dad too?"

"He always followed her lead."

"And you... did you not see Em for all that time?"

"I still did. Just not when Mom was around." I'm good at keeping secrets, I guess.

"Oh." Kaylee takes another step forward. Another. Another. She stops in front of the building. Looks to her phone then to the stone sign. "This is it."

"First stop tomorrow."

She nods. "It looks good. Traditional." She gives the tall brick building a long once over. "Were you... were you hanging out with the kinds of people Em shouldn't be around?"

"Sometimes. I wasn't choosy about my friends. Or the way I spent my time."

"You mean..." She presses her lips together.

"You can ask."

She looks up at me. Runs her fingertips over my jawline. "You mean drugs?"

"Sometimes. It was never my thing."

"You'd rather be in control?"

"How the fuck did you know?"

It's strange. I never want to share anything. And certainly not with Kay. The way she looks at me—like I'm a guy worth loving—is too intoxicating. I can't bring myself to convince her otherwise.

But I want to tell her this.

I want her to know how many people I disappointed.

How many people I continue to disappoint.

It's still fucking heavy.

"Brendon?" She tugs at my t-shirt. Her eyes meet mine. *Are you okay?*

"What's next?"

"Oh." She looks to her cell. Taps the screen a few times. "The English building is this way. I think... It would be stupid, majoring in English."

"No."

"Yeah. Reading and writing aren't jobs."

"They are. But even if that's not what you do—so what? All jobs are communication. That's English."

"Maybe. I don't know. I think... I think my parents expect more."

"They just want you to be happy."

"How do you know?"

"You'll get it if you have kids one day."

"Is that what you want?"

"I don't know. I'm Emma's dad as much as I'm her brother."

"You're good at it. Whatever it is."

"Maybe." I try. It would be fucking amazing, having a

family of my own. One day. But I'm not sure I'm the kind of guy who should be a dad. Or a husband. "Do you want kids?"

"I don't know. It's hard enough taking care of myself. That's so far off... I want to figure out this semester before I move on to the rest of my life."

I follow her along the concrete path.

The campus is beautiful this late. Big green lawn. Dark blue sky. Yellow streetlamps. Brick and concrete everywhere.

Every few minutes, we pass a student. Half are heading to or from the library. The other half are on their way home from a night of over indulging. It's in their messy steps and their habit of staring too long.

We go past every building in her schedule, even the one where her adviser is.

Finally, we stop at the building where Kaylee is taking her creative writing class.

She stares up at it. "I never would have taken this if you hadn't pushed me."

"Is that a thank you?"

"We'll see how it goes." She turns back to me. "I remember when you were younger."

I raise a brow, incredulous.

"There were times when you stormed to your room, all pissed off. But most of the time, you were sitting on the couch, scribbling in your sketchbook. You were a good guy."

I wasn't. That's what she doesn't get.

A good brother, maybe.

But not a good guy.

I used friends for drugs or booze.

I fucked women then threw them away.

I lied to my parents.

"I wasn't." I stare back at Kay. At all that trust in her eyes. I don't deserve it, but I still want every fucking drop of it. "I was an asshole. I treated people like shit."

"Even if that's true... does it really matter?" She presses her lips together. "Things can get better. People can get better."

"In theory."

"You... you were different before you had ink. You're more yourself now."

"I've had ink as long as you've known me."

She shakes her head.

I turn toward her, pull my jeans down my hip to show off my *sic transit gloria* quote. "Pretentious high school shit."

"Excuse you."

"For me. Not like I took Latin."

"You wanted the world to know glory is bullshit?"

Basically. I nod.

She moves under the street lamp. "I... I have ugly parts too. Things I don't want anyone knowing."

It's hard to believe. Kay is sunshine and cotton candy. She's the sweetest person I've ever met. Hands down. I shake my head.

She nods. "I guess that's fair. Since I don't believe you were ever a bad guy."

"It is." I move toward her. Until my hands are skimming her hips.

She looks up at me with those doe eyes.

Her lips part.

She nods.

It's like she's begging me to kiss her, touch her, fuck her.

Her arms slide around my neck. "I like the guy you are now." She reaches up to run her fingers through my hair. "A lot."

"Kay..."

She nods. "I know."

But she doesn't. Because I'm not gonna say shit about how this can't happen.

She looks up at me. "You... you're—"

I cut her off with my lips.

She's soft.

Eager.

Pliable.

I feel her everywhere. In my heart and my head and my bones.

My palm goes flat against her lower back.

I pull her body against mine.

Kiss her harder.

Deeper.

Fuck, she tastes good. Like mint and like Kaylee.

Her lips part to make way for my tongue.

Her fingers tug at my hair.

Her nails dig into my back, pressing the cotton of my t-shirt into my skin.

It's like she's begging for more.

Like she's begging to do away with every layer of fabric between us.

My hands move of their own accord.

One slides over her ass.

The other slips under her t-shirt.

She groans as my fingers skim her stomach.

She arches her back to rock her hips against mine. Shudders as she rubs against my hard-on.

There are only a few layers of fabric between my cock and her cunt.

It's too much.

I need her naked.

I need her on her back on that cold concrete bench, looking up at me like I'm the center of her universe.

She pulls back with a sigh. Looks up at me with every ounce of trust in the world. "I..." She leans into my touch. "I looked at your sketchbook."

What?

"Fuck." She jumps back. Covers her mouth with her hand. "I... Oh God." Her eyes go to the ground. "I'm sorry."

She...

What the fuck?

Time grinds to a halt.

I can feel every brush of the breeze.

Hear every distant footstep.

See every one of her lip quivers.

It's written all over her face.

She saw the drawings of her.

Where the fuck does she get off?

Could be with you. She's still here. That's why she's hinting at all this shit about being ordered around and tied up. She's into it. She wants it. She likes that you're a sick fuck.

Her chest heaves. "I'm sorry. It was wrong. A total invasion of privacy. But... if you want things to be even, we can do that. Look at my journal." Her voice cracks. Her eyes fill with terror. "Anything you want."

No. That isn't what I want. I don't know what the fuck I want. My head is spinning.

She knows how I want her.

And she's here.

She's into it.

My body is screaming for me to pin her to the wall. To push her jeans to her knees and plunge my fingers into her cunt. To growl *you want it rough, angel? I'll show you rough.*

But my head...

My heart...

"I'm sorry. I just... I want to know what you're thinking and feeling. I want it so badly. That's no excuse, but..."

"How much did you see?"

"Everything."

"And you..." My tongue trips over itself. There's nothing I can ask.

This is the only reasonable explanation for her behavior the last few weeks.

But it doesn't make any fucking sense.

Kay is sweet. Innocent.

She doesn't want it dirty and rough.

She doesn't cross the line like this.

She knows better.

"Do you?" Her voice is soft. Apologetic. "Do you really want me like that?"

The world is red. I blink, but that does nothing to help.

I pull my keys from my pocket. "Take the car home."

"But—"

"Now, Kay."

"Where are you—"

"I've got it under control."

"But..."

"Now."

Chapter Twenty-Three

BRENDON

The next thirty minutes are a blur. I'm not sure what I say to the Uber driver that drops me off in front of Walker's place.

I go straight to his apartment. Number three. My hand curls into a fist. Pounds on the door. It's doing it of its own accord. It knows something I don't, something about being willing to talk, about asking for help.

Walker mutters something. "If I owe you money, come back tomorrow."

"You have a gambling problem I should know about?"

"Fuck." Surprise drips from his voice. "Brendon?"

"Yeah."

Walker pulls the door open. Rubs his eyes. Stares back at me. "Don't tell me you owe someone money."

I shake my head.

He motions to his attire. Boxers. Just boxers. "You know how it is." He nods to the closed bedroom door at the end of the hallway behind him. "Keep it down. She's sleeping."

"You're a gentleman."

He chuckles. "Hey, just because it's one night, doesn't mean I can't show her a good time. Or do you even remember that shit?"

"It hasn't been that long."

He motions to the door behind me. "Three months? Four? Six? That's a fucking eternity. Remember when Dean got his Prince Albert? He nearly died doing six weeks."

"I try not to think about Dean's dick."

"Hard to avoid when he's always bragging."

"Yeah." I press the door closed. Click the lock. I want to tell him to fuck off, but it's not like I can deny the allegations. It's been a while.

He moves into the kitchen. "You look like hell."

I feel like hell.

"You want coffee?"

"Yeah."

Walker's walls are covered in *Star Wars* posters.

"You okay?" He spoons coffee into a reusable filter.

"Saving the planet?"

He cocks a half smile. "You just figure that out? I talk about saving for a Tesla every fucking day."

"It's flashy."

"True. It's gonna be awhile now. All that money is going to Inked Hearts."

"You regret that?"

"Fuck no."

"It's a lot. But it's..." I want to say *it's perfect*. It is. It's everything. But my head is a mess. Kay read my journal. The betrayal of that stings. But it's not what has me all fucked up.

It's thinking of her poring over the pages.

She knows every dirty thing I want to do to her.

And she's still around.

She fucking wants it.

Kay, the sweet girl who can't cook anything but almond butter and jelly sandwiches, who chooses vanilla ice cream, who owns a fucking rainbow of cardigans—

She wants it rough.

"Earth to Brendon?" Walker asks.

"Yeah?"

"You okay?"

I don't say anything.

"You don't look okay," he mumbles.

"I'm not." It's all I can get out. This is such a fucking head trip. I can't sew my thoughts together. I can't reconcile the two versions of her in my head—the virgin who blushes at the mere mention of sex and the dirty girl who wants to be tied to my bed.

"Fuck." He laughs. "That must be bad."

Yeah. It must. I've known the guy for ten years, and I've never admitted I'm not okay.

"Go." He motions to the couch. "Sit. I don't want to watch you mope while standing." He tries to play it off as a joke, but concern seeps into his voice.

I plop on the couch. Tap my fingers against the armrest. This is a nice apartment. Leather furniture. Sleek appliances. Framed posters all over the walls. A bookshelf overflowing with DVDs. Mostly sci-fi.

I motion to the box set of Star Trek. The Matrix trilogy. Japanese films I've never heard of. A whole row of action movies. "How come we never watch this shit together?"

The coffee maker drips. Walker moves forward. Rests his ass against the kitchen island. "You know you can just ask for help."

I say nothing.

"You can just invite me to do shit."

"I know."

"Do you?"

In theory, yeah. In practice... I motion to the closed bedroom door. "How was it?"

Walker chuckles. "You're so bad at this."

I arch a brow.

He mocks my tone. "How was it?" He laughs. Shakes his head. "Fuck. You know, I always thought you had your shit together. But I guess you're even denser than the rest of us."

"Been telling you that."

"Guess I should have listened." He brings the mugs to the coffee table then takes a seat. "I'm gonna put on something. If you beg, I might have mercy on you and make it an action movie."

"You really want *me* begging?"

"Yeah. I don't get off on that shit like you." He chuckles. "Not even gonna deny it?"

"Why would I?"

He shrugs. "You never talk about it either."

"What's to say?"

"*Fuck, Walker, you should have seen the woman I fucked last night. I had her tied to my bed. I had her coming so hard she nearly snapped my neck.*"

"Sounds more like Dean."

Walker laughs. "True." He settles into the couch. "Fuck. You're too pathetic. I'll have to put on *The Matrix* or some shit. I feel guilty."

"You're kind."

He laughs. "I know." He motions to the bedroom door. "She was sweet. Shy. Your type."

I flip him off.

He turns toward me, folds one leg over the other,

shakes his head. "Are you going to make me guess what happened?"

"Are you interested?"

"Fuck. What the hell is wrong with you? We've been friends for ten years. If I didn't care, I would have left you waiting outside."

I say nothing.

Walker shakes his head. "Have it your way." He grabs the remote. Flips on the TV.

It's an infomercial for one of those ab toning belts. A man is showing off his brand spanking new six pack next to a picture of his formally round midsection.

"Not sure what's more BS. This product. Or you acting like—what the fuck happened anyway?"

"It's complicated."

"Bullshit. Bet I can spell in three letters." He brings his mug to his lips and takes a long sip. It's a Star Wars mug. Black with a white X-wing logo. "What did you do?"

"It was her."

He shoots me an incredulous look.

I nod.

"Fuck. Really?"

Not exactly. It's both of us. It's my fucking head. "It's complicated, but yeah."

He sets his mug on the coffee table. "No fucking way. She's crazy about you. And you're crazy about her. You're just both idiots."

I bring my mug to my lips. Take a long sip. The coffee is perfect. Bold. Just sweet and creamy enough. But it doesn't do anything to get my mind working. I still don't know how to explain this in a way that makes sense to someone else. Or to myself.

"What happened? She cheat on you or some shit? I

can't see Kay doing that, but then I couldn't see Bree going the way she did."

Walker's sister got into drugs when she was a teenager. She's still a mess, flitting in and out of rehab, generally causing havoc.

"Didn't she turn eighteen like three weeks ago? Were you really fucking her when she was jailbait?" he asks.

"No. We haven't—"

"You haven't touched her?" He arches a brow. "Really?"

"I haven't." I run my hand through my hair. "She's so fucking young."

"Yeah. But she's not a kid. Kay has been taking care of herself for a long time."

"She's sweet."

"Your type."

"Yeah, but... I'm a fucking pervert," I say.

"No shit. You're into your little sister's best friend."

"No, I mean—"

"What? You like it rough so you're a pervert?"

Yeah, basically.

"Lots of girls like it rough. You should know. You've fucked most of them."

"Yeah."

"But, what, none of them were Kaylee? She's too sweet, too good to be into that shit?"

How the fuck does he have my number?

"Get over yourself, Brendon. You don't have a monopoly on dirty thoughts."

"That's not—"

"With any other woman, you'd be into her inexperience. How is Kay different?"

"She's Kay."

"That's retrograde shit. You're better than that."

No. I'm really not. I shake my head.

"Yeah. You are. Kaylee is an adult. She knows what she wants. If you can't handle that, then you don't deserve to be around her at all."

"Fuck off."

"Strong words for someone who needs my help so badly he's here at four a.m.," he says.

"We're about to be business partners. You're stuck with me."

He chuckles. "No. I want to work with you. I come into work every day because I want to be there. And you do too. You think Ryan or Dean does anything they don't want to do?"

"You have a point?"

"What happened with Kay? What did she do?"

"Crossed a line she shouldn't have." But that isn't the problem. Not exactly. It's my fucking head.

"For good reason?"

"Yeah." I get it. I want to peel back every wall around her heart. I've seen her journal and thought about taking a peek. I've been tempted.

"You really aren't a talker."

"You just figuring that out?"

He shakes his head. "Everybody makes mistakes. Fuck knows I've made a lot. You too. But it doesn't have to be a life sentence. We can all grow. Change. Get better."

I squirm in my seat. This kind of earnesty is not my thing. "Thanks."

"You want to watch this weight loss bullshit or you want to watch something good?"

"Depends on your definition of good?"

He chuckles. "Trust me."

"Not sure I do."

"You should. You need somebody's help to figure this shit out. And I don't see you calling Ryan or Dean."

"Have you always been this much of a know it all?"

He nods. "But it's very fucking lucky for you that I do know everything."

Chapter Twenty-Four

KAYLEE

A shower, makeup, and the perfect skater dress oxford shoes outfit do wonders to hide the ache in my gut.

But they do nothing to lessen it.

This is all my fault.

I fucked up.

I need to find a way to fix it.

Later.

Right now, I have to survive my first day. And that starts with choking down breakfast.

I do one more makeup check. My eyes look perfectly awake.

My lips and cheeks wear just the hint of color.

I look cute, effortless, vibrant.

Hell, with my glasses on, I'm a bona fide cute nerd.

But my smiling reflection only twists the knife in my gut.

"Hey," Emma calls from downstairs. "You need to leave soon."

"You too." I force myself to head to the kitchen.

She jumps to her feet and throws her arms around me. "I wanted to see you off."

I squeeze her back.

"You okay, Kay? You seem... sad." The word is a struggle. It sounds odd on her tongue. She's as bad at talking about feelings as I am.

"Tired."

"You sure that's it?"

No. I want to tell her more. To tell her everything. But she can't know about my depression. And she certainly can't know what happened between me and her brother. I can't take her hating me too. "We can talk later."

She steps back with a smile. "Boy trouble?"

"Sorta."

Her jaw drops. Her dark eyes light up. "You like someone?"

"It's more compli—"

"Oh my God! You like someone." She squeezes me again. "We're going to talk about this all night. Can you help me go red?"

"Of course. How red?"

"More crimson. Like a vampire."

"It will suit you."

"I think so too." She smiles as she picks up her backpack and slides it over one shoulder. "You want a ride?"

"I'd rather bike." I motion to the clock. Her first class is in half an hour. I have an extra hour after that. "Go. Kick ass."

"Okay." She blows me a kiss as she steps backward. "I love you, Kay." She reaches for the door. Pulls it open. "Don't worry. We'll put our heads together. Figure out this boy problem."

I swallow the confession that rises up in my throat. "I trust you."

She blows me a kiss as she makes her way out the door.

The lock clicks. Her car turns on and pulls away.

I fix a cup of tea. Pour my own bowl of cereal. Watch as my Trader Joe's brand frosted wheat cereal goes from hard to soft. Force myself to eat the shredded wheat until it's soft instead of rough.

Then I clean up all the dishes. Make another cup of tea. Stare at the text from Brendon on my phone.

Brendon: Spending the night at Walker's place. I'll be home late.

I can still see that look on his face. Like I stabbed him in the gut.

I need to fix this.

But how do I convince him I'm worth trusting again?

That I did it because I want all of him—especially those parts he won't show anyone. Especially the parts he thinks are ugly. Especially the secrets.

I need to prove I can be that person. The one who sees him. That lets him see me.

But the thought of confessing *that* sends shredded wheat back up my throat.

I can barely admit it to myself, much less to him. I have episodes. Where I think about hurting myself. About making everything stop.

I can't even use the word.

It's too ugly.

It scares me.

It will terrify him.

And then...

He might leave.

I want him to know the truth.

I want to be like Ariel, strong enough to sing my fucking heart out.

Strong enough to go after what I want.

To show off my scars.

My secrets.

I'm not ready yet. But I can get there.

I can let him in. Or at least try. Or start to try.

I rush to my bedroom. Pore over my journal for just the right thing. Not a poem. Not a story. An entry. One about him. One that shows off something ugly, something I can stand him knowing.

It takes half an hour, but I find it.

I tear the pages out. Grab a silver Sharpie. Sign my name with an *I'm sorry* and slide it under his bedroom door.

That's something.

I just hope it's enough.

———

I'M HALFWAY THROUGH MY ALMOND BUTTER AND JELLY sandwich when my cell starts buzzing. Dammit. I'm going to have to come up with a lie, a believable lie, if I want Emma to drop this.

But it's not a text from Emma.

It's my mom.

My stomach twists. I don't have the energy to pretend everything's okay. Or to hold my tongue.

I pick up anyway. "Hey."

"Kay. Hey." Mom's voice is soft. Loving. "How are you? How was your first day?"

"Okay. It's been Latin and American lit. Tomorrow is chemistry and creative writing."

Her voice perks. "Yeah?"

My shoulders rise to my ears. Is that a *why would you waste your time* or *interesting, tell me more.* "It's just an elective."

"No, sweetie. That's great. You've always been such a

wonderful writer. Your grandma keeps going on and on about your stories. She misses them."

"Are you going to tell me the truth?"

"What?"

"About how she's doing?" I don't have the energy to pretend like I'm okay not knowing. Or to deny that things are fucked. They are. And I need to know how fucked.

"We're not sure. Honestly, I don't understand half of what the doctors say. Something about heart disease and clogged arteries. Her condition is terminal, but they're not sure if it will be months or years."

"Oh." It might only be months. It might be nothing at all.

"I asked Mr. Kane about the best time to fly you out. He wasn't sure."

It's so weird, her calling Brendon Mr. Kane. "Any weekend. I just need to know in advance. Jake will give me the time off." Probably. But even if he doesn't, I'm taking it. I've worked at The Pizza Kitchen long enough. I can find a better job if I have to.

"You're just starting now. You need time to adjust."

"I need to see Grandma."

"I'll check flights. See what I can do with miles. But school needs to come first, sweetie."

School can wait. School can happen next year. Grandma might not be around next year.

But this is the best I'm going to get from Mom.

That's okay. I have my own money. I can buy my own ticket to Jersey. She's not going to stop me once I'm there.

"Okay." My voice is a whisper. It's a million degrees today, but I feel cold. It might be months. And if it might be months, it might be weeks.

"Grandma wants to talk to you. I'll hand the phone over soon. When's your next class?"

"Half an hour."

"Tell me about it."

I do. I spill all the details of my day. My inability to sleep. My talk with Emma this morning. My professor bragging about all her Latin tattoos.

I don't say anything about how awful it feels, knowing Grandma might only have months.

Or about how bullshit it is that they've been keeping that from me.

I don't want to focus on that.

I want to focus on the good. On soaking up what I have while I have it.

"I really am proud of you, Kay. You're such a talented young woman. I wish you could be here," she says.

"I could be there."

"I know, baby. But then you wouldn't be at school. And I didn't want that weight on your conscious. Grandma either. We don't want you to feel guilty for choosing school over family. We don't want you to give up your life."

Something flutters in my chest. Not quite warmth or forgiveness but something close to it.

Mom didn't want guilt on my shoulders.

That's why she didn't give me a choice.

It doesn't excuse everyone treating me like a child.

It doesn't do shit about the realities of the situation.

But it does lessen the sting.

Just enough to make it bearable.

"I love you," she says.

"I love you too."

"I'll grab Nana."

"Okay." I press my fingers into the back of my cell. The anger in my gut fades to a dull ache. This is a shitty situation and Mom is making the best of it. Or trying to.

"Kay-bear." Grandma's voice fills the speakers. "Tell

me the truth about your classes. One of them was boring."

Her voice is rich. Light. Full of life. Like she has decades.

"No. Latin was tough. I'm rusty."

Grandma scoffs. "It's a dead language."

"I know."

"Pointless."

"Like life?"

Grandma laughs. "You know me too well, Kay-Bear." Her voice drops to something sincere. "You doing okay staying with that hot friend of yours?"

"Brendon?"

"Hmm."

"Huh?"

"Your voice changed. Something's wrong. Don't tell me it's school."

"No. It's good. Really."

"Work?"

"No. Jake gave me the schedule I requested. Friday, Saturday, and Sunday night. Closing shifts."

"No wonder you're cranky. Who wants to work all weekend?"

"People who want money."

She laughs. "You and Em okay?"

"I think so."

"Kay." Her voice lifts. "It's that boy, isn't it? Things going okay with him?"

"I don't know."

"They're not. I know that tone. I was your age once, you know. I remember how it felt, those early crushes. It was like he moved the stars."

That's a good way of putting it. "I miss you."

"I miss you too, Kay-Bear. But you need to focus on school."

"But—"

"No buts. You have a bright future. You're the first woman in my family to go to college. That's what I want for you."

I have a million objections. I can start school next year. She might not be here next year. What's an extra year of education compared to time with Grandma?

"Tell me you've got something good to read me. Something *Days of Our Lives*."

"I haven't been watching."

"Then another one about Peeta and Gale double-timing Katniss."

"Grandma!" My cheeks flush. "I didn't write that one. It was something I found on that fan fiction website."

"Why not write the sequel?"

"I'll think about it."

"Anything good with Draco and Harry?"

"I'm working on it."

"How dirty?"

"Oh my God, Grandma. It's about the relationship, not the sex."

"No. It's about the sex."

I laugh. Talking to her makes me warm all over.

It's like this empty part of me is full.

But I can't think too hard about it. Or I'll think about how she's running out of time...

I won't be able to talk to her like this soon.

I...

"Tell me about the boy. Same one you mentioned last time?" Her voice gets mischievous. Like she's a teenager.

"Yeah."

"And?"

"He's... I messed up."

"You?"

"Yeah. I did."

"Is it unforgivable?"

"I don't know. I don't think so, but he's hard to read. He's..."

"It's him, isn't it?"

"Who?" I ask.

"Your hot friend. The one who's supposed to watch out for you."

"It's not like that. He... He's always saying that we can't. That it's wrong—"

"Always? You nagging him?"

"No. He said it once. But he kissed me too."

"You think it's wrong?"

"I don't know. I... I get that he's older. That he's supposed to be in charge of my well-being. That he's paying for my place to stay and my food. Well, I'm trying to pay my share of the food, but he argues about it."

"Kay-bear, do you think it's wrong?"

"No... I... I really like him."

"He's hot. I don't blame you."

"Does Mom know?" My chest is heavy. Not from the threat of Mom coming between me and Brendon. But from how good it feels talking to Grandma like this. From knowing there's a time limit on that.

"You think I'd narc on you?"

"No. But she might realize—"

"She doesn't."

"Oh. Good." I check the time. Only five minutes until I need to leave for class. Damn. I want to tell Grandma everything. Well, some things. She always gets it. And she won't feel betrayed the way Emma will.

"Does he want you too or is he an idiot?"

"He does. But it's complicated."

"It's never complicated. Not unless you make it that way."

"He used to say that."

"Smart man. But stupid if he hasn't scooped you up yet."

"There are good reasons."

"Still. He cares about you?"

"I think so."

"Then find a way to make it uncomplicated."

It's good advice, even if I have no idea how to accomplish it. "I have to go. Class. I love you, Grandma."

"Gigi."

"I love you, *Grandma*."

"Love you too, Kay-Bear. Give him hell for me."

Chapter Twenty-Five

BRENDON

The pen is heavy in my hands. It's sleek. Silver. One of those hundred-dollar fountain pens.

Honestly, I don't see the appeal.

It spills ink the same as any other pen.

And there's my name on the dotted line.

This is the last form.

As soon as the transfer goes through, I'm officially an Inked Hearts co-owner.

This is everything I want.

It should thrill me.

But my thoughts are stuck on Kay.

Dean picks up the pen and signs. He's in the chair next to me.

He hands it off to Walker. "You look cranky as fuck, Brendon."

Walker shoots him a *drop it* look.

I can practically hear Ryan rolling his eyes. "You ever shut the fuck up?" He looks to the lawyer sitting behind the desk. "Sorry."

"I've heard worse." The lawyer's voice is flat. Like he only cares about dollar signs and dotted lines.

Dean is fucking annoying.

But he's right.

I should be over the moon.

I shouldn't be thinking about all that desire in Kay's eyes.

I've had half a day to get over it, but I haven't.

I've thought about Kay a million times, but I always knew it was a fantasy. That I wouldn't throw her on the bed and split her in half. That I wouldn't order her onto her knees and fuck that pretty pink mouth. That I wouldn't slam her against the wall and fuck her hard enough to leave bruises on her cheek.

But I could.

She knows every dirty thing I want to do to her.

And she wants that too.

Chapter Twenty-Six

KAYLEE

I don't go home after school.
I go straight to the shop.

Park my bike at the rack out front. Smooth my dress. Run my fingers through my hair. Switch from my prescription sunglasses to my regular glasses.

Brendon is in there somewhere.

I can handle looking him in the eyes.

Really, I can.

The bell rings as I pull the door open.

At once, the room quiets.

Conversations cease.

Tattoo guns stop buzzing.

Footsteps move into the lobby.

There's Ryan.

Walker.

Brendon. He's in the back. Leaning against the wall. Looking straight through me.

Leighton's blue eyes find mine. She tilts her head to one side. Mouths *are you okay?*

I nod a yes, even though it doesn't feel accurate.

"I just wanted to... uh..." I play with my backpack strap. "Give this back." I set Brendon's keys on the counter.

Leighton turns toward the brooding tattoo artist. "You want to grab those now, Brendon?"

"Yeah." His voice is even. Like he doesn't hate me. Like he doesn't feel anything toward me.

"Did you guys sign the paperwork?" I bite my lip. He hates me. I know it.

"Yeah. We did," he says.

"That's great. Congratulations."

He pushes off the wall. Takes a dozen steps toward the counter. Slides his keys into his pocket without looking at me.

It's like I don't exist.

His coldness is contagious. It sucks all the warmth from the room.

Walker steps forward. "Hey, Kay. You coming to our celebration?"

"Huh?" There's a celebration?

"For signing the paperwork. It's tonight. I know just the thing. It will be fun." He looks back to Brendon with a smile. "For all of us."

"You really step up when Dean isn't here," Ryan says.

"Do what I can." Walker turns to me. "It's my treat. Bring Emma too. And any other hot friends."

I shake my head. "I'd never sink that low."

He chuckles. "Fair enough." He smiles at Brendon. Then at me. "Tonight. Meet here at eight. Then we'll... well, it's a surprise."

———

"It's Walker, isn't it?" Emma pulls open a Vitamin C capsule and lets the powder fall into the glass below it.

"No." I bite my lip. That's a good lie. Maybe I should say it's Walker. Dean. Ryan even. Emma wouldn't try to make things happen with Ryan. I think.

"Hmm..." She opens another cap.

"That's enough." I motion to the dozen cellulose caps in the sink. Then to the glass filled with orange power.

"I don't want to do it again." She glances in the mirror, pushing now light purple hair behind her ear.

This is her third Vitamin C wash. For whatever reason, mixing vitamin C with your shampoo is a great way to gently fade color from hair.

After doing Emma's hair for the last few years, I'm an expert.

"One more," I bargain.

She nods. Cracks another capsule. Tosses its remains in the sink. Motions to the shower. "Will you?"

"Of course."

She pulls her bathrobe over her dress. Pushes the shower curtain aside, places a towel over the edge of the bathtub, then leans back. "Maybe Walker is into Leighton."

"Possible."

"But they don't have it. Something is up with him. And Brendon. He didn't come home last night. That's never happened before."

"Oh."

"Yeah. It's probably nothing. A *date*. But all he texted was—" She drops her voice two octaves to imitate Brendon. "Staying at Walker's place. I'll see you tomorrow." She moves back to her normal tone. "Like that's supposed to convince me he's not out getting laid."

"It's better that way. Or would you rather hear about his sex life?" I squeeze dandruff shampoo—another good way to fade hair color—into the glass and stir with a metal spoon. There. It's a nice pale orange.

"Yeah, that's true. But I'm still worried."

"It's probably nothing."

"You would know, I guess. You two have been hanging out a lot."

"Only because his work schedule aligns with mine and yours doesn't."

"Yeah. You... you like hanging out with him?"

"You don't?"

"I guess he's all right."

"He's good company." If he ever talks to me again.

She lifts her neck to look at me. "You haven't said anything about school."

"What's there to say?"

"Like you don't love every second of learning."

"I don't hate it." I move to the tub. Grab the handheld shower head and turn the water on. And test it against my palm. Too hot. I turn the cold.

"You. Love. It."

"Maybe."

"Just admit it."

"Okay. I love it." There. Perfect. I kneel next to Emma. "Lean back."

She does.

I focus on rinsing her hair. It makes it easier not to spill everything rising up in my throat.

"What about your grandma?" she asks. "Do you have any more info."

"Sort of. It's... it's not good, but they're not sure how not good."

"Fuck, I'm sorry."

"Thanks." My chest gets tight. I need less of that. "Can we talk about something else?"

"Okay." She's quiet for a while.

I rinse her hair.

She squirms as water hits her ears.

The silence is nice. Even if it's heavy with all sorts of unsaid things.

"I thought about this. More than I should have." She looks up at me. "All the guys you know are from work or school. All except the guys at Inked Hearts."

"Maybe."

"So, if it's not someone from work or school, it's Walker, Ryan, Dean, or Brendon." She cringes as her brother's name falls off her lips.

"It's not going to happen. It doesn't matter."

"It is. And it does."

I finish rinsing her hair. Move on to shampoo.

"Why... why don't you want to tell me?"

I press my lips together. Rub Emma's scalp a little harder. Avoid her attempts to look me in the eyes.

"You'd tell me if you were into my brother."

"Don't be ridiculous, Em."

"Is it though? You guys have been hanging out a lot."

"Because he's always here."

"You're different around him. Nervous. Giggly."

"I don't giggle."

"You do. You... I mean, I get that he's hot. You're not the first person who's said that."

"They're all hot."

"True. But you look at him in this way. Not like he's your brother."

"He's not my brother. He's your brother. He's my..." Well, he's my nothing right now. "He's my friend." I grab the shower head and bring it to her hairline. "Close your eyes."

She does. "You keep insisting he's hot and not annoying."

"I take the latter back."

"You can tell me, Kay. I won't be pissed you like him. It's not like you'd ever act on it."

Right. It's not like I'd kiss him in the middle of the night.

I try to focus on rinsing Emma's hair. On anything but the feelings whirring around my gut.

There. She's done.

I turn the shower head off. "You want to do this now." I motion to the bottle of Special Effects dye sitting on the bathroom counter.

"Let's air dry a little first." She sits up. Gathers her hair in one hand and squeezes. "Whatever it is that's bugging you, you can tell me." Her voice is soft. Earnest. Hurt.

She thinks I'm locking her out.

God, the way she's looking at me like I don't trust her anymore.

I can't take it.

I can't lose Em too.

Words jump out of my mouth without stopping in my brain. "It's Dean."

Her jaw drops. "Really?"

"I know. He's too old. He sleeps with a different woman every night. He doesn't take anything seriously. But—"

"He's hot. Confident. Funny. I get it."

"Yeah. But I don't actually want to be with him. That would be terrible."

She nods. "Oh." Her eyes light up with an epiphany. "No wonder he bet Brendon you're not a virgin. Then offered to pop that cherry." She laughs over his dirty words. "You should take him up on it."

"I don't know."

"Or maybe not." She sets her hand on my shoulder. "When you like someone, you get attached. And Dean isn't the kind of guy you want to be attached to."

I nod.

"But if you do want him to be your first... I can help." Her eyes light up. "Think about it."

"Sure."

"And think about how we're going to hide it from Brendon. Pretty sure he'd kill Dean for that."

"Right."

"You have any idea what he's pissed about?"

"Brendon?"

"Yeah."

"Who knows with him?"

She nods. "You think he'll get over it soon?"

"I hope so."

Chapter Twenty-Seven

KAYLEE

Emma (now with hair in the perfect cool shade of red) and I (still dirty blond) arrive at the shop a few minutes after eight. Walker and Dean are quick about insisting we ride with them. And about making conversation. Mostly with Emma. Mostly about nothing important.

They get almost all the way to the 405 then turn left. On Sawtelle. Toward Little Osaka.

Oh no.

I turn toward Em. "Don't tell me."

"Don't tell her we're doing karaoke?" Dean teases. "Okay. I won't tell you that, Kay."

Karaoke. Ugh. I can't sing in front of people. I can't even sing in the shower if I know someone is home.

"We're counting on you rocking some emo songs," Walker says. "Really selling that pain."

Emma laughs. "You can admit you're jealous of guys who can pull off eyeliner."

Walker chuckles.

"You two should do a duet," Dean says. "Which of you is Aladdin and which is Jasmine?"

Uh...

"I won't make a joke about wanting to ride your carpet." Dean winks at Emma. Turns back to the road. Pulls into the tiny parking lot of the strip mall on the right.

The private room karaoke place is right there. I know it well. How could I not? It's the only all ages place on this side of town. I can't even begin to count how many parties I've been to at this place.

And how many times I've avoided singing or only joined in on the big, group numbers.

I love music. I love singing. It's just I don't love singing with other people around. It's too personal.

Songs dig at my guts. They force me to confront feelings deep inside me. I'm not about to do that for show.

Especially not when my guts are such a mess.

Brendon.

Grandma.

My parents.

I don't want to feel any of that. I want it far away. I want to forget everything.

I try to come up with something I can sing, something that will label me a good sport without making me feel anything, as we park and make our way to the karaoke joint.

It's as divey as it's ever been. Narrow halls with bright carpet. Beige walls. Blue doors.

Our suite is at the back of the hall. A shiny silver disco ball casts light over the powder blue couches. The song books are sitting on the low table, right next to a bunch of two liter bottles of soda and a large carafe of water.

Emma plops on the couch and pours us two glasses of diet. "So." She hands me my glass then looks to Dean with a smile. "What are you singing?"

"Good things come to those who wait." He winks at us.

She nudges me. *See. He totally likes you.*

I shake my head. This is a bad lie. I need to set her straight. Without giving away how badly I want to fuck her brother.

"What about you, Walker?" Emma sips her drink. "What kind of music do you like anyway?"

"Metal." Dean laughs. "Have we never brought you to karaoke?"

"Never. Fuck you for that by the way." She flips him off.

Dean laughs. "You close your eyes and listen to Walker you think James Hetfield—"

"Who?" Emma asks.

"Fuck, kids today." Dean shakes his head. "Lead singer of Metallica."

"Oh. Yeah. The *Enter Sandman* guys." Emma sticks her tongue out. "I don't like that stuff. Too loud."

"Not enough boys in eyeliner?" Dean offers.

"I was thinking skinny jeans." She nudges me. "But that's an irresistible combination. Right, Kay?"

"Right." Or Brendon in anything. Or nothing. Nothing would be ideal, really. Not that I'll ever have the chance to see that.

"You should try that look." She motions to Dean. "Some espresso would bring out your eyes."

The door swings open. Ryan and Leighton step inside. Ryan looks slightly less glum than usual. Leighton is wearing her usual pleasant smile, the customer service one required for working at the front desk.

And there's Brendon.

His eye catch mine. "Who's up first."

"James over here." Dean nods to Walker.

Walker grabs the mic. "You mock because you're jeal-ous." He grabs the keypad. Taps the song in from memory.

A moment later, the title card flashes on screen. *Enter Sandman, As Made Famous by Metallica.*

The room fills with the song's epic intro. Only it's practically polyphonic.

Then Walker is singing with his voice two octaves lower than it normally is. All gruff and angry a la the original song—everyone knows this one.

Emma lets out one of her full body laughs.

Leighton chuckles.

Even Ryan cracks a smile. "You do look jealous, Dean."

Dean flips his brother off.

The tension in my chest eases. This is normal. Distracting even.

So long as I keep my gaze off Brendon, this feels good.

I cross my legs. Tap my toes together.

When Walker finishes, he hands the mic to Dean. And Ryan picks up the other one.

Huh. Ryan sings.

Strange.

Walker plops next to Emma. Pics up the karaoke book, studies it closely, finds the song to plug into the machine.

The lyrics to a classic grunge song flash on screen. Dean jumps onto the table in the middle of the room as he belts out the first line.

He motions to Ryan *let's go*.

Ryan shakes his head, but he does get off the couch, move to the front of the room, and sing.

He really sings.

With passion and zest and enthusiasm.

It's like he's a different person.

The two of them are both *there*. In the song. Feeling every word.

The two of them aren't exactly great singers, but they're swinging for the fences.

And they're working together.

Like brothers who actually love each other.

Like it makes sense they have matching forearm tattoos.

Like they can fight and make up and everything can be okay.

I check to make sure no one is watching then I pull out my cell and shoot him a text.

Kaylee: I really am sorry.

His phone buzzes in his pocket. He looks up at me.

I nod *check it*.

He pulls out his cell. Glances at the screen. Then he's tapping a reply.

Buzz.

Brendon: I know. We'll talk later.

Kaylee: What does that mean?

Dean takes a bow as the song ends. He nods and waves to his adoring audience—we're clapping a little—then blows us kiss after kiss.

He winks at me. "Your turn."

"It's your turn, Kay." Emma takes my free hand. "Pick something or I'll pick for you." Her voice lifts to that encouraging tone.

She thinks this is my opportunity to finally tell Dean to be the one to "pop that cherry."

Dean is undeniably attractive. Tall. Tan. Piercing blue eyes, long, shaggy hair. He's funny. Confident.

Supposedly, he has a cock piercing.

And he has that colorful sleeve tattoo. Fuck, there's something about a full sleeve that makes me weak in the knees.

But even with all that—the thought of Dean's hands on my body makes me cringe.

The sight of Brendon's shoulders in that snug t-shirt—

My heartbeat is already picking up.

My lips are already parting.

My body is already screaming *more*.

"Kay? You there?" Emma asks.

"Yeah." Sort of.

She motions to Dean. Then to the karaoke book, currently up to Britney Spears.

She taps *I'm A Slave 4 U*.

Uh...

There's no way I'm singing anything that sexual. And certainly not to Dean. But it's a good idea.

I need the right song.

One I know.

One I can sell.

One that says everything I want to say.

"You don't have to sing, Kay," Walker says. "It is your party."

"Yeah," Leighton agrees. "Not all of us get off on blackmail."

"Get off? Huh?" Dean jumps to his feet. "Am I needed?"

She laughs. "You think you're that good?"

"Think? Honey, I don't think shit—"

"That isn't news," she says.

"I know." He motions *come here* to Leighton. "I'm more than happy to prove it."

She sticks out her tongue *no thanks*.

Emma shoots me a concerned look.

I shake my head *it's fine*.

'Cause I'm in love with Dean. Yeah. Right.

I'm running out of energy to sell this.

Time to sell... well...

I just hope this gets through to him.

"Thanks. But I'm looking forward to my debut." I plug

the number into the machine. Take the mic from Emma. Step up to the front of the room.

The TV flashes with my song.

I force myself to turn back to the room.

To stare into Brendon's dark eyes.

And I let Ariel's words fall of my lips.

I find the intention to sell every line of *Part Of Your World*.

When I'm done, my body is buzzing with nervous energy. I can barely hear everyone clapping. Yelling. Teasing.

I can't see anything but the softening in Brendon's expression.

He knows I'm sorry.

And maybe he forgives me.

But that doesn't mean he'll be mine.

He might never be mine.

Chapter Twenty-Eight

BRENDON

My eyes stay glued to Kay.

She moves back to her seat. Crosses one leg over the other. Smooths her skirt.

Fuck, that blouse is cut low. It does things to me. Makes me forget every one of the reasons why this shouldn't happen.

I have more self-control than this.

In theory.

Now that I know Kay wants it hard and rough—

Fuck, she owns my thoughts.

She leans in to whisper something in Em's ear.

Whatever Em whispers back gets Kay blushing.

I hate being away from her.

Hate being pissed at her.

Hate that I'm actually thinking about tossing aside every rational thought in my head.

I'm not *that* much of a caveman.

Even if my cock is making a hell of a compelling argument.

She could be pinned to the bathroom wall. Bound to

my bed. Bent over my knee.

Dean kneels in front of Kay. He holds out his hand. "If you'll please, madame."

"I prefer Miss," she teases.

He chuckles. "I didn't know you were into this."

"Huh?" Kaylee places the mic in his hands.

"Men on their knees." He winks and he jumps—actually jumps—to his feet.

Kay blushes.

Ryan jumps in. "You didn't get the message the first time?"

Walker nods. "You repulse her."

Dean shakes his head. Motions to the screen. "We'll see."

A familiar melody flows from the speakers. Dean holds up one arm.

Looks right at Kaylee.

Belts out the lyrics to *S&M*.

Winks at me.

Then all his attention is on Kay.

He shakes his hips.

Sucks on his index finger.

Stares at her with *fuck me* eyes.

And she's watching him.

Laughing.

Blushing.

Pressing her knees together.

He's doing it to fuck with me. I know that.

But it's fucking working.

When the song ends, Dean drops to his knees in front of Kaylee. He taps her thigh with the mic. "Offer stands."

"Oh... I... uh..." Kaylee takes the mic. Passes it to Em.

Em nudges her. Whispers something in her ear.

Ryan rolls his eyes. "Fuck, you're annoying."

"At least I'm entertaining," Dean says.

"I don't know. Ryan is pretty entertaining when he's threatening you," Leighton says.

Walker shrugs.

"And when you two start fighting," Leighton goes on. "That's gold."

Everyone nods. Except Kay and Em. They're too busy trading whispers.

Kaylee shakes her head. Stands. "Excuse me. I need to make a call." Her eyes catch mine as she makes her way to the door.

Walker chuckles. "You still repulse her."

"Nah. She just doesn't want you to know the truth," he says.

Ryan bursts into a fit of laughter.

Leighton too.

"You remember that guy who came in yesterday? The one who hadn't showered in weeks?" Walker asks.

"Yeah?" Dean arches a brow.

"You're more repulsive than he is."

"Wanna bet?"

"Fuck yeah. Find him."

"A hundred bucks says she'd rather fuck me."

"I'll take that," Leighton says.

Dean flips her off.

Fuck, these guys are assholes.

Kaylee's feelings are a joke to them.

It's not like I can talk. I'm the one that started this bullshit.

But I've had enough.

"I gotta piss." I push myself to my feet. Do my best not to storm out of the room.

Fucking Dean.

Bane of my fucking existence.

I try to shake it off. This shit isn't his fault. It's mine.

But that knowledge does nothing to untangle the knot in my gut.

Where the hell is she?

Nowhere in this hallway. Or the next.

I move through the lobby. Step outside.

She's not out front. Not anywhere outside the stores of this strip mall.

Fuck, I'm going to hit something. Or someone.

I find the nearest quiet spot. The alley next to the frozen yogurt place.

There.

I step around the corner ready to deck the fucking wall.

But she's there.

God, the sight of her eases every ugly thought in my head.

The green eyes, the blue glasses, the short skirt—that's Kaylee.

My Kay.

"Brendon." Her voice is a whisper. A plea. A *stop hurting me*.

"Kay." I close the distance between us. Ten feet. Five. Two. One.

She looks up at me. "You know Dean is just messing with you."

"It's working." My body takes over. One palm plants on her hips. Presses hard enough to pin her to the wall.

Her breath catches in her throat. "Brendon... I... I'm sorry. Tell me what I can do. Please. Anything."

"You saw every single one of my drawings?"

She nods.

"And you're sure you want that?"

"Yes. I know what it means. I've read books. Fiction. And non-fiction. And I... it's all I've thought about."

It doesn't make sense. The Kaylee in my head is sweet. Soft. Innocent. This—this is dirty, depraved, fucked up shit.

But Kay isn't the sweet girl in my head.

She's a woman.

With desires. With demands.

That's what I want for her.

And this is certainly what I want for me.

"This is it, Kay. If you want to back out, you need to do it now. 'Cause once I start, I won't be able to stop myself." I cup the back of her head with my palm. "I haven't slept right in weeks. All I can think about is the taste of your lips. What you look like when you come—"

"You haven't seen—"

"But I imagine it every fucking night." I slide my hand over her hip. "I think about you coming on my hand. On my lips. On my cock."

"Brendon." She tugs at my t-shirt. Presses her palm against my stomach. Her eyes meet mine. She nods. *Yes.*

I study her expression as I shift my hips against hers.

Those green eyes are hazy with lust.

She's ready to let go.

To make me the center of her universe.

Kaylee trusts me. I need every fucking ounce of that trust. I need every fucking ounce of her.

Fuck, this is Kay, the sweet girl who mocks my love of action movies.

Who can't cook to save her life.

Who looks at me like I hang the moon.

And she's about to be mine.

My blood is pumping. My heart is pounding. My body is buzzing with the kind of energy that comes with getting new ink.

I bring one hand to her ass and pull her body against

mine. So I can feel every soft inch of her.

She rises to her tiptoes.

Closes her eyes.

Presses her lips to mine.

It's different than our last kiss.

Softer. Deeper. More.

She's pouring into me.

And I'm pouring into her.

There's need and affection and months of unsaid shit pouring between us. Filling me from head to toe.

That's what she does—she fills this hole inside me. Nothing else does.

Her lips part to make way for my tongue.

She arches her back, melting into my touch, begging me to take her.

The rest of the world slips away. My universe is Kay. Her soft body. Her lush lips. Her palm against my stomach.

Her groan as she pulls back. "Please."

She stares at me with those doe eyes.

Begging me with those sweet eyes.

"Take off your panties." I step back enough to make it possible.

She looks around the alley. "Here?" It's empty, but we're sandwiched between a busy street and a parking lot.

My voice drops to a demanding tone. "Here."

Her lip quivers. Her brow knits. She's considering it.

Of course she is. Kay is cautious.

But if I'm going to teach her...

She isn't going to blink after an order.

She's going to trust me to lead her anywhere.

"Now." I drop another octave. Fuck, I'm impatient. I need her coming around my fingers. I need her groaning my name. I need her so wracked with pleasure she can't see straight.

She answers with a heavy nod.

Bends. Reaches under her skirt. Pushes her panties to her knees.

She shudders as I drop to one knee and peel her panties to her ankles.

I help her out of them, one foot at a time, then I slide them into my back pocket.

Her voice is soft. Uncertain. "I've never done this before."

"I know."

"Any of it." She clutches at my t-shirt like it's a lifeline. "No one's touched me but me. And I've never touched anyone."

There goes my last coherent thought. Being the first guy inside her, the first to make her come—

Fuck.

"Trust me." I cup her cheek with my palm. "I've got you."

She nods.

"All you need to do is breathe."

"Just breathe?" Her thighs shake against my fingertips.

My hand goes to the hem of her skirt. I push it up an inch. Another. Another. Until it's as high as it can be without putting her on display.

Fuck, those soft thighs.

I need them wrapped around me.

I stroke her inner thigh until her eyelids flutter together. "Can you stay quiet?"

Her fingers dig into my t-shirt, pressing the cotton against my skin. "Yes. I... Please..."

"Look at me."

Her eyes glue to mine.

I've thought about her like this a thousand times. A million even.

But the real thing is so much fucking better.

I drag my fingertips higher.

Higher.

Higher.

She shakes against my skin.

Tugs at my t-shirt.

Pulls my body against hers.

"Arms over your head." I guide her motions. One arm. Then the other.

My palm closes around her wrists.

I pin her arms to the wall.

Her pupils dilate. Her hips rock against mine. Her tongue slides over her lips.

She likes being at my mercy.

Needs it even.

Fuck, I can't remember the last time I was this hard.

She's so fucking beautiful like this.

I stroke her inner thigh until her legs are shaking. Until she's staring at me with that plea in her eyes.

I'm the only thing in her universe.

This moment—her on the edge, desperate for my touch—it's the only thing in her universe.

Then it's rolling off her lips. "Please, Brendon. Please."

"Please what?"

Her thighs squeeze my hand. "Make me come."

Fuck, that sounds good on her lips.

My cock screams for attention. For every soft, sweet part of her.

Still, I torture her. Stroke her soft thigh until she's shaking with so much desire *I* can't take it.

I stare back at her as I bring my thumb to her clit.

"Fuck." Her eyelids press together. A groan rolls off her lips. Loud. Then softer. "Please."

I rub her with slow circles. Until she's squirming against my hand. Until her wrists are shaking.

Then I bring my index finger to her cunt.

And I tease her.

Her teeth sink into her lip.

Again.

Her hips buck against me.

Again.

Her groan vibrates down her chest.

I add another finger.

Go a little deeper.

Deeper.

There.

I'm officially the first inside her.

Fuck, it does something to me.

Wakes up every nerve in my body.

Sends that last remaining bit of blood to my cock.

Fills my head with all sorts of caveman thoughts.

Her eyes burst open. Catch mine.

They're hazy with pleasure. Need. Lust.

Satisfaction.

I watch it spread across her face as I fuck her with my fingers.

Her lips part with a groan.

A sigh so heavy her entire body is shaking.

Fuck, she's close.

I pin her wrists to the wall.

Rub her harder.

Fuck her deeper.

Her eyelids flutter together.

Her fingers curl into themselves.

"Brendon. I... Fuck." She bucks against my hand. "Fuck."

There.

Her hands go slack as she pulses around me.

God dammit, she's even more fucking beautiful coming on my hand.

I soak up every bit of her bliss. Every groan. Every shake. Every sigh.

Once she's come down, I drop her arms.

I bring my fingers to my lips and I taste every drop of her.

Then I wrap my arms around her and I pull her close.

And I soak up every ounce of her.

———

I let Kay go back first.

I even have the courtesy to wash my hands.

Okay, that's bullshit. It's not courtesy. It's more that I need an ocean of cold water to convince my cock to settle down.

Those groans, the need filling her eyes, the way her wrists flexed against my hand—she's burnt into my brain.

When I get back to the suite, Kaylee is already sitting next to Emma. Her knees are glued together. Her cheeks are flushed. Half *I might accidentally flash the room.* Half *I can't believe I did that.*

Her eyes catch mine.

Her lips curl into a smile.

That blush spreads all the way to her cheeks.

This is our secret.

Or—

Dean looks to me and cocks a brow.

I say nothing as I take my seat next to him.

"You did," he whispers.

I shrug. "Mind your own business."

Walker chuckles. "About time, Kane."

Chapter Twenty-Nine

BRENDON

The next morning, I drop Kaylee off at school.
I think about her every break in my day.

By my last appointment, I'm chomping at the bit.

"What was it like?" Dean moves into my suite. Leans against the wall. "As good as you imagined?"

"Fuck off. I'm working." I try to add irritation to my voice, but it won't happen. I love that Dean is desperate for details. There's so much I want to say about her. I'm bursting at the seams.

Too bad this client is a mutual friend. And an old friend. One of our oldest and most loyal clients.

Joel lives and dies for this kind of conversation.

I can't use him as an excuse.

Shit, I better—

"Don't hold back for me. I want to hear," Joel says. His voice has that effortless breeziness. Like Walker's, but brighter. Richer. More famous. "Sounds dirty."

"Very." Dean chuckles. "Sex in an alley. That's a hell of a way to lose it."

"Why do you ruin everything beautiful?" Damn, I'm

smiling. I can't help it. Life is too fucking good right now. And I'm about to see Kay. One more line and this thing is done.

"You can't know light without darkness," Dean says.

Joel's wavy hair whips his cheeks as he shakes his head. He looks every bit the effortless playboy rock star. He even has the *let's not talk about my band* shrug down pat.

I didn't know shit about Dangerous Noise until Emma decided it was her favorite band. She's had a few choice posters up on her bedroom walls. Men on beds, stripping out of their clothes, shooting come hither looks.

Joel looks to me. "You buy this shit?"

"Does anyone?" There. I set the gun down. Examine the work.

He turns to the ink. "Fuck, no wonder I keep coming back here. You do good shit."

"And you live four blocks away," I offer.

"Take more credit." His green eyes light up as he laughs. They're lighter than Kaylee's. Greyer.

Hers are more blue.

But it still sends all my thoughts racing back to her—

The way she groaned my name.

Those blue nails sinking into my skin.

The need filling her eyes.

Fuck, I need to get ahold of myself or I'm not going to survive this conversation.

"If it was me, the bragging would never end." He smiles that effortless, casual smile. "This alley girl the one you've been pining over?"

"I don't pine," I say.

Dean scoffs.

Joel too.

"Yeah. He's been pussy free for months now. More

even." Dean shakes his head. "I don't know how you do it. One woman. Forever."

"She's the right woman." He holds up his left hand like his wedding ring is an Olympic medal. "You'd get it if any woman could tolerate you for more than—"

"Three minutes," I offer.

"That's cruel. Three minutes?" Joel looks to Dean. "Tell me you do better than that."

Dean laughs. "You make a woman come, she forgets how obnoxious you are."

"Not sure about that." Joel shakes his head. "Not in your case." He turns back to me. "She's the one who was hanging at the counter last time? Blond hair. Librarian look. Fuck, I love the librarian look."

"Watch it. He'll punch you," Dean says.

"On *my* wife." Joel lets out a dreamy sigh.

"Yeah, 'cause a married man has never looked elsewhere," Dean says.

"I'll hit you." Joel curls his hands into fists, but his smile is too wide for him to sell it. "Not as hard as I'd like to, but I will hit you. We're recording shit tomorrow."

"How many times you mention that to Brendon?" Dean asks.

"I didn't know we could be talking about deflowering virgins in alleys." Joel turns to me. "You offering details? As disgusting as possible, preferably."

"If I'm not offering this asshole details, you think you have a good chance?" I ask.

He nods. "I'm only half as obnoxious."

I'm not sure about that.

I've never been one to brag, but fuck, the chance to replay Kaylee under my command... "She was mine."

Joel nods. "Go on."

"That's it," I say.

"Fuck. Maybe Dean is right. Maybe you aren't any fun," Joel teases.

I'm fine with that label. But I did make Kay a promise. "You have any upcoming shows?"

"Always. Why?" he asks.

"Get me tickets and I'll spill."

"Fuck, I'll get you whatever you want. Bella is gonna flip when she sees this." He stares at his new ink. "She'll want one."

"I'll squeeze her in whenever," I say.

He shakes his head. "I don't want you touching her now that I know you have a thing for chicks with glasses."

"You want someone else here touching her?" I ask.

"Good point. There really aren't enough female artists. It's sexist bullshit." Joel turns to Dean. "How come you guys only hire dicks?"

"Nepotism," Dean says.

"It makes the world go round." Joel looks to me. "I'll send over your shit tomorrow. Any date, any venue you want."

"Anything here?"

"Fuck, nobody tells me the details. You think they keep me around for my brains?" Joel laughs.

"Nobody thinks that," Dean agrees.

Joel laughs. "Right back at you."

Dean nods. "It hurts, being this beautiful. Doesn't it?"

"It's our cross to bear." Joel's shrug is playful. Joyful. He's that kind of guy. One who always cracks a joke. "I'm sure we've got something coming up." He lowers his voice. "Now. Tell me... was it good dirty alley sex? Or fucking amazing dirty alley sex?"

My head fills with every detail. "It was perfect."

———

KAYLEE SETS HER BACKPACK ON THE PASSENGER SIDE floor as she slides into the car.

Her eyes light up as they meet mine. "You look like a tool with your sunglasses hanging in your t-shirt."

"This better?" I slide them on and offer her my best cocky smile.

"Much better." She pulls the door closed. Clicks her seatbelt. "First name dropping. Then designer sunglasses—"

"Em gave me these for my birthday."

"I remember."

"That doesn't buy me anything?"

"Not a thing." She smiles as she plays with her seatbelt. "Where are we going?"

"Somewhere you love."

"Which is..."

I put the car in park and pull onto the street. "A surprise."

Kaylee's laugh fills the car. "How long will it take to get there."

"Depends on traffic."

"Hmm. That's not the best hint."

"What if I tell you something else?"

"If it's something good."

"I got tickets to a show."

"Oh, tell me, Brendon the name dropper. Who are we going to see?"

"Hey, if you don't want backstage passes—"

Her eyes light up. "Really?"

"And I'm the celebrity obsessed one?"

She nods.

"Dangerous Noise."

"What?" Her eyes go wide. Her jaw drops. She stammers something incomprehensible.

Kay is actually speechless.

Fuck, it's adorable.

Slowly, she presses her lips together. Nods. "Really?"

"Yeah."

Her voice jumps higher than I've ever heard it. "Me, you, and Em?"

"If it works for her schedule."

"That's so... Oh my God. I can't even... When?"

"In a few weeks."

She nods. "I just... I need to get tickets to Jersey. So I'll make sure it's not the same dates. You can tell me when I buy them. Tonight, I think."

"You want to talk about it?"

"No. This is good. And we... you... I want to think about happy things for a while."

I want to ask about her Grandma. To know how that's going. To help her work through all the messy shit in her head.

But this is good.

And shit's been hard for Kay.

If she needs a break, I'm more than happy to distract her from every other fucking thing in the world.

"I might have mentioned you to Joel." Or replayed every second of her coming on my hand. Same difference.

"Really?" Her expression gets hazy. Starstruck. "What about me?"

"How much you drive me out of my mind."

"Oh my God."

"He might have stupid shit to say if you go backstage."

"A rock star has stupid shit to say to me. This is..." Her eyes go wide. She's back to speechless.

"Awesome?"

"Yeah." Her chest spills over her tank top as she leans in to turn on the radio.

It's playing a particularly obnoxious pop-rock song.

Kaylee sticks her tongue out. "You... um... Sorry, I'm still on this whole, you're talking about me with rock stars thing."

"He's just as guy."

"A famous guy."

"Even so."

"Ugh, you're so cool. It's obnoxious." Her laugh is nervous. Distracted. "You mind if I plug this in?" She pulls her cell from her pocket and shows it off.

"What you're going to play." I pull onto the main drag. This is going to take forever. I need to be there with her now. I need all of her now. She makes me so fucking greedy.

"Hmm." Her voice is almost all the way back to normal. To mine. She taps the screen a few times. "What would you hate the most?"

"Too many options there."

"True." She plugs the aux cable into her cell. "I'll have mercy."

Rihanna spills from the speaks. *S&M.*

"You call this mercy?" I stop at a red light, turn to Kay, watch her eyes light up as she smiles.

"It's our song now."

"I'll think of Dean sucking on his index finger every time I hear it."

"I won't." Her voice drops. "I'll think about you..." Her cheeks flush. "I can't say it."

"You can."

"I... No..."

"Sucking the taste of you off my fingers?"

She nods. "How do you make it sound so hot?"

"It was hot." I give her a long once-over. "I'm dying to

pin you to the bed, spread your legs, and lick you until you're coming on my face."

A groan falls off her lips. "And that. I want to be able to do that."

"Try it."

"No." She shakes her head. "It's too embarrassing."

"What about it is embarrassing?"

"You're much smarter than that question."

"You picked a song about whips and chains."

"Just wait until the next one."

"Yeah?" The light turns green and I hit the gas.

Kaylee laughs. "I haven't worked this hard at cultivating a playlist since high school."

I don't remind her that high school was four months ago. I don't want to think about the practicalities right now.

There are still a million reasons why this can't happen.

But my heart is hearing none of it.

And my cock—

Fuck, I need to make her come again.

"All sexy stuff." She sets her cell in the cup holder. "If I do say so myself."

"Perfect background for this."

She groans. "I don't like the sound of that."

"You managed it before."

"Yeah, I wasn't even blushing the entire time."

Fuck, she was, and it was adorable. "Tell me what you want to do to me."

"Uh..."

"What you want me to do to you."

She taps her thighs with her fingertips. "I want you to... you're driving, right?"

I chuckle. "Right."

"You have to keep your eyes on the road. And not on me."

"True."

"Okay." Her sigh is heavy with relief. "I want you to—"

She's cut off by the song switching. The sultry beat of *Let's Get it On*.

"Classic," I say.

"Thanks." Nervousness spills into her voice. "Okay. I can do this." She takes a deep breath. Exhales slowly. "I want you to... to fuck me."

It sounds more like a question than a statement. It's certainly not a demand.

Even so, my body threatens to take over.

Pull over. Find an empty spot. Drag her to the backseat.

"Tomorrow," I say.

Her sigh echoes around the car. "Tomorrow?"

"You want to do it here?" I nod to the backseat of the car.

"Isn't that the classic losing your virginity experience?"

I shrug. "I couldn't drive yet."

"Do you remember that?" She presses her lips together. "The details?"

"It was a long time ago."

"Did you care about her?"

I shake my head. "It was a hook up at a party. Didn't mean anything." It was fun. Scary. Exciting. But not particularly meaningful. I can remember her name and the way she looked at me like I was fresh meat, but everything else is a blur.

"How... um... how long did you last."

"Damn, Kay."

"What?" She blushes. "Isn't that the kind of thing people ask?"

"People, yeah? You?"

"Well? How long?"

"Not long."

"And now?"

I chuckle. "High expectations."

"Well, yeah. You're basically a sex god." She turns toward me. "So... how long?"

"Long enough to get you begging me to stop."

That blush spreads to her chest. "Oh."

"I want to fuck you, Kay. It's driving me out of my fucking mind how badly I want to bury myself in you."

"But..."

"I want to make you wait."

Chapter Thirty

BRENDON

Twenty minutes later, I park on the street overlooking the secluded beach. It's picturesque. Deep blue water. Bright sky. Lemon sun. Waves crashing into the pristine sand.

And Kaylee stepping out of the car with a squeal.

Nobody else gets this happy, jubilant version of her.

It's mine.

All right, maybe it's Em's too. I hear the two of them giggling in my sister's room almost every night.

But that's another ugly practicality.

The whole my little sister will freak the fuck out if she finds out I'm fucking her best friend.

I push it aside as I step out of the car and grab our stuff from the backseat.

The sun bounces off Kaylee's light hair. She really does look like an angel. Like my angel.

It used to be her nickname. Kay was the angel and Em was the devil.

It suits her.

A little too much.

It's filling my head with all sorts of thoughts about making the good girl bad.

I hold up my backpack. "I packed your swimsuit."

"You went into my room?" She arches a brow.

"Straight to your underwear drawer."

Her cheeks flush. "I guess you already saw most of it."

"Most, but not all."

She forces herself to look into my eyes. "You like that all my stuff is cotton and lace?"

Fuck yeah. I nod.

"You like that I'm innocent. That I'm a virgin."

"Yeah. But it's mostly that you're Kay. That you rant about *The Hunger Games*, and eat nothing but almond butter and jelly sandwiches, and mumble Latin quotes when you're tired."

"*Serva me, servabo te.*"

"What's that mean?"

"My secret."

I play with the hem of her shirt. "I'll torture it out of you?"

"That sounds more like a reward."

I shake my head.

She nods.

"You have no idea how far I can push you to the edge."

I slide my hand over her ass.

Her pupils dilate. Her lips purse. "It still sounds like a reward." She grabs the backpack, finds her bikini and a towel and hands it back to me.

I take her hand to lead her down the steep path.

She squeezes my palm as she steps onto the sand. Her eyes get wide. Her smile too.

She kicks off her shoes. Wraps the towel around her chest and loses layer after layer. Her bra falls on top of her t-shirt. Her panties on top of that.

Her eyes catch mine. "Are you just going to stand there?" She nods to the backpack.

I have no plans of watching while she runs around the waves. Not when I could have my hands on her soft body. My lips on her neck. My promises in her ears.

But it's fun to torture her.

"Maybe." I pull my black board shorts from the backpack.

She nods. "You really do look ridiculous in those."

"I could skip them."

"You should." She calls my bluff.

Fuck, I want to. I want every inch of my flesh pressed against hers. But it's going to be hard enough resisting dragging her to the backseat with my clothes on.

And I didn't pack condoms.

My genius idea. No condoms means I won't fuck her.

But now it means I can't fuck her.

She drops her towel to show off her bikini. It's so fucking Kay. A shiny green bottom with a scale print and a soft skirt. A shiny purple top that ties around her neck and on her back.

It's Ariel's fucking bikini.

And fuck does she fill it out.

I want those soft tits in my hands.

My mouth.

Around my cock.

She motions to my jeans. "You're a tease."

"You have no fucking idea."

That gets her breath catching in her throat. She forces herself to turn toward the beach. There are a dozen people here, but none are near us. "I guess I don't want you to get arrested. Not until I've had my way with you." She folds her glasses on her towel. Pushes herself to her feet. Dusts the sand off her ass.

I want my hands on that ass.

I want it pressed against my cock as I pin her to the wall.

I want to paint it red with my palm.

Fuck. I need to stop this train of thought or I'm going to get both of us arrested.

I focus on the waves crashing into the beach.

I pull my t-shirt over my head.

Wrap the towel around my hips. Shimmy out of my jeans and boxers and into my board shorts.

Let the towel fall to the ground.

Kay offers her hand.

I take it.

And I lead her right to the edge of the water.

She dips a toe in the surf. Cringes as water hits her ankle. "It's freezing."

"This is as warm as it gets."

"Still." She takes another step into the water. Another. "How come this was so much easier when I was a kid?"

"What wasn't?"

"True." She squeezes my hand, pulling me into the surf with her.

We wade until we're knee deep. Well, I'm knee deep. The water comes up to her thighs. Almost to—

She steps into a tiny wave. Yelps as the water rushes over her waist.

She turns to me with a smile. Wraps her arms around my waist. "I jump, you jump?"

"Always."

———

KAYLEE NEARLY RUNS BACK TO OUR BLANKET. SHE WRAPS herself in her towel like it's a hug she needs desperately.

254

I towel dry my hair. My shoulders. My chest. "Check the backpack."

She drops to her knees, slides on her glasses, leans over my backpack, and looks up at me. "What am I looking for?"

My command for you to suck me off.

Fuck, if there were less people here—

"This." I drop to one knee, pull my thermos from the main pouch, and hand it to her.

She turns the lid open and takes a sip. "Vanilla black."

"Still perfect for you."

She shakes her head. Digs into the backpack until she finds the other stuff in there—a few bars of chocolate and a box of strawberries. "Romantic."

"And I'm not?"

"I guess I've never thought about it." She sits cross legged as she unwraps a bar of seventy percent dark. "Have you been romancing your one-night stands all these years?"

"Depends on your definition of romance."

She pats the spot next to her. "I'm not sure I have one."

I sit. Steal a square of her chocolate and let it melt on my tongue.

"Chocolate. Strawberries. Trips to the beach."

"Making sure she comes at least three times?"

Kaylee laughs. "Five. It's not romantic until you get to five."

"You're going to regret those words."

"I don't think so." She breaks a square of chocolate in half and places it on her tongue. Her eyelids flutter together as she lets out a soft moan. "This one is my favorite."

"I know."

She picks up the tea and takes a long sip. "This too."

"I know. I know you."

"Yeah. You do." She taps her fingers against the thermos. "But, um, did you... did you read my note?"

"No." I reach into the backpack and find the neatly folded pages.

She stares at me like I'm crazy as I hand them to her. "But I..." Her voice streaks with surprise. "I left this for you. To apologize."

"You were desperate."

"Maybe."

"Yeah."

"Don't you... don't you want to read it?"

"I'm fucking dying to read it." I stare into those soft green eyes. "I want every thought in your head, Kay. But I can't take them. I need you to give them to me."

"I did."

"Because you want to let me in. Not because you think it's the only way."

"Oh." She unfolds the paper. Her attention drifts to it as she rereads her words.

I give her space. Suck every bit of sweetness from a strawberry. It only makes me more desperate to taste her.

"I... I want you to read it. This." Her voice rises from a whisper. "I do. I'm sure." She just stops herself from handing the paper to me. "Or... I could read it. I want to."

I nod. Fuck knows I want in her head.

She takes a deep breath and exhales slowly. "Okay. Here goes nothing." Her attention goes back to the page. Her voice shifts into something soft and rhythmic. "I don't even want to write this, but I need to get it out. It's not like I can tell anyone. I certainly can't tell Em."

She presses her lips together.

"I looked at Brendon's sketchbook. I know it was fucked up. I'd die if he was reading this, if he was reading anything in here. But I had to know if I was right about the way he looks at me or if it was all in my head. And I was right. It was full of pictures of me. Stripping. Naked. Bound. He wants me tied to his bed. Or at least, he thinks about it."

Guilt seeps into her voice. It's in her eyes, her shoulders, her jaw.

It was fucked, her looking at my sketchbook.

But it was nothing this bad.

Her fingers curl into the paper. "I stopped thinking about him for a while. Last year. When it all started. But then when I started feeling better, it was worse. Harder to get him out of my head. Then when I changed things last month... All of a sudden, I think about sex all the time. It's not always with him. Sometimes it's Kit Harrington or Chris Evans or some faceless guy. But a lot of times it's Brendon." Her cheeks flush.

"I think about you too."

"All the time?"

"Every fucking night."

Her teeth sink into her lip. Her attention goes back to the paper. Her voice gets stronger as she reads. "He's thinking about me too. He wants me too. I don't know what to do. I can't act on it. He and Emma are the two most important people in my life. I can't risk that. And it's not like we have the potential for a future. If he knew the truth... He doesn't want to be with someone like me. He doesn't want to be with someone complicated."

"Kay—"

Her stare cuts me off.

She knows what I'm asking.

What the hell does she mean I don't want to be with someone like her?

She's sweet. Smart. Tenacious. Funny. Beautiful.

A little uptight, yeah, but that only makes me want to undo her.

"I want to tell you. I do." She plays with the wrapper of her chocolate bar. "But I'm afraid you'll leave."

"I won't."

"I know this ends in something complicated. With Em finding out. Or you realizing you'd rather be with someone your own age." She traces the edge of her square until her finger is streaked with melting chocolate.

I want to tell her it doesn't, but I can't promise that. I can't promise anything. I want Kay. Forever. But she's got a big, bright future ahead of her. And I'm not letting anything hold her back. Even me.

Especially me.

"I'd rather have a taste than nothing." She offers me half the square.

I take it.

She places the chocolate on her tongue. Chews. Swallows. "*Serva me, servabo te*. It means *save me and I'll save you*."

Fuck, that is a romantic notion.

But what the hell does Kaylee need saving from?

Chapter Thirty-One

KAYLEE

The words are clawing at my throat.

At my fingers.

I pace around my room. It's been hours since we got back from the beach. And he hasn't said another word about the journal entry I read him.

We went right back to teasing about music.

To talking about the concert.

About how desperate he's going to make me.

But this has been on the tip of my tongue all night.

I finish my last bit of Latin homework and put my textbook away. There. The night is mine.

Officially.

And he's... he's somewhere. With Dean, I think. One of the guys. Or several of them.

I grab my journal. Pick up my pen. Let all the thoughts spill from my fingers.

Brendon, I should tell you this. No, I want to. I want it off my chest.

It's just I don't want you to leave.

That's why I haven't told anyone. Because it's better swallowing it deep than losing another person I love.

I'd rather you care about the person you think I am than you not care about me at all.

But, really, I want all your love.

And I want it for the real me. Not the girl you see when you look at me, the one who can read two books a day and offer up a Latin quip anytime.

I've been on medication the last year.

I have depression.

It didn't start with anything. I let my therapist believe it started when Grandma had that heart attack and insisted I stay here for the summer. I let my parents believe that I needed help because I wasn't dealing with her illness well. But that isn't true. It was already there. I was already having all these ugly thoughts about making it all go away.

Whenever I would borrow Mom's car, when I was driving up or down the 405, I'd think about how easy it would be to crash into the divider. To not feel anything anymore.

I don't have as many of those thoughts anymore. That voice that tells me I'm worthless, a failure, that no one loves me, that I'm a drain, that everyone is better off without me—it's quieter now.

But it's not gone.

It will never be gone.

Sometimes it's stronger. One day, it might be strong enough to convince me to act on it.

Medications stop working. My doctor warned me about that. Offered a bunch of hotlines.

It's hard to imagine swallowing a bottle of sleeping pills. Or taking a razor blade to my wrists. Or finding some tall building.

But it's possible.

That voice was so loud and so ugly.

If it comes back...

How can you love someone who might kill herself?

How can I ask that of you?

I haven't told anyone except my therapist.

But I want you to know.

I want you to know and not run away.

I'm always going to be broken.

A knock on my door breaks my concentration.

I snap the notebook shut. "Hey."

"Hey." Emma taps her fingers against the door. "Can I come in?"

"Yeah." I push up from my desk. "I'll come out. Let's watch something."

She pulls the door open. Leans against the frame. "I was going to ask you that."

"That's why we're soul mates," I tease.

"Really?" Her voice brightens. "I've beaten out Katniss?"

"Katniss doesn't make me chocolate chip pancakes."

Emma laughs. She takes my hand and leads me down the stairs.

The room is the same as always. Clean. Quiet. Still.

She motions to the couch. Then to the kitchen. "Or you can help."

"Sure." I follow her into the tiny space and get out all the wet ingredients.

She grabs the dry ones. Measures them into a giant white bowl. "You have a look."

"It's craving for chocolate."

"No. It's something else. Contemplation."

"Is that different than normal?"

Emma laughs as she licks sugar from a spoon. "Good point."

I crack two eggs and start whisking. I *am* contemplative. I need to talk to someone. And I want to talk to her. She's my best friend. "You think I could tell you anything that would change your opinion of me?"

"Sure." She takes the eggs, pours them into the bowl, stirs. "If you killed someone. Or if you failed a class. Or if you fucked Dean." Her eyes light up as she turns to me. "Did you fuck Dean?"

"No."

"You're blushing."

I am?

"You did something!" The spoon drops with a splat. Her hand goes over her mouth. "Oh my God, Kay, you did!"

I try a coy shrug.

"Bullshit. What did you do with Dean?"

"Nothing."

"Liar."

Maybe there is a way to say this without lying. At least technically. "I might have let someone..." I motion to my shorts.

"You let someone finger you?" She nearly shouts it.

"God, Em, you're gross."

She laughs. "You're the one letting Dean finger you."

I can't keep up the stern expression. I'm laughing too. This is normal. Girl talk. Only she doesn't realize it's about her brother.

I fill a measuring cup with chocolate chips then hand them to Emma.

"Was it good?" She plops a chip in her mouth.

I nod.

"Great?"

"Amazing."

"Damn, Dean gives amazing... finger, I guess?"

"I would know?"

"Apparently." She motions to the stove.

I turn it on then grab a pan and the oil.

"Wow. You and Dean. I can't believe it."

"Me either." There. The pan is hot enough. I add the oil and tilt the pan so it coats the surface.

"So are you two going to—" She clicks her tongue twice.

"I think so."

Emma squeals and throws her arms around me. "My little girl's all grown up."

"Stop it, Mom, you're embarrassing me."

She giggles. "Now, listen, honey." She takes on a perfect Mom voice. "I don't care what he tells you about pulling out or how clean he is. Unless you've seen a test result, you make sure he wraps it up. And since he's a manwhore, you make sure he wraps it up either way. No glove, no love."

"God, Mom! You think I'm a kid or something?"

"You know I only remind you because I love you."

"I know."

Emma laughs as she squeezes me again. "I think you did. I'm seeing you in a new light. A Kaylee gets hers light."

"Good?"

"Great. I'm proud. You're blossoming."

"A slut in training?"

"No. A woman who knows what she wants."

My glance shifts upstairs, toward Brendon's room. "True."

"I know I've told you a million times, but don't let anyone tell you what you want is wrong. Not me. Not Mr. Brooding Bad Boy. Not your teachers. And not Dean. If you're into freaky shit—"

"Like what?"

"I dunno. Having your toes sucked. Dressing like a baby. There are tons of fetishes. And it's always the quiet ones. Like Brendon. He's into whips and chains and all that stuff. I've heard the guys talking about it a million times."

"Oh?" God, my cheeks are burning.

"Don't tell me I scared you. I mean, you're getting hand jobs in—" She gasps. "Did this happen at karaoke."

"Maybe."

"Oh my God. This is what I get for touching up my makeup in that shitty bathroom with no light." She shakes her head with regret. "I could have seen the signs."

"Oh. Well. It was fast."

"Yeah? He's that good?"

"Better."

"You know he has that piercing. Did you see it? Tell me you saw it."

"No. It was just him."

"Dean's a gentleman?"

"I guess so."

"Are you into it?"

"Huh?"

"The piercing."

"Oh. Maybe."

She laughs. "Oh my God, Kinky Kaylee! You're into it."

"What? No. I... I mean, sorta."

"So, when are you—" She adopts Dean's *I'm fucking with you voice.* "Popping that cherry?"

"Tomorrow." He said tomorrow. I'm demanding tomorrow.

Her jaw drops. "Already? We're not prepared. We need makeup. And lingerie. And I need to go over this with you. You're not gonna have some shitty first time. You're going to come, even if you have to explain it to him."

"Is it that serious?"

"Hell yeah." She turns back to the batter and scoops a

spoonful onto the pan. "Good thing I have you all night. And after we'll get ice cream and you'll tell me if the rumors are true."

"Huh?"

"About his Prince Albert."

"Oh. Yeah. Sure."

"You promise you won't hold back on details?"

"About the sex? No. I promise. I'll tell you everything."

———

I BARELY MANAGE BREAKFAST OR LUNCH.

I struggle to concentrate on studying for next week's Latin quiz.

My creative writing project remains a blank page.

My Kindle offers no solace. I read the same line twenty times before I give up on concentration and sit in front of the TV.

I can't even think about Grandma. I stare at a dozen ticket options. There are too many airports here and near Grandma's place. LAX or Long Beach or John Wayne. Newark or JFK or La Guardia. Nonstops. One stops. Two stops. Red eyes. Early morning flights. Ones that leave in the afternoon and get in late.

I give up on figuring it out now. Tune to *Days of Our Lives*. The soap grabs almost none of my attention.

But it's enough to take the edge off the nerves fluttering around my stomach.

Today.

It's happening today.

Soon.

With every commercial break, those nerves smack into each other a little harder.

I nearly jump when the door handle turns.

He steps inside all tall, tattooed, and handsome.

He's in his usual outfit. Black jeans. Black converse. And a v-neck, a powder blue one that matches my glasses.

Wicked *I'm going to have my way with you* smile on his beautiful face.

He kicks the door closed. Tosses his keys on the table. "Hey."

"Hey." My voice barely eeks out. "How was work?"

"Fucking awful."

"Oh."

"Couldn't stop thinking about you." He leaves his shoes by the door. "It took me forever to do a fucking heart tattoo."

"An anatomical heart?"

He shakes his head. "A tiny black outline." He holds his fingers in the shape of a heart. "You own my thoughts. You know that?"

"You do too."

He closes the distance between us.

I take his hand and let him pull me to my feet.

He presses his palm into my lower back, holding my body against his. "You think about anything besides fucking me today?"

Fuck, the pressure from his palm—

The intensity in his dark eyes—

The demanding edge to his voice—

I only barely manage to respond. "No."

His voice softens. "You're nervous."

"A little."

He slides his hand over my ass and thighs then traces the hem of my dress. "I'll walk you through it."

I just barely nod. It's too much. Too intense. And too many other thoughts are screaming for my attention. I need him erasing them. I need him making me forget.

He leans down to brush his lips against mine. It's soft. Barely a kiss. Barely a taste.

He brings his lips to my ear. "I want you so lost in me you forget yourself." His breath warms my skin. "I want you to follow my commands without thinking. I want that much of your trust."

I slide my hand under his t-shirt and press my palm against his back. He's so hard and strong. He could tear me in half without a second thought.

But he wouldn't.

I already trust him not to hurt me.

Trust him with almost everything.

I want to give my body over to him.

To be his.

To lose track of everything but his words, his touch, his kiss.

He pulls my dress over my thighs. "What do you want, angel?"

The pet name makes me blush. Words rise up in my throat, but they're a tangled mess. I want everything.

"You want your hands around my cock?"

"Yes."

"Your lips?"

"Yes."

"You want to come on my cock?"

"Everything, Brendon. Everything."

"Then go to my room, take off your dress, and wait for me on the bed." His voice drops back to that demanding tone.

His expression changes. More in control.

More everything.

He gives me a long once-over. "Don't make me ask twice."

Chapter Thirty-Two

KAYLEE

Now. I'm going to go to his bed and strip now.

Why does that set me on fire?

I'm hot everywhere.

Every part of me is desperate to strip in Brendon's room. To wait for him. To be on display for him.

It's scary how much I want to follow his orders.

But it's too exhilarating for me too care.

I make my way up the stairs, down the hall, into his room.

It's quiet. Empty. Just that big four-poster bed, the dresser, the desk in the corner.

I undo my zipper, step out of my dress, and sit on the bed.

My reflection is there, staring back at me from the mirror opposite his bed. I never thought about its placement, but now it makes perfect sense.

It's so he can watch.

So I can watch.

I stare back at reflection Kaylee. Her eyes are on fire.

Her knees are pressed together. Her chipped nails are sinking into her thighs.

All of her—all of me is already begging for release.

I bite my tongue. My bottom lip. My index finger.

Nothing takes the edge off.

I need him here.

Touching me.

Kissing me.

Fucking me.

Now.

I cross my legs. Uncross them. Press them together. Pry them apart.

It only amplifies the ache between them.

I can't wait any longer.

I'm going to burst if I don't get him now.

There are footsteps downstairs. They're far away. They stay far away for too long.

Then they move closer.

Up the stairs.

Down the hall.

He pulls the door open and shuts it behind him.

It's just us, alone in here, the rest of the world far away.

It's just me and Brendon alone in his bedroom.

About to have sex.

Fuck, it's hot in here. I'm so wracked with desire I can barely move.

"Good girl." His voice is heavy with approval.

It makes my sex clench.

He moves toward me. "Stand up."

I do.

"Turn around."

It's strange, spinning on my heels, but I like everything about the heat of his gaze.

He runs his fingers over the waistband of my panties. "Fucking beautiful, angel."

My breath catches in my throat.

"Look at me."

I turn back to him. I study every inch of him. The intensity in his dark eyes. The short, dark hair. Perfect for my hands. Perfect for pulling when his face is between my legs.

Where the hell did that come from?

Some dirty version of me is taking over.

One who demands what she wants.

One without nerves or hang-ups.

"Take off your bra," he commands.

I hesitate. But I need more of that look in his eyes—the one that says the sight of me sets him on fire.

I reach behind my back to unhook my bra then let it fall off my shoulders.

I'm topless for him.

On display for him.

He drinks me in like I'm cool water and he's a desert traveler. He savors every inch of me. Then his gaze fixes on my chest.

"Fuck, Kay. You have no idea how much I want those nipples in my mouth."

"Why don't you?"

"This first." He drags his hand over my side. His touch is soft. Slow. With utmost control.

He cups my breast with his hand. His thumb stops just short of my nipple.

It's a tease.

A delicious, agonizing tease.

He draws circles with his thumb, so, so close to where it needs to be. He does it until I'm panting. Until I'm clutching at his t-shirt.

Then he moves to my other breast and does it again.

Again.

Again.

"Brendon," I breathe. "Please."

"Take off your panties."

I slide them off my hips. Kick them from my ankles.

He drags his hand down my side, over my hip. "Turn around."

This time, I don't hesitate.

"Touch the ground."

My... Uh...

"Now."

I must be going out of my mind. Because I'm not stopping him. I'm not saying *what's wrong with you?*

There isn't a single part of me that objects.

I want to be on display for him.

This on display for him.

I roll from my hips as slowly as I can.

There.

My fingers skim the hardwood.

Then it's my palms.

Thank God for my exercise routine. I can hold this position for as long as I need to.

He moves closer. So his crotch is against mine. So I can feel his hard-on against my sex.

He's hard from the sight of me.

Fuck, it's thrilling.

Intoxicating.

Those damn jeans are in the way, but still, that's Brendon pressed against me.

Almost mine.

God, I need him to be mine.

This is the kind of pure, overwhelming desire I've been missing the last year.

It hurts.

But in the best possible way.

He brings his hands to my waist and peels my torso up. Until it's pressed against his, my back against his chest, my ass against his crotch, my head against his chin.

He holds me in place with one hand.

Runs the other up and down my side. My hip. My ass. My chest.

This time, his thumb brushes my nipple.

Fuck, that feels good.

I let out a groan.

Another.

Another.

He toys with me like I'm made for him. Then it's his index finger. Middle. Ring. Pinkie.

He moves to my other breast and does the same.

He shifts his hips so his cock grinds against my ass.

He was right.

I do feel like I'm his.

And I trust him to lead me anywhere.

It's scary how much I trust him with my body. But I feel too good to care.

He drags his lips over my neck as he toys with my nipples.

He toys and toys and toys.

Fuck, my sex is aching.

"Please," I breathe.

"You'll come when I say you come."

The demanding tone makes my sex clench.

God, he's so sexy in control.

I want it. All of it.

His rocks his hips against me, his cock against the flesh of my ass.

Those jeans are in the way.

There's too much in the way.

He teases and teases and teases.

I'm panting when he pulls his arm to his side.

"On the bed," he growls. "On your back. Now."

I sit on the bed. My eyes lock with his as I slide up it. Then they lose his as I lower myself onto my back.

"Fuck, Kay." He places his body between my legs. Drags his fingertips over my calf, up my inner thigh. "You have no fucking idea how badly I want to taste your cunt."

My breath catches in my throat.

His fingers dig into my inner thighs. One. Then the other.

He pins my legs to the bed.

Leans down to drag his lips over the inside of my knee.

Up my thigh.

Almost.

Almost.

Almost—

I gasp as his lips brush my clit. Fuck, that's intense.

My hands reach for something. The sheets.

His hair.

But he grabs my wrist.

Pins my arm to the bed.

Fuck. The pressure of his palm against my wrist—

The way he's holding me down—

It pushes me to the edge.

He teases me again.

Another soft brush of his lips.

Another tease.

Another.

Another.

Then he's moving over every inch of me. Feather light. It sets my nerves on fire. It has every part of me awake and alive. Alive in a way I haven't been in a very, very long time.

I reach for him with my free hand.

He reacts instantly. Grabs my wrist. "Do that again and I'll have to tie you up."

Mmm.

Yes.

Please.

I bring both hands to his head. Tug at his hair.

He looks up at me with his eyes on fire. He's assessing me. Figuring something out.

But what?

I don't know.

He nods. "Hands over your head."

Slowly, he shifts off my body. He reaches into the bedside drawer. Pulls something out. A pair of padded black handcuffs.

My breath catches in my throat.

It's so fucking hot, Brendon holding handcuffs.

He slides them over my wrists then pulls, then slides two fingers under the right cuff. Pulls them tight.

Does the same with the left.

I shift my wrists, testing the restraints. They're not tight enough to hurt, but they're tight enough to keep me bound.

I can still move my arms.

But...

He moves to the foot of the bed. Stares down at me. "Those stay over your head. Understand?"

"Or?"

"Or I stop."

No... anything but that.

I nod. I understand. And, God, I want it too.

I want all of him.

He climbs back onto the bed.

Places himself between my legs.

Slowly, he drags his lips up my inner thigh, over my sex, down my other leg to the inside of my knee.

He traces his path. Again. Again.

Again.

He gets harder.

Harder.

Fuck, I'm aching.

I need him.

I need to come.

I need everything.

He nips at my inner thigh. So, so close to where he needs to be.

Again.

Again.

Again.

Fuck—

His tongue flicks against my clit.

It's soft.

Slow.

My body floods with pleasure as he laps at me.

I let his name fall off my lips.

I buck against his mouth.

More. I need more.

He plants one palm against my hip bone, holding me in place.

And he licks me harder. Faster.

Fuck, that soft, wet tongue—

All that pressure in my sex winds and winds.

Tighter and tighter.

And tighter.

And—

There.

Everything releases.

I see white.

Nothing but bliss.

My sex pulses as pleasure spreads through my torso.

But he...

He's not stopping.

"Brendon."

He groans against me.

Like he can't get enough.

My hips fight his hands.

My thighs too.

But he's stronger than I am.

I'm stuck in place.

The thought tightens everything inside me. I'm at his mercy. And—

Fuck.

The tension knots.

Again.

Again.

Again.

With the next flick of his tongue, I go over the edge. I groan his name as I come. I shake through my orgasm, soaking up every bit of pleasure.

He drags his lips over my inner thigh.

He places a kiss on my pelvis. My stomach. My breastbone.

I tug at his t-shirt.

He pins my wrists to the bed. Straddles me. Stares down at me with that intense, demanding look in his eyes. "Keep your hands over your head."

I nod.

Fuck, the weight of him—

He tosses his t-shirt aside. Reaches around his back to pull something from his pocket.

A condom.

He tosses it on the bed next to him.

Slides off me for long enough to shimmy out of his jeans. Then the boxers.

Fuck, that's...

That's Brendon naked.

He's...

Fuck.

His fingers curl around my wrist. He takes my hand and brings my arms over my body.

Brings my hand to his cock.

Slowly, I wrap my fingers around him.

His skin is soft but he's so hard.

And that's...

The thought keeps screaming in my head.

That's Brendon.

He's in my hand.

He's lying next to me.

He's kissing me, claiming my mouth with his tongue.

He tastes like me.

Brendon tastes like me. It's wonderful and thrilling and absurd.

His hand stays on my wrist. He guides my movements as I stroke him.

Then he's groaning against my lips.

Tugging at my hair.

He tears the wrapper and rolls the condom over his cock.

He pushes my arms over my head and holds them against the bed.

His knees push my thighs apart.

Then he's lowering his body onto mine.

His eyes stay glued to mine as his cock nudges against my sex.

With one swift motion, he thrusts inside me.

Fuck. That's intense. It doesn't hurt, not exactly. It's more like a lot of pressure. Almost too much to take.

"Fuck." I need more. All of him. Even if it hurts.

He's slow about moving inside me. It's a tiny movement. But it still feels intense.

I hold his gaze as he moves faster. Harder. Until I'm getting the full force of him. Until it feels more good than uncomfortable.

Until pleasure is knotting in my core.

"Fuck, Kay." He leans down to press his lips to mine.

He claims my tongue as he claims my sex.

It screams through my head. *That's Brendon inside you.*

That's Brendon.

That's—

Fuck.

It hurts but it feels good too.

He feels good.

And mine.

It's like the universe is just the two of us.

Like we really are one.

I rock my hips to move with him.

I suck on his lip.

Groan against his mouth.

I soak up every inch of him. Every groan. Every thrust. Every bit of pressure.

He moves harder.

I wrap my legs around his waist.

It's too intense.

I have to pull back.

To groan his name as I go over the edge.

That last bit of discomfort fades.

So the only thing in my body is pleasure.

So much I can barely take it.

He thrusts through my orgasm.

Then he's wrapping his arms around me, moving harder, faster.

"Fuck, Kay." He groans against my neck as he comes.

I can feel it in the way he's pulsing inside me.

It's strange and wonderful and everything.

He's everything.

He's mine.

Right now, he's all mine.

Chapter Thirty-Three

BRENDON

I t feels so fucking good having Kaylee's body against mine.

I pull her a little closer.

Soak in a little more of her.

Fuck, I can't remember the last time I wanted to cuddle after sex.

That I fucked someone I cared about.

I'm not used to the feelings flooding my gut.

I want to lay like this with her forever.

I want to get my hands on every thought in her head.

I thought I had it bad before.

I had no fucking idea.

———

WHAT IS IT KAYLEE ISN'T TELLING ME?

Em might know. She's sitting on the couch, tapping away at her laptop, quiet concentration spread over her face.

The device sings with the Facebook notification sound. She isn't working. We can talk.

But it's not like I can ask her *hey, know any secrets Kaylee's keeping?* I need to be smart about this.

I plop on the couch and turn on the TV. "You think Kaylee's happy here?"

"I didn't realize you cared." She closes her laptop, stands, leaves it on the table. Then she collects the dishes on the table and brings them to the sink.

I can't help but chuckle. "You wouldn't have done that last month."

"I like her more than I like you."

"Who wouldn't?"

The water in the kitchen runs. Ceramic clinks together. "Are you really spending Friday night at home?"

"You have a point?"

She moves into the living room. Brushes her red hair behind her ears. "You've been staying home more."

"And you're here because?"

"Did your last date scar you or something?"

"No. Just busy. With the shop."

"Like that *Seinfeld* episode?"

I arch a brow. Emma loves 90s sitcoms. And 90s Disney movies. And music. It's weird.

"Where George's girlfriend has mono, so he doesn't have sex for weeks, and it makes him smarter."

"Maybe. Am I smarter?"

"I don't think so. Maybe you need to wait longer." Her voice is light. Teasing. Like normal.

"I'll keep that in mind."

Emma takes a seat on the couch. She looks to the TV. "Can we watch *The Americans* instead?"

I nod. "Why are you home?" I copy her words. "Your

last date scar you?" Shit, I usually don't worry about Emma and men. She's tough. She can hold her own. And I'd rather not think about what exactly my sister does in dark movie theaters. But guys can be shit. If someone crossed the line, hurt her— "Do I need to kick someone's ass?"

"No. I'm just kinda... I'm more matchmaking right now." She turns to me with a curious expression. "You've been weird."

"I thought I was always weird."

"Well, yeah. Extra weird." She studies me. "You and Kay have been hanging out a lot."

"And?"

"It's just weird, don't you think?"

"Why?"

"You're kinda old."

"Wise."

"Eh."

I chuckle as I flip her off.

She laughs as she returns the gesture. "It's been making me think about Mom and Dad, what's happening to Kay's grandmother."

"Me too."

"I miss them. I know they were assholes to you, but—"

"They're still your parents." Only I don't miss them. Not exactly. I never let my head go to that place.

They're gone.

Our chance to reconcile is gone.

But was there ever a fucking chance?

Nothing would have convinced me to be the clean cut, high achieving son they wanted.

They had points. I skipped too much school, hung out with too many burn outs and druggies, gave too much lip.

But there was a fucking ocean between who I was and who they wanted me to be.

And I was never going to cross that.

It's easier to push everything aside.

They're gone. I don't dwell on that. I've never had the mental space. Not really. I had no fucking idea how to take care of someone when I was appointed Emma's legal guardian. And taking care of a teenage girl who'd just lost her parents—that wasn't easy.

It filled that space. Kept me from thinking about what it meant, Mom and Dad no longer existing.

I still don't let my head go to that place.

And I don't want to.

"I hated them too," Emma says. "For a long time. It was their fault. I always knew it was their decisions to lock you out."

"It was both of us." I don't want Emma picking up my baggage. Things were still good with her and our parents. That should be her lasting memory.

"But you showed whenever they didn't. You wouldn't have done that if you didn't want to be around."

It's true. I always want to support Emma. Even when she pisses me off. "It was complicated." But it wasn't, not really. Mom didn't want me around my young, impressionable sister.

"Was it? Why'd they have to draw that line."

"You have to draw it somewhere." I get it, now. I really do. It's hard being a parent. You try your best, but a lot of times you fuck that up.

"I guess." She leans back into the couch. "Maybe you are wise."

"Only maybe?"

She nods. "You... you annoy the crap out of me, Brendon, but you... you're a good brother."

"High praise."

"I'm trying to be earnest. It's not my forte." She stares into my eyes. "I know I was pissed about everything with Kaylee, but I was wrong. I'm sorry. You were just looking out for her. And for me. I don't know what I'd do without her."

"Me either."

"Huh?"

"She's half the reason why you're in college now."

Emma nods. "You push college a lot for someone who barely graduated high school."

"And?"

"It's very parent like."

"I'm your legal guardian."

"Not anymore. I'm eighteen."

"You want to move out and pay your own rent?"

"Are you really throwing down an ultimatum?"

"No." I'd never do that to Em.

"It's just. I do appreciate you taking care of her. Even if I think it's weird you two are hanging out so much."

"Thanks."

"And... I do appreciate you taking care of me too." She leans in for a hug. "I love you."

"Love you too."

She settles back into her seat and nods to the TV. "Okay. Enough feelings. Let's watch some spy action."

I chuckle. Em is funny nervous. It's rare. "You working two Thursdays from now?"

"Why?"

"I have a surprise. For me, you, and Kay."

"Same as every Thursday. Four to eight."

"Good. You two can meet me at the shop. We'll go together."

"What is it?"

I shrug *who knows*.

"Don't make me take back everything I said."

"You won't."

"Try me."

"I am."

She folds her arms. "Fine. I won't take it back. This time. But only for Kay's sake."

"She's my saving grace."

"She really is."

———

I DISAPPEAR INTO MY ROOM TO WORK ON A MOCKUP. When I reappear downstairs, Emma and Kaylee are giggling over ice cream sundaes.

Emma nods to me then motions *cut it*.

Kaylee's eyes light up with that *we have a secret* look.

"I miss something exciting?" I ask.

Emma shakes her head. "Hair stuff."

"Girl talk." Kaylee nods.

Emma waits for me to move into the kitchen. She leans in to not quite whisper to Kay. "You think you're going to do it again?" She looks to me. Motions *go away*. "The hairstyle."

"Yeah. I think this is my new hairstyle."

"But you... Uh..." My sister's brow furrows.

She's not exactly being subtle. They're obviously talking about sex.

But Emma is staring at me like it would be hell if I found out.

Huh.

Emma leans in to whisper.

Kaylee whispers back. She stands up and smooths her jeans. "I'm going to see how it goes. See how long I want to keep up this..." She pats her tight ponytail. "Hairstyle." She picks up her empty mug. "You want more?"

Emma shakes her head. "No. Sugar will keep me up all night. And some of us have work in the morning. Why do I get all the early shifts?"

"You request them," Kay says.

"No. That was some weirdo who inhabited my body. I hate mornings."

"You hate working nights."

"Mmm. Maybe." She stands to throw her arms around Kaylee.

They exchange another set of whispers.

Then Emma is nodding good night and heading toward the stairs. "Don't grill her, Brendon. Consider it a personal favor."

"What do I get out of it?" I tease.

"I'll watch *Lethal Weapon* with you," Emma says.

"And the sequel?" I tease.

Emma groans. "Fine."

She's been objecting to the possibility of watching Mel Gibson as a cop who plays by his own rules forever.

Kaylee watches Emma move up the stairs. Crosses to the kitchen. "Hey."

"Hey." I wait until Emma's door slams shut. Then I grab onto Kay's hips, pin her to the counter, and press my lips to hers.

She tastes good. Like sugar and salt and chocolate.

She groans as she pulls back. "We should be careful."

I nod as I pin her hips to the counter.

"Brendon."

"You want me to stop?"

She looks up at me with those doe eyes. "God no."

I don't. I let my tongue claim her mouth. I let my hands untuck her over-sized button up shirt then roam

287

beneath it. Fuck, her skin is soft and the way she groans against my lips as I slide my hand into her bra—

This is reckless.

But I need her too much to care.

"You should have warned me." She rises to her tiptoes to whisper in my ear.

"That?"

"I'd become even more obsessed with you." She slides her hand into my hair. Her touch is eager. Needy. "I want you again. I want you to fuck me right now." Her voice is confident. Her blush is slight. I'm already corrupting her.

The thought makes my balls tighten. "Can you stay quiet?"

"I don't know." She sighs as she tugs at my t-shirt. "I'm tempted to try."

Fuck, I love the sight of her wracked with desire.

But I need to be smart here.

I step backward. "Tomorrow."

She nods. "I... uh..." She grabs her mug. Places it in the sink. "You want to watch something?"

"Who is it Emma thinks you fucked today?"

Her cheeks flush. "Well. I kind of let her believe I'm into Dean."

"Dean?"

She nods. "And that we, ahem, today."

"She thinks you fucked Dean?"

"Yeah."

"Shit. I thought Em had a higher opinion of you."

Kaylee play swats me. "He's not that bad."

"He's not?"

She nods.

"News to me."

"You really think he's awful?"

"He has moments." I motion to the TV. "It's my turn to pick."

"Oh no. It is. How incoherent are we talking?"

"We'll see." I slide my arm around her waist. To lead her to the couch. But I'm not doing that.

I'm sliding my hand under her shirt.

Pressing my palm against her bare skin.

"Brendon..." She sighs as her hips rock against mine. Her fingers skim my thigh. It's a soft touch, but it's enough to wake up every nerve in my body.

I pin her to the kitchen counter. "We shouldn't." But I'm already undoing her top button.

"I know." She rocks her hips, sighing as she rubs against my hard-on.

"Em just went to sleep."

"I'll be quiet. I promise."

I get to the last button. My hands find her lower back. One slides between her shoulder blades. It unclasps her bra.

She shrugs her shirt and her bra off her shoulders.

She's topless in the middle of the fucking kitchen.

That smart part of me—the one that's supposed to remind me this is a bad idea—is gone.

I'm too fucking enraptured by the sight of her.

"Fuck, Kay." I undo her ponytail and slide my fingers through her hair. My palm cups the back of her head. I pull her into a slow, deep kiss.

She groans into my mouth.

I drag my lips down her neck. Over her collarbone. Over her breast.

She groans as I take her nipple into my mouth.

Fuck, she tastes good.

I toy with her. Flicks of my tongue. The scrape of my teeth. Sucking on that tender bud.

Her groan is music, but it's way too loud.

I bring my hand to her mouth. Slide my thumb between her lips.

She sucks on the pad of my finger.

Groans against my flesh.

Fuck, that feels good.

I move to her other nipple. Toy with it until I can't stand the way she's sucking on my digit.

I drag my lips over her collarbone, up her neck, right to her ear. "Turn around and place your hands on the counter."

Her nod is trusting. Obedient.

She brushes her ass against me as she turns.

Her ass feels so fucking good against my crotch.

I hold her body against mine and explore very inch of her torso. Her tits are perfect in my hand. Soft. Responsive. Mine.

It echoes through my head.

Mine, mine, mine.

I want every inch. Every groan. Every thought in her gorgeous head.

Slowly, I slide my hand over her side.

I undo her jeans and push them to her thighs.

She sighs. Arches her back. Presses her ass against me.

Fuck, those cotton panties. Sweet. Like her.

I push them off her hips.

Slide my hand up her thigh.

Fuck, I need to be inside her.

I bring one hand to her mouth, to muffle her groans, and rub her with the other.

She shudders. Shakes. Nips at my fingertips.

But she keeps her hands on the counter.

"Good girl." I suck on her earlobe.

"Brendon," she groans into my hand.

She's wet. Ready. But I need her on the edge. I need to be the only fucking thing she wants. I need my name to be the only thought in her head.

I rub her slowly. Softly.

She rocks her ass against my crotch. Driving me out of my fucking mind with her soft flesh.

Still, I toy with her.

I rub her until she's shaking. Until her fingers are digging into the counter. Until my hand is only barely muffling her groans.

She's about to come.

This is exactly where I want her.

I pull a condom from my back pocket and push my jeans to my knees. Then the boxers.

Her bottoms are still at her knees. They're binding her legs.

"Please," she whispers. "Fuck me. Now."

"Quiet."

She nods. "I can. I will. I promise."

I bring one hand to her pelvis. Pull her body against mine.

She sighs as my cock presses against her ass.

Fuck, that feels good.

Her flesh against mine.

Nothing in the way. I need that. Soon.

But right now—

I bring the foil packet to my teeth and tear it open.

Slowly, I roll the condom over my cock.

Then I place one hand over her mouth and the other on her hip.

She leans forward, arching her back, presenting herself to me.

I'm about to fuck Kay in the fucking kitchen.

And there isn't a single voice in my head telling me it's a bad idea.

She wakes up a reckless part of me.

A happy part of me.

I slide a finger into her mouth. She sucks. Greedy. Eager.

My tip strains against her.

Slowly, I slide inside her.

Fuck, she feels good.

I drive into her again and again.

Harder.

Faster.

Hard enough to pin her to the counter.

She sucks on my finger.

Groans against the digit.

Fuck, the feel of her soft body against mine.

Of her groans against my flesh.

It's fucking heaven.

I fill her with steady thrusts. Again and again.

She pulls back to gasp.

I claw at her back.

She rocks her hips. Groans my name.

It's a whisper. But it's enough to send me over the edge.

I bring my lips to her neck to suck on her skin.

Thrusting into her as I come.

I spill every drop.

Fuck.

It's like I haven't come in months.

Every part of me feels good. Relaxed. Spent.

But I need her coming too.

I muffle her with one hand. Slide the other down her torso.

And I stroke her. Harder and harder. Until she's groaning against my palm.

There. I keep that same pressure. That same pace.

I stroke her until she's coming on my hand, groaning against my palm, clutching at the tile.

I keep her pressed against the counter.

And I tilt her head and bring my lips to hers.

And I kiss her likc I'll never get enough of her.

Because I won't.

Not ever.

Chapter Thirty-Four

KAYLEE

"You sound happy," Grandma says. "Boy problems must be over."

I am happy. At least about the boy problems. The continuing vagueness about her condition—not so much. "It's good. He's... we're good."

"Good how?"

I fall onto my bed on my back. Press my cell to my ear. It's just good. What else is there to explain? "He forgave me and we—"

"Had makeup sex?"

"Grandma! I swear. You're a pervert."

"Everyone's a pervert, Kay-bear. It's just I don't give a fuck about hiding it. You won't either when you're my age."

"Maybe." A lot of my thoughts are about sex. Dirty sex. And so are Brendon's. And Em is always talking about it. And Dean is obviously dirty as hell. "There's merit to that argument."

"I hate to be a parent—"

"Then don't."

"But if your mother finds out about this—"

"I know. But she can't. I can't afford to rent my own place. And she and Dad can't afford to cover my expenses. This is the only way."

"What if it doesn't work out?"

That's a strong possibility. Brendon doesn't want complicated. And I'm complicated. This whole situation is hopelessly complicated. "I'll figure it out."

"You have somewhere to stay if you need to?"

"Why would I?"

"You never know with men."

"I know."

"You have a place or not?"

"Yeah." Ryan, Dean, and Walker have all made blanket *you can crash at my place anytime* offers. And plenty of my coworkers like me enough to offer their couch. "I have places."

"Good. Then tell me more about the boy."

"After you help me pick a weekend to visit. The prices are crazy for the next two weeks. But all the weekends after are good. All the way until Thanksgiving. And after. But you won't talk me out of coming before Thanksgiving."

"You should be focusing on school."

"It's a weekend."

She lets out a soft sigh. "It's too expensive."

"It's only a few hundred dollars. I have money saved."

She's quiet for a minute. "Anytime is fine."

"You sure?"

"Yeah."

I look to my computer screen. There are a million options. I find the soonest one that doesn't cost a fortune. It leaves on a Friday morning. The Friday morning after that concert.

I'll be tired at the airport, but that's all the better for sleeping on the plane.

"You think Mom can pick me up from Newark?" I fill in the form. Name. Address. Credit card.

"You're telling her about this?"

"I guess so." Mom has been arguing I shouldn't come. Grandma too. It doesn't make sense. At all. But I can't piece things together from voice alone. I need to look them in the eyes. I need to see for myself. And I will. I'll know in two and a half weeks. "There. I did it. I'll forward you the itinerary."

"Sure. Now tell me more about the guy."

"You know everything about him."

"I know he's tall and hot. That's it."

"He's quiet. Usually, with other people, he's more to himself. But when he's with me, he laughs. And when he smiles... it's like the clouds part and the birds sing. He has the most beautiful smile."

"You're smitten."

"I know. He... he's everything." I get caught up in my gushing. And, for a while, I forget why I'm flying back to Jersey.

I forget that Grandma is sick.

That she won't tell me how sick.

I forget that everything isn't going to be okay.

———

AFTER I HANG UP WITH GRANDMA, AND FINISH MOST OF my homework, I boot up a project that's been kicking around my head forever.

My first real piece of original fiction.

Only it's currently three sentences.

He has beautiful lips. They're soft, plush, the perfect shade of rose-pink. I want to dive into those lips and swim forever.

It's supposed to be a coming of age story. About a girl who wants a boy she shouldn't have.

I know, I know, it sounds autobiographical. But it's not. That's the problem. Everyone who reads this will think it's about me.

Or worse, that it's about me and Brendon.

This is the scene where they meet. I have it all in my head. He's across the room at a coffee shop. Sitting there. Reading. Some stranger she never expects to see again.

Until her best friends comes in. Kisses him. Introduces him as her boyfriend, the one who just moved to town.

I have plenty to say about his eyes. His concentration. His hands.

But after that...

It's scary, jumping into a project that will be all mine.

What if I can't do it?

I want to. I want to prove I can. To myself and to Grandma. If she's sicker than she's letting on, if there really isn't much time, then I want her to know I'll be okay.

That I'll keep doing the thing I love, the thing that brings us together.

It's an ugly thought.

If Grandma's dying.

But I let it flow through me. I let it tighten my throat. I let it sit on my chest. I let it make the warm room cold.

I let it make the—

Oh.

There's a knock on my door. Then Brendon's voice. "Hey."

"Hey yourself." My voice is soft. It's hitting me there. "Come in."

He steps inside. Presses the door closed with his back. He looks the same as always—jeans, t-shirt, bare feet—but there's something different about him today. An expression. I don't know how else to explain it.

"Kay." He moves to me. Drops to his knees in front of me. His palm presses against my cheek. A tear catches on his thumb. "What's wrong, angel?"

I want to collapse in his arms and tell him everything. Not just Grandma but all the other ugly stuff in my head. Those words are clutching at my throat.

I need someone to know.

I need them to know and to stay.

"Grandma. I don't know. She keeps saying she's okay. That Mom is over-reacting. That she has plenty of time. But I don't know if I believe her."

He takes my hand between his. Rubs the space between my thumb and forefinger with his thumb. "I'm sorry, Kay."

"Thanks." I blink and a tear catches on my lashes. I've been pushing this away for so long. Can I really hit the release valve? I might overflow. "I just... I don't know what to do. Everyone is treating me like a kid. Like they need to protect me from reality. So I don't know how bad it is. If she's dying... how am I supposed to live in the world without her?"

His eyes meet mine. He nods. An *I'm listening* kind of nod.

I like that he does that.

That he lets me talk.

Okay, I like almost everything about him.

More even.

"She was my first friend," I say. "She taught me so much. And she's still my confidant. As much as Em is. As much as you are."

"I remember her. She was—"

"Weird?"

His laugh is soft. "Yeah. Fun."

"She is. She's bold and strong and alive. How can someone like that be dying?"

He rubs my hand with his thumb. "It happens to all of us. I know that doesn't help. But—"

"I know. I just... I don't want it to be her. She's supposed to be around to read my first novel. To see my college graduation. To see my wedding. To meet my... well, I don't know if I'll have kids. But if I do. Their lives will be so much richer if they can meet her." I blink back another tear. "I'm sorry. You don't... you don't have anything and I'm—"

"It's not a contest."

"But—"

"Even if it was, you love your Grandma. She loves you. My parents—"

"You didn't love them?"

His eyes go to the hardwood floor. "Things were bad for so long. It's hard to remember anything but my mom staring at me like I was toxic."

"You're not."

He reaches up to brush a hair behind my ear. "Everybody hurts, Kay."

"Like the REM song?"

He laughs. "No. Well, yeah. You can tell me. Anything. You never need to apologize for what's in your head."

I hope that's true.

That he'll accept anything.

I press my lips together. I practice the words in my head. *Brendon, I have to tell you something. Something I've never told anyone. I'm broken. I'll always be broken. But I want you to love me anyway.*

I can't do it.

I can't open that valve either.

I need to shove *all* these feelings back to the box where they belong.

So I can make it through...

Through something. I don't know.

His fingers skim my temples as he pulls my glasses off my face. "You miss her?"

"Yeah. It's been good talking more on the phone. But she sounds so alive. Every time she laughs, I think it might be the last time."

He nods. "Are you going to see her?"

"I finally got tickets. In two weekends. It's the day after the concert actually."

"I'll take you to the airport."

"Yeah?"

"Of course." He runs his fingers through my hair. "Anything."

"Will you be there? If she... if she does die."

He stares up at me. "Your parents will realize—"

"I know."

"They won't let you stay here."

"I know."

"You're okay with that?"

Maybe. I don't know. But— "I'll need you there. I'm not sure I'll survive any other way."

"Then I'll be there."

It calms something in me. More than it should. I do trust him. With almost anything. "What was it like when you found out?"

"I got a call that they were in critical condition. By the time I got to the hospital, they were gone."

"Do you wish you'd said goodbye?"

"I don't think about it. I didn't have time. I had to figure out how to be a fucking parent. By the time I had space to breathe, it hurt less."

So he stayed busy. That's good advice. I can do that. I can do busy. But then— "Have you ever stopped and felt it?"

"It's hard to find a part of me that misses them."

"Really?"

"I know. I sound like a piece of shit—"

"No, I get it."

"I'm sure it will be worse for you, Kay. But I'll be there. With whatever you need."

I slink off my chair and wrap my arms around him.

He presses his lips to my forehead.

We stay linked together, breathing together, hearts beating together for ages.

Until there's a sound downstairs. The door opening. And Emma announcing her arrival.

Brendon plants a soft kiss on my lips. "Tomorrow."

I'm not sure what he's promising, just that I want it.

He pushes himself to his feet and slips into the hallway. His footsteps move toward his room.

I push myself into my chair.

Then Emma's footsteps are moving up the stairs and she's knocking on my open door. She peeks inside. "Kay. What happened?"

"Grandma."

She moves into my room and sits on the bed. "You want to talk about it?"

I nod.

And I do.

I tell her a lot.

But it's not enough.

I'm still lying to her about Brendon.

I'm still hiding a huge piece of myself from her. From everyone.

Chapter Thirty-Five

KAYLEE

I fall asleep with puffy eyes and a sore throat and I wake up lonely.

As long as I keep this to myself, I'm alone.

Brendon doesn't belong to me. He belongs to the version of Kaylee I convince him I am.

But that isn't me.

I need to tell him everything.

Soon.

Really, really soon.

———

IT'S A BEAUTIFUL MORNING. SOFT LIGHT FLOODS THE room. It bounces off the TV, casting glare over the incomprehensible action movie.

But it's not like I'm paying attention.

I'm sitting next to Brendon, turning over all my thoughts.

Wanting more.

More of... just more.

I need to *feel* he's mine. Because I'm not ready to tell him. Not yet.

My body is going to have to get this across.

He turns toward me. Brings his hand to my chin and pulls me into a kiss.

A deep, hard *you're mine* kind of kiss.

An *I love you* kind of kiss.

I've never said those words before. Not romantically.

I'm still not sure exactly what it means to love someone.

I press my lips to his. I tug at his t-shirt. "Emma's at work."

He nods.

"We could... I want to..." My cheeks flame. I'm still not good at this dirty talk thing.

His expression shifts. The doubt in his eyes fades into something a lot more demanding. "Tell me what you want, angel."

To be sure you're mine. I stare back into his eyes. I know exactly what I want. Now I have to ask for it.

He stares back at me. "Well?"

"I... I want to suck you off."

His pupils dilate. "Fuck, Kay, you know how to bury the lead."

My cheeks flush. "I'm sorry. I just. I've never, and—"

"Don't fucking apologize." He slides his hand into my hair and pulls me into a slow, deep kiss. "I love how earnest you are."

Love. The word does things to me. Things it didn't do yesterday.

My confession nags at my throat.

I want to tell him.

I'm going to.

Just... after this.

I swear.

He nips at my lips. "Fuck, you have no idea what you do to me."

"Right back at you." I press my forehead to his nose so I won't have to look him in the eyes. "I've never... will you teach me?"

He nods. "I like it rough."

"Are you going to keep warning me?"

"Probably." He wraps his arms around my waist and pulls me off the couch with him.

Brendon nods to the window. "You want the blinds closed?"

I bite my lip. "No." We're blocks from the beach. People might walk by. They might see. But the thought doesn't scare me. It makes my sex clench. It makes my pulse race.

"You want people to see you on your knees, angel?"

I swallow hard. "Yes."

He motions *come here.*

I do.

His lips crash into mine. It's a hard, hungry kiss. Need rises up from my stomach and pours from my lips to his.

Right now, I need to *feel* he's mine.

He breaks our kiss to pull my t-shirt over my head. Then he's undoing my bra and pushing the straps off my shoulders.

Desire races through my body as Brendon cups my breasts.

My eyes flutter closed as he draws circles around my nipples. His hands are strong, but they're gentle too. Every brush of his fingers sends another wave of desire straight to my core.

"Brendon..." I grab onto his t-shirt.

"Say it again, angel."

"Brendon..." Right now, the only thing I know is that I want him touching me.

He presses his hips against mine so I can feel his erection. Still, he keeps his focus on my chest as he toys with my nipples. His touch gets lighter and lighter until it's so light I can barely feel it. Then it's harder.

Harder.

Hard enough it hurts as much as it feels good.

But it feels really fucking good.

He drags his fingers over my collarbones. His eyes fix on mine.

His voice is as demanding as his gaze. "On your knees."

My sex clenches. I want to be on my knees for him. I want him in my mouth.

I don't know how it's possible, but somehow, I'm even hotter.

I lower myself onto my knees.

Brendon's hand curls into my hair. "I'm going to fuck that pretty mouth of yours."

Yes. Hell yes. I nod.

"Unzip my jeans and take out my cock."

I bring my hands to the waistband of his jeans and unzip. My palm presses against his boxers. That's Brendon under that thin layer of cotton.

Desire pools in my core. I want this more than I want to get off.

I pull his jeans to his feet. Then the boxers.

I take a moment to soak in the sight of him. He's thick. Long. My fingers go to the arrow-head shaped tip.

He feels good in my hand.

I lean in to brush my lips against him. At first, it's just a taste, and fuck does he taste good. Like skin and sweat and something distinctly him.

"Open your mouth," he commands.

I do.

He brings his other hand to my head. "Keep your hands at your sides, angel. I'm in control here. If it's too much, tug on my wrist."

"Yes." I press my palms into my sides and pull my lips apart.

His holds my head in place as he shifts into my mouth. I run my tongue over his head, savoring every groan that falls off his lips.

He tastes good and that's Brendon in my mouth.

I want him.

I want this.

His grip tightens as he thrusts deeper. My lips stretch around him. My tongue presses against the underside of his tip.

His pace stays slow, but, still, I have to relax my throat to keep from gagging.

I have to press my palms into my hips to keep from reaching out to touch him.

He looks down at me, his expression equal parts caring and ravenous. He runs his hand through my hair.

It settles on the back of my head. "I'm going to come in that pretty mouth of yours."

My sex clenches. I want that too.

I nod, sucking on him. I suck harder. Harder. I need more of him. I need him coming in my mouth.

Something in Brendon's expression shifts. Some animal part of him takes over as he presses his palm into the back of my head.

His movements get harder. He thrusts into my mouth hard and fast. He thrusts deep enough I gag. But I fucking like it.

I like how dirty I feel.

I like being a vessel for his pleasure.

Feeling like I'm his.

I dig my nails into my skin to contain the desire building in my core. To keep from gagging.

I look up at him. Watch his dark eyes fill with pleasure, his lips part with a groan.

"Fuck, Kaylee." He tugs at my hair.

His movements get harder, faster. He's close.

And then he's there, filling my mouth. He tastes good and it feels good, knowing I brought Brendon all that pleasure.

Once I'm sure he's spilled every drop, I swallow hard.

He reaches down to take my hands. Then he pulls me up and presses my body against his.

His lips find mine. His tongue claims my mouth.

He pushes my shorts to my knees as he breaks the kiss. "Sit on the couch and spread your legs."

I stumble, falling back onto the soft couch. I've sat here a hundred times. No, a thousand.

But never like this.

Brendon's dark eyes light up as he takes a long look at me. He moves closer. Closer.

Then he's kneeling in front of me.

He pulls my shorts off my feet. His hands close around my thighs, just above my knees.

In one swift motion, he pushes my legs apart. My knees press into the slick leather fabric of the couch. I fall onto the cushion.

Brendon drags his lips up my inner thigh. Closer. Closer. Closer.

There.

His lips brush against me.

My thighs fight his hands. I want more. I want all of him.

But I also want to give myself to him.

I want to be his.

He teases me mercilessly. He blows hot air against my clit. Then cold. Then he's brushing his lips against me. Then it's slow flicks of his tongue, so soft I can barely feel them. He gets every inch of me.

Pleasure builds in my core. I'm ready to overflow, but he's not pushing me toward the edge. He's only building my need.

"Please." I tug at his hair.

Still, he teases me. His tongue stays soft and slow. The pleasure is diffuse. It's everywhere. I feel good in a way that hurts. In a way that begs for release.

"Brendon, please." I press my legs against his hands.

His grip stays firm. He looks up at me, his brown eyes on fire. "You'll come when I say you come, angel."

The edge to his voice makes my sex clench. I can't believe it, but I want him in control of my orgasm.

I can't believe how much I'm willing to give myself to him.

How deeply I trust him.

Still, he teases me. I tug at his hair and press my thighs against his hands. It does nothing to contain how badly I need release. I'm wound up. I'm close. And I desperately need to go over the edge.

It's like he can read me. His motions get harder. Faster. He takes his time ramping up his speed and pressure. The intensity makes it feel like hours pass.

He goes faster.

Harder.

His soft, wet tongue is heaven.

His fingers curl into my thighs as he licks me.

The tension in my sex builds to a crescendo. Almost. So fucking close.

There.

With the next flick of his tongue, I unravel.

I groan. I writhe. I tug his hair hard enough to rip it out.

He holds me in place, still flicking his tongue against me. It's too much pressure. I can't take it.

"Brendon." I try to press my legs against him, but his grip is too firm.

I'm staying on this couch, his mouth on me, as long as he wants me here.

Fuck, the pressure is intense. I can barely take it. But I can. As painful as it is, I don't want him to stop.

He flicks his tongue against me. His motions get harder. Faster. It's still intense. It still hurts. But now the pleasure outweighs everything else.

I get lost in the bliss growing inside me. A few more flicks of his tongue and I'm there.

I scream his name as I go over the edge.

I shake. I writhe. I tug at his hair.

I feel my orgasm all the way in the tips of my toes.

This time, Brendon releases me. He pushes himself up, takes my hands, and pulls me into his arms.

His touch gets soft. Gentle.

Like he thinks I'm his.

But I'm not.

Not until he knows every part of me.

Chapter Thirty-Six

KAYLEE

Saturday night is busy. And I'm closing. I get caught up in the noise and the demands. I don't stop to rest or to think until I'm tallying my receipts. Even then, it takes all my mental energy to tap the numbers into my phone.

The chatter of work drifts away on my ride home. I park my bike in the garage. Slip into the house. Climb the stairs as quietly as possible.

All the lights are out except for the one in Brendon's bedroom.

Emma's asleep.

I'm about to slip into my room and find a way to stay busy—to keep that confession from rising up my throat, to keep my thoughts of Grandma stuffed into the box where they belong—when Brendon pulls his door open.

He's standing there, one hand in the front pocket of his jeans, the other on the doorframe, his t-shirt hugging his shoulders just so.

There's practically a *beautiful distraction* arrow pointing at his head. Like something in a cartoon.

Already, the words are clawing at my throat.

I need to tell him.

I need him to know and to stay.

To still love me.

Does he love me now?

I don't know. I'm sure he loves me as a friend, that he has for a long time, but this whole *in love* thing is new. Confusing.

He reaches for me. His arm slides around my waist. In one quick motion, he pulls me inside his.

He stares down at me with those intense, dark eyes. Right now, I know exactly what's in them. Affection. Trust. Need.

His eyelids flutter together.

He leans down.

I rise to my tiptoes.

Our lips brush. Just barely. But it's enough to fill my body with warmth. With need. With love.

My fingers go slack. My bag hits the hardwood floor with a light thud. It's loud enough to wake Emma, but I don't care.

I don't care about anything but getting my hands in his thick, dark hair.

I don't care about anything but kissing him back.

He tastes like whiskey. It shouldn't taste good, but it does. It tastes like him.

I kiss him harder.

Deeper.

I shift my hips against his. Tug at his hair. Groan against his lips.

He feels better than he tastes.

He's everything I want.

Well, almost.

I can't risk that.

But, then, I can't swallow this down much longer.

I kiss him until my lips are numb. When I finally come up for air, he's staring back into my eyes.

"Nice to see you too." He pulls the elastic band from my hair, undoing my ponytail. "Work good?"

"Busy." *I have to tell you something. I'm broken. I know you won't believe me, so let me explain.* I rise to my tiptoes. Kiss him again. Anything to keep the words from spilling.

He untucks my shirt. Undoes the top button. Then the next. His fingers brush my collarbones. My chest. My stomach.

I need those hands on my body.

I need one more time pressed against him—just in case he doesn't keep loving me.

Just in case he runs away.

I pull back with a heavy sigh. My eyes go straight to his. *Brendon, I have to tell you something.*

It's been eating at me for weeks. Longer even. I wanted to tell him when it happened. I wanted to tell him the first time I had an ugly thought.

I want him to save me from it.

I know it doesn't work that way. I get it now. But there's still a part of me that thinks he can wipe everything away.

No, I know he can.

Just only for a little while.

"You're thinking something." His fingertips skim my jawline.

I'm thinking a lot. And it's all on the tip of my tongue. Either I go back to my room or I tell him. Those are the two options. I'm not sure which is worse.

His palm presses against my cheek.

Fuck, his skin against mine—

The comfort of the gesture—

I need that right now.

And I need him to know.

I stare back at him. "That I need a shower."

He motions to his bathroom. "I'll join you."

Yes. That's perfect.

I nod. Follow him into the bathroom. Take my time stripping him out of every layer. He does the same.

Then I step into the tub and I soak up every drop of him.

AFTER, WE HELP EACH OTHER TOWEL DRY AND COLLAPSE in his bed.

I shouldn't sleep here. I shouldn't even be here with Emma in the next room.

But I can't tear myself away.

It feels too good, having his warm, wet skin pressed against mine.

He wraps his arms around me. One under the crook of my neck. The other over my waist, his palm resting on my stomach.

I'm in his arms, my back against his chest, his breath warming my neck.

I should be melting.

I should be forgetting everything.

But those words are screaming at me.

Brendon, I have to tell you something.

It's a simple enough start. Ominous, yeah, but simple.

"Hey." He runs his fingers through my wet hair. They skim my ear. My neck. My shoulder. It's impossibly soft. Like he's trying to drive me crazy.

"Hey yourself." I lean into his touch. My eyelids flutter together. Fuck, that feels good. He feels good. All of this— I can't lose it.

But I can't keep hiding this.

I need him to know.

It should be simple. I need Brendon to know. So I tell him.

But my mouth is sticky.

My hands are numb.

Everything is heavy.

"Your grandma?" He traces a line down my arm, all the way to the tip of my index finger, then back up to my shoulder. It's slow. Sweet. Affectionate.

He does it again, only this time he traces my middle finger.

Then my ring.

Then my pinkie.

We lie in silence for minutes. Until I can't feel the bliss of his touch. Until I can't feel anything but the weight of this secret crushing my chest.

It's everywhere. In the air. In the moonlight. In the soft cotton sheets. In his fingertips.

On my lips.

"Kay." His lips brush my ear. My neck. "Whatever it is, you don't have to talk about it."

I nod.

He kisses me again. It's a sweet kiss. Not *I want you* or *I need you* or *I'm going to fuck you again*.

It's *I love you*.

"But you can." He draws circles on my shoulder. "Anything."

"I want to." I do. Really, I do. My desire is so big and bright it's casting everything else in glare. Every single one of my thoughts is tuned to this frequency.

"Yeah?" He places a kiss on my shoulder.

"But I don't want you to look at me differently."

"I won't."

"How can you promise that?"

"Did you kill someone?"

"No."

"Do you really want to fuck Dean?"

My laugh breaks up the tension in my shoulders. "Murder and lust for Dean are equally bad in your eyes?"

"Fuck no." He presses his palm into my stomach to pull me closer. "Lust for Dean is a million times worse."

"Really?"

"You have no fucking idea what it does to me, the way he flirts with you."

But I do. I see the way his jaw cricks, the way his fists form, the way his eyes fill with jealousy. "He does it to get to you."

"It works."

"It did work. We're here."

"You're giving him credit for this?"

"Well... doesn't he deserve a little?"

"Maybe." The playfulness falls from his voice. It's back to soft and sweet. "But I'm not giving him credit."

"That doesn't seem fair."

"What is?"

"True." None of this is fair. Not that I need a pill to feel okay. Not that Grandma is sick. Not that my parents are middle class when Brendon and Emma's are rich.

But it's not fair that their parents are gone. Or that I was born smart. Or with a nice figure.

Or that he's almost mine.

That really isn't fair and it's all in my favor.

"Life isn't fair. But you can't use that as an argument for everything," I say. "Otherwise, what's the point of fairness? Of justice?"

"You're such a smart girl, Kay."

"Why don't I like the sound of that?"

"You should." He intertwines his fingers with mine.

"There's nothing you can tell me that will change the way I look at you."

I shake my head. "You can't promise that."

"Maybe I lack imagination, but I can't think of a single thing."

Because he'd never think of this. I have everyone convinced I have my shit together. And, mostly, I do.

It's just, sometimes I don't.

I've been healthy for a long time now. But that can't last forever.

"I don't want you to promise that." It's more that I know he can't. That it will hurt too much if he does. "I don't want you to promise you won't leave. Because you might. And I don't want you to stay out of obligation."

"Kay..."

"Don't tell me there's nothing. Because you don't know what this is."

"Okay." His voice is some tone I've never heard. An understanding one.

He drags his fingertips back up my arm. All the way to my shoulder.

It's funny. I'm naked. I've been naked this whole conversation, but I feel like I'm about to strip out of everything.

This might scare him away.

I might lose him forever.

I suck a breath between my teeth. My exhale is heavy enough my hands shake. No. They're still shaking.

I'm shaking.

"I..." Too many words rise up in my throat. They knock together. They take over my head and my lips and my heart.

Then he's running his fingers through my hair with that impossibly soft touch.

And I'm still terrified to lose him.

But it's scarier, the thought of being alone with this forever.

"I don't know a better way to say this." My hands are shaking, but I press on. "I'm broken."

He doesn't say anything. He just combs his fingers through my hair again.

"I have depression. I guess that's normal. Relatively. But I... last year. That was when it started. It was before Grandma's heart attack. It wasn't because of anything. Everything got hard. Heavy. Food didn't taste as good. My favorite books no longer entertained. It was like I was moving through water. It took so much energy to make dinner or clean my room. Or even get out of bed in the morning. I couldn't sleep, but I didn't want to do anything else."

His fingertips brush my neck. My shoulders.

I can't see his face. I have no idea how he's taking this. But I can't wait to know.

I need to get this out. All of it.

"Then I started having these thoughts. I'd be driving Mom's car up the 405 and I'd think about crashing into the divider. Or I'd see sleeping pills in the cabinet and think about downing the bottle. Or look at some tall building, and try to figure out if I could actually get to the roof. I didn't make plans to kill myself. But the thought of it—of not hurting anymore—it was tempting. And I... I felt like everyone would be better off if I wasn't dragging them down. Then I'd think about how sad my parents would be and I'd feel guilty and that would only make it worse."

He pulls me closer.

"I understand now. It's my messed-up brain chemistry. I take medication. I see a therapist. She helped me under-stand a lot of it. And the medications stops most of the thoughts. But not always. Sometimes they flood my head, and I can't stop thinking I'll never be good enough. Sometimes, things get heavy again. It's short phases now. But it might be longer one day. Medications stop working. Life gets stressful. And I... one day, those voices might be loud enough to convince me to do it."

I'm still shaking.

I want, so badly, to turn around and look in his eyes. To figure out what he's thinking. But I can't. If it's bad, I'll lose my nerve. Then I'll never get this out.

I take a deep breath and exhale slowly. "I need you to know. It's not a phase. It's forever. I'm always going to be broken—"

"You're not broken."

"You can use another word, but it will mean the same thing. My brain is fucked up. It will always be fucked up. I'm always going to be fighting the voice that tells me I'm worthless. That everyone would be better off if I wasn't around. Can you really love someone like that? Someone who might fall and end everything?"

"Are you thinking about it now?"

"No. It's been awhile since I've really considered it. But I still have fleeting thoughts. And I always will. I just... I want you to know the reality. I see how you look at me. Like I'm heaven sent. But I'm not."

Slowly, he turns me around. His hand goes to my chin. He tilts my head so we're face-to-face.

I keep my gaze on his chest for as long as I can stand it.

My eyes meet his.

He's... I don't know. I just don't.

He cups the back of my head with his hand. "Thank you."

What?

I...

Huh?

"It's an honor, you sharing that with me."

What? I blink a few times. Everything gets blurry.

I'm crying.

"You... you don't want to leave?" A tear rolls down my cheek and falls off my jaw. It lands on my shoulder.

"Never."

"But I... You... You hate complicated."

"No. I just never met someone worth complicated." He stares back into my eyes. "Are you taking care of yourself? Taking your meds? Seeing your therapist?"

"Yeah."

"And everything else?"

I nod. "Aren't... aren't you scared?"

"I'm always scared of bad shit happening to you. But this, no—I'm not scared that you have depression. Or that you've been suicidal."

"But one day... I might... what if I..."

"You think about it that much?"

"I did. It was scary. I didn't trust myself. I guess I still don't."

He stares back into my eyes. "Nobody can promise they'll be okay forever. I don't care that you need a little chemical help, Kay. You're still the sun in my sky. You're gonna struggle, yeah, but I want to be there for that. I want to be the person holding you up when shit is bad."

"I... you... you're not leaving?"

"No."

I stare back at him, blinking away tears until my vision is blurry.

He rests his palm on my check and wipes my eyes. "Are these happy or sad?"

"Both. And everything else. I... I just can't. I thought... I thought you'd leave."

He shakes his head. "There isn't a single part of me that wonders if you're good enough for me."

"Really?"

"Not even a molecule."

The weight lifts off my chest.

My hands stop shaking.

I...

He...

Maybe things will be okay.

He leans in to press his lips to mine.

It's an *I love you*.

We haven't said the words.

But I can feel it.

He knows.

And he's staying.

And he loves me anyway.

Chapter Thirty-Seven

BRENDON

K aylee steps onto the stairs with the world's most content smile. She's already in some adorable sundress. One with a blue floral print and thin straps.

Her eyes brighten as they meet mine.

I have to force myself to direct my attention back to my sister.

This is giving too much away.

And I'm not doing enough to check in with Em. The school year isn't as big a deal for her—she started college officially back in June with summer courses, and she's only going part-time—but it's still a transition.

"You've been working more." I snap my piece of bacon in half and take a bite. It's salty, chewy, rich. Perfect.

"I like money." Emma stirs another splash of cream into her coffee. "I'm not going to suffer another 'you should be in school full-time lecture,' so if that's where you're going you can save your breath." She turns to watch Kay step into the main room. "Where are you going dressed like that?"

Kay's laugh is nervous. She twirls a long, blond strand around her finger. "With my hair a mess and no makeup?"

"That's a mess?" Emma shakes her head, sending crimson hair in every direction. "Life is unfair."

"True." Kay's eyes meet mine. Her smile gets wider. She's stupid happy.

Last night meant a lot to her.

I'm still turning it over. I'm going to be turning it over for a long fucking time.

It terrifies me, the thought of Kay doing anything to hurt herself. It hits me like a punch to the gut.

But, mostly, I'm humbled by her sharing that with me.

Fuck, I want to find every place she hurts and destroy it.

I don't think she's broken. But if she is, I want to be the glue that holds her together. I want that as much as I want the shop to succeed. As much as I want Em to thrive. As much as I want anything.

"There's more eggs and bacon in the pan." I nod to the kitchen. "And coffee."

"I'll make a tea." She nearly floats into the kitchen.

Is that all from spilling her secret?

Fuck, I can't imagine the weight of that.

Taking all that on her own—she's so fucking strong, so fucking brave.

Emma turns back to me. "Really? No lecture?"

"You want to stay part-time." I bring my mug to my lips. Damn. This coffee is good. Nutty. Rich. With that hint of toffee. It's the best fucking coffee I've ever had. Or maybe that's the smile on Kay's face. The honor and responsibility of her placing all her trust in me.

"Nothing about how I should work a little harder and get done in four years instead of languish for eight?" Emma takes a long sip. "Really?"

"You've worked retail for two years. You know what it's like. You know you'll be doing that forever if you don't go to college." The coffee warms me everywhere. No, that's Kay. "If you want to own a boutique one day, you'll need those business classes. Trust me."

"I do. It's just..." She scoops her eggs onto her fork. "Weird that you're being reasonable."

"I'm always reasonable." I eat the other half of my bacon slice.

Emma laughs so hard she slaps the table. "No." She turns to Kaylee, now pouring hot water into her mug. "Back me up here."

Kay laughs. "Always isn't the right word."

"Yeah. It's weird. It's like... like you're happy." Emma stares at me like she's picking me apart.

"I am." I really fucking am.

Emma tilts her head to one side. "Why? You're never happy."

"I own a quarter of the shop. We're putting a new sign up next Friday. With a logo I designed. We're getting rid of all the old shit that doesn't suit us. I finally talked Ryan into interviewing another artist or two." My eyes meet Kay's as she takes her seat. And that. Her. "Why wouldn't I be happy?"

"Because you're Brendon." Emma brings another scoop of eggs to her lips. Chews. Swallows. "It's good. I'm happy for you. Just weird."

"He's always weird." Kaylee smiles at me. "That isn't new."

"True." Emma turns to Kay. "And you're happy too. Satisfied. Like you... like that hairstyle is really working for you."

"It is." Kaylee dunks her tea bag. "It's great."

"When did you... try it out yesterday? Weren't you working all night?" Emma asks.

Kay giggles. "After."

"After. Hmm." Emma shoots me a *stop eavesdropping* look.

I should let them talk. I finish my last bite. Even these eggs taste better than usual. The room is brighter, the air is sweeter, the coffee's bolder.

Everything is better.

I bring my plate to the sink. Finish my last cup of coffee. Watch Emma and Kaylee giggle over their incredibly obvious metaphor.

"I have an appointment." I look to Emma. "You're working this afternoon?"

"Yeah, till closing. I'll get dinner at work." Emma turns to Kay. "Are you closing again?"

Kaylee nods. "It's the best shift in the summers."

"But it means I don't see you weekends," Emma says.

"Except early." Kaylee motions to the table.

"Yeah, except early." Emma leans in to whisper to Kay.

The two of them giggle.

"Keep an eye on her, all right, Kay?" I grab my keys and take a step toward the door.

"Sure." Kay smiles back at me.

"Hey!" Emma feigns offense. "Why don't you ever tell me to watch Kay?"

"Keep an eye on Kay. All right?" I ask.

Emma laughs. "Perfect."

I slide into my shoes and I slip out the door.

And I nearly float to the fucking shop.

I wait until I'm inside to text Kay.

Brendon: I'll be done at noon. I'll meet you at home.

Kaylee: You think I wait around for you all day?

Brendon: I think you read, study, or watch TV when Emma is at work.

Kaylee: Maybe.

Brendon: Aren't you writing a novel?

Kaylee: Yeah, but not right now. It's the weekend. I need a little incentive if you want me at your beck and call.

Brendon: Trust me. You want to meet me at noon.

Kaylee: For...?

Brendon: For a surprise.

Kaylee: Which is?

Brendon: I'll see you at noon.

Kaylee: Maybe. Or maybe I'll be out.

Brendon: You won't.

Kaylee: How do you know?

Brendon: You can't come on my cock if I'm not there.

———

KAYLEE TAPS HER FINGERS AGAINST THE DASH. "YOU really aren't going to tell me?"

"You struggle with the concept of surprise," I tease.

"No. I just like knowing." She grabs the aux cable and plugs it into her phone. A moment later *S&M* is pouring from the speakers. She looks to me with a coy smile. "Who are you imagining?"

I arch a brow.

"Me or Dean."

"You." I leave one hand on the wheel and place the other on her leg. I rub her soft skin with my finger.

It makes her shudder.

Fuck, the moan that falls off her lips is distracting.

All that heavy shit is still in the air. We'll have to ride through the storm soon. But not yet. She's facing reality as soon as she gets off that plane.

I want to make the next two weeks—well, nearly two weeks—as blissful as possible.

Rhianna purrs about her love of whips and chains.

I slide my hand under Kaylee's dress. Higher and higher, until my thumb is brushing the edges of her panties.

Her fingers dig into the seat. "You're a tease."

"You just figuring that out?"

She shakes her head. "It's more obvious some times than others."

I can't help but smile. She does that to me. She makes me stupid happy.

I turn my attention back, but I keep my hand on her thigh, my thumb tracing the edge of her panties.

Marvin Gaye serenades us.

I turn on Santa Monica Boulevard.

Then into the little strip mall on the right and grab the first spot I find.

Kaylee looks around carefully. First, the donut shop. Then the juice place. Then our destination. Then the liquor store. "I don't really like donuts."

"Guess again."

She motions to the juice place. "Lunch."

"No."

Her eyes go to our destination. A Perfect Romance. "Brendon Kane. You... you're not..."

"I am."

I pull my hand away.

Her sigh is heavy. Needy. "You... you're... why..."

I undo my seatbelt and step out of the car. Fuck, there are a million reasons why. "Because I want to be sure you're thinking of me every fucking night."

She gets out of the car and presses the door shut. Her eyes find mine. They're still dumbfounded.

"You don't have a vibrator."

Her cheeks flush. "People can hear you."

I hit the lock and slide my keys into my pocket. "People should hear me." I slide my arm around her waist. "People should know how much I love it when you come."

Her blush deepens. "You... you do this on purpose."

"Maybe."

"Yeah. You do." She rests her head on my shoulder. "I'm not sure why I talk to you."

"You want people knowing."

"No." She shakes her head. "I... aren't you supposed to do this somewhere dark and quiet? Or online? It's the twenty-first century."

I lead her toward the store, pull the door open for her. "I want it now." I lean in to whisper in her ear. "I want to go straight home and use whatever we buy to make you come until you pass out."

"Oh." Her blush spreads to her chest. Her teeth sink into her lower lip. "I guess that's acceptable."

"Just acceptable?"

She nods. "Don't push your luck."

"My luck?"

"Yeah. Your luck." Her eyes go wide as she takes in the store. She presses her lips together. "I... I'm on birth control. If you... if you're sure you're clean."

"I got tested last month." A few days before her birthday. Three months earlier than scheduled. Yeah, I knew exactly what I was doing. And it was fucked. But at least I'm safe. "There hasn't been anyone for a long time."

"I want to try it without a condom. If you do." She looks up at me. "Do you?"

My cock threatens to take over. "Yeah." Why are we here? I could be fucking her in the backseat. I could feel every inch of her flesh against mine.

"Oh. Good."

"Fucking great."

"Fucking great." She moves to the racks of lingerie in front. Flips through a set of animal print thongs. "Why is cheetah print sexy?" Her voice is nervous. But it's plenty loud.

We are the only people in here, besides the salesgirl.

But still...

Her confidence fills me with a pride that goes all the way to my bones.

"Brendon?" She holds up a cheetah print thong. "Can you explain it to me?"

"It's a thong."

She laughs. "I get that part. But the animal print?"

I shrug. "Fuck if I know." I join her at the rack. Go straight to a row filled with lacy pink stuff. "Now this—" I pick out a sheer pink bra and panty set. "This is sexy."

"Why?"

"You really have to ask?"

"Have to is relative."

"It's sweet. Innocent. Angelic."

Her cheeks flush. "It's too small. I'm the next size up."

I trade it in for the next size. "I'm buying this for you."

"I thought we were here for a—" She lowers her voice. "For something else."

"You can say vibrator. They have a whole wall of them."

"An entire wall?" She scans the room for said wall. "How am I supposed to know what to get?"

"We could ask the salesgirl for help."

Kaylee's eyes go wide. Her lips press together. She shakes her head *no way*. "I can ask you for help."

Perfect. I press my palm into her lower back and lead her toward said wall. Only I take the long way.

Kaylee gawks as we pass a wall of porn. She stops to stare at all the lifelike dildos.

"It... it has veins." She reaches out to touch one of the packages. It's modeled after some porn star. "Is that sexy?"

"I'd know?"

"True. But... it's just..." She tilts her head to the other side. "Why?"

"Capitalism."

She laughs. "Of course." She looks up at me. "I like punk rock anarchist commie Brendon. But I think... I think whatever you'd call this guy—the small business owner who shops at Ikea—I think he's more you."

"You'd feel different if you appreciated The Ramones—"

She laughs. "And you'd feel differently if you appreciated The Smiths. But no one is perfect." She turns to check out the rack behind us. Ball gags. Then bondage gear. She picks up an under the bed restraints kit. "Do you have one of these?"

"Of course."

"Or... do you use rope with the bed?"

"Both."

She turns it over to read the label. "You, um, we haven't that much. Maybe we could... try it again? Soon."

"Today?"

"Today is soon."

"You sure?" I'm already thinking about it. Fuck, I'm already getting hard.

"Positive." She replaces the restraints kit then moves forward. Right to the wall of vibrators—and it really is a wall of demo units. "Shit. You weren't kidding."

I nod.

"How do I pick just one..."

"How do you fuck yourself?"

"Uh, well, I just... you mean, specifically?"

I force myself to stare into her eyes. "Yeah."

"I guess I..." Her cheeks flush, but she pushes through. "I rub my clit."

"You ever fuck yourself with your fingers?"

"No. Not usually."

"You want to?"

She picks up a bullet vibrator and turns it over in her hand. "Um... I wouldn't mind. But I'd rather... I'd rather it be you."

I reach over her to pick up a demo unit. It's big enough to fuck her with, but it's still small and sleek. "Something like this?" I turn it on and press it against her fingertip.

She stares up at me. "Maybe."

I turn it off. Set it down. Find the rabbit style vibrator at the end of the row.

Kaylee's eyes go wide as she takes it in. "Oh. So that's... and then that's... and it just..."

"Yeah."

She swallows hard. "That seems intense."

"It is." At least, that's what I hear. "You want to try it?"

"Yeah. I do."

Chapter Thirty-Eight

BRENDON

Kaylee's cheeks flush a deeper red with every step she takes upstairs. Her gait speeds. She stumbles over the top step. "I, uh... I'm kind of distracted."

"Thinking about being tied to my bed?"

She takes an unsteady step into the hallway. "You know that. Don't brag."

No deal. Thinking about her tied to my bed, forced to take every ounce of pleasure I want to give her—

If I can't brag about that then what good is bragging?

Her hips sway as she moves into the bedroom. Fuck, her ass is perfect. I want to watch it slam into my pelvis as I fuck her from behind.

I want her every fucking way I can have her.

I tear off the toy's packaging as I step into my bedroom. Cardboard and paper flutters to the ground. I need to clean up all the evidence of that. But not now.

Now, I need her coming until she can't take it anymore.

"Take off your dress," I demand.

She nods. Her eyes get bright. Bold. She stares back at

me, daring me to resist touching her, as she unzips her dress and slides it to her ankles.

Fuck, she's wearing that pair of panties. The one with *Paradise* plastered on the crotch.

My voice drops right to that demanding tone. "You wear that for me, angel?"

She nods.

I move close enough to touch her. Toss the vibrator on the bed. Trace the outline of her bra with my fingertips. "This too?"

"Yes." Her voice is dripping with confidence. "I wore my dress to torture you too." She slides her hand under my t-shirt and presses her palm against my stomach. "It gets me off, driving you out of your mind."

"What else gets you off, angel?"

"Thinking about you."

"Specifically."

"About you pinning me against the wall so hard my cheek is pressed against it. Us in some semi-secluded public place. You exposing my breasts, playing with them like you need me on display."

Blood rushes to my cock. "What else?"

"You throwing me on the bed. Peeling off my jeans. Spanking me. Holding me down and fucking me from behind." Her cheeks flush. "You're not the only one with dirty thoughts, Brendon. You're not the only one who fantasizes about it rough."

Two weeks ago, I wouldn't have believed her.

But now, I do.

It's still hard for me to wrap my head around sweet, innocent Kay wanting it as rough as I do.

But the fire in her eyes—

The way she's standing strong and proud—

She's not a clueless girl.

She's a woman who knows what she wants.

And, fuck, I love her even more like this.

I blink a few times.

I love her.

It's so fucking obvious, but I've never put it together. I've never thought about loving someone. Not like this.

I love every fucking inch of her.

Everything that brings her joy.

Everyplace she hurts.

I want her happy before I want me happy.

But then that's been the case for a long fucking time.

"Brendon." She slides her hand up my stomach, over my chest. "Are you going to leave me waiting?"

"What do you think?"

"I don't think you have it in you. Not today." She rises to her tiptoes and presses her lips to mine. Her other hand goes to my hips. Then she's cupping my cock over my jeans. "You're so hard."

"Yeah."

"Fuck me."

"Not yet." I bring my hands to her waist and pull her body against mine. My lips find hers. Fuck, she tastes so good, and the way she groans against my lips—

She's needy.

Eager.

I want to fuck her. I want to bury myself inside her.

But I want her screaming for it first.

I want her so desperate for my cock that she doesn't have another thought in her head.

That she's sure she'll never think anything again.

I slide my hands up her back, unhook her bra, and slide it off her shoulders.

Kaylee's arms drop to her sides. Then they're on my hips and she's arching her back, rubbing against me.

She purrs as I toy with her nipple.

I bring my lips to hers.

Her kiss is hard. Hungry. Needy.

I tease her as I slide my tongue around hers.

I tease her until she's shaking. Then I move to her nipple and tease her more.

Her pink nails dig into my skin.

Her hips rock against mine.

She needs me so fucking badly.

I drag my lips down her neck, over her collarbone, to her chest. I take her nipple into my mouth and suck softly.

Her hands find my hair. "Fuck."

I do it again.

"Brendon." Her hips rock against me. Her hand knots in my hair. "God."

I suck harder.

Her groan echoes around the room.

I toy with her until she's shaking. Then I bring my hand between her thighs and I stroke her over her panties.

She's fucking dripping.

I can feel it even with all that cotton in the way.

"Fuck." She tugs at my hair.

She bucks against me. Again and again.

I push her closer to the edge.

Suck a little harder.

Stroke a little softer.

I watch need spill over her expression. Her eyelids press together. Her brow knits. Her teeth sink into her lip.

She's so fucking close.

But she's not coming on my hand.

Not today.

I bring my hands to her hips and push her onto the bed.

She falls onto her back. Looks up at me with a mix of need and affection in her eyes.

"Scoot up and put your hands over your head," I demand.

She holds my gaze as she moves up the bed.

Her hands go to her hips.

She pushes her panties to her knees then kicks them off her ankles.

Then she brings her hands over her head.

Fuck, she's baiting me.

If it was someone else, it would annoy me.

But on her I fucking love it.

I pull my bondage rope from the bedside table and place my body next to hers.

She looks up at me, watching me tie a knot around her wrists and tie it to the railing of the bed.

Her breath hitches in her throat as I test the restraints.

Her fingers curl into her palms.

Her teeth sink into her lips.

She fucking likes being bound.

It's not exactly news. I could tell that last time. But I was too caught up in finally having her to notice just how much she wanted it.

Kay.

My angel.

My demanding dirty girl.

Fuck, the desire in her eyes is making my balls tight.

I need to be inside her.

But this first.

This for as long as she can fucking stand it.

I press her knees apart and kneel between them.

She looks up at me with a plea in her soft green eyes. "Brendon. Please."

Fuck, the way my name rolls off her lips.

Like she needs me more than she's ever needed anything.

Like I really do replace all the hurt in her life with pleasure.

I know I can't do that everywhere. The whole supportive boyfriend thing—fuck, I have no idea if I'm capable of that.

But I can do this.

I can satisfy her here.

I pick up the vibrator and turn it on.

Kaylee gasps at the sound of the buzz.

Nervousness spills into her expression.

But there's trust in her eyes.

Fuck, I need every ounce of that.

I need it in my bones.

I need it a hell of a lot more than I need to be inside her.

And I really fucking need to be inside her.

I tap the toy against her inner thigh. It's on the lowest setting, but, still, it makes her jump. Well, as much as she can jump bound to my bed.

My eyes lock with hers.

She nods *keep going*.

I bring it higher. Press it against her soft skin.

Her toes curl.

Again, she nods *keep going*.

Higher.

Higher.

Almost.

I press it against her clit.

"Fuck." Her pupils dilate. Her nails sink into her palm.

I keep it pressed against her.

Her eyelids flutter together.

A groan falls off her lips.

Another.

She tugs at her restrains. "More."

I grab the lube from the bedside table, slather it over the toy, and bring it to her cunt.

The brush of it makes her jump.

"Fuck." She arches her back, rocking her hips. Her eyes meet mine. They plead *now*.

Slowly, I slide the toy inside her.

Her eyes go wide.

Her thighs press against my legs.

Her toes curl into the bed.

Fuck, it's so beautiful watching pleasure spill over her face.

I bring the rabbit ears to her clit.

Her breath catches in her throat.

A groan falls off her lips.

She arches her back, pushing the toy deeper.

Every single part of her is begging for more.

It's the best thing I've ever seen.

Slowly, I push the toy deeper.

Then I bring it out, all the way to the tip.

Her eyelids flutter open. She stares up at me, those green eyes heavy with need. "Please."

I push the toy inside her then pull it out.

I do it again.

A little harder.

There. Her teeth sink into her lips. Her groan vibrates down her chest. This is exactly how she needs it.

I push the toy deeper.

A few thrusts and she's tugging at her restraints.

A few more and her eyelids flutter closed.

Her groans get louder. Lower.

With the next thrust, she comes. It's so fucking beautiful watching pleasure spill all the way to her fingers and toes.

She shakes. She pants. She groans my name again and again.

I give her a moment to catch her breath, then I thrust the toy inside her again. I fill her with steady thrusts. Until I'm jealous of the fucking vibrator. Until I'm desperate to toss it aside and bury myself in her.

Then I thrust it into her again.

Her lips part. "Fuck. God. I... Uh..." She tries to reach for me. Rubs against the restraints instead. It makes her groan. It makes her legs shake. It makes her hips buck.

She fucking likes being at my mercy.

It's a good thing, because I fucking love it. I need it. Every drop of it.

She rocks through her next orgasm, groaning my name, shaking as she pulses.

This time, I don't give her a chance to catch her breath.

I fuck her harder. Deeper.

"Brendon. Fuck..." She bites her lips. "It's... I..."

"You want me to stop?" My voice is a dare. It's a lot to take. But she can handle it.

I drive the toy into her again.

Again.

Again.

"Uh... I... Uh... no." She bucks her hips. "Oh. Fuck. Fuck."

She goes fucking crazy. Panting. Shaking. Groaning my name loud enough to get the neighbors calling in a noise complaint.

I watch every bit of pleasure spill over her face as she comes again.

The I pull the toy away, turn it off, toss it aside.

"Please." She looks up at me. Watches with rapt attention as I pull my t-shirt over my head. Undo my jeans and slide them off my hips.

I don't have the fucking time to lose them completely. I need to be inside her.

I nudge her knees apart and bring my body onto hers.

Her chest presses against mine. She kisses me hard and deep. She kisses me like she's claiming me. Like she'll never get enough of my lips and my hands and my cock and my torture.

My hands plant outside her shoulders.

My tip strains against her.

Fuck, there's nothing in the way.

Just my flesh against hers.

It feels too fucking good.

And I'm too fucking close to the edge.

I have to pull back. To kiss her harder. To knot my hand in her long blond hair.

She groans against my mouth. Rocking her hips. Begging me for more. Begging me to take her.

I shift my hips.

Fill her with one hard, deep thrust.

She pulls back to gasp. "Fuck." Her eyes meet mine. They're hazy with lust, need, love—every fucking thing in the world. "Don't stop."

Like hell. "Fuck, Kay, you feel good."

There's nothing in the way.

My cock against her cunt.

Her soft, slick walls enveloping me.

Fuck—

My body takes over.

I rock into her with steady thrusts.

Her hips buck in time with mine.

She groans as she pushes me deeper.

As her wrists strain against the restraints.

As I tug at her hair.

I stare back into her eyes until I can't take it anymore.

My lids press together.

And my lips find hers.

I kiss her as I drive into her.

We stay locked like that until she's groaning against my lips, her cunt pulsing around my cock.

Fuck.

It pushes me over the edge.

With my next thrust, I come.

Pleasure spreads through my torso.

I rock through my orgasm, spilling inside her.

Fuck, the satisfaction goes all the way to my bones.

Her body is mine.

And mine is hers.

And it really is fucking perfect.

I stay inside her until I'm going soft. Then I undo her restraints and pull her body against mine.

She drags her fingers over my chest, tracing the lines of my ink. "That was—"

"Yeah."

"You..." She looks up at me. "Just thanks. For the toy. And for... for everything."

Chapter Thirty-Nine

KAYLEE

I get lost in my routine. Breakfast with Emma. School. Homework. Watching movies with Brendon on the couch. Writing. Reading. Bed—sometimes his, sometimes mine, sometimes without much sleeping involved.

Long weekend mornings with him. Work. Shower. Crashing in his bed.

Stopping by the shop after school so I can see him before he gets home.

Even though it means *if you're going to hang out, help out* stares from Ryan.

And *attagirl* winks from Dean.

Okay, I kind of like the *attagirl* winks.

It's Thursday, the night of the concert, the night before I leave for New Jersey, and the shop is about to close. I'm already in my *I'm totally a rocker chick* denim skirt, converse, artfully torn up (by Emma) band t-shirt combination. I'm even wearing heavy makeup.

And I'm sitting behind the counter, watching Brendon work on a sleeve. The tattoo is meant to look like a robot arm, like skin stretched over metal. It's intricate and grueling, and the guy in the chair is gritting his teeth, refusing a break.

God, Brendon looks so handsome with that stern yet caring expression.

"Kinky Kaylee." Dean taps the front desk. He nods to the laptop—my laptop—sitting in front of me. "What are you writing there?"

Em calls me Kinky Kaylee. Sometimes. Why is Dean? Oh. "Did Em—"

He nods. "She came up to me all giggly. Asked if I'd been seeing anyone lately."

"I can explain."

"Nah. Don't. Apparently, I'm the reason you're walking around with that satisfied look on your face."

My cheeks flush.

"I must be quite the fuck."

"You have no idea."

"I'd like to."

I shake my head.

He pushes himself onto the counter. Turns so he's facing the same direction I am. "How long have you been staring at him?"

"I wouldn't call it staring."

"I've been watching. It's staring."

"It's loving appreciation."

"Of his ass."

"Well." I motion to said ass—Brendon is standing to grab something off a shelf. His customer is finally taking a break. "Look at it." It really is a thing of beauty.

"I've seen it."

"Try seeing it without the clothes."

"Been there, done that."

I clear my throat.

"You don't want to know."

"Actually, I do."

He shakes his head. "Nah, Kinky K. It's too kinky even for you."

"Then wouldn't that make me un-kinky K? Vanilla K?"

"Special K?"

I stick my tongue out. "Say it again and I'll—"

"Sic your boyfriend on me?"

Boyfriend. That's a nice word. It makes me warm everywhere. Brendon as my boyfriend. He basically is my boyfriend. Except for the matter of this being a secret from my best friend slash his sister.

And all of my family.

My mom will flip when she finds out.

Okay. The warmth is receding.

"Why have you seen Brendon's ass?" I ask. "Don't tell me you two—"

"Threesome."

"What?" I turn so I can examine Dean's expression. It's earnest. Well, not exactly. But he's not lying. Probably. He's hard to read what with his penchant for fucking with people. "You and Brendon had a threesome?"

"Forever ago."

"Oh."

"It was a nice ass."

"Don't even."

"This guy bothering you?" Walker moves behind the counter. Motions to the appointment book to my left. "You mind if I do some actual business?"

"Who died and made you Ryan?" Dean asks.

Walker looks from Dean to me. "You and Dean, huh? Pretty crazy, how Em seems to think he's blowing your mind."

"Crazy," I agree.

"Must be some book you're working on," Walker says.

"To be as kinky as—" He nods to Brendon, now back in the chair, working on the sleeve. "*Dean*."

"Is this a lecture?" I gather my hair on my right shoulder. "Because I'm not sure I can take a lecture about not lying or about sex or about anything, really from either of you."

"Really, Kay? I can't lecture you about not swimming after getting fresh ink?" Dean chuckles. "That's a good way to get a wicked infection."

"I don't have any ink," I say.

"Yet. With you and Brendon all kissy face, I give it..." Dean scrunches his brow. "Two weeks."

"A hundred bucks says it's longer," Walker offers.

"Can I get in on this?" I ask.

Dean shakes his head. "Third parties only."

Okay. That's fair. And I'm not even pissed about Dean and Brendon betting about my virginity.

Dean did it to push Brendon.

It worked.

Everything worked out.

Everything is perfect.

With Brendon.

Tomorrow...

I'll face tomorrow's realities then.

Dean turns to me. "I'm more than happy to be your beard, but Emma is gonna figure it out. And you know Emma when she gets pissed."

"Yeah." I do. Everyone knows but her. That's going to hurt.

"Damn, Kay. You're looking at him the way a dog looks at a bone," Walker says.

"Well, look at him? Can you blame me?" I ask.

"She used that one on me." Dean laughs. "You're getting my sloppy seconds."

Walker cringes. "No fucking way." He looks to me. "He has a certain charm."

"Emma calls him Mr. Look at What a Brooding Bad Boy I Am," I say.

"She's got him pegged," Walker says.

"Yeah. But he's so much more." I tap my toes together. God, the way that shirt stretches over his strong shoulders. The way all his focus and attention is turned toward his work... He's perfect.

"You're gonna make her jealous," Dean teases.

"Brooding isn't my type." Walker shakes his head.

"You have a type?" I ask. Walker isn't exactly... discriminating.

"Breathing," Dean offers.

"And your type?" Walker asks.

"Breathing and hot." Dean chuckles.

I turn my attention to my laptop. I'm up to four chapters. And it's actually coming together. Even if this book never amounts to more than a file on my computer, it feels good working on it.

"I can't help it I love watching a woman come." Walker's sigh is dreamy. "The groaning. The shaking. The screaming my name—it's fucking poetry."

"They remember your name?" Dean teases.

"Yeah, I know that's never happened to you."

"It's easy. Four letters. Starts with the thing they're begging for."

"D? That's awful."

"Fuck off."

"You first."

Dean turns to me. "Why are you here, Kay?"

"We're going to a concert," I say. "Me, Brendon, and Em."

"Shit." Dean slides off the counter. So he's next to me.

Right next to me—there isn't a lot of space behind the counter. "I need to play my part?"

"No. We're picking Emma up on the way." I close my laptop and slide it into my backpack. "But thanks." I'm pretty sure Dean is trying to help. Just in a Dean kind of way.

"Joel's band, right?" Dean asks.

"Dangerous Noise, yeah." I zip my backpack and bring it to the counter. I'm almost ready. It's almost eight. As soon as Brendon finishes, we can go.

And I get a precious few minutes alone in his car before we grab Emma.

God, I've been craving him more and more every day.

There's something about knowing he really sees me, even the ugly parts—it's addicting.

"You know, Joel was asking about you," Dean says.

"What?" I bite my lip to keep from blushing.

"Brendon filled him in on all sorts of details."

"You mean—"

"Gotta say, Kay. It was pretty fucking hot. I can see why you're into him. Man's got a mouth."

"You have no idea."

Dean chuckles. "If he ever gives you shit, you call me."

I study Dean's expression. He's actually sincere. Sweet even. Weird. "Okay."

"Me too." Walker offers me a hug.

I take it.

"You're a good kid," Walker says. "You ever need ink, you know who to call."

Dean takes his turn giving me an *attagirl* hug. "Or breakup sex."

"You have a problem." Walker shakes his head.

"Just want the girl to know she has options," Dean insists.

"Look at her." Walker turns to me. "Kay, you've got options in spades. You're hot. And guys dig the librarian thing."

I adjust my glasses instinctively. "Are these really librarian glasses?"

"Fuck, like we know? We don't read," Walker says.

I motion to the Kindle in his suite. "You read all the time."

"Genre fiction," he says.

"What's wrong with genre fiction?"

"You seem more highbrow," he says.

I shake my head.

Dean chuckles. "Told you. She's writing some dirty book like the ones she's always reading."

"No." That blush threatens to inflame my cheeks. "It's a coming of age story."

"Sexually?" Dean raises a brow.

"That's part of it." A lot of it. "Sex is a part of life."

"Erotica. Nice." Dean nods.

"Just 'cause something has sex, doesn't make it erotica." Walker shakes his head. "Fucking plebeians, huh?"

I nod.

"Okay, Kay. Let me ask you this. What words are you using?" Dean asks.

"For?"

He motions to his crotch.

"Uh..."

"Cock?"

"Sometimes."

"Cunt?"

"I need to hit someone?" Brendon's steady voice flows into my ears. He's right there. In front of the counter. His eyes meet mine. *You good?*

I nod. This is actually kinda fun.

He looks to Dean. Then to Walker. "Why are you here? We're closed."

"For the show." Dean motions to the two of us. "And to hang with my girl. Haven't you heard? I'm giving it to Kay real good. Even promised to tie her up and spank her if she writes her dirty book."

"It's not dirty." Okay, it's a little dirty.

"He's gonna hit you," Walker says.

"Nah. Look how happy he is." Dean motions to Brendon's attempt at a stern expression. It's failing. He's too smiley.

He is.

And I am too.

It's just... perfect.

Dean laughs. "Kinky Kaylee. You're using 'cunt' aren't you?"

"Well." I wink at Brendon. "It's a powerful word."

Chapter Forty

KAYLEE

Brendon's hands go to my hips. Then his body is against mine and he's pinning me to the passenger side door.

"Fuck, Kay." His voice is breathy, heavy. "You wear that to torture me?"

I nod.

"I'm gonna have to punish you for that."

This time, I only barely manage to nod.

He rocks his hips against mine as he kisses me. It's hard. Deep. Hungry.

"Brendon. We shouldn't. Em..." I can't finish my sentence. I'm too busy sliding my hands into his hair and pressing my lips to his.

He tastes so good.

Like he's mine.

I never get enough of it.

He traces the hem of my skirt. Then his hands are sliding beneath it. And he's pressing his palm against me, over my panties.

His tongue slides around mine.

His hand knots in my hair.

He pulls back with a heavy sigh.

My glasses are tilted. My lipstick is smeared all over his face.

"Here." I wipe his lips with my thumb. But the feel of those soft lips against the pad of my digit only makes me more desperate to have him. "Is it too late to ditch this concert?"

He nods.

"To—" I nod to the backseat.

"We'd get arrested even if it weren't."

"Worth it."

He nods. "For me, yeah. But for you—" He steps backward.

My body cries for his. My heart is singing from the whole him protecting me from my raging libido thing. But my body is having none of it.

"Come on." He motions to the door. "Get in. Let's pick up Em."

"Okay." I slide into my seat. Click my seatbelt. Fix my smeared makeup in the mirror.

We're quiet as he turns the car on and pulls onto the street. We don't have to say anything. That *I want to fuck you* tension is hanging heavy in the air. It's all I can think.

Brendon pulls into the parking garage and stops by the elevators.

Emma bounces to the car. She's wearing skinny jeans and a ripped up, cropped shirt adorned with the logo of her second favorite band. *Darkest Days.* Its red logo matches her hair. And her lipstick.

She slides into the backseat. "Hey."

"Hey." That *I need to fuck you* tone seeps into my voice.

Emma shoots me a *what's up with you* look.

I shrug.

"Earth to Brendon?" She clicks her seatbelt. When he doesn't respond, she presses on. "You two get into a fight or something?"

Or something, yeah. "You know your brother and his music taste."

"Yeah." She looks to him. Examines him the way she examined me. "You can drop us at the show if you prefer that."

He doesn't say anything.

"Brendon? Hello." Emma taps him on the shoulder. "Are you okay?"

"Yeah." His voice still has that breathy edge. He shakes it off. "Why are you wearing another band's shirt?"

"Duh. Everyone knows it's lame to wear the same band's t-shirt to a concert," she says.

"Do they?" His voice is almost back to normal.

"Everyone cool," I say. "That must not include you."

He chuckles. It's too rich. Too hearty. Too full of affection.

Emma shakes her head. "I swear, if I didn't know better..." *I'd swear you're fucking.*

Something flares in her eyes.

Like she's considering the possibility of us fucking.

Like it's the only reasonable explanation for our behavior the last month and change.

———

Damn, this is one packed club.

There must be two thousand people crammed into a space that usually holds far less. Everything is black—the floor, the walls, the stage, the attire of most of the patrons.

The opening band is playing. I recognize the song from the radio, but I can't put a name to it.

The lead singer has his hand around the mic. He's pouring his heart into his performance. And he's cute. He has the rocker hottie thing going in spades. Skinny jeans. Black t-shirt. Leather jacket. Spikey hair. Facial piercings.

"Think he's got the tongue too?" Emma asks.

"What is that like?" I ask.

"Are you calling me a slut, babe? Because I take that as a compliment." She laughs.

"You wish you were a slut," I say.

"You know I'm right here," Brendon chimes in.

She shrugs. "And a shining example of slut." She turns to her brother with a coy smile. "I'll never live up to your standards."

He rolls his eyes.

"You had a long dry streak there." She folds her arms over her chest. "Who finally broke it?"

Brendon arches a brow. *What are you talking about?*

"There were condom wrappers in your bathroom trash can." She shrugs like this is a normal thing to notice.

"You have your own bathroom," he says.

"Kay was using it."

"There's one downstairs."

"She was using the shower." Emma's eyes narrow as she stares at her brother. "It's not like I opened your drawers or something. They were right there in the open. That's um... in plain sight. It's legal."

"You been watching *Law and Order*?" he asks.

She nods. "That's also legal." Her eyes go to me then back to him. "Just kinda funny. The two of you getting laid at the same time."

"Hilarious." Unease seeps into his voice.

Emma turns toward the stage. Watches as the guitarist steps forward to shred through his solo. He's also cute. Tall. Broad. Stoic in that Brendon kind of way.

Emma tilts her head to one side. "Maybe I should get an eyebrow piercing."

"Cute." I nod.

She lets her voice get loud. "Or maybe my nipples."

"You trying to piss me off?" Brendon asks.

"No. I'm trying to talk to my best friend. No one invited you to eavesdrop." She does nothing to hide the irritation in her voice.

But it's not the eavesdropping.

It's the suspicion.

She knows.

Or she's going to know soon.

This isn't good.

I squeeze Emma's arm. "Shh. I love this song."

She play swats me.

I play swat her back.

Her smile is normal. Like she's not trying to figure out if I'm sleeping with her brother.

I *do* love this song.

I focus on the guys on stage. On the music flowing into my ears. On the sway of my hips.

Then on belting out the chorus. The one I've heard a million times.

Emma sings with me.

And everything is normal.

All the way through the end of the song.

The singer smiles. "We've got a few more. You guys excited to hear Dangerous Noise?"

The crowd cheers.

Emma too.

"We've had a blast this tour. We want to thank them for inviting us. And to thank all of you for showing up tonight." He turns back to his band and shoots them a thumbs up.

Then the bassline is kicking in.

And the drums are pounding.

A guitar riff fills the air.

Then this low roar of a verse.

Emma turns back to Brendon. "Are you sticking around?"

"How else can I ruin your good time," he teases.

"Oh." Her eyes light up. "We're on the list. Why are we here. We could be backstage."

"Because here is fun?" I offer.

"And backstage isn't?" She motions to the hall where we came in. "Only a few songs left. Now is our chance."

He looks to me for permission.

I nod. This will be fun. And it won't advance Emma's suspicion. I think.

He nods back. "Follow me."

Emma steps forward. "No, follow me."

She cuts through the crowd expertly. I follow just as swiftly. We've got a lot of experience weaving through crowded venues.

The lighting dims as we step into the hallway. There's a security guy guarding a door at the other end of the hall. The one opposite where we came in. He has an earpiece and a clipboard. A *this is the list* kind of clipboard.

Emma squeals. "Oh my God, this is... oh my God. They're all so hot. I can't even. What am I going to say?"

"Fuck me please." I laugh.

"No, they're all taken." She pouts. "What would possess a smoking hot rock god to settle down?"

"The right woman," Brendon offers.

That shakes her out of her starstruck daze. She turns back to Brendon. Examines his expression. "You have a secret girlfriend I should know about?"

He shoots her a *really* look.

She returns it.

Uh uh. My night is not heading down this path. Not when everything is perfect.

This is my chance to be happy before everything goes to shit tomorrow.

I'm not losing that.

I move toward clipboard guy. "Excuse me. Um. I'm Kaylee Hart and this is my friend Brendon Kane. We're on the list."

He looks to Em. "And you, sweetheart?"

"Emma Kane." Her smile is equally parts sexy and sweet.

He glances at the clipboard. "Looks like you are." He moves aside from the door. "Head in. But stay out of the way."

I nod as I step through the door. "Thank you."

Emma and Brendon follow.

We're actually backstage.

It's a lot more crowded than I'd expect. There are roadies and other crew type people milling around.

And there's the opening band's dressing room on our right.

And just beyond it, a sign taped to a door reads *Dangerous Noise*.

Emma squeezes my hand. "That's it." She skips forward.

I follow her into the room.

Oh my God.

That's actually Joel Young, Brendon's supposed client.

And he's actually looking at Brendon like he recognizes him.

And at me like he—

He has this knowing smile. This mischief in his green

eyes. Like Brendon did fill him in on all sorts of dirty details about me.

"Didn't think you'd show." He moves forward. Nods hello to Brendon then looks to me and Emma. "I'm Joel."

"I know." My tongue sticks to the roof of my mouth.

Emma nods.

"You must be Kaylee," he says.

"Yeah." It's all I can say. He knows my name. A famous rock star knows my name.

"I dig the glasses." He holds up his left hand and wiggles his adorned ring finger. "If only you'd found me before Bella did."

"Huh." I giggle. If only I'd met him before he was married, then he would have slept with me.

With the way he's smiling in Brendon's direction, I'm pretty sure this is for my not exactly a boyfriend's benefit.

But still...

A rock star is flirting with me.

"This is Emma." I nod to my best friend. "She's a big fan. We both are."

"Thanks." He offers me a hug.

I take it.

I'm hugging Joel Young.

This is so weird.

Then he's hugging Emma.

He opens his arms to Brendon. Chuckles when Brendon shakes his head. "It's been what, six years now? Still can't get any affection from the guy. Must be hard living with a brother like that."

"You have no idea," Emma says.

"Nah, I do. My older sister is a tough cookie. And she's a shrink. Count your blessings," he says.

Emma laughs.

"He doesn't talk much, does he?" Joel asks.

Emma shakes her head. "Not usually."

"So sometimes?" Joel cocks a brow. "Go on. But only if it gets juicy."

"There's someone he talks about a lot." Emma presses her lips together. "A girl."

A voice echoes through the room. "Five minutes."

"Damn." Joel shakes his head. "They really gotta warn us about this shit. Pretty sure Ethan is still fingering Vi off some place."

"Oh... Uh..." My mouth gets sticky. How can he be so casual with that information? It's just... Umm... Uh...

"It was nice to meet you, Kaylee. Emma." He winks. "Give your brother a hard time, for me."

She laughs. "Will do."

The three of us make our way back to the main room. We cut through the crowd just in time for the lights to go down and the band to step on stage.

Emma and I get lost in the music for the entire set. Even Brendon seems to enjoy it.

Everything is perfect.

Until we're on our way out.

And Emma is dragging me into the bathroom. "Come on, Kay. We need to talk."

Chapter Forty-One

KAYLEE

Emma goes straight to the sink. She sets her purse on the counter and digs through it until she finds her lipstick.

I lean against the wall. Watch her add another coat of red. Try to wipe the guilt from my eyes.

It's not working.

I find the lipstick in my purse and apply another coat. But my hands are shaking. The line is messy. Like it was after I was making out with her brother.

"So..." She zips her purse and taps her fingers against it.

"So...?"

Her chest heaves with her sigh.

I keep my lips pressed together.

I can't say anything.

She can't know.

It's just not an option.

"Whatever is happening, you can tell me." She turns toward me. "I won't be mad."

I don't believe that. I force my lips into a smile. "Nothing is happening."

"You... you and Brendon are being weird. And your lipstick was smudged in the car."

"I had a snack at Inked Hearts."

"Nobody snacks at Inked Hearts."

"In the lobby."

She shakes her head. "What is it, Kay? Why don't you want to tell me?"

"It's nothing." Shakiness seeps into my voice. I want it to be nothing. Or at least nothing important. But it's huge.

"It's something." She presses her ass against the counter. Folds her arms. Frustration creeps into her eyes.

It's hurting her that I'm keeping a secret.

This is my chance.

I can confess everything.

Or I can double down on the lie.

I take a deep breath and exhale slowly.

Her dark eyes stay fixed on mine.

"I... uh... Brendon... uh. Brendon caught me and Dean." Guilt nags at my throat. It takes everything I have to keep my expression neutral.

"Oh." Emma tilts her head, turning over the so called admission.

"Yeah." I dig into my lie. "We were just kissing, but he got pissed."

"What did he say?"

"Dean's a whore. I can do better. That kind of thing."

"Did he threaten to kill Dean?"

"More or less." Or a lot less.

Emma's eyes bore into mine. "Really?"

I barely nod.

"Look me in the eyes, Kay."

"Why?" My gaze goes right to my shoes. They're grey. Canvas and rubber. Comfortable. Perfect for a concert.

"Kay."

"What?" I force myself to stare back into Emma's dark eyes. They're lighter than Brendon's. Wider. But still a lot like his.

"Tell me the truth. Whatever it is."

"I..." My voice cracks. The words claw at my gut. They make it all the way up my throat, but I stop them with a swallow.

"You..."

"I..."

"Are you fucking my brother?"

"Em..."

Her eyes go wide. She shakes her head. "Kaylee, what the fuck?"

"It's not like that."

"You had sex with my brother."

"Yeah, but—"

"He was the one at karaoke?"

I nod.

"And the one... oh God, he was offering to, ew..." Her nose scrunches. Her eyes fill with disgust.

All the details I've spilled have been about her brother.

And her best friend is a liar.

Of course she's disgusted.

I...

"I'm sorry." I don't know what else to say.

"You and Brendon..." Emma shakes her head. "How long have you—"

"A long time."

"And he?"

"I don't know. A long time too."

"And everyone else knows?"

"I didn't tell them."

Emma steps away. "So, what, you don't trust me?"

"No, Em. I thought you'd freak."

"You. Don't. Trust. Me."

"I'm sorry. But I... I love him."

She shakes her head. "No. You do not love my brother."

"Yeah, I do."

"He's fucking ancient!"

"But he... he's a good person. You know he is."

"No." She grabs her purse and moves toward the exit. "I know that he's a liar. That you're both liars."

"Em. Please."

She shakes her head. "Don't talk to me."

"Em—"

The door swings shut behind her.

Chapter Forty-Two

BRENDON

"What the fuck is wrong with you?" Emma grabs my arm and pulls me from the theater entrance.

"Where's Kay?"

Her eyes narrow. "Is that the only thing you care about?"

"What are you—"

"What am *I*? You're fucking my best friend."

"Em—"

"Don't. I don't want to hear it. You're supposed to be the guy who keeps shit like this from happening."

She's right. It's completely fucked, me and Kaylee.

"I'm so stupid. You two have been hanging out all this time. And I just... I actually believed that you care about her. That you want the best for her."

"I do."

"She's eight years younger than you. What the fuck would you do if it was me and Dean?" She folds her arms. "She trusts you, Brendon. She trusts you like family. And you used that to fuck her."

"I care about her."

"If you cared about her, you'd keep your fly zipped." She moves to the street. "Don't wait up."

"Where the hell are you going?"

"None of your business. I'm eighteen. I'm an adult. Those are clearly your standards. I don't need to tell you shit." She turns and runs toward the Hollywood and Highland center.

She's pissed.

She needs to cool off.

But I'm not going to let my sister do something stupid.

I run after her.

———

SHE'S GONE.

I check every club on Highland.

I check every store at the strip mall.

I call every one of Emma's friends.

And, still, I keep looking. Find another store. Another bar. Another shady fucking alley.

I don't stop until my phone is buzzing.

It's a text from Walker.

Walker: Emma's at my place. She's gonna stay here.

Brendon: She okay?

Walker: No. But she will be. Is Kay okay?

Brendon: I don't know.

Walker: Fuck. You better figure that out.

Brendon: Take care of Em, okay.

Walker: Good luck.

I slide my phone into my pocket and make my way back to the venue.

But it's already closed. Lights off. Everybody—even the crew—is gone.

I call Kaylee.

Voicemail.
Again.
Voicemail.
Again.
Nothing.
I shoot her a text.
Brendon: Where are you?
Nothing.

Chapter Forty-Three

BRENDON

The house is dark.

The only sound is coming from upstairs. From Kaylee's bedroom.

She's crying.

Fuck, I've never been this happy to hear someone crying.

I nearly run up the stairs.

Nearly break her door pushing it open.

She's curled up in her bed in the dark.

Hugging her knees.

Blinking back another set of tears.

"Kay." I sit next to her. Rub her shoulder with my palm. I need to fix this. Somehow.

"I'm sorry." She pulls her knees into her chest. "She asked. And I wanted to lie, but I couldn't. I couldn't say anything. I just stared."

This is my fault. This whole fucking thing is my fault.

Em is right.

I'm the adult here.

I'm the person who is supposed to protect Kaylee.

If there was some other twenty-six-year-old guy trying to get in her pants, I'd kick his ass.

"It's not your fault." I run my fingers through her hair. "This has been inevitable."

She nods. "Still."

"No, Kay. This is on me."

She shakes her head. "I didn't have to make up that stuff about Dean. I... I'm sorry. I made everything complicated. And you... you don't want complicated."

"Come here."

She pushes herself up and buries her head in my chest. "She's never going to talk to me again."

"She'll get over it."

Kaylee shakes her head. "No. She looked so betrayed. I've never seen that before."

"She will. I promise."

"No. I'm going to leave tomorrow, and everything is going to be fucked, and I'm going to come back here and everything will still be fucked." Kay clutches at my arms. She holds me tighter. Pulls me closer. "I'm sorry. I..."

"It's not your fault."

Again, she shakes her head.

She's not going to get it.

Not like this.

She needs someone to walk her through this.

To occupy all her thoughts.

Or maybe that's my cock talking.

I run my fingers through her hair.

I hold her body against mine until she stops shaking.

Is this for me or her?

I'm not sure.

She has me so fucked up.

I don't know up or down anymore.

I certainly don't know right or wrong.

"You want to feel better, Kay?"

She looks up at me with all that trust in her eyes. "Yeah, but I don't see——"

"You want out of your head or not?"

"I do."

"You trust me?"

"Of course."

"Then go to my room."

Understanding fills her eyes. "You mean——"

"Yeah."

"Oh. Well. Um. Yeah. Okay." She pushes herself to her feet. "Okay. Is Em okay?"

"She's staying with Walker."

"Okay. Good. I, uh... Okay. Do we need a safeword or something?"

It never hurts. "You have something in mind?"

"Tattoo."

Fuck, it's like she's trying to be adorable.

How the hell am I supposed to give her up?

I nod. "Tattoo."

"Okay." Her voice is halfway back to normal. Her posture too.

She's slow about moving into the hallway.

Then into my room.

The door shuts.

She's waiting in there.

For me to hurt her.

But not the way she thinks I'm going to.

Chapter Forty-Four

KAYLEE

*E*mma is never going to forgive you.

It's the only thought in my brain.

No matter how hard I try to focus on Brendon's smooth sheets, or the way his scent is lingering in the bed, or the mirror I can use to watch him fuck me, or even that he's about to come in here and—

I don't know what he's going to do.

Only that I trust him to steal all my other thoughts away.

Emma is never going to forgive you.

Thoughts of my wrists tied to this bed, of his palm on my ass, of his hand around my throat—

Nothing can stop that angry voice in my head.

This is your fault.

You ruined everything.

You begged him for this.

He said it couldn't happen and you begged him.

You're ruining his relationship with his sister.

With the only family he has left.

You really think he'll forgive you for that?

That either one of them will?

Grandma is gonna die and Mom is gonna find out about this. And then you'll have nothing. You'll come back to LA and you'll be alone.

He steps through the door.

He's still in the same outfit. Skinny jeans. T-shirt. Bare feet.

He has the same dark hair and dark eyes.

The same sleeve tattoo.

But he's different than the Brendon of a few minutes ago.

He's demanding. In control.

And that look in his eyes, the one that screams *you're mine and I'll do whatever I want with you*—

It sucks up all my attention.

It's exactly what I need.

His eyes fix on me. "You wore that skirt to drive me out of my fucking mind."

It's a minor infraction compared to everything else I've done, but it's enough.

"Answer me."

"Yes."

"You knew I couldn't touch you in front of Em."

Her name is a dagger to my chest. I push up the walls around my heart. Something, anything, to stop that guilt from flooding my body.

"Kaylee. Answer me." His voice is stern. It's a promise. An *answer me or you'll regret it.*

"Yes."

He takes a seat on the bed next to me. His hand rests on my thigh. It doesn't stroke or tease. It just sits there. "What did you want to happen?"

"I don't know."

"You do."

I shake my head. I really don't.

"Did you want me to fuck you?"

"Yes?"

"To drag you to the alley and split you in half?"

"Yes."

"What else?"

"I don't know. I just want you. It's all I can think sometimes."

"How?"

"Huh?"

His hand knots in my hair. He turns me so we're eye to eye. "Tell me how you wanted me. You were staring at me all night. You were thinking about me."

"I was."

"How?"

"About you bending me over the counter. Or the chair. Or ordering me onto my knees."

"And coming on those pretty, pink lips?"

"Yes."

"You like to tease me, angel?"

"Yes."

"You have to pay for that."

I nod. Yes. Please. I need to pay for... for everything.

He presses his palm against the back of my head to guide my body over his. So I'm bent over his knee, my stomach against his thighs, my face against the bed, my ass in the air.

Brendon rolls my skirt up my thighs. Over my ass.

He traces the outline of my thong. "You wear this to torture me too?"

"Yes."

"Bad girl."

I nod.

He rubs me over my panties.

"You want to hurt, angel?"

"Yes."

He brings his hand into the air.

I squeeze my eyes closed.

Sink my teeth into my lower lip.

I've never.

I mean, I've thought about it. Fuck, how I've thought about it.

But I've never...

What if I can't...

His hand comes down hard on my ass. It stings. I feel the slap in my sex. In my nipples. In my fingers and toes.

Fuck, that hurts so good.

He does it again.

Again.

I cry out. It's not a word. It's a yes and a no. A please and please make this stop. And then just a please.

He spanks me again.

"Brendon," I breathe. "Please."

"Tell me you need this, angel."

"I do. Please."

"Tell me why."

"I ruined everything. Us. Em. Just... everything."

"No."

"No?" Anything but no.

He traces the line of my thong over my ass, my sex, my clit, my pelvis, then back again. "Tell me exactly."

"You told me no. That this couldn't happen. But I begged you."

He brings his hand into the air then brings it down hard on my ass. "No, Kay. Tell me how it really happened."

"But it did. You did, and I did, and—"

He spanks me again. Harder this time. Hard enough it hurts as much as it feels good.

"I..." I'm not sure what I'm asking for. Only that he'll give it to me.

"I wanted you. I was desperate for you. I still am. This is on me too."

"Oh. But I... I lied to Em."

He brings his hand down hard on my ass. "What else?"

"I... I don't know. I kept so many things from everyone. All this time, and I... I'm here and not in New Jersey, and—"

He spanks me again. Hard.

Fuck, that hurts.

"I ruined everything. Everything." That dam breaks and guilt floods my body. It's in every pore. In every molecule.

"You need to hurt."

"Yes."

He brings his hand into the air then brings it down against my ass. "I'll tell you when it's enough."

"Yes."

He spanks me again.

Again.

Again.

I get lost in the smack of his palm against my flesh.

In the rush of pain and the pleasure that follows.

My sex is aching.

My skin is screaming for more and for less.

For everything.

He spanks me again.

Again.

Again.

"Please. I... I need you." It's the only thing I know.

"Tell me you deserve it."

"What?"

"That you deserve my fingers in your cunt."

"I..."

"That you deserve to come on my cock." His hand comes down hard on my ass.

"I don't know."

Again.

"I... please."

He holds his hand in the air. "Tell me, Kay. Tell me you deserve to feel good."

I don't know. I want to believe that. But my head is still a mess. "Again."

He presses my body against his with his other hand. It's like he's reminding me he's in control. That he's got me. That I'm safe.

Not just my body. But all of me.

"Tell me, Kay." His voice is equal parts stern and caring. "Tell me what you deserve."

"To hurt."

He spanks me again. "And then?"

"I don't know. I want to believe it. I do. Please... just please."

His palm comes down hard on my ass. "Tell me."

"I deserve..." This. I deserve hurting. But then I...

Smack! "Tell me."

"I..."

"Repeat after me."

"Okay."

"I deserve to come."

All my breath leaves my body as his palm smacks against my flesh. "I deserve to come."

"I deserve you."

"I deserve you."

"Good girl." He brings his palm into the air.

"Last one."

"Please." There it is again. I still don't know what I'm asking for, only that I need it desperately.

Smack! His palm comes down hard on my ass.

Then he's pushing my panties aside.

Teasing my sex with one finger.

Two.

Three.

"Please."

"Beg me."

"Please."

He teases again.

Again.

Again.

"Please what?" His voice is low, demanding.

He teases again.

God, my sex is aching.

I feel so empty.

So incredibly desperate to be full.

"Please, I want to come on your hand. Please."

He pushes a little deeper.

"Please. More."

Deeper.

"Please."

There. He drives his fingers into me.

Then he's pulling them out.

Another thrust.

Another.

My body relaxes. He's giving me what I need. Exactly what I need.

He fucks me with his fingers.

It's rough. Hard. Fast.

And it feels so fucking good.

"Brendon," I breathe. "Please."

"Say it again, angel."

"Brendon."

He drives his fingers into me. Again. Again. Again.

All that tension in my sex knots.

Almost.

Almost.

There.

I groan his name again and again as all that tension unwinds. An orgasm rocks through me. It pushes every last inhibition from my brain.

He throws me onto the bed on my stomach.

Peels my panties to my knees.

I hear his zipper undo.

Then his hand is around my throat.

And his body is on top of mine, his chest against my back, his cock nudging my thigh.

Nudging my sex.

There.

With one swift movement, he drives inside me.

I get the full force of him.

Fuck.

It's intense.

But it feels so fucking good.

He goes deeper.

Harder.

Again.

Again.

His grip around my neck tightens.

He has me pinned.

I can barely move my legs—my panties are around my knees. And he's between then.

I'm completely at his mercy.

But there isn't a single part of me that's scared.

He drives into me again and again.

It's overwhelming, that sense of being full.

Or being held down.

Of being under his control.

He nips at my neck, holding my body against his as he drives into me again and again.

Fuck, he feels so good.

And the way he groans against my neck—

I do believe I deserve this.

That I have done penance.

That everything is going to be okay.

He keeps me pinned to the bed as he fucks me.

That last bit of guilt fades away. Until my body is nothing but pleasure. But the ache of desperately needing to come.

I clutch at the sheets.

I buck my hips against his.

He pins me harder.

Tightens his grip around my throat.

Almost.

He drives harder.

Deeper.

My eyelids press together. "Don't stop." It's all I can get out.

He drives into me with those same steady thrusts.

Again.

Again.

There.

The tension in my sex unfurls. I'm pulsing so hard I can feel it in my fingertips. I'm sure I'm going to push him from my body.

But he keeps that same steady thrust.

Keeps me pinned to the bed.

His lips find my neck. He groans my name against my skin as he thrusts through his orgasm.

His cock pulses as he spills inside me.

He's giving me everything he has.

I feel so full, so whole, I can't stand it.

Once he's spilled every drop, he collapses next to me.

He wraps his arms around me and pulls my body into his.

His lips find mine.

And he kisses me like he's never going to let me go.

Chapter Forty-Five

KAYLEE

Sleep eludes me. I lie in bed—in my bed, just in case Em comes home and decides finding me in Brendon's bed is adding insult to injury—staring at the white-blue glow of those little plastic stars. Their light is soft. Ghostly almost.

I turn over. Press my eyelids together. Try to chase the image of Emma's face from my mind.

It won't go. All I see is the hurt in her dark eyes. All I can hear is the betrayal in her voice.

Kaylee, what the fuck?

No, I know he's a liar.

You're both liars.

Like I slapped her in the face.

No, I did. I didn't just lie to Emma about this. I stomped the ground and dug my heels into it. I dug a fucking grave with my heels.

Now it's time to lie in it.

Light peeks through the dark curtains. First a deep shade of blue. Then lighter. Some mix of red, pink, and orange. Then enough to keep the stars from shining.

I give up on sleep and crawl out of bed.

All the downstairs lights are on. Brendon is on the couch in his jeans and t-shirt, his head on a pillow, his eyes closed. A bright, colorful infomercial flashes on the TV. Some sponge. It's a happy face that makes it easier to clean. So you can drag happiness over dirt until it's as grimy as everything else.

I let him sleep. Brush my teeth. Wash my face. Shower. The water is hot, but I don't feel it. The release of last night is gone. It keeps replaying through my head.

Emma is never going to forgive you.

I press my eyelids together, tilt my head back to rinse my hair. Water streams down my face, off my chin. Still it screams in my head.

Emma isn't going to forgive you. And whatever's happening with Grandma—you're going to have to get through that alone.

I *know* I have my parents.

But I still can't get over them keeping this from me. And I know how awful it feels—someone keeping a secret to protect you. Only I don't know the reality. I don't know how much of their words are sugar coating and how much are straight up lies.

I guess it runs in the Hart family.

After I towel dry, I finish packing. There. That's everything. Meds. Clothes. Kindle. Laptop. Toiletries. It's still hot here. But what about in New Jersey? I check the weather report, pack a few sweaters just in case.

I find my phone and text Emma for the hundredth time.

Kaylee: I'm sorry. Can we talk? Please.

Nothing.

I stare until my eyes are dry.

Nothing.

It's still early. She's probably not even up. Brendon's here. That must mean she's still at Walkers. That she's still okay.

It means more. I don't know. My head is fuzzy. Full. My thoughts are going in circles. They're fast but they're slow. I need sleep. And tea. In that order.

It's not an option.

I lug my stuff downstairs and put the kettle on.

Brendon stirs. I can't see him from here but I can hear him.

"Fuck. What time is it?" he asks.

"Early." I grab a mug from the cabinet. The one I made at that paint it yourself pottery place. With Emma. A million years ago. It has a mermaid on it. Well, it's supposed to be a mermaid. It looks more like a blur of beige, green, purple, and red on a blue background. "You can go back to sleep."

"No. We should go soon. There's always traffic."

That's true enough. I stare at the shiny silver kettle, willing it to work faster. I need comfort. Tea. And his arms around me. But when I open my lips to request it, I can't force any words out.

"I better get ready."

"Okay. You want coffee?"

"Thanks." His footsteps move closer. Closer. He steps into the kitchen, wraps his arms around me, pulls my body against his. "I'm sorry, Kay. This is my fault."

No. It's not. He said no. He said this couldn't happen. And I begged him.

Maybe it's not all my fault.

But we share the blame.

He didn't tell me to dig into my lies.

That was all me.

I shake my head.

He runs his fingers through my wet hair.

Tears well up in my eyes. It feels too good being in his arms. It reminds me of how bad everything else is. But I don't want to say any of it. I just want to soak in this comfort while I have it.

The kettle whistles.

I pour hot water over my bag of vanilla black.

"Go." I press my lips to his neck. "Get ready. I can leave as soon as I finish my tea."

"Eat something."

"I'm not hungry."

"Kay, eat something."

"It's my body. Not yours."

He steps back. Hurt flashes in his eyes. But it can't be over that comment. At least, I don't think so.

He turns and moves toward the living room.

"At least make a sandwich for the plane." He climbs up the stairs and disappears into his bedroom.

It's not the worst advice.

I fill the coffee maker with fresh grounds and filtered water and turn it on.

Slowly, the smell of java wafts over the room.

I find the bread in the fridge and focus all my energy on spreading almond butter over one side and raspberry jelly over the other.

By the time Brendon rushes downstairs all showered and fresh I have my sandwich wrapped in plastic. But my tea is still too fucking hot.

He steps into the kitchen. His eyes catch the sandwich then they meet mine. "Good?"

"Yeah." I bring my lips and take a sip. It's too hot, but it's tolerable. "Have you heard from Emma?"

"No, but Walker said he'd text as soon as she was up. She has work today. She won't skip that."

"You sure?"

"Yeah. She's a responsible kid. And she loves her discount."

I try to muster up a laugh. I'm not sure if he's joking. Emma does love her employee discount. And she's also responsible. But she also ran off last night. She's never done that before. We've fought a lot—who hasn't—but she's never run off without telling me where she was going.

Brendon brings his hand to my jaw. He tilts my head so I'm looking up at him. "It will be okay, Kay."

"How do you know?"

"I know."

I want to believe him, but I'm not sure I do.

———

TRAFFIC IS A CRAWL. IT'S FRIDAY MORNING. TRAFFIC IS always a crawl at this time.

The sun bounces off the pavement, flowing into Brendon's sedan, making it hard to read my cell screen.

Not that there's anything to read.

Emma still hasn't texted back.

My parents' *have a safe flight, can't wait to see you, let me know when you've boarded* texts are the same.

The only thing changing is the time in the top bar of my cell screen.

I stare at it until the screen goes dark then I wake my cell and do it all over again.

Brendon reaches over and wraps his fingers around my wrist. "Kay, put your phone away. You're driving yourself crazy."

"I know. But—"

"Emma's not gonna text back today. You have to give her time."

I know that. I do. But my heart isn't getting the message. And when I let my thoughts float away from Emma, they go straight to Grandma. To the question mark and all the possible answers. They're too scary. I can't take that.

He rubs my wrist with his thumb. It pulls my thoughts back to the moment.

Brendon is such a loving person, but he doesn't see himself that way. No one else sees him that way.

But it's there. It's just hidden, like the stars on the ceiling.

He rubs my wrist through the last stretch of the 405. As we take the LAX exit. Even through the crawl to *Departures* then to my terminal.

God, this airport is a mess.

It's constantly in construction.

It will be better one day. But right now the improvement is only making things worse.

There. He pulls into the short-term parking lot and finds a space on the second level. Even though it's a bright day, it's dark in here. The sun can't get through the walls of concrete.

His hand goes back to his side. All the warmth in my body goes with it. Something changes in his posture as he turns off the car. Something that makes him harder. Further away.

Or maybe that's my imagination.

It's possible sleep deprivation is getting to me.

God, I'm actually looking forward to being on that plane. That's six hours to close my eyes and block out the world. Or six hours for the world to invade my thoughts. One of the two.

"I'll get your bag." Brendon steps out of the car. He grabs my rolling duffel from the backseat then slams the door shut.

I pull my cardigan tighter as I step into the parking lot. The air here is cool. I hug my purse to my shoulder and adjust my jeans. This is weird. I'm flying to New Jersey. That's how things are supposed to go today.

But they're supposed to be different too.

Brendon takes my hand and leads me through the parking lot. It's bright on the sidewalk. The sky is a brilliant blue. The sun is a luminous yellow. There isn't a cloud in sight.

And his hand is on mine.

His touch still feels so fucking good.

Even though something—everything—else is wrong.

The red hand at the cross walk disappears as the walk sign flashes on.

I follow Brendon across the street. Then over the loading zone. We take the escalator to departures, step into the air-conditioned terminal, and go straight to the machines against the wall.

Shit, that security line stretches on for ages. This is going to take forever. And we're no longer early.

I slide my credit card into the machine and follow the instructions. It spits out my boarding pass and a message to proceed to security.

Brendon rubs my shoulders. "You have everything you need for your flight?"

I nod. I think so.

"Load up your playlist with Linkin Park?"

I shake my head. "Joy Division."

He chuckles but his eyes stay sad. "Call me when you get in. And let me know how your grandma is doing."

"Of course." I wrap my arms around his waist. "You'll let me know what happens with Em? Whatever it is?"

"Yeah."

"Good." I rise to my tiptoes. My eyelids flutter closed as I press my lips to his. He tastes good. Like coffee and like Brendon. I don't usually like the taste of coffee, but it's another thing that makes me think of him.

I pull back with a sigh.

My eyes fix on his. They're like coffee, his eyes. Rich. Dark. Deep.

He's here with me.

Holding my hand.

Kissing me off.

He's everything.

"I don't want to say goodbye, but I guess I have to." I rise to my tiptoes and kiss him again. It's not enough. I need more of him. I need all of him.

This time, he's the one who pulls back. He runs his fingers through my hair. His voice gets soft. "Me either."

"I... I'll miss you." I lean into his touch. Words rise up in my throat. Ones I've been avoiding.

I try to swallow them down.

I kiss him one more time. Something to keep my lips occupied.

But that doesn't work.

I'm shaking when I pull back.

My eyes meet his.

And those words spill from my lips.

"Brendon, I love you."

Chapter Forty-Six

KAYLEE

S hit.
My cheeks flush.

My stomach drops.

Not the right time.

Not at all.

And the look in his eyes.

That's not the right look.

"Kay..." His eyes go to the floor.

"You don't have to say it. It just came out. I, uh... I mean, I do love you. But it's okay if you're not sure yet. Or if you're not there yet."

"No." He runs a hand through his hair. Slowly, his eyes meet mine. "Kay..."

No. That's not the right tone. "What do you mean *Kay*...?"

"Don't worry about us. Go see your grandma."

I shake my head. "No. The way you said that... it's like there isn't an us." I stare into his eyes. I pick apart the way they turn down. It's barely anything, but it's enough. It's bad. "If there's not an us—"

"There shouldn't be."

"What?" My heart rises in my throat. There has to be an us. Otherwise, I really don't have anything.

"Em was right. I'm supposed to protect you from guys like me."

"Em said that?"

"Yeah. But that doesn't matter." His voice gets stronger. Like he's sure. "I am supposed to protect you from guys like me."

"What the fuck does that mean? You're strong and sweet and supportive—"

"I'm not the kind of guy you should love." Hurt streaks over his face. It seeps into his voice. But he stays strong. Confident.

"No, Brendon. You're exactly the kind of guy I should love."

He shakes his head. "I'm not."

"Well too fucking bad. I do love you."

"You shouldn't."

"And you should love me?"

"Kay—"

"No, you don't get to say my name like that." My fingers curl into fists. He's still standing there all strong and sure and stoic. Like he's doing this for me. But that's bullshit. This is the last thing I need. "Am I the kind of girl someone should love?"

"Kay—"

"Don't say my name like that!" My voice rises. It's too loud for the airport. People are staring. Even a security guard. I swallow hard. I force myself to be quiet. "How am I a girl you should love?"

"You're smart, strong—"

"I think about hurting myself."

"That's different."

"How?"

"It just is." He places one hand on my shoulder. Stares back into my eyes.

His stupid gesture is calming.

I hate that it's calming.

How can he calm me when he's ripping my heart out?

I stare back at him, daring him to explain, daring him to see what an idiot he's being.

He doesn't.

"It isn't different." I try to whisper, but my voice is still too loud. "If you're no good then neither am I. My brain is broken. I think about hurting myself. I might one day."

"You won't."

"You don't know that."

"I know enough."

I shake my head. "Why should anyone love a girl who might swallow a bottle of sleeping pills?"

He stares back at me.

"Is that it? You don't want to be with someone like me?"

"No."

"You could at least have the courtesy to be honest when you break my heart." I take a step backward. "Don't tell me this is for me. Because it's not. I know what I want. I want you."

"Kay—"

"DON'T SAY MY NAME LIKE THAT!" I press my lips together. Fuck. I'm causing a scene. I need to get shit under control or I'm going to be escorted to some scary secret TSA room. "Tell me the truth, Brendon. Is this really because I shouldn't be with you? Or is it because you could never love someone like me?"

"No, Kay. This is because I love you."

"Bullshit." I stare into his eyes, begging him to budge.

But he doesn't.

He just stares back. Apology streaks his expression, but he stays silent.

It feels like we stare forever.

Eventually, he takes a step backward. "You're going to miss your flight."

"But... but you love me."

"It doesn't matter."

"Of course it does."

"You shouldn't be with me." His voice is dripping with hurt, but it's still confident. Sure.

"I get to decide that."

"Yeah. But I do too." He takes a step backward. "I'm sorry, Kay. Have a safe flight."

Then he turns and leaves.

And takes my heart with him.

Chapter Forty-Seven

BRENDON

I sit in my car for a fucking eternity.

I check the flight notice again and again.

Boarding.

Boarded.

On its way.

I turn my car on. Plug my cell into the stereo. Blast something by The Descendants.

The parking fee is a fucking crime.

But I don't care.

I take the streets to Lincoln and I drive. I drive until the street becomes Pacific Coast Highway proper. I drive until I'm curving around Pacific Palisades then the Malibu hills.

It doesn't help my thoughts come together.

I keep seeing the hurt on Kaylee's face.

Like I ripped her heart in half.

I was sure I was right. That hurting her was a necessary evil. That she shouldn't be with me much less love me.

But the more I drive, the less sense it makes.

Chapter Forty-Eight

KAYLEE

I rest my head against the window and watch the clouds roll by.

It's strange. I'm empty. But my thoughts have nowhere to go.

My head is only more of a mess.

Brendon insisting I shouldn't love him.

Emma calling me a liar.

Grandma promising she's fine.

I pull out my Kindle and try to read. The words are fuzzy. They're nothing. They're pointless.

This isn't happening.

I find my journal—the one he bought for me. And I put my purple pen to the page.

None of this makes sense.

I let my thoughts pour from my fingers.

And I don't stop until I don't feel anything anymore.

Chapter Forty-Nine

KAYLEE

M om is waiting at baggage claim.

Her eyes are puffy. Red. She's been crying.

From the way she's looking at me, I'm pretty sure mine are the same.

Fuck.

I knew things might be bad.

But not this bad.

———

MOM MAKES SMALL TALK.

And I let her.

Until we take an early exit.

She turns on an unfamiliar street.

Then down another.

The hospital comes into view.

"Mom..." I place my hands in my lap. "What... What the hell?"

She pulls into the hospital parking lot. "I can explain."

"How can you explain?" Grandma is supposed to be

okay. Okay people aren't in the hospital. That's a fucking fact.

"Your Grandma had another heart attack last week." Mom pulls into an end space and turns the car off. Her hands stay glued to the steering wheel. Her gaze stays on the windshield. "We knew you were coming. We figured it would be better to wait until you were here."

"And all the stuff you've said the last few months about her being okay?"

"She was okay—"

"Mom." I blink and a tear catches on my lashes. I don't have the emotional energy for this. For anything. I need a million hours of sleep. "Tell me the truth. How long have things been bad?"

"Bad is relative."

"She's dying."

"She..."

"Mom. Tell me the truth. Is Grandma dying?"

She turns to me, tears rolling down her cheeks. Her lips quiver.

Mom usually looks so put together. Pretty. Trendy.

But she's in leggings and a hoodie. Her hair is in a ponytail. Her only makeup is a little lipstick. It's not like her.

"Mom..." My voice cracks. I know the answer, but I need to hear her say it.

"I'm sorry, Kay." She shakes her head. "We thought it would be better if you didn't know. It's what Mom wanted."

"But—"

"She didn't want you to see her like this."

"But—"

"She only has a few weeks, max. Or maybe a few days. It's hard to say."

My hands are shaking again. A tear stings my eye. It's hot and salty. Then there's another. Another.

Words rise up in my throat.

But what is there to say?

Grandma is dying.

There isn't a word in the universe that will make that better.

I unclick my seatbelt and move toward Mom.

She wraps her arms around me. "I'm so sorry, Kay. We thought we were protecting you."

"Well stop." I tug at her hoodie. "Stop making decisions for me. Stop protecting me. I'm an adult and I can tell you what I can handle. Or what I want. Or who I love."

"Kay?"

"He... he isn't here."

"Who?"

"He loves me, but he won't be with me."

"Who loves you, Kay?"

"It doesn't matter." Not anymore. I have to get through this without him. That's his decision. It's probably for the best. Otherwise, I'll fall more in love with him.

I stop chocking back sobs.

I hold onto my mom and I cry until I can't cry anymore.

Chapter Fifty

BRENDON

T his is taking every ounce of my concentration.

It's a simple tattoo. Black line art. Three colors. No shading.

Fuck, it's like I'm apprenticing again.

I pull back to check on my client. Allison. She's a tall girl with short hair and a quiet smile. Her boyfriend is sitting opposite her, holding her hand, whispering words of comfort.

"You okay?" Sweat is gathering on my brow. It's not the heat. The air conditioning's hum is competing with the buzz of Walker's gun.

It's the devil on my shoulder, telling me I fucked up.

And the angel arguing that this is for the best, no matter how badly it hurts right now.

Allison grunts a yes.

Her boyfriend smiles at her. Squeezes her hand. "It looks awesome."

"Yeah?" She turns toward the mirror to catch a glimpse of the ink forming on her shoulder blade. It's two dinosaurs facing each other with a heart between them.

She must be able to see because her eyes light up. "That's perfect." She looks to me. "How much longer?"

"Ten minutes." It's a small piece and we're halfway there.

She nods. "Ten minutes. I can do that." She lies back down. Rests her head on her hands. "Do you get a lot of people saying it doesn't hurt?"

All the time. "Mostly guys."

"They think it makes them tough?" she asks.

"Yeah." I check the work. The green dino is done. Now it's the pink one and the red heart between them. "You know men."

She looks to her boyfriend with a smile. "I do."

"Hey." He folds his arms. Throws her a look of faux irritation. "I told you it would hurt like a bitch."

"Stay still." My voice drops to that demanding tone. Damn. I don't have enough focus to keep shit professional.

She doesn't notice. She's too busy smiling at her boyfriend.

"You ready?" I hold her back in place with my free hand.

"Ready," she says.

I get to work on the pink dinosaur. She lies there, squeezing her boyfriend's hand as he distracts her with conversation about their upcoming vacation.

Usually, I love it when the boyfriend comes. Wife, daughter, mom, best friend, coworker—it doesn't matter. Talking keeps people distracted from the pain. If they're here alone, that's my job.

I should appreciate it more right now—I don't have a shred of comfort in me.

But, fuck, I hate seeing them happy.

I hate the way they're smiling at each other.

I hate that the sun is shining.

I hate the music flowing from our speakers.

I hate that Kay is hurting alone.

It only takes eight minutes to finish. I clean and bandage her, go through my aftercare routine, take her to the register.

She throws her arms around me. "Thank you. Thank you. Thank you."

The boyfriend shoots me a friendly nod. "Thanks for taking care of her." He offers his hand.

I shake. "Just doing my job." I motion to Leighton, standing behind the counter. "Will you get them some A+D ointment?"

"Sure. But you should—" She motions to Walker, leaning against the wall, staring at me like he's thinking about how he's gonna deck me.

On anyone else, that expression would be *you're mildly annoying*. But Walker never shows that he's pissed. Or hurt. Or annoyed even.

That look might be *I'm gonna kill you*.

He waits until the clients are out the door to approach me.

His eyes narrow.

His voice drops to a threatening tone. "What the fuck is wrong with you?"

"A lot. You need to be more specific," I say.

Leighton clears her throat. "We have customers."

Walker shakes his head *I don't care*. "What the fuck is this?" He shows off his cell. With a text from Emma.

Emma: Kaylee said Brendon ended things.

"And?" I press my lips together. I'm not defending my decision to him. Or to anyone.

"What the fuck, Brendon?"

"Not a question."

"Is Em talking to Kay now?"

"No. Just fielding texts. She said she sent something to you. But you know that."

Fuck. My stomach drops. "No. My phone is charging in the office."

Leighton clears her throat. Nods to the short guy waiting in the lobby.

Walker ignores her. Continues staring at me like I'm the devil.

He's probably right.

But I'm finally fixing that.

"That's not an explanation." He stares back at me. "I'm not going to watch while you throw away the only person who makes you happy."

Leighton joins his glaring. "You really dumped her?"

"Yeah. And I don't see how it's your business," I say.

"You're my friend, you idiot. And she is too." She runs a hand through her short hair. "I don't get it. You pine for her for months. She follows you around like a lovesick puppy. You finally have her, and you're both happy. Then, what, you dump her because you're bored of her?"

"No." It's not even close to that.

"What reason could you possibly have for leaving Kay?" Leighton asks. "You're worse than my ex."

"No arguments there." I have no idea what Leighton's ex did to hurt her, but right now I feel like the scum of the Earth. Fuck, the way Kaylee stared at me like I tore her heart out.

"What the fuck, Brendon? Are you going to explain?" Walker asks.

"How many times are you going to ask the same question?" This isn't what I want. It's how things have to be.

"Until I get a straight answer." He shakes his head. "Why would you break up with Kaylee?"

"She shouldn't be with someone like me," I say.

"What the hell does that mean?" Leighton asks.

"God. Still with this shit? Get the fuck over yourself." Walker's voice gets angry. "Do you treat her well?"

"Of course," I say.

"You make her smile?" he asks.

"Yeah. And?" I fold my arms.

"You support her?" he asks.

"I try." I do.

"You listen when she needs that?" he asks.

"You make her come?" Leighton jumps in.

"Of course. That's a stupid fucking question," I say.

"You're a stupid fucking idiot." She slams the table. "You make her laugh. You make her feel safe. You make her come. Explain to me how she shouldn't be around you."

I... I can't.

"She lights up like a pinball machine when you're around," Walker says. "She loves you. You love her. The two of you are a million fucking times more pleasant when you're around each other. Whatever bullshit you're selling about her being better off without you—nobody is buying it but you."

Chapter Fifty-One

KAYLEE

"Kay-bear." Grandma's voice is soft. Quiet. She's smiling. Her eyes are a little fuzzy.

According to Mom, she's on a lot of painkillers.

But she doesn't look like she's dying.

She just looks tired.

How can she only have weeks left?

Or less?

I swallow hard. "Hey, Grandma."

Mom squeezes my hand.

"You look terrible, Kay. Haven't you heard of under-eye concealer?" Grandma teases.

It's the same as always. Except for the circumstances.

"I just got off a plane. Give me a break." I move closer to her bed. "I'm tea deprived."

"Nothing good here," Grandma says. "But there is a Starbucks up the street." She looks to Mom. "Get us something, honey?"

Mom nods. She pulls me into a tight hug. "Take as long as you need."

Because this is it.

This might be one of a few weeks of conversations—there's no way I'm flying back to LA now. Not until...

This might be our last conversation.

Tears threaten to hit my eyes, but I swallow them down. If this is our last conversation, I want to savor it.

I want it to be about more than Grandma dying.

But I still have to say a goodbye. "I love you, Grandma. I'm... I just want you to know how much I love you. And how much I've missed our conversations. And spending summers with you. And reading you my *Days of Our Lives* fan fiction. I'm up to chapter five in my book. I wrote a little on the plane."

"Yeah?"

I nod. "It's been a nice distraction."

"From this?"

"Yeah, and... I don't want to talk about my problems."

"I do." She sits up a little straighter. "You know I love giving you advice, Kay-Bear."

"You mean telling me what to do?"

She laughs. It's hearty. Alive. "Tell me what happened. It's that hot friend of yours?"

I nod. "Emma realized. She freaked. She stopped talking to me. Then I... I thought we were okay, but he..."

"Oh, Kay—"

"I told him I loved him. And it scared him, I guess. I don't know. He kept saying he's not good for me. That I shouldn't love him. But that's ridiculous. He's the sweetest guy I've ever known."

Grandma squeezes my hand. "I'm sorry, baby. Some people won't get out of their own way. You can't always stop that."

"I know. But it sucks."

"That it does." She laughs. "There will be other guys."

"Is it that hopeless?"

410

"Maybe not." She pats my hand. "You're a catch, Kay-bear. Pretty. Smart. Sweet. He's a fool to let you go."

"He's trying to say it's for me. Because he's bad for me. Or something. I'm not sure."

"The hot ones are never smart."

I laugh. "He is. Just—"

"We've all got our baggage. After your grandfather left, I wouldn't even look at men. I'd get write ups at work for being disrespectful to my supervisors."

I smile. That sounds like Grandma.

"Once your mom was older, I tried dating, but I was still angry at the world. I wasn't ready to trust someone to be my partner. I lost a few good things because I wouldn't get out of my way. But there was nothing any of those guys could do."

"Nothing? You sure?"

She laughs. "You think he loves you?"

"He said he did, but I don't know... if he loves me then why doesn't he want to be with me?"

"I don't know, baby. I'm sorry. Sometimes it takes a while to get over past hurt. I never did. I was never brave enough to risk my heart again."

"Maybe that's it. He... his parents were awful to him before they died. Made him feel worthless. Then they died suddenly. I mean, sorry—"

"It's okay. I know I'm dying."

A tear catches on my lashes. "And you... are you ready?"

She presses her lips together. "I've been too weak to live a long time. I'm ready."

Oh God.

"But I'd rather talk about your hot friend."

I wipe a tear from my cheek. "Okay. I just... You have

to know how much I appreciate you. You were my best friend for a long time. You still are."

She squeezes my hand. "It's been an honor watching you grow, Kay. You're such a bright young woman." She blinks back a tear. "It's good you take after your mother and not me."

I shake my head. "I wish I was more like you."

She wipes her cheeks with her free hand. "That's about all I can take—"

"Okay. I do... I do need advice about Brendon."

She nods. "You think he's worth the trouble?"

"You've seen his picture."

She smiles. "Not lately."

I pull out my phone to grab one of us. There's a text from Emma. A few actually.

Emma: I'm sorry. Brendon is so stupid. I can't believe he did that. Did you get to Jersey okay? How is your grandma? Call me, Kay. I'm so sorry about flipping out. I just... I guess I did freak out. I love you.

"That him?" Grandma asks.

"No. Emma."

"You're smiling."

"She apologized. She forgives me for lying to her."

"Good. Now let me see the hottie."

My laugh hurts. These pictures are salt in the wound. We look so happy. So right together.

I pick one of us at Inked Hearts. I'm sitting on the stool behind the counter, and he has his arms around me, and we're both smiling like we're happy enough to die.

I hand my cell to grandma.

"Mmm. Yes. I can see why you look so miserable." She taps the screen. "Anything good in here?" She raises her brows twice.

"Oh my God, Grandma! No. If there was, do you think I'd show you?"

"You'd deprive a dying woman of a juicy pic?"

"If it was meant for my eyes only, yes."

"You're not convincing me to stop looking."

I laugh as I steal my cell back. "You're sick. You know that?"

"Of course." She smiles. "How is school?"

"Good. Hard. But good."

"And work?"

"It's fine. I... um... I might extend my trip and—"

"Don't miss school for me."

"Grandma. You're... I'm staying here as long as I need to be here. You won't talk me out of it."

She looks up at me with a sad smile. "You really are a strong young woman."

I wipe my tears. "I try. But I don't feel that way. Not usually."

"If your boss gives you shit, tell me. I'll call him. Cough a lot. Guilt him."

I shake my head. "No. I can find a place with better tips, so I can drop to two days a week."

"You should, Kay-bear. And play up the flirting. You'll never go broke appealing to a wealthy man's ego."

"I'll keep that in mind."

"You won't. If things were different, you'd lecture me about integrity."

"They aren't different." I press my lips together. "You were a single mom. I get it."

She nods. "You're such a good kid. And so strong, going through everything on your own. But it doesn't have to be like that, Kay-bear. Don't make the same mistakes I did. Let people in. Let them see when you hurt. Even if it means risking your heart."

"I'm trying."

"Your mom told me about your depression."

"What?" How does mom know?

"You're on SSRIs. Insurance, they send a summary of benefits. Billing codes. All that shit. She wanted me to know, so I could look for signs that you might be thinking about hurting yourself."

"Oh."

"Let her think it was our secret."

I nod. If things were different, I'd argue. But they're not. "Okay."

"Your mom probably never told you, but she had terrible postpartum depression. She couldn't get out of bed. And she felt so guilty, thinking there must be something wrong with her. She had a new baby. She was supposed to be happy."

"Oh."

"I guess you can blame my genetics. The same thing happened to me." Grandma squeezes my hand. "It's the human condition, Kay. We're all a little bit broken. Don't let that stop you from going after what you want."

I nod.

"Promise."

"I promise."

"You mean that?"

I nod. I really do.

Chapter Fifty-Two

BRENDON

After hours of driving mindlessly, I end up where I'm supposed to be. The cemetery in Culver City. It's the perfect place for my parents to rest forever.

The freeway is on one side. The mall is on another. A pocket of expensive houses is on the third.

The shiny billboards tacked to the mall cast a soft glow over the lush green grass. It's fucked how green this grass is —our entire state is out of water—but it would be more fucked if it was as dead as the people buried here.

I clutch the bouquet of roses. Mom's favorite. A cliché, yeah, but it's hard to do anything but love roses. They spread open, invite your touch, then reward you with a prick to the fingertip.

They're a perfect fucking metaphor. Beautiful. Guarded. Dangerous.

I've lost track of how many rose tattoos I've done. Hell, of how many I've done this month. Everyone wants that strong, barbed feminine beauty on their skin.

It suits Mom.

Strong. Beautiful. Viscous.

My canvas shoes soak up every drop of dew on the grass. It's a cool night. It should be dark, but those stupid fucking billboards are as bright as a dozen full moons.

My feet remember the path. I'm not sure how. It's been an eternity since I've been here. The funeral. A few times when Em wanted to go the first year. Then never.

I've certainly never come here alone.

There. Almost all the way at the back, halfway down the row. Josephine Kane. Elliot Kane.

My memories of Mom are sharper than my memories of Dad. But then she was so much sharper than Dad. She was always the picture of the perfect trophy wife. Educated. Pretty. Dark hair cut in a chic straight line. The latest designer clothes. A schedule filled with proper hobbies and volunteering.

When I was a kid, she spent a lot of time with me. She'd read to me. Take me to the park. Bring me on all her lunches and community meetings. Then she had Emma, and it was the three of us together. Dad was always busy. Working. But Mom poured time into us.

She loved us.

She loved me. At least that guy I was then.

It wasn't until I discovered punk music and insisted on wearing ripped jeans that I lost her affection.

It wasn't all at once. It was a little bit at a time. She'd look at me like my decisions were wrong. Like they disgusted her. Then like there was no coming back for me.

I guess there wasn't.

I get why she asked me not to come around anymore. I get that she was protecting Emma. Fuck, if there's anything I get it's protecting Emma.

It was bullshit.

She didn't look past what she saw.

But then I didn't either.

Mom always seemed unbreakable. But she wasn't. There were cracks. A quiver in her voice here. A too strong drink there. A sad look at the door when I asked when Dad would be home.

She was lonely. She was lashing out. She was trying to put shit together.

I peel the plastic from the bouquet and drop the roses on her grave.

"I don't know what you'd think of me if you were still around. I guess I wouldn't be this guy. I wouldn't have changed everything in my life to take care of Emma." I press my hand to her gravestone. "I get it now, how hard it is to be a parent, to try to do the best for the people you love. I get that you were trying to help me and Emma in your way. I get that you looked at me like I was a piece of shit because you wanted something better for me." I lean back on my heels. "I understand. And I forgive you."

The tension in my shoulders melts. Fuck, it's weird talking to a tombstone, but if I squint, I can convince myself Mom is hearing this somehow.

"I know you didn't mean to fuck with my head. But you did. There's still a huge part of me convinced I'm worthless. That I'll never deserve the love of the kind of woman who wears cardigans and gets straight As. Fuck, I think I just threw away the best thing that ever happened to me because of it."

My exhale is heavy.

"But even with all that fucked up shit you did, I wish you were still around. I miss you. I can't believe it, but I do. I'm not sure if you'd believe me, but I'm trying to do better. For me. For Em. For you and Dad. For all of us."

———

Emma's locked in her room.

I knock on her door.

She doesn't answer.

"Em. I can open this door. I need to know you're okay."

"Okay is relative."

"Physically, okay."

She says nothing.

"Em." All these doors are child proof. A bobby pin is enough to trip the lock. But I'd rather not invade my sister's privacy. That's one of the million ways I want to do better. "You don't have to talk to me. Just tell me if you're okay."

"Yeah."

"Thanks."

Her footsteps move toward the door. "Why did you break up with Kaylee?"

"You were right. I'm supposed to protect her from guys like me." At least that's what my head was telling me. Now... it doesn't feel as right. It feels like Mom's voice.

"Really?" Emma pulls her door open. "Are you fucking serious?"

"You said it."

"Because I was pissed." She smooths her hair. Wipes her puffy, bloodshot eyes. "I thought about it. And... well, I was wrong. I was shocked and pissed and, well, you don't exactly have a good track record with relationships."

Fair enough. "Yeah."

"I thought... well, Kay is really pretty. And she's all sweet and innocent. And your reputation... I thought you just wanted to corrupt her. Or some sick shit like that. I couldn't imagine you really loving her. But I knew... I think, deep down, I knew she liked you."

"Yeah?"

"Yeah. I wanted to believe it was someone else. Even Dean. But I think I knew. And I even understood. She's happy around you. She laughs. She relaxes. She... she tells you stuff. Stuff she doesn't tell me. That pissed me off. I'm her best friend and you're some hot, tall guy who will probably throw her away."

"You're tall."

"Yeah. I... I was jealous of you, I guess. That you were getting more of her. I just... You've both been spending so much time together. And then you both lied to me about it. It hurt. But now that I step back from that. I think you're good together."

What? I blink a dozen times.

"Don't give me that look, Brendon. You must see it. She's happy around you. And you—you're normally trying to audition to play Jess on some *Gilmore Girls* reboot."

"What?"

"Oh my God, everyone knows *Gilmore Girls*! You watched it over my shoulder."

I shake my head. I vaguely remember the mom and daughter eating a lot of junk food, but that's it.

"You sit around with your sketchbook like it's the only thing that gets your pain. But that isn't true. Kay does. I don't know what you tell her, but you're different around her too. You're happy. And, no offense, but you're usually miserable enough you're annoying to be around. I mean, I still love you, but it can be a drag."

"No offense though?"

She laughs. "Yeah. Of course not. I mean, you're no Ryan, but you were kinda on your way there. The last six months at least. And Kay... I'm just glad she has someone to help her right now. Well. That she did. But if you're breaking up with her for her then you're a fucking idiot. Who takes advice from their eighteen-year-old sister?"

I can't help but laugh. "You're wiser than you think."

"Well, yeah, if you need some help with your makeup or wardrobe. We have some great skinny jeans on sale. If you want a new pair, I can help with that. With Kay—"

"You know you're giving me advice right now."

"Okay. Let's say I'm wise. You should listen to me."

Yeah. I'm pretty sure I should.

Emma pulls out her cell. "Did you get this?"

It's a text from Kaylee's mom.

Mrs. Hart: Kaylee is going to be staying with us for a few extra days. She's doing okay. I'm sure she'd appreciate a call from you, Emma. I'm not sure she's in a place to reach out.

"It sounds bad." Emma's gaze goes to her screen. "I called a bunch, but she didn't pick up."

"It's late on the East Coast."

"You think it's bad news with her grandma?"

"Hard to say." But probably.

"We should be there. Shouldn't we?" Emma pushes her door wide open and steps into her room. She goes straight to her laptop. "I looked at tickets. And I talked to my manager. We could leave tomorrow night. Get in first thing in the morning. Or... well... if you really don't want to be with Kay, then you probably shouldn't come."

No shit. I nod.

"So, what's it going to be? Are you coming or not?"

Chapter Fifty-Three

KAYLEE

I spend the entire day in Grandma's hospital room, talking about everything and nothing. Mom gives me the morning with Grandma. She joins me in the afternoon. We share stories and they team up to give me life advice.

Grandma stays quiet about things with Brendon. But I know Mom is going to find out. And that's going to be the end of me living at his place.

Not that I could live there with things as they are.

I... I'll just have to work more. Take out another student loan. Commute a little farther. Do whatever it takes to make it work.

We don't leave until the nurse insists.

It's so quiet at home. It's strange. Usually the house is full of Grandma's laugh. Or some loud, exciting show she's watching. This whole place is her. The walls are bright jewel tones. The blankets on the black leather couch are hot pink.

She's always so bright and vibrant.

It's scary that soon she won't be alive.

But I'm starting to accept it.

———

I'M HALFWAY THROUGH MY MORNING TEA—SHITTY generic tea—when the doorbell rings.

Mom is making eggs in the kitchen.

Dad is asleep in the bedroom.

It's early. Seven-something. Who the hell could that be?

"Can you get that, Kay?" Mom's voice is even. Knowing.

Huh.

I take one more sip and push myself to my feet.

This is a small place. It's only a dozen footsteps to the door. "Hello."

"Hey."

That's Brendon's voice.

What the hell?

My stomach gets all light and floating. Nervous energy spills through my limbs. He's here. Why is he here? What does that mean?

I need his comfort so badly.

But I...

If he's not here to kiss and makeup...

I can't take falling more in love with him.

I pull the door open. "Hey."

He's standing there in jeans and a t-shirt. Like it's a normal day. Like we're about to walk to the shop.

But then...

His shirt is wrinkled. His hair is a mess. His eyes are heavy. Tired.

"We just got in." He nods to the black suitcase next to

him. Then to the car parked on the street. A rental car. Emma is in the passenger seat, staring at the mirror. "Emma insisted on fixing her makeup. I told her I wouldn't wait."

I nod. That's so them.

"Your mom told me what's going on. I'm sorry, Kay. I wish things were different."

"Me too."

His eyes meet mine. They promise that everything will be different. But he doesn't say anything.

I try to find the words, but I can't. Mom is moving toward us.

She stops at the door. Smiles at Brendon. "Mr. Kane. You didn't have to come."

His eyes meet mine. He raises a brow. *She doesn't know?*

I shake my head. She doesn't. Not yet. But I'm going to tell her. I'm going to stop taking on the whole world by myself.

"I get a little protective of Emma," he says.

Mom nods. "I can imagine. She's a spitfire."

"You have no idea," he says.

Mom laughs. It's the first time she's laughed since I've been here. "Well, come in. We've already got a pot of coffee on." She looks out to the car. Waves. "Hey, Emma. Come in whenever you're ready."

Emma steps out of the passenger seat. Taps the key fob. The car beeps locked. Her eyes meet mine. She mouths *I'm sorry*. I think. She's far away.

"We'll put out the air mattress for you. And there's the couch. It's very comfortable." Mom leads Brendon into the kitchen.

"We have a hotel," he says.

"Nonsense. You've been so hospitable this year. Kaylee

sent me pictures of her room. It's beautiful. And I remember your house. This is the least we could do."

His eyes meet mine. He raises a brow, offering me a chance to object.

I want him here. Fuck, I want him here so badly it hurts. But I want him here as mine. If he's not...

I don't know.

God, the sight of his dark eyes and his soft lips is enough to comfort me. To remind me that there are beautiful things in the world. That one day it's going to be okay.

"You should stay here," I say. "We have good coffee. Dad's obsessed."

He nods. "I'm sold."

Emma rushes in through the door. She presses it closed behind her, rests her suitcase against it.

She goes straight to me and throws her arms around me. "I'm so fucking sorry, Kay."

"Me too."

"I love you."

"I love you too."

She leans in to whisper. "And I'm sorry my brother is an idiot. He... I think he's going to come around. But I get it if you don't forgive him."

I don't know what I forgive. I'm not ready to ask myself that yet. I release Emma. "You want coffee?"

"Of course." She smiles. "You look good."

"You too."

She smacks her lips. "It's not too much?"

"That's in your vocabulary?" I tease.

Mom laughs. "Your hair is darling, Emma. I wish I could pull that off."

"You could, Mrs. Hart. Though I think purple would suit your complexion better. There's this great new brand with smokey colors. The purple would look fierce on you," Emma says.

Mom laughs. "I'll think about that."

Brendon's eyes meet mine. I'm not sure exactly what he's saying, only that I want to hear every drop of it.

Chapter Fifty-Four

KAYLEE

We go straight to the hospital with Grandma. Brendon and Emma introduce themselves and say hello then they wait in the lobby.

Mom and I stay with her all morning. Dad joins in the evening. We get home, have dinner together, make small talk about nothing, sleep in separate spaces.

It's like that for days. We spend every minute of visiting hours in the hospital. Emma and I talk all night. Brendon is just there. Waiting for me. Ready for when I need him.

It's like that all week.

Until Friday.

I wake to Mom standing over my bed, tears running down her cheeks.

I don't have to ask to know. It's written all over her face.

Grandma is gone.

The world is a little colder.

A little darker.

A little uglier.

I WANT TO BE STRONG FOR MOM. SO SHE CAN FALL apart. But I can't bring myself to leave my bed.

Dad brings me breakfast and tea.

I force myself to brush my teeth. Wash my face.

Then I collapse back in my bed. It whispers of Grandma too. The hot pink sheets. The landline phone in the shape of lips. The boy band posters all over the walls.

She'd want me to celebrate her life, not mourn her death.

And I want to do that.

But it hurts, knowing she's not here anymore.

That I can never go to her for advice. Or read her another chapter. Or argue about whether or not I'll call her Gigi.

Emma brings me lunch and dinner. She sits with me as I pour my heart out. Hugs me as I cry.

But I don't fall apart until the sun sets. Night falls over the house slowly. My room is silent. I can hear my parents go to bed. My mom sobbing. My dad comforting her.

Emma turning on the TV.

Footsteps moving toward my door.

A soft knock.

Brendon's voice. "Hey."

"Come in." I pull the sheets a little higher. I'm not ready to face him, but I need his comfort. It's confusing. My first thought is that Grandma would know what to do.

But she's not here.

She's never giving me advice again.

She...

I choke back a sob.

Brendon steps into my room and presses the door shut behind him.

He lays in my bed behind me. Wraps his arms around my waist and pulls my body into his.

And he holds me as I sob.

As I release every bit of hurt.

I fall apart in his arms.

Even with everything between us, he's the only person I trust to piece me back together.

Chapter Fifty-Five

KAYLEE

I wake up alone.

Even so, the world is a little less cold.

A little less dark.

It hurts a little less, Grandma being gone.

I manage to drag myself out of bed. I brush my teeth, shower, put on makeup, blow dry my hair. I feel better. Not great. But better. Like I can actually face the world.

I pull on an old dress. It's a little small, but it's stretchy enough to be comfortable. I'm about to move into the hallway when I see it.

A note on my desk.

Meet me at the boardwalk at noon. I have something to show you.
- Brendon

And there's the exact address. And a detailed drawing. A blooming rose in the shape of a heart, covered in thorns. It's beautiful. Intricate. Incredibly Brendon.

My stomach flutters. It pushes away the darkness flowing through me. I actually feel warm. Alive. Like the world is a place where good things can happen.

It still hurts.

But I'm pretty sure I can survive it.

———

MOM IS STRANGELY OKAY WITH MY REQUEST TO BORROW
the car. Emma too. She doesn't ask where I'm going or
insist on coming. Dad either.

It's weird.

Like they know what Brendon's up to. And are
somehow okay with it. But that isn't possible. If my parents
knew we were sleeping together, they'd kill him.

Or maybe...

I mean, I told Grandma.

She might have narced on me. And I wasn't exactly
subtle about crying to Mom about a guy who didn't
love me.

The sad promise of *Love Will Tear Us Apart* flows
through the speakers. Joy Division is the only band
Brendon and I like. Well, the only band he'll admit to
liking. He hates the indie pop and pop-rock I play. (Sue me,
I like vaguely pop sounding things). But he's different with
some of the pop-punk bands. Maybe it's all high school
nostalgia. Or maybe it's a secret love of well-recorded,
melodic music.

I'm going to call him on it one day.

But not today.

Love has already torn me apart.

I'm just hoping it puts me back together.

I check the address again. Almost there. My fingers
curl around the steering wheel. My heartbeat picks up. I
don't know what this is, but guys don't leave beautiful
drawings and promises as break up notes. I think. I don't
know anything about guys.

Grandma would tell me to be brave. To go with it.

She'd say something cliché about how she regrets all the things she didn't do. All her mistakes taught her things or brought her joy. Even her ex-husband. He brought her Mom. And that was worth everything.

I turn into the beach parking lot. It's half empty. And there, in the corner—that's Brendon's rental car. I think. It's some generic black sedan with a big yellow sticker advertising the rental company. It could be anyone's rental car.

I park at an end space. Turn the car off. Force my hands into my lap.

They're shaking.

But it's a good shaking.

A nervous energy *I'm capable of feeling alive* shaking.

I climb out of the car, tap the lock, hug my purse.

A breeze blows over my shoulders. It's a cool day and the ocean breeze isn't helping matters. This dress isn't nearly warm enough. And it's not a boardwalk dress. My hair isn't right. Or my makeup. Or my shoes.

No. This is fine. It's clothes. They aren't what matters.

I cross the parking lot and climb the wooden steps to the boardwalk.

He's standing there against the railing, the sand and the ocean and the sky his backdrop.

He looks so good. All tall, dark, and handsome.

Those same black jeans.

Those same coffee eyes.

That soft smile curling over his lips.

I move toward him. Until I can smell his soap. My fingers curl around the note. "It's a beautiful drawing. New?"

He nods. "Had something in my head I had to get out."

"What does it mean?"

"I'll get there." He takes my hand. "I promise. But give me a minute."

I nod. A minute is too long. A second is too long. All this air between us—it's too much. But I need to hear everything.

"Your mom and I talked."

"Oh. You told her?"

"Not everything. But I will. We agreed that you and Em should move in together. If you want."

Me and Em with our own place? We always talked about that. But once I started working, I realized it would be forever before I could afford it.

"Emma refused to let me cover her half."

"Of course."

"Your Mom... Your grandma took out a life insurance policy awhile back. It's a few hundred thousand dollars. And you're the sole beneficiary."

"What?"

"She wanted to make sure you'd have enough to study whatever you wanted."

"Oh."

"I tried to get your old place back, but the subletor refused to leave before the lease is up. It can be yours next September. But I figured you'd rather find one place and make it home."

I nod.

"I found you two a place. It's in Santa Monica. It's halfway between the beach and SMC. If you'd rather save everything, I can find you a cheaper place." He pulls out his cell and hands it to me.

I flip through the pictures of the apartment. It's small, but it's nice. Big windows. Hardwood floors. Two little bedrooms. A balcony. An ocean view if you look from just the right angle.

"It's yours if you want it."

I nod. "I do."

"And I..." He stares back into my eyes. "That night Emma found out, she said something—"

"Said?"

"Yelled something that stuck with me. I'm supposed to protect you from guys like me."

"But you—"

"Let me finish." His voice is strong. Even. Sure.

But I can't wait.

I need to know that he's mine.

I force myself to nod.

"I couldn't stop thinking about it. I've believed that I'm no good for a long time. My mom made sure of it. That was why I tried to stay away from you, Kay. Not just because you were young or because you were Emma's friend or because it would fuck up everything in my life. Because I didn't want to hurt you."

Words claw at my throat. Somehow, I manage to nod instead of speaking.

"But the more time I spent with you, the more I wanted to peel back all your walls. I wanted to find the things that hurt you and destroy them. I wanted your heart."

"I wanted to give it to you."

"I know. You trusted me."

"I still do."

His lips curl into a half smile. "That was everything I wanted. Still is. But it's also everything that terrifies me. You're as bright as the sun, Kay. You have this big, beautiful life ahead of you. And the thought of snuffing out even a hint of your boundless potential—it guts me."

He moves closer.

Until I can feel all the heat of his body.

His hand goes to the neckline of his t-shirt.

"It still does. But I want to get through that. If you're willing to have me. If you have the patience for it."

He pulls his t-shirt down his chest.

There's fresh ink on his skin.

Right on the spot I chose.

Serva me, servabo te.

Save me and I'll save you.

"Brendon." I reach for his skin. "Can I?"

He nods.

I trace the lines of the ink. "When?"

"Before I left. Walker did it."

"Yeah?"

"Told me he'd kick my ass if I fucked this up."

A sob rises up in my throat. "He meant it?"

"I think so. Pretty sure Dean and Ryan will join him."

My heart warms. The guys look out for me. They support me. I do have people who love me. Who want me to be okay. None of them can replace Grandma, but it helps, knowing I have support.

"I mean it, Kay. I know you'll always feel a little broken. And I'll always worry I don't deserve you. But I want to be there, by your side, to help you through every ugly moment. And I want you by mine."

A tear rolls down my cheek. "I want that too."

He cups my cheek with his palm. Wipes a tear with my thumb. "Those happy or sad?"

"Both."

"I love you. I have for a long time. And I will for longer."

I nod. "I love you too."

He wraps his arms around me and he kisses me like he can't get enough of my lips.

Like he can't get enough of me.

God, he tastes good.

I don't come up for air until I'm dizzy.

With love and lust and the comfort of knowing he's by my side.

For everything.

Forever.

FIFTY-SIX

Epilogue

BRENDON

Kaylee steps out of the humanities building with stars in her eyes. She stretches her arms over her head as she lets out a soft yawn.

Her lips spread into a smile as her eyes catch mine. Her movements get faster. The exhaustion fades from her expression.

I move toward her. Meet her at the halfway point of the sidewalk.

She jumps into my arms and squeezes me tightly. "I thought you had to work."

"I finished early." I soak up the feeling of her body against mine. She's so warm and soft. And she's mine.

All mine.

Fuck, it's still hard to believe.

I set her down on the concrete, but I keep my arms around her.

Her green eyes fill with affection as she looks up at me. "I missed you."

"I missed you." I bring one hand to the back of her

head, undo her ponytail, and run my fingers through her hair. "How was it?"

She smiles. "Easy peasy."

"Easy?"

"Relatively speaking."

She's been locked in her studying cave for the last two weeks. It's been torture. But it's worth it for the look on her face.

I cup the back of her head. "Straight As?"

"I think so. But we'll see." She slides her arm around my waist and rests her head on my chest. "Tell me we're going straight to your place."

"My place? What would we do there?" I play dumb.

"Brendon Kane, this is not the time to be a tease."

"There go my plans for the afternoon."

Kay laughs so hard she shakes. "Okay. You can tease. But not until we're at your place."

"I'm not following."

"You are too." She slides her hand under my t-shirt and presses her palm against my stomach.

"I have a surprise for you."

"Yeah?" Her voice lifts. "Something, ahem..."

I chuckle. "No. After."

"After." She looks up at me. "I like after."

"Me too."

———

KAYLEE GIGGLES AS SHE STEPS INTO THE HOUSE. SHE surveys the living room like she hasn't seen it in weeks. I guess she hasn't. I'm not sure she's done anything but work, sleep, and study for the last two weeks.

"It's so much cleaner without Em here." She runs her

fingers over the spotless dining table. "Almost freakishly clean."

"And your room?"

"Good point." She takes my hand and follows me to the stairs. "I miss this place."

"I miss you here." Nearly every night, I fall asleep wishing she was in my bed. But I made her mom a promise, that Kaylee would live with Emma until she graduated from college.

Today was Kaylee's last final. The last day of freshman year. That leaves three years to go.

Fuck, three years until I have her around twenty-four seven.

If I'm lucky, she'll graduate early.

No, I'm lucky either way.

I whisper in her ear. "Go to my room, strip, and sit on the bed."

She stops short. "Strip to what?"

"I want you naked on my bed."

Her tongue slides over her lips.

"I want you coming on my face until you can't take it anymore."

Her pupils dilate. She nods and takes a shaky step forward.

I watch her climb the stairs and move down the hallway. She's practically bouncing. She wants me that badly.

Fuck knows I want her... I'm not sure I have words for how much I want her.

It's been two weeks since I've watched Kay come.

That's two weeks too long.

I wait until I can't stand it anymore, then I make my way to my bedroom.

She's sitting on the black sheets. Naked. Her legs

spread. Her palms on her thighs. Her gaze on the mirror opposite her.

My balls tighten.

Fuck.

I need to be inside her now.

But this first.

My voice drops to that demanding tone. "You want to watch as you come on my face, angel?"

She nods.

I don't have any fucking patience today.

I move right to the bed. Sit next to her, pull her into my lap, and bring my lips to hers.

She kisses back hard and hungry.

I let my hands roam her body. It feels like it's been months since I've touched her.

She groans against my mouth as I toy with her breasts. As I drag my hand down her stomach.

Slowly, I lower her onto her back. I pull her to the edge of the bed, spread her legs, and kneel between then.

Her back arches as I dig my fingers into her thighs.

Fuck, I love the sight of her.

I push her knees apart as I drag my lips up her inner thigh. I go higher and higher, until she's squirming against my hands.

Then I move to her other leg and do it again.

Her groan is half agony, half ecstasy.

I do it again.

Again.

I do it until she's shaking. Until she's groaning my name like it's a curse. Like I'm evil.

I am.

But she fucking loves it.

Once I've tortured her thoroughly, I bring my mouth to her cunt.

Relief drips from her sigh.

That feels so fucking good.

And she tastes so fucking good.

I take my time licking her up and down. I do it slowly, mercilessly slowly.

I wind her up again.

I bring her right to the edge.

She squirms against my hands. She bucks her hips. She tugs at my hair.

"Please," she breathes.

But I don't relent.

I do it again.

"Please." Her hand knots in my hair. Her groans run together. *Please, sigh, please, sigh, please.*

I kiss on her inner thigh. "You watching, angel?"

"No. I..."

"Watch."

She presses herself onto her elbows. Her pupils dilate as her gaze goes to the mirror.

She looks down at me, begging me with her eyes. "I need you."

Fuck, that's music to my ears. Kaylee on the edge is the best thing I've ever seen, heard, smelled, tasted.

I drag my lips a little higher.

She groans a *you're evil* groan.

Still, I do it again.

I do it until all those curses are running together.

Until I'm sure this is as much as she can take.

Then I bring my mouth to her clit.

I flick my tongue against her.

A soft tease.

Then another.

Another.

"Brendon... Please."

One more tease.

Then I lick her exactly how she needs me.

"Fuck," she breathes.

She fights my hands.

She bucks against me.

I keep her pinned to the bed as I lick her. A little harder. A little faster.

There.

Her groan echoes around the room.

Her thighs press against my hands.

Her breath gets ragged. Needy.

A few more flicks of my tongue and she's there.

Her elbows slip. She falls back on the bed. Tugs at the sheets.

Groans my name as she comes.

I lick her through her orgasm.

But that's not enough. I need her coming again.

I give her a few seconds to catch her breath, then I place my head between her legs, and I suck on her clit.

"Fuck." Her hands go straight to my hair.

She tugs like she can't stand how good she feels.

I keep her pinned to the bed as I suck on her.

She shudders. She shakes. She tugs at my hair.

Then she's there. She gets sweeter. Wetter.

I savor every fucking drop of her.

Then I pull back. Stand.

Kaylee watches with rapt attention as I strip out of my jeans and t-shirt.

Her eyes go wide as I push my boxers to my knees.

She nods *please*.

I climb into the bed. Onto her.

She wraps her arms around my chest.

I nudge her legs apart.

With one swift motion, I slide inside her.

Fuck.

She's so fucking soft.

So wet.

So mine.

She rocks her hips to meet me.

We fall into a rhythm, moving together, breathing together, hearts beating together.

I bring my lips to hers.

I kiss her as I fuck her.

And we stay locked like that, limbs tangled, tongues dancing, bodies moving together.

Until she pulls back to groan against my neck. To claw at my back. To groan my name again and again as she comes.

Fuck, the way she pulses around me—

I'll never get enough of *that*.

It pushes me over the edge.

It always does.

With my next thrust, I come.

Pleasure spills through my body. From my cock to my pelvis, my thighs, my torso, my arms, my legs.

All the way to my fingers and toes.

I thrust through my orgasm. I spill every drop inside her.

Then I collapse next to her and pull her into my arms.

We stay pressed together until we catch our breath.

She looks up at me with an ocean of affection in her eyes. "Was that my surprise?"

I shake my head. "We're due there in an hour."

She nods.

I slide my hand between her legs. "I have forty-five minutes to make you come again."

"If I want to shower?"

"Thirty."

Her lips curl into a smile. "That might kill me." She presses her lips to mine. "But I'm willing to risk it."

————

INKED HEARTS IS EMPTY.

Well, that's not exactly right.

Walker is standing behind the front desk.

Kaylee's eyes dart from him to me.

Walker smiles as he shakes his head. "You really keeping her in the dark, Kane?"

"It's not a surprise if you tell someone," I say.

Kaylee's lips press together. Her brow knits then softens. "If he and you..." She looks up at me. "This is an ambush."

"Told you," Walker laughs.

"I prefer surprise." I motion to Walker. *Bring it.*

Kaylee stares back into my eyes. "A surprise with witnesses?"

I nod. "I thought about it. I can do the ink if you want. But I'd rather be the person holding your hand."

"Oh." Her eyes go wide. "You mean, you already have an idea—"

"Yeah. But only if you want it." I take the temporary tattoo from Walker and show it to Kaylee. "Right here." I drag my finger over her ribs. It presses her dress into her skin.

"Bra strap tattoo?" Her laugh is more nervous than anything.

I nod. "That way it's our secret."

Her lips press together. "I, um—"

"We can do it wherever you want. Or not. This is for you, Kay. It's your body. I'm not going to tell you how to adorn it," I say.

"I can kick his ass if you want," Walker says.

She shakes her head. "No. That... that's perfect."

"You know it's gonna hurt like a bitch," Walker says.

She nods. "You know I've seen you guys do a thousand tattoos. I think I have the pain chart memorized."

He winces. "Doesn't get much worse than ribs."

"It doesn't," I agree.

She looks up at me. "I know. But... I... I think that's perfect. Let's see it."

I nod and lead her into the suite in back. Away from the window.

She slides her dress to her waist, unhooks her bra, and holds it in place.

I'm careful about applying the temporary tattoo at the perfect spot.

She's already shaking. But it's good shaking. Excitement.

"There." I peel the paper from her skin.

Her eyes go wide as she turns to the mirror. "It's perfect."

"You sure?"

"Yeah. I am."

It is perfect.

Serva me, Servabo te.

Save me and I'll save you.

She hugs her chest. "Oh God. It's going to hurt a lot." She bites her lip. "What if I can't handle it?"

"You can," I say.

"What if I chicken out with just an *s* on my skin?"

"You won't." I stare back into her eyes. "You've survived a lot worse than a ten-minute rib tattoo."

She nods.

"Everyone is scared to get their first piece."

"You were?"

I nod. "Of course."

"Really?"

"Yeah, but I couldn't admit it. All that macho pride shit."

She laughs. "I can admit it. I'm... it's really going to hurt?"

Again, I nod.

"But I... I can handle it. I think." She motions to her bra pressed against her chest. "Can we do something about this?"

"Here." I take in the rest of the shop. Walker is still at the counter. He's making a point of not looking at us.

It's surprisingly sweet. But then he's been different lately. Ever since he switched from bringing home a different girl every night to a regular fuck buddy.

He insists I'm imagining things, but I'm not.

He's into that girl.

He wants a lot more than her body.

He'll figure it out eventually.

Until then, I'll taunt him about it.

"You two ready yet or what?" he calls out.

"Almost." I shoot him a *give me a minute*. "Avert your eyes."

He laughs. "You know I do rib tattoos all the time."

"Not on Kay, you don't." I turn back to Kaylee. Her soft green eyes are filled with an equal mix of nerves and excitement. "Here." I fasten a backless tube top out of gauze and tape it to her skin.

She laughs. "Fashionable."

I run my fingers through her hair. "You ready?"

"You're going to hold my hand the entire time?"

"Of course."

"Then I am."

I turn back to Walker. "You're needed."

"Story of my life." He laughs, goes to the sink, washes his hands, moves into the suite and motions to the bench. "Lay on your stomach for me."

"Okay." Kaylee moves onto the bench slowly. She folds her arms and rests her head on them.

I sit next to her and offer my hand.

She takes it.

My body gets light. Floaty.

Fuck. I'm as nervous as she is. More even.

Walker preps her skin then applies the stencil. It's really fucking cozy with both of us next to Kay, but there's no way in hell I'm moving.

He slides on his gloves and picks up his gun. His voice drops to a sincere tone. "You ready, Kaylee?"

Her voice is soft. "I think so."

"You'll get used to it fast. Trust me." He turns on the gun. "This is what it sounds like. I know you've heard it a million times, but it's different when it's right by your ear."

"Okay." Her lips press together.

He looks at Kay. Raises a brow. *You ready?*

She nods.

Presses her eyelids together.

"Breathe, angel." I rub the space between her thumb and forefinger with my thumb.

She sucks a deep breath through her teeth and exhales slowly.

Walker looks to me. Offers that same *you ready?* look.

Fuck, I must look as nervous as I feel.

I nod to him then turn back to Kay. "You've got this."

Still, she keeps her eyes closed.

She takes another deep breath. Another slow exhale.

"This is what it feels like." Walker brings the needle to her skin.

She mutters a curse. Squeezes my hand.

"You okay to start?" he asks.

"Stop asking. You're making me lose my nerve." She takes a shaky breath. "Just do it."

He chuckles. "On three."

She nods.

"One, two, three—"

She squeezes my hand as the needle hits her skin. Her eyes stay closed. Her lips stay pressed together.

"Breathe." I rub her hand with my thumb.

She nods as she sucks in a deep breath. Lets out a heavy exhale.

Her grip on my hand tightens.

Fuck, I'm too nervous to do my job properly. I'm supposed to keep her mind occupied. "Emma said she redecorated your place."

"Yeah." Kaylee's exhale is heavy with relief. She must need the distraction. "Mostly her room. She put up a bunch of new pictures of hot guys. She says you have to visualize what you want so the universe can bring it to you."

"You believe that?" I ask.

She grunts as Walker moves onto the second word. "Um. Well, sorta. I mean, if you don't know what you want, how are you going to get it? Besides, it's not just hot guys. She has all sorts of stuff about fashion. And she has those business text books everywhere. I think I talked her into summer school."

"Yeah?" I ask.

"I'm pretty sure she already signed up. I've been really distracted studying for finals." She squeezes my hand.

"Did she change the main room?" I ask.

"You haven't seen it? It's all ocean themed. Teal, turquoise, sand, coral, paintings of mermaids," she says.

"That will be my next one. The mermaid. Do you still have the art?"

"Of course." My chest fills with pride. She's only halfway through this tattoo and she's already desperate for another.

She grunts as Walker moves onto the third word. It's right over her rib bones. That's tender skin. It hurts like a bitch.

"These paintings any good?" I ask.

"Some of them. Some are... not up to Brendon standards." She laughs. "Emma was bragging about how you'll hate them."

"You like living with her?"

"Yeah. She's my best friend. Don't get me wrong." She pauses. Grits her teeth. "I want to live with you one day. I kinda hate you and my mom for your little *not until I graduate* agreement. But I... I understand why she's insisting. And why you agreed."

"Good," I say.

"It's just... I love you and I want you around all the time."

"I'll always be around all the time."

"You promise?"

"Yeah."

The buzzing stops.

Kaylee's shoulders relax. "That's it?"

"That's it." Walker sets the gun down. "But sit tight for a second."

She looks up at me with a smile. There's no nervousness in her expression.

It's pure joy.

She squirms through Walker's aftercare routine.

When he's done, he stands. "I'll let Brendon lecture you."

She pushes herself up and throws her arms around him. "Thank you!"

He pats her back. "Sure thing."

I stand. Swallow my growl. I don't like anyone touching her. But he did this as a favor. You can't tattoo someone without touching them.

He steps backward. "I'll leave you two alone." He nods goodbye.

I nod back.

Kaylee turns toward the mirror. Her eyes go wide as she takes in her reflection. The tattoo is bold black letters across her ribs.

I wrap my arms around her. "You like it?"

"I love it." She leans into my touch. "This is perfect. All of it."

It really is.

———

Want More?

SIGN UP FOR MY MAILING LIST TO GET AN EXCLUSIVE extended epilogue (if you're already subscribed you'll get this soon).

You can also join my Facebook group, like my page on Facebook, or friend me on Facebook.

Keep your Inked Hearts fix going with *Hooking Up*, featuring cocky tattoo artist Walker and geeky grad student Iris having a whole lot of, ahem, *fun*. Turn the page for a sample.

Hooking Up

SPECIAL PREVIEW

Chapter One

WALKER

Get Hooking Up Now

"Thanks for letting me know." My stomach drops like a stone. This is inevitable. Obvious. But it feels like a surprise.

"I'm sorry, Mr. Williams."

"Don't worry about it." My fingers curl into a fist. I press my cell to my cheek. There's nothing else to say. Nothing that will change this. Still, I'm not going to shoot the messenger. "Thanks for your help." I end the call and slide my phone into my front pocket.

The cool air gets hot.

The sounds of the party flow into my ears. Laughter. Conversation. Booming bass.

Bullshit.

It's all bullshit.

This isn't fun.

It's toxic.

The loud music fails to fill my head.

To drown out the thought running through my mind.

Again?

She pulled this shit again.

I'm surprised again.

My heart is a lead weight again.

I'm not taking this anymore.

She's on her own.

She wants to destroy herself. Fine.

I'm done being collateral damage.

I take a deep breath and let out a heavy exhale. Peel my shoulders from my ears. Perfect my poker face.

I step through the open door. Back into Sandy's living room.

She's over the moon. Dancing with her boyfriend, amber beer bottle pressed to her bright pink lips.

We're here to celebrate their new place, them moving in together. I'm happy for them. Really.

Love is great for other people.

I'm not interested.

Don't get me wrong. I love women. I love diving between a woman's legs, throwing her on my bed, getting her screaming my name.

But that's where my relationships stop and end.

Sandy's eyes catch mine. She pulls the bottle from her lips. Mouths *you okay?*

I nod *of course.* I will be. As soon as I find someone to get me out of my head.

I grab a plastic cup from the bar and fill it with room temperature whiskey. It's not good shit. It burns my throat.

Someone is behind me. Pressing her chest against me. "Are you okay, Walker?"

I turn to face a pretty woman with a red pout. One of Bree's friends. An old one. Her name escapes me.

"Fine, yeah." I take another swig. Let the drink sand

off the rough edges. I'm a hypocrite, yeah, but it's necessary.

"How is Bree? I haven't seen her in forever."

"She's Bree." And this conversation is over. I nod a goodbye and move through the makeshift dance floor. The song flows into the next one. I think. I can't tell this music apart.

Friends chat on the couch.

A couple is sitting in the arm chair, making out.

A woman is leaning against the wall, her fingers wrapped around her plastic cup, her lips curled into a frown.

She looks as miserable as I feel.

And as desperate to be somewhere else.

Perfect.

I move closer. She's curvy. Pretty. Dark hair in one of those asymmetrical cuts. Like Leighton's, but shorter. Blue eyes. Soft lips.

She looks smart. Serious. Like a suit.

But there's something else about her. The tight jeans, the leather jacket, the purple gem hanging between her tits.

Fuck, she has nice tits.

There goes my train of thought.

Good riddance.

I move next to her. Copy her stance.

She looks to me. Gives me a long once-over. It's slow. Deliberate.

I bring my glass to my lips. "Let me in on your secret. This *is* where the cool kids hang."

"What makes you think I'm a cool kid?" She taps her glass with her purple fingernail.

"I don't."

"You don't?"

"Not yet. Just want to make sure I'm in the right place."

She laughs. "Because you're cool?"

"You think otherwise?" I run a hand through my wavy hair. This is easy mode shit, but I'm not in the mood for a challenge tonight.

"I spend most of my time with PhD candidates. My cool scale is skewed."

"What are you studying?"

She stares back into my eyes, assessing something. She nods like she's sure. "Psychology. If you want a fighting chance don't make a dumb comment about it."

"A fighting chance?"

"At taking me home."

I laugh. "You have me figured out?"

She takes a long sip of her drink. "Just that."

"You don't like people making comments about you studying psychology but you guess their motivations."

"Are you suggesting there's a correlation?"

"It's possible."

Her lips curl into a smile. Her eyes fix on my chest. My forearms. My eyes. "And you…"

"And I…"

"What do you do?"

"Does it matter?"

She laughs. "No."

"How do you know Sandy?"

"I live next door."

"You want to get out of here?"

She finishes her glass. Her eyes fix on mine. She nods. "Yeah."

I take her hand and lead her to the door.

Chapter Two

IRIS

T he cool air is a welcome reprieve from the heat of
the party.

My heels click against the walkway. What am I doing in
these things? They're job interview heels. They're comfortable, yeah, but they're something Mom would wear. I'm
pretty sure Mom has this exact pair in her closet.

It's only a few dozen steps to my apartment.

Thankfully, it's quiet.

I pull my key from my purse and slide it into the door. I
don't want to be at that party. Going home is the right call.

But inviting a stranger with me?

I press my lips together.

I turn back to… him. "I never asked your name."

"Walker." He offers his hand to shake.

"Iris." My palm presses against his. It does something
to me. Makes the air feel hot again.

His dark eyes fix on mine. They light up with desire.
Anticipation.

He seems like a good time.

And he's hot.

Obscenely hot.

Tall. Broad shoulders. Strong arms covered in ink. And I mean *covered* in ink. I've never found it appealing before— Lily and I used to argue about that all the time, back when she spoke to me—but it looks good on him. It makes him seem even more carefree. Even more like a perfect distraction.

God knows I don't want to listen to the thoughts racing around my head.

I turn the key and press the door open. "Come in." I suck a breath between my teeth. It's been a long time since I've slept with anyone. And that was Ross. I've never slept with a stranger.

Am I out of my mind?

"Thanks." He steps inside and presses the door closed behind him. His eyes move over my apartment slowly, like he's assessing every detail. His gaze stops on the bookshelf. His lips curl into a smile.

"What?"

"You read extended universe books."

My cheeks flush. I've been trying to re-connect with all the things I used to love. It's not going well. "*Star Wars* is mainstream now."

"You're embarrassed by it?"

"No." Maybe. Definitely.

He laughs as he pushes his t-shirt up his arm. He taps his shoulder with his finger.

Oh.

Right there, on his shoulder, that's a *Star Wars* tattoo. It's part of a sleeve of movie and pop-culture themed tattoos.

It's cool too. Well, as far as nerdy tattoos go.

Okay, who am I kidding?

The framed scene of Luke on Tattooine, looking out at

the setting suns, is the coolest ink I've seen in forever. And I've been staring at ink nonstop for the last few months.

"You're a nerd?" I ask.

"And you are too."

"Maybe." I pull my cell out. "Hold on." Walker seems like a normal, non-ax-murderer, but safety first.

I text Sandy.

Iris: I invited your friend Walker over.

Shit. How does this go? I'm telling her where to find me. And him. That's it. I think.

Sandy: OMG! Girl, get some. He's fine. If I wasn't with John, I'd be first in line.

Iris: He's safe?

Sandy: He's a good guy. I've known him forever. But he is a slut. Make sure he wraps it up ;) Have fun xoxo.

I set my cell on the dining slash coffee slash studying table.

My apartment is a decent size for Brentwood, but that isn't exactly huge. The main room is cozy.

He raises a brow. "Someone you want to talk to?"

"Checking in with Sandy."

"Did she tell you to sleep with me?"

"Yeah. How did you know?"

"It's not the first time."

I can't help but laugh. "You're that irresistible?"

"You did invite me here."

He is. And he knows it.

Usually, that annoys me.

But I kind of like it on him.

Walker.

The tattooed, slutty sci-fi fan.

He's intriguing.

Too intriguing. I'm not opening myself up to heartbreak again.

I know I shouldn't stereotype, but the tattoos and the man-whoring don't suggest stable, supportive boyfriend material.

Then again, clean-cut guys haven't exactly been good to me.

I move to the kitchen—it's on the other side of the coffee table—and grab a glass. "You want water?"

"Sure."

I pour two glasses and hand one to him.

He's smiling.

"What?"

"Women don't usually offer water."

"That's bad strategy."

"Yeah?"

"You need to stay hydrated if you want peak performance."

He chuckles. "True."

"You keep laughing."

"With you."

"With me?"

"I promise. I like you, Iris." He takes a long sip and sets his glass on the table. He moves toward me. Closer. Closer.

There.

He peels my fingers from my glass and sets it on the counter.

His hands go to my hips.

He leans in close.

My eyelids flutter together.

I rise to my tiptoes and press my lips to his.

He tastes good. Like whiskey. Fuck, it's been too long since I've really savored a sip.

Or a kiss.

He slides one hand under my blouse and presses his palm against my lower back.

He pulls me closer.

Sucks on my bottom lip. Softly. Then harder.

I bring my hand to his hair. Part my lips to make way for his tongue.

Lust pushes aside every other desire. I don't want good whiskey. Or understanding. Or dinner.

I only want this tall, handsome stranger's body pressed against mine. Erasing every thought in my head.

I slide my hand under his t-shirt. He's hard. Strong.

My hand explores the lines of his torso.

The other knots in his hair.

Desire spreads through my body as his tongue dances with mine.

As he peels off my leather jacket and tosses it on the coffee table.

He cups my breasts with his palm. Slides his thumb into my bra to play with my nipple.

Fuck.

This is intense. It's different like this. Good different. But scary different too.

Slowly, he backs me into the wall.

He pins me with his hips. His tongue plays with mine. His thumb toys with my nipples, one then the other.

I don't know his last name.

And I don't care.

Some free, uninhibited Iris is taking over. No, I know that Iris. It's just she usually only comes out after four or five shots.

He pulls back.

I stare into his eyes. "Bedroom."

He nods. Steps backward to release me.

I move through the living room.

My bedroom is small, but it's nice. I flip the switch for the string lights. The soft glow of the white paper lanterns bounces off my plain grey bedspread and sheets. Off my Ikea vanity and dresser.

They make the room feel homey.

Comfortable.

Like a place for old lovers.

Walker shuts the bedroom door and leans against it. His dark eyes pass over me. He drinks me in.

His eyes find mine. "Take off your jeans."

"What?"

"Your jeans. Lose them."

"No." I press my lips together. Where the hell is this objection coming from? This guy is hot as hell and he's already setting me on fire. I very much want to lose my jeans.

"No?"

"I don't do that."

"You have sex with your pants on?"

"No. I don't do the whole guy barking orders thing." That was Ross's thing. It was always weird. Awkward.

His voice gets light. "Barking?"

"Yeah." I can't help but laugh. Okay, he isn't exactly *barking*, but the point stands. I copy his posture.

It doesn't work standing.

I sit on the bed and spread my legs in that *blow me* position guys love.

"Take off your jeans," I demand.

His eyes brighten. "Not sure I need to for that."

"Yeah?"

"Yeah." He takes another step toward me. Drops to his knees between my legs.

"You... you're not one of those guys who doesn't—"

"Fuck no." He presses his palms against my thighs and pushes my legs apart. "You're gonna have to pull me away."

"Yeah?" My tongue slides over my lips. My limbs get light. It's been a long, long time since I've come from someone's mouth.

Longer since I've enjoyed it.

He undoes the button of my jeans. His eyes meet mine. "I don't bark orders."

"Then what was—"

"A request." He looks up at me. "Lift your hips."

"And that's a request?"

"I can't do this with your jeans on."

"True." I lift my hips.

He unzips my jeans and rolls them to my knees. My ankles.

His fingertips skim my skin as he drags his hands up my calves, my knees, my thighs.

His fingers curl into the straps of my thong.

Genius decision. Thank you, past Iris. For once, we're on the same page.

"You're not into dirty talk?" he asks.

"I am. Just not—"

"Ruff. Ruff."

What? I stare back at him.

"That's barking."

I laugh. "You know what I mean."

"I do." He nips at my inner thigh. "Would you like to come on my face?"

"You're teasing me, aren't you?"

He laughs. "Yeah. You're fun to tease." His voice drops. "I'll have to see how fun."

He tugs at the straps of my thong then slides the garment to my ankles.

"I mean it, Iris." He brings his hands to my hips and pulls me to the edge of the bed. "You're gonna have to drag me away."

I try to find a response, but I don't have anything. I want it. Him. Everything.

He places a kiss on the inside of my knee.

I pull my blouse over my head and toss it aside.

Then the bra.

My breath hitches as he drags his lips up my thigh.

Fuck. I'm already buzzing with anticipation.

"Lie back," he mumbles into my thigh. It's softer, but it's still demanding. Needy.

Like he really is desperate to dive between my legs.

I fall onto my back.

Slowly, he brings his mouth to me.

My hand goes to his dark, wavy hair. It's the perfect length for grabbing.

He pins my legs to the bed as he licks me from bottom to top then top to bottom.

He's takes his time.

Like he's savoring it.

Like he—

Fuck.

He flicks his tongue against my clit.

My legs fight his hands.

He pins me harder. He pries my thighs apart. Keeps them pressed against the edge of the bed.

It's strange, feeling this vulnerable with some guy I barely know.

Good.

But strange.

Every flick of his tongue pushes away my concerns. My nerves fade. I forget that I barely know him. I forget the last few months. And the three years before that. I forget everything but his soft, wet mouth against me.

Mmm.

I tug at his hair.

Buck my hips against his mouth.

He holds me in place. Groans against me. Licks me hard. Soft. Fast. Slow. Up. Down. Left. There.

"Fuck." My thighs fight his hands.

He scrapes his nails against my skin. He has me pinned. He's in control. I shouldn't like it—I never like that kind of thing—but I do.

"Walker." I buck against his mouth.

He stays on just the spot. Licks me with long, soft strokes. Then harder. Harder.

There.

"Don't stop," I breathe.

He doesn't.

He keeps that same rhythm. That same speed.

Tension pools in my sex.

It's intense. Different. Good different.

He takes me higher. Winds me tighter. I tug at his hair, holding his mouth against me.

Almost.

There.

The next flick of his tongue pushes me over the edge.

I groan his name as I come.

My sex pulses. Everything goes white, this beautiful, bright, blinding shade of pleasure. It's the only thing in my world. The only thing in the universe.

He's still going.

Licking me with those hard, steady strokes.

It's intense. Too intense.

I tug at his hair. "Fuck me. Now."

He pulls away. Nips at my thigh. Pushes himself to his feet.

I watch as he tosses his t-shirt over his head.

Pulls a condom from his back pocket.

Unzips his jeans and slides them—and his boxers—to his feet.

Fuck.

He's big.

And it's been a long time.

He stares down at me as he tears the wrapper and slides the condom over his cock. "Turn over."

I stare back at him.

"Please." His voice is heavy. Needy. Like he's not sure if he wants to tease me or *tease* me.

I push myself up.

He brings his hands to my legs. Helps me flip over. Onto my hands and knees.

I plant my feet on the floor. Arch my back to bring my ass into the air.

"Fuck, Iris." He drags his fingertips over my sex. "You always get this wet?"

My response is a groan.

God, that's hot. How can five words be that hot?

He teases me with one finger.

Then two.

I clutch at the sheets to stay upright.

That feels good.

Too good.

I need him inside me. His fingers. His cock. His everything.

I need it too much. The way I used to need—

"You like it rough?" He slides one finger inside me. Then two.

Fuck.

My eyelids flutter together.

I rock my hips. Rise onto my tiptoes.

How do I like it?

I don't even know.

I always went along with whatever Ross wanted.

He pushes his fingers inside me. It's slow. Deep. Intense.

"Slow at first." I swallow hard. How does he talk about this stuff so casually?

I mean, I appreciate his excellent communication skills.

And how much his dirty talk sets me on fire.

But I can't return it. Not with that kind of confidence.

"Then harder." I rock my hips.

He murmurs a yes as he drives his fingers inside me.

It feels good. But I need more.

"Fuck me," I breathe.

"This first." He drives his fingers into me. Again. Again. Again.

It pushes me toward the edge.

Fills me with this strange mix of satisfaction and need.

It's good.

But I need *him* inside me.

"Walker. Please." I arch my hips. Heel—toe my feet to spread my legs. "I need you inside me."

He lets out a low heavy groan and brings his hands to my hips. He holds me steady as he brings his body onto mine.

His tip strains against me.

Desire floods my senses. Yes. More. Everything.

He pulls back and does it again.

Again.

Again.

I dig my fingers into the sheets. I rise onto my tiptoes. I get dizzy from anticipation.

"More." I push aside my inhibitions. "Harder."

His fingers dig into my hips.

He thrusts into me full force.

Fuck. He's big. It's intense. But good intense.

He holds me in place as he pulls back and drives into me again.

Again.

He fills me with deep, steady thrusts.

Each winds me up. Each sends bliss to my fingers and toes.

He slides one hand around my hip and slips it between my legs.

He rubs my clit with his thumb as he drives into me.

Damn. That's intense.

He's good at this.

Way too good at this.

It defies explanation.

But then logic isn't all that interesting at the moment.

I…

He…

His thumb finds just the right spot.

"There," I breathe.

His groans fill the room as he drives into me. As he rubs me right where I need him.

He's bringing me all this pleasure. And it's making him groan. And he…

Fuck.

His name rolls off my lips.

It makes his groan lower. Louder.

The tension in my sex builds with every thrust and brush of his thumb.

It winds tighter and tighter.

"Harder," I breathe.

He digs his nails into my thigh as he drives into me. Harder. Faster. Deeper.

Mmm.

A few more thrusts and I'm there.

All that tension winds tighter than I can take. Then everything releases.

A wave of pleasure rocks through me.

My sex pulses. It pulls him closer. Makes him groan.

I moan his name as I come.

My grip on the sheets releases. My arms go slack.

"On your back." He pushes me flat on the bed.

I spread my arms. My legs. Arch my back.

He places his body on top of mine. One hand on my hip. The other on my shoulder.

With one quick motion, he drives inside me.

The weight of him pushes me into the bed.

It feels good. Safe. Comforting.

It's just physical. Just sex. It doesn't mean anything. You're never going to see him again.

I can't push the thoughts away.

This is too intimate. Too good.

I rock my hips to meet him.

He drives into me.

His movements get faster.

He loses control of his breath. Pulls me closer. Groans into my neck.

He's almost there.

And I need him there.

"Come for me." The words fall off my lips. A wave of nerves follow, but they disappear with his next thrust.

I can dirty talk.

At least when it's someone I'll never see again.

It makes him groan.

And go harder.

And pull me closer.

A few more thrusts and he's there. He shakes and shudders and groans my name as he comes.

He pulses inside me.

It's satisfying in a way it never has been.

Slowly, Walker peels his body off mine. "You have a trash can?"

"Yeah." I motion to the one next to my bed. "There's tissues—"

"I see them."

He takes care of the condom then sits on the bed next to me.

I roll onto my elbow and look up at him.

His dark eyes are so pretty.

His everything is so pretty. Not that he's really *pretty*. He's more handsome. Exactly handsome. Exactly halfway between rugged and pretty.

He brushes my hair behind my ear. "You want to go for round two?"

"You can?"

His laugh is soft. "I need ten minutes."

I nod. Yes. Round two is a good idea. And maybe three.

But that's it.

Tonight.

Only tonight.

Get Hooking Up Now

Author's Note

When I started writing Brendon and Kaylee's story, I was sure it was going to be a palate cleanser, something short and smutty to clear my head. I was going to add a little meat to the original novella *Bound to the Bad Boy* and finish as quickly as possible. I had a falling out with one of the authors in the *Begging for Bad Boys* bundle and I wanted to erase every memory of it from my mind and my life ASAP.

But my brain refused to keep the story breezy and casual. My brain always refuses to smooth out the edges that make my books quirky and offbeat. I set out with plans to write something by the numbers, and all of a sudden, I'm writing a scene where the hero is daring the heroine to say cunt in a shopping mall. It's a good thing I prefer unique to normal, because I don't really have a choice in the matter.

I didn't plan for Brendon and Kaylee's story to get this personal, but this was what it had to be. During the beta reading phase for this book, I was shocked by how many readers told me they appreciated my frank depiction of depression and suicidal thoughts. I was shocked by how many readers had dealt with depression or anxiety.

Depression morphs your brain (though I probably don't have to tell you that). I write books very much inspired by how badly I wanted to save the broken bad boy —the depressed/manic depressive lyricists I fell in love with in high school—but, sometimes, I still believe I'm the only person who's ever felt this way. That no one else could ever understand.

But people understand a lot more than they let on. They hurt a lot deeper than they let on.

I've always wanted to be a writer. I've always wanted to examine the fragility of relationships, how easy it is to ruin something beautiful and how hard it is to nurse it back to health. I love writing about characters who keep getting in their own way, because they're damaged or hurting or carting around too much baggage. But this was my first time, in a long time, writing a heroine with a specific mental illness. Kaylee is a person, not a representation of depression, and her feelings are not meant to reflect those of everyone with depression. This is just one story—her story. I hope it's brings comfort to those who have suffered from depression and illumination to those who haven't. But, mostly, I hope it helped you forget the world for a few hours.

If you're interested in learning more about depression, take a look at the National Institute for Mental Health. The National Suicide Prevention Hotline is always a phone call away for those who are considering self-harm. Phone: 800.273.8255

As always, thank you for reading.

I hope I'll see you for *Hooking Up*, a fun, sexy fuck buddy romance featuring Walker and his heroine.

If you'd like to stay up to date on the latest Inked Hearts or Crystal Kaswell news, please join my mailing list, join my Facebook group, like my page on Facebook, or friend me on Facebook.

Acknowledgements

My first thanks goes to my husband, for his support when I'm lost in bookland and for generally being the sun in my sky. Sweetheart, you're better than all the broken bad boys in the world. (Even though you're wrong about which Brendon is hotter).

The second goes to my father, for insisting I go to the best film school in the country, everything else be damned. I wouldn't love movies, writing, or storytelling half as much if not for all our afternoon trips to the bookstore and weekends at the movies. You've always been supportive of my goals, and that means the world to me.

A big shout out to all my beta readers. You helped give me the confidence to put out a book a little more heartbreaking than usual. And also to my ARC readers for helping spread the word to everyone else in the world.

A special thanks to my fellow pop-punk addict, Molle, for fangirling over music with me, for talking me through my business decisions, and for reminding me that loving my work matters as much as all the marketing money in the world.

Athena Wright, you are the best author BFF a girl could ask for. Thank you for your feedback, for being my chat buddy, and for always being there to give me the perspective I need. And thank you for mocking me when I deserve it and telling me no when I need to hear it. (Though I still think a reference to Panic would have been hilarious).

To my cover designer Letita, thank you for your work in making my rock star series perfect. And thank you so much to Wander and Jonny James for the perfect image. To my editor Marla, thank you for whipping the story and the prose into shape. And thanks to all the other book bloggers who helped get the word out.

As always, my biggest thanks goes to my readers. Thank you for picking up *Tempting*. I hope you'll be back for *Hooking Up*.

Stay in Touch

Sign up for <u>my mailing list</u> to get an exclusive extended epilogue (if you're already subscribed you'll get this soon).

You can also <u>join my Facebook group</u>, <u>like my page on Facebook</u>, or <u>friend me on Facebook</u>.

More books about the men of Inked Hearts are coming soon. *Hooking Up*, featuring Walker and his heroine, <u>is out now</u>.

Also by Crystal Kaswell

Sinful Serenade

Sing Your Heart Out - Miles

Strum Your Heart Out - Drew

Rock Your Heart Out - Tom

Play Your Heart Out - Pete

Sinful Ever After – series sequel

Dangerous Noise

Dangerous Kiss - Ethan

Dangerous Crush – Kit

Dangerous Rock – Joel

Dangerous Fling – Mal

Dangerous Encore - series sequel

Inked Hearts

Tempting - Brendon

Hooking Up - Walker

Pretend You're Mine - Ryan

Hating You, Loving You - Dean

Breaking the Rules - Hunter

Losing It - Wes - coming 2019

more coming in 2019

Standalones

Dirty Rich

Sign up for the Crystal Kaswell mailing list